DEAD MAN'S TALE

By *Quintin Jardine* and available from Headline

Bob Skinner series:
Skinner's Rules
Skinner's Festival
Skinner's Trail
Skinner's Round
Skinner's Ordeal
Skinner's Mission
Skinner's Ghosts
Murmuring the Judges
Gallery Whispers
Thursday Legends
Autographs in the Rain
Head Shot
Fallen Gods
Stay of Execution
Lethal Intent
Dead and Buried
Death's Door
Aftershock
Fatal Last Words
A Rush of Blood
Grievous Angel
Funeral Note
Pray for the Dying
Hour of Darkness
Last Resort
Private Investigations
Game Over
State Secrets
A Brush with Death
Cold Case

The Bad Fire
The Roots of Evil
Deadlock
Open Season
The Cage
Secrets and Lies
Dead Man's Tale

Primavera Blackstone series:
Inhuman Remains
Blood Red
As Easy as Murder
Deadly Business
As Serious as Death

Oz Blackstone series:
Blackstone's Pursuits
A Coffin for Two
Wearing Purple
Screen Savers
On Honeymoon with Death
Poisoned Cherries
Unnatural Justice
Alarm Call
For the Death of Me

The Loner
Mathew's Tale

QUINTIN JARDINE

DEAD MAN'S TALE

HEADLINE

First published in 2025 by Headline Publishing Group Limited

1

Cataloguing in Publication Data is available from the British Library

Hardback ISBN 978 1 0354 1993 7
Trade Paperback ISBN 978 1 0354 1994 4

Typeset in 12.18/16.31pt Electra LT Std by Six Red Marbles UK, Thetford, Norfolk

Printed and bound in Great Britain by Clays Ltd, Elcograf S.p.A.

MIX
Paper | Supporting
responsible forestry
FSC
www.fsc.org   FSC® C104740

Headline's policy is to use papers that are natural, renewable and recyclable
products and made from wood grown in well-managed forests and other
controlled sources. The logging and manufacturing processes are expected to
conform to the environmental regulations of the country of origin.

Headline Publishing Group Limited
An Hachette UK Company
Carmelite House
50 Victoria Embankment
London EC4Y 0DZ

The authorised representative in the EEA is Hachette Ireland,
8 Castlecourt Centre, Dublin 15, D15 XTP3, Ireland (email: info@hbgi.ie)

www.headline.co.uk
www.hachette.co.uk

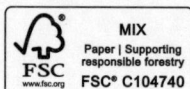

This is for Anne.

One

'Thank the Lord you're back,' DI Tarvil Singh boomed as his colleague stepped into the Serious Crimes office in Govan. 'At last I can get back to Edinburgh. The bloody commute's been killing me.'

As he spoke his colleagues rose to their feet at their workstations, and spontaneous applause broke out. Detective Superintendent Harold 'Sauce' Haddock, the unit's national commander, and DCI Lottie Mann, the Glasgow bureau chief, joined in, framed in the doorway of Mann's small office. Deputy Chief Constable Mario McGuire had been standing beside them, but he stepped forward towards the newcomer, hand outstretched.

'Detective Sergeant,' he said, loudly enough for his voice to carry to the furthest corners of the room. 'Welcome; you've been missed. Chief Constable McIlhenney would have been here, but unlike you he's still on sick leave. It's really good that you're back.'

John Stirling's face reddened; to his surprise he felt tears coming but he managed to hold them at bay, by the simple expedient of smiling at Detective Constable Maya Smith. It had been six months since he had seen some of the people in the room, but in her case, it had been only an hour. She had left their home immediately after breakfast, wanting to be in the office with the rest when he returned to work.

'Thanks, sir,' he replied as the greetings subsided. 'Trust me, it's even better to see all of you. The time's been dragging. You all know I'd have been back sooner if the Crown Office hadn't sequestered me as a key prosecution witness.'

'I know,' McGuire agreed. 'And in not one but two trials. We got the right result in both of them, thank Christ.'

Stirling nodded. 'Echoed.'

'Are you sure you feel okay now, John?' Haddock asked. 'You know you can pick your own slot in the unit,' he added. 'It can be office only if that's what you want, a co-ordinator role. Equally if you want to walk away from criminal investigation, that would be understandable. I know that HR have spoken to you about that already, and offered you a suitable transfer.'

The DS grinned. 'In that case you'll know what I told them. I want to be here, sir, nowhere else. Physically, I'm fine. Maya'll vouch for that. We've bagged eight Munros in the last six weeks; a couple more and it'll be the equivalent in height terms of having climbed Everest.'

His partner nodded agreement. 'It's true,' she confirmed. 'He was a bit slow when we started but he's got stronger with every one.'

'Maybe I'll come with the two of you on your next one,' the DCC said, leading Stirling and his senior colleagues away from the group and towards Mann's office. He raised his eyebrows. 'And then again, maybe not. John, I know you passed the physical . . . you wouldn't be here otherwise . . . and I know you've had counselling, but psychologically,' he asked quietly, 'are you sure you're a hundred per cent? I have to ask you this, because we have a duty to your colleagues as well. It could be that you'll be sharing a stressful situation with one of them, and . . .' The rest of the sentence hung unspoken in the air.

'I'm living with one of those colleagues, sir,' Stirling reminded him. 'I've asked myself that question, and Maya's asked me too. I'll

2

tell you and anyone else who needs to hear it what I told her. To me, any situation is what it is: just something to be dealt with, no more no less. I've never been a panic merchant. Any time I'm challenged, I ask myself "What's the problem? What's the solution? What do I need to do to get there." Once I work it out I do what I have to. Nothing's happened to change that. If anything it's been reinforced.'

'How d'you mean?' Lottie Mann asked.

'Work it out, ma'am,' he told her. 'When I was stabbed and I went down, the one thing I knew was that I didn't want to be fucking stabbed again . . . pardon my French. I decided that the best way to prevent that was to play dead, and hope that my assailant bought the act. That's what I did, and it worked. As I lay there, in my own blood on that kitchen floor, I heard a phone call being made, I heard a call for help, in disposing of my body I suppose, and then I heard a door close. I sneaked a look to check that I really was alone. When I saw that I was I crawled across to the back door. I was in shock, obviously, so it hurt less than you might expect. I was a lucky boy, for the door was unlocked. The blood flow had slowed, and I was able to pull myself to my feet using the handle. I dragged myself outside, then hauled my arse around the house and into my car. I'd left my phone there, plugged in and charging. My brain was working better by that time, and I knew I had to act fast, rather than go through the emergency services rigmarole with all the time that takes, I called your mobile, and told you where I was and what had happened. There was still no sign that my escape had been discovered, but I decided it wouldn't be wise to wait for the cavalry, so I packed my wound with a towel from my sports bag and drove to A and E at the Queen Elizabeth Infirmary . . . which fortunately wasn't too far away. When I got there, I was actually pleased with myself, would you believe?'

'I'm not surprised,' Mann agreed. 'You'd just solved a murder that had us tied in knots.'

He shook his head. 'No, not because of that.' He grinned, shyly. 'That's an exaggeration anyway, boss; I just found a connection, and completely by accident, I didn't go looking for it. No, I was chuffed with the way I had handled myself.'

'Were you not scared, John?' McGuire asked. 'I got shot once, when I was a DC, and I don't mind admitting that I was terrified.'

'Honestly, I wasn't; it never occurred to me to be frightened. Thing is, when I was at university I joined the Territorial Army; I was a weekend warrior, mainly because it kept me out the pub. As part of it we were given some training in battlefield first aid, including how to handle significant wounds. I think I knew from that where mine was, and that it was survivable, for a while at least.' He frowned, remembering. 'Yes, I was lucky, no question. I knew it then, and the surgeon who operated on me confirmed it. The weapon went under my ribcage and straight into my gall bladder: you couldn't do that if you tried, the way it's tucked under your liver. I don't have the thing any more . . . the doc actually showed me what was left of it . . . but so what? It's one of those bits you don't really need. If it had hit my liver, the surgeon said, or nicked an artery, yes, the show would have been over. But it didn't, so . . . there's no point dwelling on it. So . . .' he said, looking at Mann, 'what's in my in-tray, ma'am?'

She shrugged her broad shoulders. 'Nothing,' she replied. 'DI Singh wrapped up an armed robbery last week. He even got a confession, so unless it's withdrawn he won't have to come back to the High Court for a trial.'

'It doesn't matter,' Sauce Haddock interjected. 'You have to be office duties only for the next six months.'

'Aw, come on, sir,' Stirling moaned. 'I'm fit for active duty, honestly. I should be fully operational.'

'Sorry, John,' his superintendent said. 'That's how it's got to be.'

The young detective sergeant knew better than to go over his boss's head, but could not resist a single raised eyebrow, aimed at the acting chief constable.

McGuire smiled, and nodded towards Haddock. 'What he said,' he chuckled. 'Sergeant, I know you're frustrated, and I know your instinct is to prove us all wrong. But it's not Detective Superintendent Haddock who's put this condition on your return to work, and it's not me either. The decision was taken by our Human Resources department and, trust me, there would be no point in Sauce, or me, or even Chief Constable McIlhenney, if he was here, getting into a pissing contest with that lot. We'd only wind up with wet feet, and you'd still be chained to your desk for six months.'

'Thanks for leaving me out of that analogy,' Lottie Mann drawled.

Stirling sighed. 'Could I go to the Police Federation?' he asked.

'You could, but you'd wind up wringing out your socks as well.' He paused, his eyes narrowing. 'However . . . and I apologise for not thinking of this before . . . there's a two-week command course beginning this morning at the police college in Jackton. It'll be the shortest of notice for them, but I could wedge you in there as a late entrant, if you were up for it. That might help you deal with your frustration, and it might even do you good in the longer term. It won't fast track you through the system, but if you do well it could speed the promotion process. Would you be up for that? If so I can tell them to delay the start by an hour.'

'Jackton,' the DS murmured. 'Just outside East Kilbride. Sir, I can be there in thirty minutes.'

Two

Sir Robert Skinner gazed at the face on his tablet screen.

'Are you sure he's ready?' he asked.

'If I wasn't he wouldn't be going,' the editor of the *Saltire* newspaper assured her group executive chairman. 'I know Ignacio's inexperienced, but his work's really been outstanding in the four months that he's been with us. Plus,' June Crampsey added, 'the newsroom's stretched; I've got two staff on holiday and this morning another two reporters called in sick with bloody norovirus. That's five this week, after the three on the sports desk. It's ripping through the office, Bob. I'm probably doing him a favour by sending him.'

'He doesn't speak Swedish,' Skinner pointed out.

'Who does, apart from the Swedes? That's why most of them speak English.'

'Couldn't you use an agency reporter?'

'Yes, I could,' Crampsey conceded, 'but whoever they gave me wouldn't have background knowledge of the Scottish infrastructure. This is Richard Ralston, our First Minister, visiting Malmo to inaugurate a new ferry route between Malmo and Edinburgh, one that he's driven through pretty much by himself. It's a big story, a good news story; we need to cover it appropriately. I trust Ignacio to do that.'

'And it's your call,' he conceded.

'Exactly. I'm only telling you because he's your son.' She allowed him one of her infrequent smiles. 'That, and because you're the big boss,' she added. 'You should be proud of him, Bob,' she insisted. 'He's a natural. Look, if Xavi Aislado was still sitting in your chair, he'd agree with me; and you know what a great journalist he was.'

'How are you going to bill him?' Skinner asked. 'He's never had a byline before.'

The editor frowned. 'What do you mean?'

'What are you going to call him in the paper, and the online edition? The name on his passport and on his Spanish birth certificate is Ignacio Watson Skinner.'

'And on his employment contract,' she added. 'Yes, I get it; in the office he's just Ignacio. Nobody but me and HR know that you're his dad.'

'I'd like to keep it that way, and I'm pretty sure he would too. That means his byline should be just Ignacio Watson. You okay with that?'

She nodded. 'One hundred per cent.'

'When does he leave? How does he get there?'

'Sparrowfart tomorrow. It's a flight to Copenhagen, then the train to Malmo, across the bridge, the one in the TV series. Oh, and he wants to take his girlfriend. I've said okay . . . but he pays her fare.'

'Absolutely. As it happens, I'm with Pilar's father as we speak. I'll let him know. Cheers, June. I'll look out for the coverage.'

Skinner ended the WhatsApp call, returned the iPad to his document case, and turned back to his companion, who had been listening. 'What do you think of that, Raul?' he asked. 'My boy's new career seems to be blossoming. When he told me he wanted to go into journalism, my first assumption was that he meant via social media, but he said no, that he fancied the traditional route.

7

He never asked me to find him a place with InterMedia, but . . . My first thought was to find him a slot with the Girona paper, since he's a dual national and Spanish is his first language. But the fact that he's not literate in Catalan could have been a problem, so instead I asked June if she'd consider him for the *Saltire*. She interviewed him and was so impressed that she gave him a twelve-month trainee contract on the spot. I'm happy for him,' he said, 'but as you might imagine I'm sensitive to accusations of nepotism. That's probably a carry-over from my previous career in the police. In my early days, I saw a few people get special treatment because of who their dad was.'

Raul Sanchez nodded. 'Of course,' he murmured. 'You know, Bob, in my mind's eye I can still see you in a police uniform.'

He laughed. 'In real life not many people did. I hated it, so I hardly ever wore it. Being CID that was okay, but even when I was at command rank, assistant chief and up, it mostly stayed in the wardrobe. By then I was . . . in theory . . . well away from criminal investigation, but that never worked in practice. I could never keep my hands off.' He leaned back in his chair, smiling. 'On reflection I was a bloody awful chief constable. I delegated all the stuff that bored me and second-guessed everyone else. I must have been a right pain in the arse. Mind you, I couldn't have done that within the new Scottish national set-up,' he paused, for a second. 'I should stop calling it "new",' he added. 'It's been around for a few years now, for better or worse, although I for one can't see where it's better. How can you convince people in Shetland that they have accountable community policing when the high command is hundreds of miles away in offices in the central belt? The politicians could never answer that question but they went ahead anyway, and that's why I walked away.'

'Would you have become the national chief if you hadn't left?' Sanchez asked.

His friend nodded. 'No false modesty, but I reckon I would. Okay, they could have parachuted someone in from England, but I doubt that. If I had toed the political line, they'd have owed me. Whatever, I've never regretted my choice. But I am pleased that I left a number of alternative appointees behind me, people who'd worked under me. The first one, Andy Martin, he didn't work out too well, probably for the same reasons that I wouldn't have, but his successors, Maggie Steele, and now Neil McIlhenney, they've been successful. I trained them both, them and the current deputy. It's ironic that he, Mario McGuire, didn't go for the top job when Maggie left. He said he didn't want it, but he's doing it now anyway, since Neil's been away with long covid.'

'For all that you say now,' Sanchez observed, 'it must have been a wrench to leave. I can tell, the way you talk about your old job.'

'Sure it was,' Skinner agreed. 'It was an even bigger wrench when I left Edinburgh to take over the Glasgow job, to close it down, so to speak. Afterwards, I don't mind admitting that I was lost for a couple of years, until my buddy Xavi threw me a lifeline by making me chair of InterMedia's Scottish subsidiary.'

'And then made you his successor when he backed off from running the company,' his guest added, 'a role in which you are excelling.'

'Nah,' the big Scot murmured, with a deprecatory smile. 'I'm executive chair, that's all. Hector Sureda's the CEO; he and his team, they run the business. They're journalists, I'm just a broken-down old cop.'

Sanchez raised an eyebrow. 'That's not what the analysts say. I'm a commercial banker, Bob. I study these things. InterMedia is still a privately owned company, but . . .'

'And always will be,' Skinner interjected. 'Paloma Aislado Craig will inherit everything. Xavi's plan is that she'll be running the business by the time she's thirty. Part of my role is to prepare her for it.'

'That may be so, and InterMedia may be cash rich, but it still requires substantial borrowing facilities. Your successful American expansion, for example. That was supported by your bankers in Spain and in the US, but only because they have confidence in your leadership. Xavi Aislado is not an idiot. When he asked you to take over from him, it was based on ability, not friendship. And you know it too, my friend. I say this kindly, but your modesty is a cloak you wear, to hide your absolute self-confidence.'

'Hah! Is that so? Try telling my wife that.'

'I will, when finally I get to meet her,' Sanchez promised.

Skinner frowned. 'I'd hoped she might join us today,' he said. He glanced around the place in which they sat. 'She would have too; Siete Portes is her favourite restaurant in Barcelona, but unfortunately she has a lecture at the university, and her students come first. That and,' he added, cautiously, 'given that we will inevitably get round to discussing my oldest son's mother . . .'

'They don't get on, Sarah and Mia?'

'They tolerate each other, on the rare occasions that they meet, but they're not a good mix. Sarah's fine with Ignacio, she treats him like one of her own, but Mia McCullough has too much baggage for her taste.'

'Do you mean baggage with you?' The question was put delicately.

'No, not that kind. She and I didn't even have a small suitcase. Raul, the truth is that Ignacio was the product of a one-night stand, when Mia and I were both single. Very soon after that she had what I will euphemistically call family issues. On my advice, she left town in a hurry: if I'd known she was pregnant, that advice would probably have been different. I don't think she knew herself at that stage, but when she found out she didn't choose to share the news with me.'

'If she had, what would you have done?'

10

'No question,' he replied instantly. 'I'd have acknowledged my son, and been part of his upbringing. He'd have been protected.'

'From whom?'

'Ultimately, from his mother. But I couldn't do that, because she kept him secret from me, even though she put my name on his birth certificate, and in the *Libro de Familia*, the thing they give you in Spain. By the time I found out about him he was already in trouble. I was able to mitigate the damage but I couldn't make it all go away.' He looked his companion in the eye. 'You don't really know anything about Mia, do you?'

'No,' Sanchez admitted. 'When I said a few months ago that I wanted to talk to you about her, what I really meant was that I wanted to ask you about her. Inge and I have invited her to Madrid repeatedly, but she has always put us off. She has invited us to her hotel in Scotland, but she seems reluctant to visit Spain. And yet her son is Spanish.'

'And British. He has two passports.'

'I thought you couldn't do that, have dual nationality, Spain and UK.'

'You couldn't until fairly recently. The way it works now, Ignacio made a legal declaration in Spain that he intends to retain Spanish nationality, and then he applied for a UK passport. Before that, he had settled status. But Mia had nothing to do with that. It was my doing, when he came to work for us.'

'I was going to ask you about that,' the Spaniard said. 'I had thought that his future was in radio.'

Skinner grinned. 'So did his mother. Before Mia left, she was a disc jockey on an Edinburgh local station. She was known as Mia Sparkles, and she had a big teenage following, my oldest daughter Alexis among them. When she came back to Scotland, she went back to work as a radio presenter, on a station in Dundee, owned by a man named Cameron McCullough, and wound up marrying him.

When he died she inherited it, along with a life interest in that hotel, Black Shield Lodge, and enough investments to keep her in comfort, although the bulk of his wealth went to his granddaughter. Pilar probably told you that Ignacio worked on the station helping out as a runner during his university vacations. Cameron was still alive, but Mia was running the place even then. She gave him a weekend slot on air, and of course with her genes in him he turned out to be a natural. As you probably know also, when he finished uni and went in there full-time, his role expanded. Mia gave him the breakfast show, and a role in station management. She assumed that in time she'd be able to back out completely: I know that because she told me. I had my doubts,' he added, 'but I said nothing. She gave him a free rein in programming . . . basically he was his own producer . . . and he used it to introduce a current affairs element, with political guests as well as the odd showbiz drop-in. I listened to it most mornings on its app, so it didn't matter where I was. I thought it was bloody good but . . .' he smiled again and sighed. 'How much did Pilar tell you?' he asked.

'She said he was trying a new format,' Sanchez replied, 'one that involved more than just playing music. She said he wanted local radio to be part of the community, not just background music on construction sites or something that people have on when they are in the shower.'

'Yes, that's a fair description of what he was after. The problem was . . .' Skinner hesitated. 'I'm not certain, but I reckon that Dundee was the wrong place. He couldn't get enough worthwhile guests in the studio, and when he approached potential online contributors they, or their advisers, looked at the location and more often than not decided they were too busy. The audience figures dropped off, and so did the advertising. Mia couldn't let that go on. She took over the early slot herself, and relaunched it under her own brand, if that's what you call it. She moved Ignacio to drivetime, late afternoon, early evening, but insisted that he had to go back to basics. They had a big row, and last summer he quit.'

'I see,' Sanchez said. 'Pilar didn't explain all that background. And that's when he came to the *Saltire*?'

'Not directly. As I said, he never asked me for a job; he simply told me what his ambition was. Okay, he probably had his fingers crossed that I would help. But if I hadn't, he'd either have gone to one of our competitors or done his own thing on YouTube, as some people do these days, and looked to build a subscriber base big enough to attract advertisers. In the event, I did what any dad in my position would do, as far as I deemed proper. I asked June if she would meet him. She did, and you see how it's working out. Already he's been turned loose on an international story. Okay, in practice it'll be a bit of a milk run, but it'll get his name on the front page, and if the First Minister plays ball there'll be a video interview as well on *Saltire Online*, which,' Skinner added, 'has subscribers all over the fecking world, mate.'

'What does his mother think of his new career?'

'I don't really know. Mia and I aren't in regular contact, and Ignacio's said nothing about her in a while.' He glanced at his watch. 'Look, Raul, this has been excellent. It's always good to catch up, but I have to be in Girona in less than ninety minutes.' He looked at their waiter, who was standing by the doorway, surveying the terrace tables, and made eye contact.

Sanchez took hold of his friend's wrist as it moved towards an inside pocket. 'I will get this,' he said, firmly. 'It's my turn; we agreed.'

'In that case,' Skinner conceded, 'thank you. Next time, it's on me, hopefully in Madrid and with our wives there.'

He was reaching for his document case when his ringtone sounded. He took his phone from his pocket and peered at the screen, frowning as he read the caller ID. 'Mia?' he murmured. He pressed Accept.

'I've just had a call from Ignacio,' the mother of his oldest son exclaimed. The excitement in her voice took him by surprise. 'Sometimes,' she continued, 'I think I've loved you all along, and not just for about twenty minutes back then. Our boy's going to make page one? Really?'

In spite of himself, he smiled. 'That was always going to happen,' he told her. 'It's come quicker than I'd expected, that's all. So you're pleased after all?'

'Of course I am. I've always wanted him to fly, in whatever direction he chooses.'

'That's good,' Skinner said. 'And by the way,' he added. 'As far as I recall it was at least two hours.'

Three

'What is Malmo?' Pilar Sanchez Hoverstad asked her partner. Although Spanish was the first language of both, they had a pact that they would only use it when they were actually in Spain.

'What is it?' Ignacio Watson Skinner repeated. 'It's a city, the third biggest in Sweden. Population? Three hundred and fifty thousand, give or take, but if you look at the Greater Malmo area it's touching three quarters of a million. It has a big immigrant population because of Sweden's open door policy. Economically, it's thriving, partly because of the Öresund Bridge that connects it with Denmark. We'll cross it from Copenhagen Airport. Hence the new ferry route that the FM's going there to inaugurate. It won't just link Scotland with Sweden but with all of Scandinavia and with Germany when the new immersible tunnel's finished.'

'How long is the bridge?'

'Around eight kilometres. From Sweden it lands on an island on the Danish side then goes into a tunnel that takes you on to Copenhagen.'

'It must be huge. Will we be driving over it?'

'No, we'll take the train from the airport. We're booked into a hotel called the Scandic Triangeln. There's a station next to it, where we can get off. I checked it out on Google Earth. It's very close.'

'Will the First Minister be on the same flight as us? Or will he be on a private plane?'

'Why should you think that? Ralston's Holyrood, not Westminster. And even the British Prime Minister would have trouble justifying his own aircraft for such a short flight.'

'Your father has a private aircraft,' Pilar pointed out.

Ignacio laughed. 'No, he doesn't. InterMedia does. Actually, it has two,' he said, 'because it's now a transatlantic business. As executive chairman my dad gets to use them, but so do others. When the company negotiated approval for the US Hispanic news channel, the CEO headed the team that did it. They all went over in the Gulfstream.'

'I thought it was a Cessna.'

'The first one is; the Gulfstream has transatlantic range.'

She winked at him. 'Couldn't InterMedia offer one of them to the First Minister and his people for this trip, with us on board too?'

'That's not such a bad idea,' he admitted. 'It would really piss off our opposition, only you're too late. All our travel arrangements have been made. But as it happens, Ralston will be flying privately, his press office told me. The ferry company that's going to be operating the new route has an executive aircraft subsidiary. It's flying him to Sweden the day after tomorrow. The idea is that he'll do a couple of visits to local places of interest, which I'll be there to cover, then next day, mid-afternoon, he'll inaugurate the new service, and sail back to Edinburgh on the first crossing.'

'And we're sailing back with him?' she asked.

'That's the plan. The boss has asked the press office if I can have an interview with him on the way. It hasn't been confirmed yet, but it will be, I'm sure. With the election in sight, Ralston needs to keep us onside.'

Pilar frowned. 'Are you? The newspaper? On his side, I mean?'

'Officially,' he told her, 'the *Saltire* doesn't endorse any party.

16

Privately, Sue Bland, our political editor, hates the First Minister, but that can't be allowed to colour our coverage. That's why I'm going to Sweden, and not her.'

'Why is she so antagonistic?'

Ignacio beamed. 'Because they used to be married to each other, that's why. She was his first wife, when they were both in their twenties, but it didn't end well.'

Four

'Richard Ralston smiles at the mere sight of a camera,' Susan Bland declared.

'He's a politician, Sue,' her editor pointed out. 'They all do that.'

'But his facile grin is as fake as the rest of him,' she snapped. 'June, you really should let me go on this trip. I know how to wipe it off his face. This ferry link, it's a massive punt, with millions of taxpayers' money at risk and likely to go down the drain.'

'How do you know that?' Crampsey challenged.

'There's never been a proper risk-assessment done. It's a total gamble. We're putting up seventy-five per cent of the start-up cost, not including the creation of a new terminal . . .'

'The City Council's doing that,' she pointed out. 'It links directly to the tram line, taking new arrivals right into the heart of the city and helping to regenerate the local area.' She frowned, slightly. 'That's the theory,' she added.

'The tram line from the airport does exactly the same thing. And I know for a fact that at least one of the Scandinavian airlines is going to cut its timetable if the ferry's still going in a year.'

'But the project isn't all about tourism,' the editor insisted. 'It's more than just a car ferry; it takes lorries too. It's a trade link, opening up the whole Scandinavian market directly to Scottish goods, and beyond, through Denmark into Holland, Germany, Poland

and so on. It'll make Scotland a European player, that's what Ralston says.'

'What he really means is that it'll make him a European figure. It's all linked to the independence movement, June. When he's in Sweden, he's going to meet the Swedish Trade Minister, Lena Rapace. She's doing the ferry inauguration, and there's a chance that her Danish counterpart will be there too. "A courtesy visit", the programme says, but it'll be more than that. I'll bet you there'll be one item on the agenda that won't be declared in advance. Richard will propose that the Malmo and Edinburgh terminals will each be given freeport status, meaning that goods can be received and shipped free of customs duty.'

Crampsey stared at her. 'Why should you think that?'

'Because he told me, as good as, sixteen years ago. When the EU referendum was no more than a Tory pipe-dream, when he and I were married and he was still a brand new Lib Dem MSP, we were talking one night about the consequences for Scotland of leaving Europe, and potential ways around it. That's the idea he came out with then. When I told him he was daft, that there was no way his party would ever go for that, he laughed and said, "In that case I'd better find another party." At the time I didn't think he was serious. When he jumped ship . . . and how appropriate that phrase is now . . . and joined the nationalists, well, I'd forgotten about it by then. It only came back to me when he went big on the ferry link and got the Parliament to back him. A couple of days ago, I asked Joanie Cooper . . . his communications director . . .'

'I know who she is.'

'Of course, sorry. I asked her, on the record, about the agenda for the Sweden trip. She was unusually foxy about it. She said it was confidential. That's not like Joanie, not at all.'

'But Sue,' Crampsey argued, 'Customs Duty isn't a delegated

function. That's Westminster's. The UK Government would have to approve a freeport, wouldn't they?'

'Yes, but do you really think that with a Holyrood election coming up, and a national one maybe a couple of years after that, with all those Scottish seats at risk, a Labour Prime Minister could possibly refuse?'

The editor winced. 'Point taken,' she conceded. 'But . . . why am I only hearing about this now? Why haven't you run the story already?'

'Because it's better that we run it as fact, not speculation. Any sort of interest from the Swedes, Richard will take back to Holyrood and announce it there on his big stage. The boy you're sending in my place . . . yes, I accept that I can't go . . . you must make sure that when he gets face to face with Richard he puts that question. It'll piss him off, and I doubt that he'll give a straight answer, but anything short of a flat denial gives us a story. You'll brief Ignacio, yes?'

'I will,' she promised, 'don't you worry about that. Ralston's going to hate us for it, you realise?'

'Yes and I will glory in it. You're sure this kid's up to the job?'

'Too right I am,' Crampsey declared. 'That apple's fallen very close to the tree.'

Five

'Privately, I'm less worried by climate change than I should be. Publicly, as executive chair of a media organisation with a global reach, I have to acknowledge that it's a hell of a story.'

Paloma Aislado Craig stared at her godfather across the desk in his Girona office. 'Seriously, Uncle Bob?' she gasped. 'You're a denier?'

'No, love, I'm not,' Skinner reassured her. 'I've got faith in human ingenuity, that's all. Global warming's a challenge for sure, but most nations are tackling it already.'

'Apart from the Americans and the Chinese,' she pointed out.

'For now, but ultimately both of those follow the money. They won't be able to dodge compliance for ever.'

'You should talk to my professors at LSE. They're not nearly as upbeat as you are.'

He laughed, ironically. 'That's because they're academics, always arguing with each other. Those people are like lawyers; by definition half of them are wrong. If the world had fewer professors the world would be a calmer place, and none the worse for it.'

'Uncle Bob, you're the least woke person I know,' Paloma declared.

He gave her a brief nod of acknowledgement. 'Thank you, my dear. If that means not saluting when a teenager with a flair for self-publicity makes a noise, I plead guilty. Humanity might be tackling the climate problem quietly, but generally it is tackling it. Your dad's a prime example. He's ready to focus on the outside world again but he doesn't want to come back here.'

'Because he says you're running the business better than he ever did,' Paloma interjected.

'I don't think I am, but it's his call. Instead he's moving into clean energy, buying cheap land in central Spain and building solar farms.'

Paloma nodded. 'And Africa,' she added. 'He's talking to the Kenyan government about doing the same there.'

'That I did not know,' Skinner murmured. 'But I'm pleased about it.'

'Mum would be too. She'd have been mad at him going into seclusion, the way he did.'

He frowned. 'Nah, she wouldn't,' he said. 'Your mum was a very understanding woman. Bereavement's an awful thing, Paloma. People react in all sorts of ways. For some it's depression, for others it's drink or drugs. In my case . . .'

'You've been widowed?' She gazed at him.

'Yeah. Has your dad never told you? I was in my mid-twenties. Myra, Alex's mother, was killed in a car accident . . . actually it wasn't an accident, but that's a long story. I was left with a four-year-old daughter and a very demanding job. My bosses gave me as much time off as they could, but I had to go back eventually: crime never sleeps, and all that. I had help looking after Alex, from her aunt, among others, so I was able to carry on.' His eyebrows came together. 'That was bad news for the criminal classes, I can tell you. Life made me fearsome back then. If someone had a go at me, I really enjoyed it; I sent a few so-called hard men to A&E. Fortunately my clear-up rate was a hundred per cent, and my boss, Alf, was even more unwoke than you think I am, so nobody cared. At home, though, I was a pussycat. I didn't realise it at the time, nor does she, even now, but my daughter actually looked after me, as much as I took care of her.' He grinned, suddenly. 'She still does in fact. You and your dad don't know it either, but you've done the same for him.'

'That's nice to hear,' she murmured.

'But back to business,' he continued. 'How have you found the experience of shadowing Dolça Nuñez?'

'Enlightening, to say the least. She's a free spirit, she's a very gifted reporter, and she loves her job. Plus, she's still so young.'

Skinner smiled. 'I thought the two of you would get on. Dolça handled a project for us last year, and did it so well that Hector Sureda's given her a special status in the organisation. "Global correspondent", we call her. It means that she has the freedom to pop up on any of the group's news outlets, in Spain, Italy, the US, even in Scotland.'

'You and Dad both love the *Saltire*, don't you?' Paloma observed.

'You bet we do,' he replied wistfully. 'It's where his career in journalism began, after his wrecked knee finished him as a footballer. And,' he continued, with emphasis, 'it's where InterMedia took its first step towards being a multi-national business, when Xavi persuaded your uncle Joe to buy it and rescue it from bankruptcy. As for me, it's the place where my new career began, when your dad made me a director.'

'Can I go there for a while? To Edinburgh?'

He looked at her, surprised by the question. 'Paloma,' he chuckled. 'You can go anywhere you like. You will own the business one day. My most important task here is to train you to succeed me; you know that.'

'Yes, but . . . I don't want to succeed you,' she countered. 'Even when I'm through university and have a few years' experience, my aim is to take over from Hector, when he retires as CEO. When that happens I'll still need you as chairman, and as my adviser.'

'Maybe I'll want to retire too,' Skinner suggested.

'And do what? The school run with your kids? Already I know you better than that.'

Skinner drew a breath. 'Paloma, we'll deal with that as it happens. For now, why do you want to go to the *Saltire*?'

'I want to follow in my father's footsteps: as you say, it's where his career in journalism began.' She grinned. 'Part of me wants to follow his story from the beginning but I don't see myself as Hearts' goalkeeper.'

He laughed. 'Why not? Women play professionally these days.'

'I know, but I'm rubbish. I did train with a team in London for a while, long enough to find out that I have my mother's football genes.'

'But you do want to be a journalist?'

'I want to find out about it,' she replied, 'as part of the overall learning process. That's what your son Ignacio is doing, isn't it?'

'Not quite. Nacho sees it as a career path. He's done radio already; now he's taking what he learned there into newspapers. We own radio stations, we have our cable TV outlet in the US. You could embed in any one of those, all of them.'

'In time, but I want to begin with the *Saltire*.'

'Okay. When?'

'As soon as possible,' she told him. 'I'm finished at university. I have my degree; all that's left is graduation. In a couple of years I'll go back and do a Masters, but my learning the business, that began by sitting in with Dolça. On to the next . . . please.'

'Done. I'll tell June. You can have my office.'

'Can't I be in the newsroom?'

'You can spend time everywhere; you're there as a management trainee, but under your own name and treated appropriately. You're Paloma Aislado and the whole building will know that from Day One.'

'What about accommodation?' she asked. 'Where will I live? My dad still owns his place there but it's rented.'

'I'll ask Alex to take care of that; there's plenty of options. She and her partner Dominic each have their own places in Edinburgh, but mostly she's with him. That said, since Sarah and I moved the family to Spain they've been spending a lot of their time at our place in Gullane. Ignacio and Pilar have an apartment there too. Don't worry, Alex will fit you in somewhere.' He frowned. 'Unless you'd . . .'

'Unless I have a partner hidden away in London that Dad and you don't know about and would prefer to fix my own digs?'

'Well . . . yes.'

'No, I don't. I swing both ways, Uncle Bob; but there's nobody special.'

With an effort Skinner masked his surprise at her frankness. 'When do you want to start?'

'How about the day after tomorrow? If that's not too soon for Alex.'

'It shouldn't be, but if necessary we'll put you in a hotel for a couple of nights. I'll have the jet available at Girona Airport.'

'Uncle Bob . . .'

'Like I said,' he retorted, overriding her protest. 'You're Paloma Aislado, and everyone's going to know it from Day One.'

Six

Richard Ralston looked out from his window on the fifth floor of St Andrews House, where the First Minister's office was located. In times past, pre-devolution, it had been occupied by successive Secretaries of State for Scotland, and before that by Calton Jail, Edinburgh's prison. The structures had been built into a hillside; thus there were more than five levels beneath his feet, and the deepest of them was said to be a holdover from the original. He had been told that in the bowels of the building there was a storeroom that had once been an execution chamber. He had never checked the truth of that story, but there had been times on the floor of the Holyrood Parliament when he had wished that if so, it was still in use.

'Do I have to talk to the *Saltire* lad, Peter?' he asked his adviser.

'Press Office says yes,' Peter Dunbar replied.

'Sod the Press Office,' Ralston murmured. 'What do you think?'

'I think it would be politic; the editor's being nice to us. She's giving the trip staff coverage, which means page one status, and probably lead story unless some foreign crisis blows up. The paper's editorial line on the ferry service has been positive too, unlike several others, so we need to keep it onside.'

'We'll never do that completely as long as my bloody ex is the political editor. Her dislike of me is only exceeded by my passionate hatred of her.'

'June Crampsey's aware of that too; that's why she's sending someone else.'

'What's his name again?'

'Ignacio Watson.'

The First Minister turned away from the window, with its view across Waverley Station to the Old Town beyond. 'That name's familiar,' he murmured. 'Got it; I did a drop-in to a radio show in Dundee to present some award it had won, and he was there. His mother owns the station, doesn't she?'

Richard, Dunbar thought, *don't kid a kidder: the name's familiar because you're shagging his mother; on the quiet, you think, but I know, and so do most of your staff. The only person who doesn't might be the current Mrs Ralston, although things being the way they are I doubt that she'd object.*

'That's right,' he said. 'But the son's moved on. Talk about net-working,' he exclaimed. 'You know who his father is, don't you?'

Ralston shook his head.

He really doesn't, Dunbar thought. *Mia can't have told him.*

'Sir Robert Skinner, no less. Ex-chief constable, now the top guy in the group that owns the *Saltire*.'

'Skinner?' the politician exclaimed. 'The same Skinner that used to be married to one of my predecessors, Aileen de Marco? Before she found a Westminster seat and became Home Secretary?'

'There's only one Bob Skinner.'

'I didn't know he and Mrs McCullough had a connection,' he murmured.

'There's no reason why you should,' his adviser assured him. *Other than via pillow talk.*

'Can we make use of that? Politically? Like put the screws on him for the *Saltire*'s support in the next election?'

Dunbar marvelled yet again at his boss's political innocence. Perhaps it helped make him such a man of the people. 'Richard,' he said, 'let me tell you something. Bob Skinner has no enemies, and you know why? There are none left. Nobody crosses him and walks away undamaged. Let's rephrase your question. Can we make use of Skinner's position as exec chair of the fastest growing media group in Europe? Maybe we can. He and the newspaper are publicly apolitical, but he's on the record about voting against Brexit. Your unstated policy is to build as many trading alliances between Scotland and individual EU members as you possibly can. If we can get Skinner to swing the InterMedia titles behind that . . . not just the *Saltire*, all of them . . . it would be a huge help. Let's take advantage of the fact that his son's covering the ferry inauguration and give him special treatment.'

'Okay,' Ralston agreed. 'Let's feed the cub first, then move on to the lion.'

Seven

'How long will she be in Edinburgh?' Alexis Skinner asked her father.

'We haven't discussed that yet,' he told her, gazing at the screen, 'but my thinking is six months. Then a year in the Italian operation, and another in the US.'

'How long will you be doing this job, Pops?'

'For as long as Xavi and Paloma want me, or until Sarah decides that she wants to retire.'

'That's got to be at least fifteen years away. And you'll be into your seventies by then.'

'True,' he conceded, 'but I'll have outlived my usefulness here way before then.'

'And moved back to Scotland?'

'Maybe I'll never do that. I like living in Spain and so do the family.'

'Don't you miss the place at all?'

'The weather, no. The dark days of winter, no. Sometimes, though, I miss Gullane; I miss being able to walk down to the golf club and knocking a ball around there. But I'm a member of the swanky resort just outside Girona; it's only a short drive away, and an acceptable alternative. And I miss taking Sarah to the theatre, but there's a lot of cultural stuff here, and in Barcelona. Oh yes, and I miss you, but we have this thing to talk on.'

'Do you miss Edinburgh itself?'

'Not a tiny piece of it,' he replied. 'I hate what the clowns on the City Council have done to the city over the last couple of decades. Not that I'd say that to the *Saltire* readership, mind,' he added.

'Do you think this new ferry link with Sweden's going to help?'

'It'll probably help the Swedes more than us,' Skinner suggested. 'The Scottish Government spin doctor's pressing June Crampsey to run an editorial backing it, but she's not buying into it, not yet. You know that ferries are an emotive issue in Scotland; June doesn't want to be seen flag-waving for a link to Europe while people are being stuck on islands at home on a regular basis because of our elderly fleet's high breakdown rate. Yes, she's sending Nacho to cover the inauguration, but that's as far as she's prepared to go. My private view is that the guy Ralston has an agenda that he hasn't revealed yet. That's what Westminster thinks too, by the way; I was told that by the Home Secretary herself, no less.'

'You're still in touch with Aileen de Marco?' his daughter exclaimed.

'It was the other way around. She got in touch with me to ask if I had any idea what Ralston was up to. Look, Alex, I don't have a beef with Aileen. Sarah and I had some rocky patches first time around, my fault more than hers, and she was there during one of them. These things happen. She wasn't a marriage-breaker.'

'Pops, that's exactly what she did!'

'It took two, love. Look, I know you didn't like Aileen, but if I'd paid more attention to her and less to playing the big chief, our marriage might have worked, or lasted longer. On the other hand, I am very happy now, and if Aileen and I had lasted, your youngest sister would never have been born.'

'Pops, you and Aileen were never going to work,' she said. 'I could've told you that at the time. Two personalities like yours can't share the same space. It's not just me saying that: Dominic thinks

30

the same. Okay, you're right,' she conceded, 'I never liked the woman. I never liked Mia bloody Sparkles either, if you really want to know. She was great on the radio and I was a fan, but when you brought her home, I realised pretty quickly that wasn't the real her. I still don't care for her, but I'm polite when we meet, with her being Ignacio's mum.' She paused. 'What would my mum have made of it all, do you think? You had a colourful life for twenty-odd years after she died.'

'Myra had a colourful life before she died,' he shot back, 'as you well know. She'd probably have been astonished by what's happened in mine. She thought I was boring; and she was right. But,' he sighed with a wistful smile, 'all that's history.'

'I wonder what she'd have made of me and Dominic?'

'She'd have liked him, no question. How is the big guy, by the way? He and I haven't spoken in a while.'

'He's very busy,' Alex replied. 'His practice is going very well. He has quite a mix of clients; disturbed kids referred by their parents, stressed-out business people, a couple of top-fifty golfers who come to him for mental conditioning, a very high-profile football manager whose first language isn't English, and even a stable of showbiz people, the kind who think you haven't made it until you have a shrink. Plus he's done a bit of profiling, very much off the record, for British and American law enforcement. The fact is, Pops, I think he's too busy; he's not getting enough exercise, and he's easily tired. He's not young, remember.'

'Tell him to take a break.'

'I have done but the problem is he loves his work.' She smiled. 'So Mum would have approved of him, you reckon?'

'One hundred per cent,' he assured her. 'But I'll tell you one thing,' he continued. 'If she was still here, she'd approve even more of you. She'd be effusively proud of her daughter. Alexis Skinner, King's Counsel, no less.'

'That doesn't mean much,' Alex said, dismissively. 'Just a couple of letters after my name.'

'Bollocks! It means a lot more than that, and you know it. It means success and I'm as proud of you as Myra would have been.' He paused. 'Are you pleased to have finished your stint in the Crown Office?'

She nodded. 'Yes, I am. But I'm glad that you persuaded me to go there, after me swearing I never would. Prosecution's a different skill; it took me a while to acquire it.'

'Not that long. A one hundred per cent conviction rate speaks for itself.'

Her smile faded. 'Yes, it does,' she agreed, 'but you know what it really says? It says that the prosecution approval benchmark is set way too high. The Crown Office won't take a case to court unless the chances of conviction are well above fifty per cent. It's coy about the actual number, but the CPS in England works to a figure of around an eighty per cent chance of success. That's why my hundred per cent rate isn't remarkable at all. I only had to be reasonably competent and avoid procedural fuck-ups to achieve it. As a defence counsel a significant number of cases in which I'm briefed never actually get to trial. Okay, I never lost a case as a prosecutor, but so what? Mitch Laidlaw, my old boss when I was in corporate law, he never lost in court either. That's because he knew when to settle a case better than anyone else in the business.'

'Do you ever think about going back to that sector?' her father wondered. 'With your reputation and skills you could start your own corporate firm, and make a fortune.'

Alex laughed. 'No way, Pops. I left for a reason and it still stands. I'd rather have bears for clients than sharks. Speaking of which, I had a proper odd one this morning. A man came to see me. He was youngish, IC1, around thirty, give or take a year or so, well-dressed and immaculately groomed. He began by asking whether our

32

conversation would be privileged. When I told him it would be if he was my client, he said that he wanted to retain me as his defence lawyer. I asked him, "What's the charge?" He said, "There isn't one." I asked him what offence was under investigation, he said none. As far as I could tell, he wants me to defend him for a crime that he hasn't committed yet.'

'Eh?' Skinner exclaimed. 'What are you going to do?'

'I suggested that he come back when he has been arrested or charged. But as you know, technically I couldn't refuse him. I had to accept his retainer. We can't turn people away just because we don't like them. We're obligated by the thing called the cab rank rule.'

'You're no taxi, baby,' he chuckled. 'You're a Rolls Royce. This guy, did he tell you anything that might compromise you . . . or put you at risk?'

'No, he didn't, and I made a point of not asking.'

'What's his name?'

'You know I can't tell you, Pops. Lawyer–client privilege, and all that. Besides, if I did you'd probably set Sauce Haddock on him.'

Eight

Mia McCullough rolled off the spent First Minister, ruffling her tousled hair with one hand before pulling the duvet over them. 'That wasn't exactly memorable, Richard,' she said. 'A wise lady in Spain once told me that the two saddest times in a woman's life are, first, when her partner can't find her clitoris and, second, when he does.' She smiled up at the ceiling. 'Hey, do you realise,' she asked, 'that when Aileen de Marco had your job, she and Bob Skinner would have screwed in this bed.'

'But not on this mattress,' Ralston countered, clinging to as much of his self-esteem as he could. 'When I took over as party leader, and moved into the official residence, I insisted that they change it.'

'I wonder if they do that in Downing Street?' she yawned. 'Or whether they clean the bathroom thoroughly? Imagine, Labour and Tory pubes intermingled in the shower's hair trap.'

He scratched his head. 'I never thought of that,' he admitted. 'But I'm sure the housekeeper does.'

'Don't be . . . so sure, I mean. I run a hotel, remember. I know where the corners are cut. Speaking of Bob,' she added, 'or at least speaking of his newspaper, thanks for agreeing to give Ignacio an interview. He told me this morning.'

'I'll be meeting Ignacio the day after tomorrow. He'll be at the

34

airport when my flight gets in. But don't get too excited,' he told her. 'An interview is one thing, a headline's another.'

'Can't you give him a headline?'

He laughed. 'Would you like me to announce my resignation? Would that do?'

'A couple of million Scots would love it,' she said, dryly.

'I'm sure they would, but they'll have to wait until next year, if the election goes the wrong way.'

She propped herself up on an elbow and looked down at him. 'Do you think you'll lose?'

'Far from it. I think I'll gain an absolute majority and be free of those Green people, Ben and Holly. Once I am . . .'

Mia frowned. 'Richard,' she ventured, 'I'm no John Curtice, but the polls aren't saying that.'

'They're not saying that right now, because Labour still has some of the support it gathered at the last Westminster election. A year from now, that'll have gone, the incumbent Prime Minister will be as popular within his own party as a turd in a hot tub and most of that support'll have evaporated, dragging the Scottish party down with it. As my granny would have said, we will scoosh it.'

'What about these Reform characters? Aren't they a danger?'

'Not to me; their votes come from the Tories and from discontented Labour supporters who don't understand how right wing they are. My people know that they're even more pro-Union than the Unionists. Those polls you talked about . . . take a really good look and they'll tell you that.'

'When will you begin your campaign?' she asked.

'I'm campaigning already, my dear. Everything I do from now on will have one eye on the first Thursday in May next year.'

She turned on her side, reached under the duvet and took hold of him. 'Everything? If your adoring public found out about me . . .'

'Why should they?' he laughed. 'You're not going to spill the beans, are you?'

'No,' she said. 'I wouldn't want the notoriety, thanks very much . . . and strangely enough, I wouldn't want to embarrass your wife either. I have nothing against her. Is it right that she's your second wife? Ignacio said that you and a colleague of his were . . .'

He sighed deeply. 'I thought everyone knew about Susan. Yes, I was married before Amy: Sue and I met at university. Love at first sight.'

'Which one?'

'St Andrews. Where the students wear cloaks.'

'And some wear crowns, eventually,' she chuckled. 'If it was love at first sight, what happened?'

'Second sight. But mostly politics. Sue was very into it even then; she was studying it in her degree course. I was a law student. We were both Liberal Democrats, and that brought us even closer. We married before we graduated: just kids, the pair of us. After uni, I went to do an apprenticeship with my dad's law firm in Glasgow . . .'

'Indeed?' She interrupted him. 'That's one thing you have in common with Bob Skinner. His father was a lawyer too. Bob could have done what you did, but his ambitions lay elsewhere.'

'So did mine, I suppose, if you look at where I am now. Anyway, as I was saying, after St Andrews, Sue, she was focused on journalism and wanted to do a post-grad. That was at Stirling, and involved a daily commute, so we saw less of each other than was healthy for a new marriage. At the same time, we were both active in the party. As soon as I had my practising certificate, I stood in a City Council by-election and won it. Sue stayed in the background. She was working for the BBC by then and had to keep her head below the surface, although it didn't soften her commitment to the cause: it did the opposite, if anything. On the other hand, although I was in a minority group on the Council . . . or Cooncil as they all called it, I was involved in a lot of committee work, where I was exposed to the views and thinking of the other parties. Gradually I came to realise how much of a nationalist I really was. Feeling that way as a Lib Dem didn't make me a traitor, but it did make me realise that if I wanted to achieve some of the things that I wanted to nationally, I couldn't do it in that situation. And one day I said as much to Sue. She exploded: she said I had no philosophical backbone. I told her that if I wanted to win hearts and minds, I needed to figure out where my own were at. She chose that exact moment to tell me she was pregnant.'

'You have a child?' Mia exclaimed. 'I didn't know that.'

'Daniel keeps a low profile; his choice as much as mine. He runs my law practice, now that I'm full-time at Holyrood. Anyway, the pregnancy served as a sort of truce. Sue had her maternity leave, at the BBC's insistence, for she'd have gone back earlier. I carried on with my career and as a Lib Dem councillor, a good one. Ask any of my friends from those days and they'll tell you I did a good job on those committees. I chaired a couple, Education and Social Work; I was a moderating voice, I found the areas of consensus in the parties' positions, broke deadlocks on several occasions and actually got stuff done. It involved compromise on everyone's part; and that was it for Sue and me. You see, the fundamental truth about the Liberal Democrats is that they never agree with anyone. They tried it once, remember, when they parlayed a few Westminster seats into Cabinet positions and official cars rolling up to their doors every morning. They were only able to do it because the Tory leader of the day lacked the balls to form a majority government, and his Lib Dem chums sold their souls for the trappings of power. Sue would never have done that deal; she sees herself as incorruptible. I have to concede that politically she is.'

'That's why you split up?' Mia interjected. 'She thought you were politically corrupt.'

Ralston laughed. 'Hell no! Three years or so after that first big blow-up, I discovered that she was screwing an academic, a politics lecturer at Glasgow University, and had been for a while. I didn't make a fuss; just told her quietly that our definitions of liberalism really were polls apart. I tried to keep the divorce amicable, but as always she was confrontational. She had a lawyer friend send me a list of demands.' He grinned. 'Mistake. Her pal was a planning specialist . . . I think they'd had a fling too at one point . . . but my expertise is in family law, and I'm good at it. They folded pretty quickly. Sue went to BBC London as a Parliamentary reporter and I stayed put.'

'And Daniel?'

'I was given custody. Uncontested,' he added. 'Sue didn't want him, not as a single woman in London.'

'But that made you single too? Weren't you?'

'Yes, but my mother was still in her fifties, with time on her hands. And my sister had two kids, one of them a few months younger than Daniel, so I had plenty of support.'

'When did you meet Amy?'

'A few years after the divorce. She was a constituent, a divorcee like me, a survivor of an abusive marriage, but her abuse was physical rather than emotional, and I was a very new Member of the Scottish Parliament; still as a Liberal Democrat,' he added. 'If we were to separate . . .' he murmured. A question hung there.

'But you won't,' she insisted, deflecting it quickly. 'It might cost you that absolute majority.'

'Not if it was properly managed, presented as a mutual decision, a happy parting of the ways. That wouldn't be a lie, Mia; that's how it really is.'

'Are you being serious?' she exclaimed.

He nodded.

'I don't believe you. If you did that it would shaft you. It would knock a big hole in your female support.'

'Mia, my dear, if we told the truth it might actually increase it. The official story is that Amy is too shy to get involved in the active side of politics, so she prefers to remain at home. That's true, but the real story is that she left me some time ago, before I became First Minister.'

'For someone else?'

'Yes.'

'Do you know who he is?'

'Oh yes; he's pretty high profile. His name's Jesus.'

She squeezed him, hard. 'You're taking the piss!'

He gasped. His forehead wrinkled and his eyes widened. 'I'm not, honestly,' he said, hurriedly. 'Amy is a nun, an Anglican nun. She's completed her novitiate and lives in a convent in Perthshire. She used to come back home every few months, just to see that I was all right, but not any more.'

'I didn't know you could be an Anglican nun,' Mia said. 'Can you really?'

'Bloody hell, have you never watched *Call the Midwife*? Amy did, and that's how it all got started.'

'My God. Richard . . .'

'No, her God. She found Him and He filled a gap in her life that I didn't even know was there. I was always too busy, I suppose; like me, Amy has a son from her first marriage, but we have no children together and . . . well . . . she found that someone else.'

She stared at him, with a faint smile. 'When she did come home, did you still . . . have sex? Did she ever cheat on JC?'

'Celibacy isn't a requirement within the Anglican community.'

'Well? Did you?' she pressed him.

'At first, maybe; occasionally,' he admitted, returning her grin.

'It would have been the missionary position, I assume.'

'Of course. It always was.'

She released him and sat up, braced against the headboard. 'Why keep it a secret? Surely . . .'

'Amy's order prefers that we do. You can imagine why. The tabloids and the bloggers would have an absolute field day. Look, we haven't put a time frame on it, but in October, we'll have been separated legally for two years and we'll be free to divorce. It'll be a story for a couple of days but that'll be all. Then,' he said, quietly, 'maybe you and I can come out of the closet and announce our engagement.'

'Fuck off!' Mia exploded, laughing. 'Richard, if you knew all there is to know about me, you'd want to go into a monastery yourself.'

'Don't you want us to be together?' Ralston asked her, suddenly anxious.

'No more than we are already,' she replied. 'Not yet, maybe never. Listen, I've only been married once, but the way I feel at the moment, that will be enough, thanks. Marriage was nice, a new experience for me, but then Cameron died, when nobody expected it and it hurt; I don't want to be in that situation again, Richard. For the moment being a girlfriend is enough for me. If you want more than that, if you want to be . . . politically correct, if you like, well, I'm not sure it can be with me.'

'I see. I'll need to think about how that will look. I've been assuming . . .'

'You're a man, you would,' she said.

He pulled himself up and sat alongside her. 'Mia, if you're as relaxed about relationships as you seem to be,' he hesitated, then continued, 'I need to ask, if I can work out how to put it . . .'

'No,' she said.

'No what? No, I can't ask?'

'You did, without saying it. No, Richard, I am not sleeping with anybody else. If you had a sudden vision of me shagging the leader of the opposition as well as you, you can put it to bed. I'm not promiscuous, nor have I ever been. I had five lovers before you and that's including one husband. If you hadn't invited me for dinner after your visit to the radio station, that number probably wouldn't have changed.'

'And Skinner,' he murmured. 'You and he? How did you feel about him?'

She tilted her head towards his. 'Good question. One I've asked myself many times. Want to hear what I think is the answer?'

He nodded.

'For a very brief moment, at a very bad time in my life, I fell seriously in love with him. That's how Nacho came to be. But Bob can be scary, Richard. He really did frighten me, like nobody else had before or has since. He didn't set out to, he didn't even realise, but he did. He can be a very dangerous man, can Bob. If you're attuned to it, if you've had a childhood like mine, then you're aware of it. There's a sort of energy within him. It comes off him in waves. Cameron, he was the same, if not quite as intense. On the rare occasions that they were in the same room, if you'd connected the pair of them into the national grid the energy from them could have floodlit a football ground.'

'I wonder if Aileen de Marco felt it,' Ralston mused. 'When she was caught with the actor guy, Joey Morrocco, I wonder if it was because he'd scared her off too. Funny,' he chuckled, 'how life's interlinked. You and Skinner, you and me, him and de Marco, her and me.'

She stiffened. 'You and her? Have you . . .'

'No,' he rushed to say. 'Not in that way. But she is a danger to me.'

'How? What's dangerous about her?'

'Her ambition. It could cost me the election, or at least that absolute nationalist majority.'

'Are you saying she might stand in Scotland next year? How could she? She's Home Secretary and her Westminster seat's in England.'

'No, I'm not saying that at all. De Marco shook the dust of Scotland off her shoes a long time ago. She'll never be back. Her future is in London, and the chattering classes down there know what it is. The Prime Minister, Merlin Brady: he has a thumping majority, but only because his predecessor made an arse of it, and because the Reformers cost the Tories a big chunk of votes and a lot of seats. That great big majority overstates his actual support in the party and in the country, his immigration policy's a shambles and the NHS is in an even worse mess than the previous government left it. On top of that he's old and tired. He's personally very popular but if he decided to resign tomorrow, a large chunk of his Parliamentary party would be relieved. His stated intention is to fight the next election as leader, but few of his MPs really believe that'll happen. There have been rumours of a putsch for a few months now, with Brady being eased towards the door and replaced by de Marco. That, or something like it, will happen, of that I'm sure. The question is, when? Conventional wisdom is that he'll stay for another year. If he does, Labour support will erode still further and we'll kick their arses in twelve months, or sooner if I decide to bring the election forward.'

'So what's the danger?' Mia asked. 'And where does de Marco's ambition come into play?'

'I have a source who tells me that she wants to be more than just a one-term Prime Minister. That means that she has to win an election in her own right. If you go back seventy-five years you'll find nine Prime Ministers who were chosen by their party but not by the people. Seven were Conservative, and two Labour. Of those, one never fought a General Election as leader. Five of the others lost, and another kept the job but without an absolute majority. De

Marco is loyal to Brady at the moment, but my fear is that if she decides that it wouldn't be safe to keep him in office for another year, she might push the button in Cabinet and challenge him. If she does that, he won't fight her; he'll resign. There might be a leadership election or there might be a simple coronation. Either way she'll be Prime Minister, there will be a popularity bounce, and overnight Scottish Labour will have muscle again, even more with one of their own in Downing Street.'

'How good is your source?'

'The best,' Ralston replied. 'It's Joey Morrocco. He and Aileen aren't together any longer, but they're still on good terms. And he's on good terms with me too. He's a significant donor to my party.'

'Joey Morrocco,' Mia chuckled. 'The man who cuckolded Bob Skinner and still has full motor function. That said, glass houses come to mind with Bob.'

'You mean when you and he had your fling? He was married?'

'No, he was widowed. But him and de Marco, that started as an away game.'

He entwined his fingers with hers. 'You know what I'm hearing, my dear?' he said. 'I'm hearing jealousy, pure and simple. When you say that you were in love with Skinner for a very brief period, I think you're lying to yourself. I don't believe you've ever stopped loving him.'

'Funny,' she murmured. 'I said much the same thing to him this afternoon. I thought I was joking, but now that you say it . . .'

Nine

'Above us is where the body was left,' Ignacio said, as their train passed smoothly across the Oresund Bridge, on the track beneath the highway.

'What body?' Pilar asked, puzzled.

He grinned. 'The body in the TV series, *The Bridge*. This is where it begins, between Denmark and Sweden.'

'I've never heard of it,' she confessed. 'Was it shown in Spain?'

'It's been shown everywhere,' he assured her, 'and the concept's been copied in other settings in other countries. It's iconic. The story is that the corpse is found where we've just passed on the border between the two countries. But, when they take a closer look, they are actually two bodies, the top half of one and the lower half of another. The investigation involves two police forces in the different countries, and two detectives.'

'Can we stream it when we're home?'

'It'll probably be showing somewhere. I'll check.'

'Will we have any time for sightseeing in Malmo?'

'Tomorrow, none at all, but once we've checked into the hotel we can visit a couple of places. Is there anything that you want to see? My impression is that the place isn't exactly a tourist hotspot.'

Pilar shook her head, her black hair shimmering in the carriage lights. 'That is not fair,' she insisted. 'It has many things. It has an opera house, museum, a library, a castle, and it has the Turning Torso.'

'The what?' Her partner laughed.

'The Turning Torso,' she repeated. 'It's the highest residential block in Sweden, a masterpiece of architecture and engineering, so the tourist guide says. It looks like nine cubes stacked one on top of another, but in a twisting design.'

'Ah,' Ignacio exclaimed. 'There's a visit on Ralston's schedule for tomorrow to something that's referred to as TT, with an address. That must be it.'

'I'd like to see it with just us, and without you working.'

He shrugged, glancing through the window as the Swedish coast approached. 'Okay, that can be done: we'll go there first. We can walk, yes?'

'No, but when we get to the station we can buy bus passes that will last for twenty-four hours.'

He grinned. 'You have done your research, haven't you?'

'I need to make myself useful. Otherwise what am I here for?'

Ignacio looked at her, suddenly serious. 'You're here because I couldn't stand the idea of spending even a couple of days without you. Some journalist I'm going to be, eh? I'm beginning to think I should stick to being a sub-editor; that way I'd be guaranteed to be in the office all the time and I'd get to go home every night.'

'Are you that insecure?' she asked him.

'I've never thought of myself in that way, but when it comes to you . . . my great fear is of losing you. Stuck on you, love.'

She took his right hand in hers, interlinking their fingers. 'In that case,' she murmured, 'I can see only one solution.'

'And what's that?'

'You'd better marry me.'

He grinned. 'If that's the only way, then I guess I will.'

Ten

'What's the man's name?' Dominic Jackson asked his partner.

'I'm not going to tell you,' Alex Skinner replied.

His eyebrows rose as he beamed at her. 'I can understand why you didn't tell your dad but, love, this is us. I'm not going to tell anyone.'

'You can't promise me that.'

'Sure I can.'

'No, you can't,' she insisted. 'Get your great big brain around this if you can. I feel absolutely boxed in here; the cab rank rule says that I had to accept the guy as a client, even though I don't know why. Let's say something did happen with him, and that he's more than just the flash fantasist I suspect him to be. Let's say he does something really serious, like he kills the King, something like that. As soon as I stepped up as his brief, the investigating officers would be looking at all the angles. Someone like Sauce Haddock, or maybe Lottie Mann . . . I'm close to both of them, for different reasons . . . might try to have an informal word with me in the vain hope that I might slip them a clue. In terms of potential foreknowledge of a crime, I'm covered by lawyer–client privilege, so I would shoo them away. But you aren't covered, my love. It's far from inconceivable that you might be approached, in case I have let something slip domestically.'

46

'Sauce or Lottie wouldn't do that, would they?'

'Probably not, but Major Crimes might not be the investigating branch. If there was organised crime involvement . . . okay, brainstorming, let's say he's part of an international people-trafficking gang . . . then the security services might be involved.'

'Alex, isn't the head of that branch in Scotland your uncle? Or has he been moved?'

'No, he hasn't, but I wasn't talking about his outfit. If an investigation crosses our internal border or goes international, Thames House might get involved.'

'Didn't your dad have links there when he was chief?'

'I think he still does, but only as far as he and the Director General are on each other's Christmas card list.'

'Okay,' he grunted. 'Your point being?'

'That we should be careful of any situation that might put you at risk. Look, Dominic Jackson might be a respected professional figure, with a stack of qualifications and a successful practice, but it's your second identity. If anyone tried to get to me through you, it would be Lenny Plenderleith who was in the witness box. Lenny Plenderleith is a life-sentence prisoner, currently released on licence, but liable to recall at any time, as he would be if he refused a judge's order under oath. I wouldn't let that happen anyway, my love, but I am not going to do anything that makes it even faintly possible. Get it?'

He nodded. 'I get it, and I love you for it. Now, what have you found out about Mr X? For I'm sure you'll have looked by now.'

Alex smiled. 'Of course I have,' she said. 'I did a search for him online. I found a few people of that name on Facebook but none of them was him. I had a look at Companies House but there were none of those there either. It may be an alias; if he ever does come back I'll ask him for proof of identity, as I should have done today.'

'Maybe you should have shared his name with Bob,' Dominic

suggested. 'You're right. He would have reached out to Haddock or McGuire and let them check him out.'

'I've done that myself,' she confessed. 'I spoke to a friend in the Crown Office and asked her to run a search, off the record. Nobody of that name has a criminal record in Scotland or is even known to the police.' She paused, looking at him. 'As I said, I reckon he's a fantasist. Either that or a journalist or a blogger, playing a daft game. What do you think?'

'I don't think anything,' he replied. 'I'd need to meet the man and talk to him to give you a significant opinion. If you ask me to guess, I'd suggest that he might be a wannabe, someone who's watched so many TV crime dramas, that he's absorbed aspects of them into his personality. You said he was well-dressed. How well? What was he wearing?'

'A dark blue suit, over a shiny yellow waistcoat, possibly satin. Black shoes; they were shiny too. The suit fitted perfectly, so it could have been tailor made, and the shoes could have come off a last. His shirt was pale blue with white pinstripes . . . not a Marks and Spencer's job; they tend not to have monogrammed collars . . . and his tie looked as if it was silk. It matched the colour of his waistcoat,' she added. 'Overall, he reminded me of one of the equity partners in Curle Anthony Jarvis, my old firm when I was a solicitor. His working clothes cost at least three grand, back then. The mysterious Mr X's outfit was in that league, and he probably spent even more on grooming.'

'Ethnicity?'

'White.'

'His accent?'

'British, that's all I can say. Nondescript, in a literal sense. I didn't detect any regional influences. Does all that tell you anything?'

Dominic smiled. 'Yes, it tells me, yet again, that you should have a camera in your consulting room.'

'I've told you before,' she exclaimed, a little testily, 'my clients wouldn't like it.'

'And I've told you before,' he countered. 'They don't have to see it. Meantime, the best thing you can do is put him out of your thoughts, until he brings himself back into them, if he ever does, and that's questionable. One thing, though . . . and this is not my opinion as a psychologist, but as someone who's met more than a few criminals in his time. Should he consult you again, formally, it won't be about the theft of a few paper clips. It will be about something serious, something big. Yes, I know about the cab rank principle that you advocates operate under. It says that if you are, metaphorically, waiting at the kerbside, you're professionally obliged to take on as a client more or less anyone who asks you. The way I see it, there's only one thing you can do to overcome that: keep yourself as busy as you can. Make sure your taxi's full.'

'Noted, but as I said, it's too late for that. He's already in the taxi.'

Eleven

The Scottish First Minister was of above-average height, and had to duck his head to exit the Learjet 60 that had flown him and his two-person entourage from Edinburgh. As he descended the aircraft steps, another group of three approached; its leader extended a hand.

'First Minister,' the blonde woman exclaimed. 'Lena Rapace, Trade Minister. Welcome to Malmo, and to Sweden. This is an auspicious visit for both our countries. The Prime Minister regrets that she couldn't be here to welcome you herself, but she had to be in Brussels today.'

'That's understood entirely,' Richard Ralston replied. 'Indeed, I envy her. My nation voted overwhelmingly to remain in the EU, but we were dragged out of it by the Westminster Tories.'

'I sympathise with you,' the Swedish minister assured him. 'My career background was in political science. I'm aware that most of that administration didn't want to leave Europe, so I ask myself why they held the referendum at all.'

'Because they assumed they would win,' he grinned. 'That's the trouble with referendums; they're an unstable weapon; they can go off in your hand . . . unless they're fixed, as ours was by allowing English expats in Scotland to vote while disallowing Scots expats living in England and elsewhere.'

'But doesn't your party want an independence re-run in Scotland?'

'Yes, but on our terms. Meanwhile . . .' he stopped, abruptly.

'Good luck in securing them,' Rapace replied. She glanced over her shoulder, towards a small group of journalists and photographers who stood in front of the entrance to the terminal building. 'The press. Would you like to speak to them? I'm told by my media officer that they're all ours, apart from one Scottish reporter. There's no BBC, I'm afraid.'

Ralston shrugged. 'The way things are, the BBC being here would be a story in itself. Minister, I suggest that we're polite to them, but we keep a longer discussion for the inauguration ceremony. Would that be okay with you?'

'Perfectly. And it'll give us a little more time for the only visit we have scheduled for today, our visit to the Turning Torso. I was intrigued to see that you asked especially to visit it. You're a student of architecture, Mr Ralston?'

He smiled back at her. 'I wouldn't know a Frank Lloyd Wright from a Frankfurter, but I do have an ulterior motive. I wasn't going to raise it until later, but I might as well tell you now, if we have a moment.'

'Of course, please go on. I'm intrigued.'

'Thank you,' he said. 'Well, your Prime Minister, Ms Mattson, is aware that I'm keen to build links between Sweden and Scotland. The ferry service is an excellent start, but it's very much focused on Edinburgh. The last thing my party and I want to do is put Glasgow's nose out of joint. Malmo has twinning links in place with cities in seven different countries. Scotland isn't one of them, but we would like to remedy that. My people on Glasgow City Council, which we control, have worked up a proposal to twin with Malmo.'

Lena Rapace managed to shrug with her face. 'That's good to hear,' she conceded, 'but hardly earth-shattering.'

'Ah, but there's more,' the First Minister said. 'Let me explain.'

By the time he finished, her attitude had changed, dramatically. 'Does anyone in Malmo know about this?' she asked. 'Central government hasn't heard of it.'

'Oh, Malmo knows about it, be sure of that. We broached it with them months ago, at Mayoral level. If there had been no interest from your side, well, that would have been it, but they liked the idea. They bought in straight away. I'm told they see it as enhancing their own status within Sweden. It was agreed by everyone that, during the discussion phase, the proposal should be kept confidential and at civic level, but the time has come to open up and move it up. Tomorrow morning, before the inauguration ceremony, or if necessary after it but before we sail, I'd like to sit down with you and the Mayor of Malmo, and run through the detail with you both. Would you do that?'

'If I'm allowed to, yes,' Rapace replied. 'With you being involved, I'll need to tell the Prime Minister. Pernil will react in one of three ways: she'll say, "Go ahead," she'll say, "I want to be involved in this myself," or she'll say, "No". If she says no, it'll be for one of two reasons; she's from Goteborg, our second city, and wouldn't want Malmo, our third, becoming too big for its boots, as you might say, or,' she hesitated for a second, 'it's because she doesn't want to upset Merlin Brady, her UK counterpart, by being seen as too friendly with you, the Scottish First Minister, when you and he are in different camps politically.'

'If she's in Brussels, will she be available tomorrow?' Ralston wondered. He had been ahead of his counterpart in her thinking. He knew that the last of her options, if that was how it played out, would bring his long-term strategy to a full stop. 'When can you contact her?'

'I can call her directly from the car on the way into the city . . . it's a twenty-minute drive to our destination, even with a police motorcycle escort . . . brief her on the proposal and ask her how she wants to play it. Pernil's impulsive, so that's the best way to handle her. Doing it through her officials will give her time to consider all the downsides. Let's go, First Minister. I'll have my press aide tell the journalists that we're heading straight to the Turning Torso. If they want to, they can follow.'

Twelve

'What's her status, Bob?' June Crampsey asked. 'Officially, what's she doing here?'

'How do you describe her to the staff?' Skinner asked. 'Is that what you mean?'

'Yes.'

'You don't need to describe her as anything. We don't in Girona. She's Paloma to a few of the top-level staff, by whom I mean those who've known her since she was a kid, hanging around the office with her dad, and Señora Aislado to all the rest. Just put her name on her office door: that'll tell everyone all they need to know. As for how she's treated, our plan, hers and mine . . . and Xavi's,' he added, 'is that she familiarise herself with the whole InterMedia operation over the next few years, location by location. As for the detail of what she does, you can help her plan her schedule for her Edinburgh residency.'

'Will she and I get on, do you think?'

'It won't be a problem. She has an open mind, and she understands that young people aren't born with all the answers, nor do they learn them at LSE.' He gazed at the screen. 'Speaking of young people, have you had any feedback from Ignacio yet, from Sweden?'

'Yes, we have. He's just filed a very brief story about Ralston's

54

arrival at Malmo Airport, and being met getting off the plane by the Swedes' Trade Minister. It was all at a distance, though; they didn't speak to the press. It was really a waste of money having a reporter there, although Ignacio's put a decent spin on it by noting that their Prime Minister wasn't there, and suggesting that defines Ralston's place in the pecking order. He and Rapace, the Swede, had what the piece describes as an extended conversation, then it says they went off-programme, by-passing the media, getting into their cars and heading for the city and the only engagement Ralston has for the day. He's gone to look at a tower block . . . as if we need any more of those,' she added dryly.

'From what I know of Ralston, if he's agreed to the visit, there'll be something in it for him, you may be sure of that.'

'Our new political editor would agree with you there.'

'Is that woman an asset or a liability?' Skinner asked. 'Not that I'm questioning your judgement in hiring her,' he added, hastily.

Crampsey laughed. 'Of course you are, Bob, but don't worry about it. I question my judgement all the time. Broadly speaking, Sue is an asset for sure. I'll grant you that I wish I didn't have to maintain a Chinese Wall between our political ed and the First Minister, but I didn't hire her to spend all her time at Holyrood. Her experience and her expertise are at Westminster. We position ourselves as a national slash UK newspaper, so that's where I want her to focus. My plan . . . which I did mean to discuss with you, honest . . . is to appoint a deputy political editor to lead our Scottish Parliamentary coverage. The person I have in mind is . . . Ignacio. That's why I sent him to Sweden to cover Ralston there.' She paused, as she saw Skinner's frown on the screen. 'What?'

'The exec chairman's son? I would need to clear that with Xavi.'

'You and I both know that Xavi will approve.'

'Still, you might need to row back on the idea. Have you spoken to Nacho about it?'

'No, not yet. What's your concern?'

'You might need to build another Chinese Wall. They way things are going, Ralston's going to be completely boxed in.'

'I don't get you.'

'Our charismatic First Minister is in a relationship with Ignacio's mother.'

'She's what? How on earth do you know? Did Mia McCullough tell you that herself?'

'No, she didn't.'

'Then who?'

He stared at the camera on his device, then beamed. 'Mrs Crampsey, are you asking me to betray my sources? What sort of journo are you?'

'I'm the kind who doesn't want to wind up explaining myself to a Court of Session judge why I don't know the identity of a source in a story I published.'

'You won't be publishing this one,' Skinner declared, 'so it won't be an issue. Do you know who Lowell Payne is?' he asked.

'He's an assistant chief constable, isn't he?'

'That's right; with oversight of the department that we used to call Special Branch; now it's Organised Crime and Counter Terrorism. He's also Alex's uncle, my late first wife's brother-in-law. Unlike the Prime Minister and the key Westminster Cabinet members, the First Minister doesn't have obvious visible security. However they do keep an eye on him, and everything goes across Lowell's desk. That's how he was able to tell me very discreetly that Mia's become a regular visitor to the official residence, going in through the back door and staying for breakfast. Ralston's also paid a few visits to her house in the grounds of Black Shield Lodge, her hotel.'

'Ralston's married, yes?'

'He is,' Skinner confirmed, 'but he and his wife are separated, from what Lowell said. And others, for that matter.'

'Does Ignacio know?' she asked anxiously.

'I don't think so. I'm pretty sure that if he did he'd have told me . . . and you as well.'

'Bugger, bugger, bugger!' Crampsey exclaimed. 'No way can I put him into that job now. How serious do you think it is . . . the relationship?'

'I don't know, all I know is of its existence. Mia herself isn't a security threat, so Lowell isn't doing anything about it. He only told me so that I could flag up with Mia that his department is aware. I said I would when an opportunity came up, but now you say that it's compromising our son professionally, I have to act on that. When we're done, she's my next call.'

'In that case,' the editor said, 'we're done now. Let me know how it goes.'

Thirteen

'It's very impressive, isn't it?' the Swedish reporter said.

'It's interesting,' Ignacio Watson Skinner replied.

'Your first time here?'

'My first visit to Malmo, yes. To the Torso, no; my partner and I had a look at it after we arrived yesterday. Is it really the tallest building in Sweden, as one of the tourist guide books says?'

'It used to be, until Goteborg built a bigger one, but I believe it's still the tallest residential building. I'm from Malmo myself,' she explained. 'We're very proud of it here. It looks quirky but it's a remarkable construction if you think about it. For example, elevators don't have curves in them: their doors have to be absolutely one on top of the other. How did they achieve that?'

Ignacio grinned. 'With difficulty, I suspect.'

They were part of a group of ten journalists, reporters and photographers, marshalled into a small space by two dark-suited men. Ignacio was unsure whether they were police or press officers; the former, he suspected, since they did not engage with the media in any way. Whoever was in charge, the day had been carefully planned and executed. The attending media had been accredited in a square in the centre of Malmo, an hour before the scheduled arrival of the First Minister's flight, then taken to the airport in a bus that could have accommodated, comfortably, twice as many

58

passengers. After their long-distance view of the arrival, they had been rushed back into their transport and driven back into the city, managing somehow to arrive before the VIP group at the base of the soaring building, which was separated from them by an encircling moat.

'How long will you stay?' his colleague asked.

'As long as he's here. We're even sailing back with him on the ferry, the day after tomorrow. His media person's promised me an exclusive with Ralston once we're under way.'

'You say "we".' She looked around. 'Do you have a photographer somewhere?'

He grinned, shaking his head. 'No, I brought my partner. She's back in the hotel . . . or rather in the shopping centre beneath it.'

'That could be expensive. Whose credit card does she have?'

'Her own, don't worry.'

'Hah.' She paused. 'The shopping centre. Does that mean you're in the big hotel in Triangeln?'

'Yes. It's okay. We ate there last night; the head waiter made it seem as if he was doing us a favour, but when we were finished we had to wait forever for the bill. A crowd of at least twenty had come in after us, and he was all over them.'

His colleague smiled. 'The Opera House crowd. That's where they're from. They eat there once a week, they're famous. You should visit it if you have time: it's one of our attractions. It's a status thing really. We Scandinavians are big on classical music; if you don't have an opera house you can't call yourself a city. Do you have many in Scotland? Are you a classical nation?'

'None that I can think of,' he admitted. 'Glasgow has a big concert hall. Edinburgh has a thing called the Festival Theatre, but before that it was a bingo hall. I would say that we're more of a country-and-western nation, but I was brought up in Spain, so I am not the best person to ask.'

She glanced at his name badge. 'I wondered: "Ignacio" does not sound very Scottish as I understand it. I'm Agnetha, by the way. It's a name I share with many Swedish women of my age. Abba has much to answer for. But everyone calls me Aggie,' she added.

He winced. 'In Spain, and in my family, they call me Nacho for short, but at work I discourage that: it makes me sound like a takeaway.'

Aggie's laughter was interrupted by the arrival of two motorcycle outriders, flanking the two limousines they had seen leaving the airport. They stopped no more than twenty metres from the waiting journalists. One of the two dark-suited minders stepped briskly across to the first vehicle and opened the rear passenger door. Ralston eased himself out, smiling and looking around, managing, somehow, to convey the impression that his audience was much larger than it was. That done he stepped to the side, extending a hand to Lena Rapace as she joined him. At the same time the occupants of the second car exited. Ignacio recognised Joanie Cooper, the Scottish Parliament's media director, and another face that he guessed was that of Peter Dunbar, the First Minister's senior adviser.

The two politicians waved to the media; Ralston making a gesture indicating that they should follow. As he did so, the double doors of the Torso's entrance slid open . . . 'Would that be its navel?' Ignacio thought . . . and a small rotund man emerged, stepping on to the bridge that crossed the moat.

'That's Nicolai Lundqvist,' Ignacio's new friend murmured. 'He's the Mayor of Malmo and he looks even more pleased with himself than usual.'

As the politicians met halfway, Rapace introduced the Mayor to Ralston. 'No need,' Lundqvist said. 'We've met on another occasion, in Scotland. Of which more later,' he added.

'Ah yes,' Ignacio heard the Trade Minister say. 'Of course.

Glasgow. Excited, Nicolai?' His voice recorder was switched on: he hoped its microphone had the range to pick it up.

'Very,' the Mayor replied, 'but should we be . . .?' He turned away as he spoke, walking back towards the entrance with his guests.

'*Folja*,' one of the dark-suited minders said. 'Follow,' he repeated. As the media group took him at his word, Ignacio noticed that only seven of them were left. He assumed that the others had deadlines or had decided that it was a non-story.

The tower's foyer was wide. There were two elevators, side by side, each with its doors held open by a minder. '*People live here*,' Ignacio reminded himself. '*They must be loving this.*' As he and his colleagues were directed into the lift on the right, a figure broke off from the VIP group and joined them. Joanie Cooper interposed herself between Ignacio and his new friend, peering at his lapel badge as if in confirmation. A button was pressed and the lift began to move, picking up pace rapidly.

'I'm pleased to see you, Mr Watson,' the spin doctor murmured, 'really pleased. You, that is the *Saltire*, your being here's a message in itself to the Swedes,' she murmured. 'And I'm glad June Cramp-sey had the sense to send you rather than that political editor of yours. As far as we're concerned, she's of marginally less use than a chocolate fireguard, given her feelings about the First Minister. I take it you know about their personal background?'

He nodded. 'The boss explained.'

'And of course,' she added, with what he judged to be a trace of sarcasm, 'it's doubly good that you're here, with your own personal connection.'

Ignacio gazed down at her, puzzled. 'Excuse me?'

At that moment, the lift eased to a halt and its doors opened. Cooper left his side as quickly as she had arrived and rejoined Ralston's party. 'What the f . . .?' he whispered to himself, as he stepped out on to level forty-five; it was an open-plan area and appeared to be a mix of office and display space. As the Ministers and their media following regrouped, Nicolai Lundqvist stepped forward. 'Welcome to Malmo's pride and joy, First Minister Ralston,' he said, managing to smile at the guest and nod to the media simultaneously.

'Smooth-talking little bastard.' It was more than a whisper; heads turned. Aggie had appeared at his side once more. She looked to be at least twice his age; he wondered if he had stirred her maternal instincts.

'The internet describes the Turning Torso as the tallest residential block in Sweden,' the Mayor continued. 'That it is, certainly, thanks to its owners, HSB, our national housing association, but it is more than that. It is also a centre for exhibitions and small conferences, and this is where they happen. Let me show you around.' He turned to the seven-strong media group. 'Please, come with us.'

'That's why we're here,' Aggie muttered.

The group followed Lundqvist as he led them on a circular tour, around the pillar enclosing the lift shafts, and a door leading to a staircase: *Emergency exit*, Ignacio thought, *but it must give residents access to this floor.*

The space was flooded with natural light, streaming through floor-to-ceiling windows that displayed a panorama of the city. It was filled by photographs and exhibits telling the story of the Torso's creation; as they moved, each section was explained in detail by the Mayor.

As they walked, Aggie leaned in close again. 'Nicolai's as slippery as they come. He'll charm you with that smile but he's always after something. I can't think what it is here though.'

They stopped at a model of an eco-friendly housing project. As Lundqvist began explaining its features, Ignacio tuned out, his mind returning to Joanie Cooper's cryptic comment and her brisk exit. *What the fuck was that about?* he wondered.

Eventually they moved on; the display was well-structured, Ignacio conceded, with each section revealing more of Malmo's plans for future development. As they reached the completion of the circular tour, a large video screen flickered to life, displaying a high-definition animation of what the city might look like in another decade.

'Impressive, isn't it?' Lundqvist's voice pulled Ignacio back to the moment. The begged question was for Ralston, but as it was put the Mayor was looking at the journalists.

'I have to commend you,' Ralston replied. 'You've certainly set a high bar for sustainable urban living, much as we're trying to do in Scotland. Would that we had your resources and didn't have to rely so much on London.'

Lundqvist beamed as he led his guests to a table where cafetieres and crockery were waiting. As the refreshments were dispensed by two uniformed waitresses, Ignacio gazed out across the city, mentally composing his piece for the next morning's *Saltire*, wondering how on earth he could find the colour that June Crampsey would expect. He had decided to focus on the Mayor's undisguised attempts to ingratiate himself with Richard Ralston, when he realised that the First Minister was standing at his shoulder.

'Your colleague was right,' he murmured. 'He is a slippery little bastard, isn't he?'

Ignacio grinned. 'It's usually the politicians who say "No comment", not the journalists.'

'Fair point. He has good reason to suck up to me, though. I guess you're looking for a hook to hang the *Saltire*'s coverage of this event.'

'How did you . . .?'

Ralston raised an eyebrow. 'How did I know you were the *Saltire* reporter? Joanie Cooper told me . . . not that it could have been anyone else. So here's the promised headline, and it's exclusive. The Swedish Prime Minister, Pernil Mattson, who couldn't find the time yesterday to meet with Merlin Brady in Brussels, has changed her schedule. She's coming here tomorrow to inaugurate the Malmo Edinburgh ferry with me and after the ceremony, before we sail, she's finding time for a half-hour meeting about future relations between Sweden and Scotland. If it all goes well there'll be a much bigger story for you than the ferry. You can run that in tomorrow's paper, online whenever you like. Okay?'

'Very okay, First Minister,' Ignacio said. 'Does the Trade Minister know she's being elbowed aside?' He nodded in the direction of Rapace, who was with Lundqvist. 'She's looking relaxed if she does.'

'Not only does she know,' he replied, 'she helped arrange it. So you go and write your story. It should make page one.'

'I will. In fact I'm out of here right now. I'll take a taxi back to my hotel.'

'Do that, but before you go, do you have any plans for dinner tonight?'

He looked at the politician, surprise in his eyes. 'Not really. My partner and I were going to pick somewhere, that's all.'

'In that case,' Ralston continued, 'if you and Pilar would both care to join me, there's a restaurant slash café called Gustav Adolf that I'm told does a decent steak. See you there at seven thirty. We need to talk. On you go now and get your story written. I must get back to the Mayor.'

Ignacio stared at his retreating back. 'How did he know her name?' he murmured.

Fourteen

'Yfou're fucking sinister, Skinner,' Mia McCullough said, as she glared into her phone's camera. 'Is there anyone's private business that you don't know about?'

He laughed. He had been driving home to L'Escala when he had remembered his promise to Crampsey. He had pulled into the next service area to make the call, and had found her at home. 'Don't blame me, lady; I didn't go looking for you,' he retorted. 'I didn't ask; I was told.'

'By who?'

'You don't need to know that.'

'Is someone after Richard?' she asked. 'Is your newspaper after him?'

'It's our son's newspaper more than it is mine,' he reminded her. 'He's the employee. As far as Ralston's concerned, there's no agenda at all. Yes, he's the First Minister: we're interested in his public life; but not the private side, unless there's a legitimate story in it. That's because the *Saltire*'s an ethical publication. I've known a few tabloid hacks in my time, and freelances, who wouldn't think twice about monitoring the comings and goings at the back entrance to Bute House . . . that's a clue to my source, by the way; it wasn't a journalist. In fact one of them did just that when I was married to Aileen, and chief constable. The bloke had a very difficult conversation with Neil McIlhenney, who was Special Branch then, and decided it was a bad idea.'

'That's how you found out?'

'Yes. Seriously though, would it be a problem for you if a snooper did stake the place out?'

'Personally, no. Bob, this isn't a love story; at least I don't think it is. I'm a forty-seven-year-old menopausal widow. He's a public figure in his fifties with a marriage that's in name only. There's nothing wrong with us having a discreet fling,' she grinned unexpectedly. 'Well, not much wrong. He is still married but Mrs Ralston is out of the picture.'

'Sister Trudi, you mean?'

'Christ, you know about that too?'

'We do . . . as in the *Saltire* and me . . . from different sources, not the cops, but June Crampsey's taken an editorial decision not to publish, not yet. Amy Ralston's due to take her final vows next month. When she does, we'll run it.'

'Will any of this cause problems for Nacho?' Mia asked. 'With his job, I mean?'

'On his current assignment, no,' Skinner replied. 'But in a broader context, the fact that his mother's doing the horizontal mambo with Scotland's head of government, that's getting in the way of a role that June had in mind for him.'

'Seriously?' she said. 'In that case you can tell her that it's over.' He saw her shrug her shoulders. 'Ach, I was thinking about chucking him anyway. He's a really good guy but, honest to God, Bob, I've had better sex with nobody else in the room.'

He laughed. 'Okay. If you really mean that, I'll let her know. Maybe it'll work after all, but she might take the view that the lad's objectivity's permanently compromised as far as Ralston's concerned. If she does, well, that'll be her decision.'

'Would it help if I spoke to her?'

'Absolutely one hundred per cent not,' he declared. 'What are you going to say to Ralston though? You're not planning to tell him about being under scrutiny, are you?'

She raised an eyebrow. 'No way. "Goodbye", would seem appropriate. Ah, I don't know. I may say nothing, only . . . He's supposed to be coming up here to Black Shield Lodge on Sunday, assuming the boat from Sweden docks on time.'

'The boat that Ignacio and Pilar are also on,' Skinner observed.

Mia's mouth opened; she gasped. 'They are? Nacho never told me that!'

'It was a late twist. Do you know Joanie Cooper? Did her name ever come up when you were with Ralston?'

'Is she the press woman?' He nodded. 'Yes, she was mentioned. I never met her though, only the guy Dunbar, Richard's adviser. Why?'

'It was her idea that they should sail back with the First Minister. It's all politics, Mia. It's known and understood that the *Saltire* won't endorse anyone at the next Holyrood election, so their strategy between now and then is to be seen in the paper in the best possible light. They're all being nice to us, all the parties . . . other than the Greens, who live in their own wee magic kingdom, like Ralston said in Parliament . . . and so far Ralston's team are being nicest of all.'

She smiled. 'What you're saying is that June Crampsey has the most kissed arse in Scotland . . . metaphorically, of course . . . or will have by the time the election's over.'

'Inelegantly put, but yes,' Skinner agreed. 'And that's why our boy and his partner will be in one of the vessel's best cabins.'

'Mmm.' Her expressive eyes narrowed. 'Is anyone kissing it for real, I wonder?' she asked. 'Is there a Mr Crampsey?'

'There was,' he replied, 'but he died, in New York, in the Twin Towers, when June was young. She's been work-focused ever since. Her dad's a retired police officer, Tommy Partridge. Tommy's old now; he's in a care home. June visits him as often as she can, and so do I occasionally. Other than that, she has a couple of dinner companions, but that's it.' He paused, as a memory came to him. 'Speaking of dads, did you ever hear from yours?'

Her eyes widened as she stared at him. 'How could I? He died, remember, when I was wee.'

Instantly, Skinner empathised with Wile E. Coyote, realising three steps too late, like the cartoon character, that he had just run off a cliff. 'No, Mia,' he said, quietly, 'he didn't. I met him, back then, at your brother Marlon's funeral. Your mother never told you?'

She drew a deep breath. 'If you remember, DCI Skinner, as you were then, I never saw my mother after that funeral. Because I left town, on your advice. Like he did, I guess, from what you're saying. Is that so?'

'Yes, he did,' Skinner confirmed. 'Your uncle Gavin gave him little or no option, after your dad found out about your family's real line of business.'

'They told me he had died at sea,' she whispered.

'And they lied, which shouldn't really surprise you. He went south and joined the RFA; at least that's what he told me. In the brief time that he and I spoke, he seemed to me like a decent man.' He gazed at her; he was frowning, deeply. 'I'm sorry, Mia. I'd forgotten about that encounter, until now. I don't know, thinking of June's dad made me think of yours.'

'What's the RFA?' she asked.

'Royal Fleet Auxiliary. Supply ships, I suppose you'd call them. They belong to the Ministry of Defence, but their crew are civilians. Mind you, I'm not sure it still exists.'

'Could he still be in it if it does?' Mia frowned as she made a mental calculation. 'No, he must be over seventy by now. He'd be retired . . . or he's really dead. Fucking hell, Bob!' she hissed. 'You really are good at dropping bombshells into my life . . . no, fucking depth charges in this case.'

'I guess,' he said, remorsefully. 'But honestly, I've never thought about him, from that day in Seafield Cemetery to this. Really, I am sorry.' Even on screen he could see that her eyes were moist.

'I suppose. And for what it's worth, I'm sorry too.'

'For what?'

'For letting eighteen years go by without telling you that you had another son. I've never said sorry for that, and I should have. I didn't because I was still angry at you. Angry at you for getting me pregnant, and then getting me out of town. I've always been angry since then . . . and now I can see why. It's a barrier I put up to hide from the truth . . . that I was in love with you.'

'And are you still angry now?' he asked, uniquely anxious.

'No,' she replied. 'But I should be. For now I can't hide from that truth.'

Silence hung between them, until Mia broke it. 'Could you find him, Bob? My father? If he's still alive. It should be simple for you: nothing seems to evade you.'

He nodded. 'I can ask somebody a question; somebody who has access to pretty much everything. If you really want me to.'

'Yes. Please. Do it. He deserves to know that he has a grandson.'

'And a daughter,' Skinner added, quietly.

She nodded. 'That too.'

The silence returned, until suddenly she frowned, gazing at her phone screen but not at the camera. 'Shit,' she muttered. 'Not now, Loukas. Damn it! Bob, I've got an incoming call and I think I have to take it. It's from Loukas Adelfos, my new accommodation manager at the hotel. He wouldn't be bothering me if he didn't have to.'

'Go on then,' he said. 'You take it and I'll make my call, like I said.'

'Thanks . . . love.'

Fifteen

John Stirling frowned into his glass: perched on a high stool at the bar that divided the kitchen from the living area, he was present in body but his mind was in another place.

Maya gazed at him as she reached across to the wine cooler for a top-up. 'My Granny Smith was hit by a bus on her way to Tesco this morning,' she said, breezily.

'Mmm,' her partner mumbled.

'She's okay, but the driver braked so hard that he was thrown through the window.'

'Mmm. Eh?'

'What did I say?' she asked.

'Eh? What? Emm . . . something about apples in Tesco?'

She shook her head, slowly, a faint smile on her lips. 'Close but no bananas. Actually, she was hit by a shopping trolley being pushed by an off-duty bus driver who wasn't looking where he was going. She told him she hoped he didn't work on her route. But,' she continued, 'that's beside the point. What the hell is up, love? You've been like this since you went back. Are you having flashbacks? Should I be worried about PTSD?'

He looked up at her. 'No, I'm fine. Promise. No, it's just . . . I'm not going to hack six months of desk duty and that's for sure. Human fucking Resources can take a running . . .' He stopped in

70

mid-sentence. 'Seeing the rest of you going out on enquiries, chasing major crime . . . and by association major criminals . . . while I'm sat at a desk counting paper clips and rechecking transcripts of witness statements and other paperwork that I know in advance will all be flawless; it's doing my head in, love. It's a phoney job, completely unnecessary and one that didn't exist before Monday; I'd worked that out by Monday lunch time. Who did it before me? Tell me? No, you can't, because nobody did. We're a serious crimes team; we don't have the manpower . . .'

'Careful,' Maya cautioned cheerily, 'or the gender polis will be after you.'

'You know what they can do and what with,' he shot back. 'I challenged Lottie about it this afternoon.'

'That was brave of you, challenging DCI Mann.'

'Not at all. She agreed with me. She said that Sauce told her to do it and hinted that the DCC told him to tell me to do it. I asked if she could go back and tell HR to do one themselves, but she said that only the DCC could do that and she's not going near him, because he's under pressure filling in for the Big Chief.' He reached out for the bottle, and emptied the last of its contents into his glass. 'I've been signed off by my consultant,' he said. 'For the last month I've been working with a trainer on a fitness recovery programme, plus, you and I have been hiking up those bloody mountains. Yet some suit or skirt or whoever they are says, "No, DS Stirling. You must sit behind a desk for six months." I said that I would sign a risk acceptance form, but they said no to that too. Six months, love, six months.'

'What about your course at Jackton?' she asked. 'That's two weeks.'

'Yes, out of six months, and it's actually only eight days spread over those weeks. And what's it worth? A command course: every day spent on active duty with Lottie Mann is a command course in itself.'

'It could mean accelerated promotion.'

'I've passed my inspector's exams already. I know where I am in the queue already. Love, I could be a DI next month if I wanted to go to fucking Stornoway, but you don't want me to do that, do you? Looks lovely on the telly but it's cold, it's windy and the days in the winter are really short.'

She sighed. 'And we couldn't commute to watch St Johnstone every weekend, I know.'

'And that's another issue,' he said. 'Us. Have you ever asked yourself how you feel about being part of a police couple? A police family?'

She frowned. 'No, I can't say that I have. John, we've only been together for six months, and for some of the first of those, you were in intensive care or high dependency.'

'Yes, well, during all that time I had time to think about all sorts of things. I was grateful to have a future with you and I want to get it right. Two cops in the same kitchen? We'll always be all right but what about our kids? Would our thinking be too narrow, would it affect their attitudes and their development?'

'Jesus!' Maya snorted. 'You really do need to get back in action. Love, there are plenty of happy cop families. Look at the boss, look at Lottie Mann herself. She and Dan Provan are as happy as anything and they're both police officers; or were, him being retired.'

'Yes, but I heard it's her second cop marriage and that the first one didn't end well. He went to prison, in fact.'

'If that's true, it wouldn't have been because he was police, but because he was a wrong 'un. Come on, love, out with it, where's this going? Do you want me to quit? Are you suggesting that I choose between you and my career?'

'Hell no,' he exclaimed. 'The opposite in fact. I'm considering getting out myself.'

She looked at him in silence, skipped down from her stool and fetched another bottle of Sauvignon blanc from the fridge.

'Okay,' she said, eventually. 'To do what?'

'I could train as a primary school teacher. I could go into human bloody resources myself on a mission to change thinking or . . . I could set myself up as a security consultant and make loadsamoney. What do you think?'

'John,' she replied slowly. 'You're an exceptional police officer with a distinguished career ahead of you. I don't know anyone who doesn't see that. You are also the bravest man I've ever met. I think you should summon up enough courage to serve your six months behind a desk without doing your head in, and mine too; then when it's over, get on with our lives. I'm happy to be in a police family, as long as it's with you, but I'm telling you now, I'm not having kids until I've made detective sergeant!'

Sixteen

'What did he mean, you need to talk?' Pilar asked. She was reclining on the vast bed in their hotel room, flanked by bags that Ignacio guessed contained new clothes.

'I have no idea,' he admitted. 'He didn't hang around to explain. He shot off and then we were all ushered out by the minders . . . Trade Ministry press officers, my new pal Aggie said, but they weren't like any I've ever met, and I encountered quite a few in my time on the radio station. They told us that the Mayor, slippery bastard Lundqvist, she called him, had arranged for him to visit a couple of the Torso's residents in their homes, but without us press types tagging along. That's a direct quote from Mr Mayor, by the way: "You press types," delivered with a sneer.'

'Who's Aggie?'

'A Swedish freelance, I think. She seemed to take a shine to me.'

'Oh yes?' Pilar murmured.

'Relax, cariña; she's around the same age as my mother.'

'If you say so. Will she be there tomorrow?'

'I have no idea. It didn't occur to me to ask. She won't be sailing with us, that's for sure.'

'Yes,' she exclaimed. 'I'm really looking forward to that. You'll have little or nothing to do . . . nothing at all, apart from your

74

interview with the First Minister. Mostly it'll be like we're on a cruise. Let's do a real one on our honeymoon.'

'You were serious about getting married right away?' Ignacio asked. 'Er . . . you haven't missed a period, have you?'

'No, not yet . . . but if that's what it takes. For a woman of her generation, my mum is surprisingly old-fashioned about that sort of thing.'

'For a Scottish woman of her generation, mine doesn't give a fuck whether we're married or not,' he said, cheerfully. 'Are we talking about a big affair? A white dress, black tie? When I was a kid, Mum and I went to Sevilla once: I remember that in the area around our hotel, there was nothing but wedding shops. You in a white dress, lovely, but I'm not dressing up in a sailor suit, like I saw there.'

'A kilt, then: I want you in a kilt. You and your father!'

'I can promise you that will not happen. There is more chance of Bonnyrigg Rose winning the Champions League next season than there is of my dad ever being seen in a kilt.'

Pilar frowned. 'Who is Bonnyrigg Rose?'

'She's a football team: Scottish Division Two. Remember in my first month on the *Saltire*, the Sports Editor made me cover a football match? It was them. Trust me; Dad? Kilt? No way.'

'Then I'll settle for just a suit, and a tie. Ignacio, do you realise that I have never seen you wearing a neck-tie.'

'I was raised in Spain,' he protested. 'I don't even own a tie.'

'Then I'll buy you one, tonight. On the way to the restaurant, I'll buy you one. Do you know where it is, this restaurant?'

'Yeah, I noticed it yesterday when we were exploring the city. It's a gentle walk from the hotel.'

'Do you know where the First Minister is staying?'

Ignacio wrinkled his nose. 'He's probably in an Airbnb somewhere.'

'No!'

He chuckled. 'No, probably not. The ferry company flew him over here; I wouldn't be surprised if they're picking up his hotel bill too.'

'Is that allowed?' Pilar wondered.

'I think it is, as long as it's disclosed to Parliament as hospitality received.'

'Who's paying for dinner tonight? If you do and put it on expenses, would he have to declare that too?'

'I imagine that he would, as I'm a journalist. But it's his invitation,' he added, 'so that won't be an issue.' He glanced at the time on his phone. 'Six thirty now, fifteen minutes to file my story, twenty minutes' walk to the restaurant I reckon . . .'

Pilar sprang from the bed. 'Do your work,' she exclaimed, 'and I will do mine. For dinner with the First Minister, a girl has to look the part.'

Seventeen

'What is it, Loukas?' Mia McCullough asked, peering over the top of her spectacles at the man who stood in her doorway. There was a trace of irritability in her expression. 'Before you reply,' she added, 'you're new here so maybe I should put on the record that I like my managers to manage. Every time one comes back to me about something, I see it as a sign that they can't.'

'I'm sorry, Mrs McCullough,' the man said, 'but this one I felt I had to bring to your attention. I've had a provisional request for a booking for thirteen people for two nights. It's come from the office of the First Minister, from Mr Ralston, but the guest party's inter-national. They want to book accommodation, with dinner, breakfast and a sandwich lunch, and the use of our conference facility for one day.'

'Dates?' she shot back.

'To be confirmed, but within the next month.'

'People?'

'The stand-out name is Ms Lena Rapace; she's the Swedish Trade Minister. As well as her, there's a Mr Nicolai Lundqvist, he's the Mayor of Malmo. With them there are two officials yet to be named, both Swedish nationals.'

'Nice,' she said, 'but so what?'

'There's more,' he continued. 'As well as the Swedes, there's a

Mr Peter Dunbar, the First Minister's chief adviser, Ms Joan Cooper, the Scottish Government's director of communications. Plus, Councillor Jane Williams, the Lady Provost of Glasgow, Councillor Bert McCann, the council leader, Mr Joseph Barratt, chief executive, and Ms Anna Smith, the CFO, whatever that is.'

'Bloody hell!' McCullough muttered. 'That's quite a cast list. I wonder what it's about?'

'Beats me. I asked, of course, but she just ignored the question.'

'Hold on, you said a booking for thirteen. That's only eleven.'

'That's right, but,' he drew a heavy breath, 'they want accommodation for two Swedish security officers, both male.'

'Cops?'

'Security is how they were described, but I'd assume they are, given that there's a Cabinet minister involved. They can share a room, I was told, but it has to be close to Ms Rapace.'

'Can we do all this, Loukas?' she asked.

He nodded. 'If it's within the next month, yes, we can. There is one important proviso. We've got a bi-lateral conference at Government level and yet Mr Dunbar's secretary . . . that's who called me . . . she stressed that for the next forty-eight hours it has to be confidential, meaning that we don't use the event for our own publicity.'

'Why should we? Get back to her and say okay, we can do it within a certain date range, and we'll even give them a special rate, on the understanding that whatever they are discussing here, if it leads to anything that goes public and it's positive, our role should be acknowledged.'

'Will do, Mrs McCullough.' He paused. 'I'm sorry to be bothering you with this, but I thought . . .'

'You thought right,' she assured him. 'And it's Mia, by the way. But,' she continued a moment later, 'there is another thing that should be puzzling you. This thing's being set up by the Scottish

Government, by the First Minister himself. Dunbar's booked in, and Joanie Cooper . . . and yet, where's Richard Ralston on the list? They're political Siamese triplets.'

Loukas Adelfos frowned. 'That's a very good question. It hadn't occurred to me. I suppose Mr Ralston will commute from Edinburgh or wherever he lives.'

She grinned. 'Maybe,' she conceded, 'but my guess is that he'll be expecting to be accommodated elsewhere. If he is . . . we'll have to see about that.'

Eighteen

They arrived two minutes early. Pilar wore a sparkling, close-fitting dress, its colour somewhere between cherry red and crimson. A black shawl, protection against the evening chill, was draped around her shoulders. Ignacio had discarded the hoodie in which he had begun the day, in favour of his black leather jacket, and a crisp white shirt, open at the neck. In his pocket there was a blue silk neck-tie, bought by his partner in a shop in the arcade below the hotel. 'When I learn how to tie it, I'll wear it,' he had promised, 'but not tonight.'

Ignacio had expected their destination to be up-market but the place had a café atmosphere about it. Its outside tables, packed tightly around space heaters, were full, but several of their occupants appeared to be there for drinks alone. They eased past two waiters and made their way inside. There, the history of the restaurant was more obvious in the décor, although it was not clear whether its name referenced the square in which it was located, or one of the Swedish monarchs who had borne it.

They had made a point of being punctual, but Ralston had beaten them to it. To Ignacio's surprise, the table was set for only three. He had expected to see Peter Dunbar, who seemed always to be at the First Minister's side, and probably Joanie Cooper also, as his press liaison.

He rose as they approached. 'Hello, both,' he exclaimed. 'Welcome, Pilar; I'm so glad you could join us.'

'I am very pleased to,' she replied, smiling. 'My parents will be very impressed when I tell them that I have dined with the First Minister of Scotland. My father is a keen student of international politics . . . not just the EU,' she added.

'What does your father do?' Ralston asked her.

'He is a commercial banker.'

'Is it one of the big ones? One of the High Street banks, as we call them here?'

'No, it's purely a business bank, not retail. It's his company; his business card says "President",' Pilar smiled again, 'but it's a very small country.'

'And your mother?'

'She's in public relations. She's half of a partnership.'

He beamed. 'Very good. When you're at home the dinner table conversation must be interesting.'

'If your interests include tennis, which my mother plays, or Rayo Vallecano, the football team my father supports.'

Ralston's eyebrows rose. 'He lives in Madrid and he doesn't support Real?'

'Vallecano is a Madrid team too; like Espanyol is in Barcelona,' she explained. 'The men of my family have always supported them. Ignacio will have to also. My father says that it's a dirty job but someone has to do it. They are not always in the top league, but just now they are, in the top half. My father is very excited.'

'I'll look out for them from now on.'

There was a bottle of Prosecco on ice, in a stand by his chair. He took it out, wrapped it in a towel, filled three glasses and distributed them. 'I don't need to ask about your parentage, Ignacio,' he said. 'Your father's a very famous man. And now at the top in his second career,' he added, emphatically. 'I've never met him, you know. I'd very much like to and now . . . well, I suppose it's likely that I will.'

Ignacio frowned; he was puzzled. 'I might work for an Inter-Media newspaper, Mr Ralston, but . . .'

'Richard, please.'

He nodded. 'Richard, thank you . . . but Dad's a million miles above me in the organisation. Plus, he distances himself from anything political these days. He says that he was married to one politician too many.'

'That's probably very wise of him. How many has he been married to?'

'One.'

The First Minister chuckled. 'Ah, I see.' He paused. 'Now I think about it, I have had contact with him, although it was indirect. A few months ago, I asked Peter Dunbar, my adviser, to take discreet soundings from a few people about recommending that a young police officer who was stabbed in the line of duty should be given the King's Police Medal. The response would have been universally positive, had it not been for one man: your father. He told Peter that in his day if one of his officers had been careless enough to put himself at risk by taking his eyes off a murder suspect with a bladed weapon in her hand . . . and here I quote . . . the last fucking thing he'd have been getting would have been a fucking medal.'

There was no depth to Ignacio's smile. 'My dad will always give you a straight answer,' he murmured. 'He doesn't compromise his beliefs, ever. One of the reasons he has difficulties with politicians is that he doesn't do political correctness. I can picture him saying what he did to Mr Dunbar, and even the look on his face as he said it. However, what you don't know is that as soon as that cop, Detective Sergeant Stirling his name is, as soon as he was out of danger he was visited by my father, along with Deputy Chief Constable McGuire.'

Ralston frowned. 'You're right,' he conceded. 'That I did not know.'

'And something else, something that now I think of it binds Pilar and me even closer. He's a Motherwell supporter.' He laughed, releasing the tension.

'Let's look at the menu,' the host decreed. He raised a hand. For a moment Ignacio feared that he was about to snap his fingers to attract the waiter's attention. He had served on tables in Spain from the age of sixteen, and later, briefly, in what was now his mother's hotel. Thus he was accustomed to that gesture, and he despised it. The bond between him and his father had been strengthened in its early days by an occasion in a restaurant when a man at the next table to theirs had done so, ostentatiously, possibly to impress his girl-friend. Bob Skinner had leaned towards him and had said, quietly, 'You know, mate, if I was a waiter and you did that to me, you'd be eating with the other hand for as long as it took the fractures to heal.'

But Ralston simply waved, with an entreating smile, and a tall blonde server crossed from the bar area, carrying three menus, which she distributed. 'I'm told the plank steak is your speciality,' he said as he perused his. 'I'll have that, medium, after a herring starter, but my guests will probably need a minute.'

'Actually,' Ignacio ventured, 'I'm good with the herring too, but . . . whatever that massive plate was that your colleague just carried past us . . .'

'That was the schnitzel,' the waitress told him.

'Then it's for me.'

'And I will have the steak,' Pilar added, '*al punt*, after a crayfish cocktail.'

'I wish everyone was as decisive as you all,' the woman said as she gathered in the menus.

Ralston nodded. 'Let's hope it's as good as it looks. It should be, the Trade Minister told me about this place.' He paused to top up the three glasses. 'Were you able to meet her, Nacho? Lena Rapace?'

His guest was taken aback. 'When she arrived she said hello to the press pack, such as it was, but that was as far as it went. Her press officers . . . her minders really, I suspect . . . kept us well clear of you all, as you'll have been aware.' As he spoke, he wondered, *Why did he use my family name? How does he know my family name?*

'Mmm,' the First Minister murmured. 'Your instincts were right about those guys. Can I tell you something, absolutely off the record?'

'If it's a political matter, no,' Ignacio answered, 'because there might be a public interest issue. If it's a security matter, yes, if you feel you need to.'

'And you, Pilar?'

She smiled. 'Señor Ralston, I'm not even here.'

'Of course. Those guys, they were there, them and others you couldn't see, because there may have been a threat.'

'A threat?' Ignacio repeated. 'What kind of threat?'

'I don't really know. The Swedish security services had picked up a whisper. It may be nothing, it probably is nothing.'

'How did you hear about it?'

'The Swedes told our counter-terrorist people. They wanted to give me the opportunity of cancelling the engagements around the inauguration of the ferry service, and simply cutting a ribbon instead and sailing off into the sunset. When I was told, my reaction was that, if the Swedes weren't cancelling themselves, why the hell should I? The deputy chief constable asked me if I wanted to take my own protection officer, just in case. I said, in case of what?' He shrugged. 'Thinking about it, maybe it's a test, the whole business.'

'What kind of a test?' Ignacio asked.

'A test of me. By the Swedes, a way of sizing me up as a person they can deal with. Nacho,' he said. 'I have plans for Sweden, very ambitious plans at that. And not only Sweden, well beyond its borders. Let me explain. You must know, for my party has been shouting it from the rooftops for almost a decade now, that the Westminster government did not have a mandate to take Scotland out of the European Union. Across our country Remain polled sixty-two per cent of the vote. Now we're enduring the consequences of something we rejected. My predecessors and I have asked successive Prime Ministers to undo it. Very few of them have been polite: and since we're not an independent country there's nothing we can do about it. Well, maybe there is. I've been taking private soundings, in Stockholm, Copenhagen and other European countries about by-passing Merlin bloody Brady and his government and doing our own deals, sneaking Scotland in through the back door. What do you think of that, Nacho . . . as a journalist?'

Ignacio sat silent for a few moments; in that time the starter course arrived. Once it had been served, he looked back at Ralston. 'As a journalist, didn't I just set out what can be off the record and what can't? If that isn't covered by legitimate public interest, I don't know what is.'

'I promise you,' the First Minister insisted, 'the last thing I want is for this to be off the record. It's a matter of timing, that's all. Look, I promised your mother that I would give you a headline, an exclusive, and that I will do, in our formal interview after the inauguration ceremony, but this is much bigger, long term, and could be a whole string of front-page leads. What do you say?'

'The first thing I say is this, Richard. What the hell do you mean, you promised my mother?'

As Pilar gazed at Ralston, she recalled a saying in Spain that politicians never blush, because they have no sense of shame or embarrassment. It could not be true in Scotland, she thought, for his face had turned bright red.

'My God,' he gasped. 'You mean Mia hasn't told you?'

Nineteen

'You do keep damn good coffee,' Hector Sureda exclaimed. 'And I need it. I'm sorry that meeting dragged on so long, when I know you were planning to go home to L'Escala this evening.'

'That's okay,' Bob Skinner assured him. 'Sarah's afternoon lecture finished early enough for her to pick up the kids from school. I texted her an hour ago to let her know I'll stay in the Girona apartment tonight.'

'What will you do for dinner?'

He shrugged. 'Something. Nothing. Stop at a restaurant and have a steak. Go straight home and stick a frozen pizza in the oven. Don't give a toss really.'

'Come home with me,' the InterMedia chief executive suggested. 'Gloria will have something ready for me when I get in. It would be no trouble to set another place. After all, we have something to celebrate: the first quarter of the US news channel and the returns are way above expectation.'

'That's kind of you, Hector,' Skinner said, 'but I'll just go home and crash. We should probably hold the celebration for another quarter. We had a friend in the White House when we launched. We don't any longer. Let's see how things are moving forward.'

Sureda frowned. 'Could we be under threat if they don't like our coverage?'

'No, I don't see that at all. We're telling it like it is; we're the antithesis of Fox News but in Spanish, addressing and reflecting the views of an ethnic group where conservatives are definitely in the minority. The more noise the Executive makes, the more it will alert the non-Hispanic population to our existence and our political position. If the guy knows anything at all, he knows TV. He's not going to do anything that will draw attention to us.'

'Could he cancel our White House accreditation? He's done that with others.'

'What did I just say?' Skinner countered. 'We carry on as we've begun, we sit tight for a year and wait for what might be the most important mid-term elections in history. Anyway, Hector, what the fuck, it's late so let's both of us get our arses down the road.'

'Agreed, but . . . there's something I wanted to mention to you. I had a call this morning from our Financial Editor, Sonya Arizamendi. She had a whisper from a colleague of hers that our name was dropped to a Parliamentary committee as a prospective supporter of a fairly controversial leisure development in the south of Spain . . . well, actually your name was. The man who brought it up is trying to win approval for the project in Madrid but, more important, in the Andalusian Parliament in Sevilla. He's a banker, but he isn't from one of the big investment houses. In fact, nobody really knows where he's from or what he's about, not even Sonya and she knows everyone and everything. His name is Sanchez, Raul Sanchez Jimenez. Does it mean anything to you?'

Skinner stared at him. 'Raul Sanchez? Yes, it does. He's my oldest son's potential father-in-law.'

'In that case, can Sonya call you? If you could brief her about the man and his background, that would be useful.'

'Jesus,' he whistled. 'I could, but I'd be asking her more questions than I'd be answering. I know Sanchez, yes, on a family basis, but I realise now that I know very little about his professional life.

He's an investment banker, that's all he's told me . . . but he's never given me the name of his business, or any other clue about it. If he's out there peddling me as a supporter, it's time I found out. Hector, do you happen to know if Dolça Nunez is still in the building?'

'I believe she is,' Sureda replied.

'In that case, on your way out can you tell her I need to see her, now.'

Twenty

'Mother, I appreciate that there is life after forty, but you should have told me,' Ignacio said. He was trying to sound severe, but he knew that his eyes were giving him away, even on the small screen of a mobile.

'How was I to know he was going to invite you to dinner?' Mia countered, grinning. 'How I wish I'd been a fly on the wall when it dawned on him.'

'If you had been, I might have swatted you. I'm sure that Richard would have. It wasn't just him that was embarrassed! I was too.' His composure cracked. 'But it was funny, the expression on his face. I knew something was wrong when he called me Nacho, but it wasn't until he said he had promised you that he'd give me a headline . . . which he did, by the way, with an even better one to come tomorrow . . . that it all came out.'

'When it did,' she asked, 'what did he say?'

'At first he said you were friends and that was all. But the colour of his face, Mum, it gave him away. He was . . . *remolacha* . . . I forget the English word.'

Mia translated for him. 'Beetroot. He was that red?'

'Yes, he really was. You should have seen it. Pilar said she had such a struggle to stop herself from laughing that she almost wet herself.'

'If she had a problem at her age it's just as well I didn't see it. When he said we were friends . . . How did you react?'

'At first I didn't say anything, just let it hang there. What's the British saying about what to do when you are in a hole? Stop digging. Well, he just carried on. I knew he'd been to Black Shield Lodge before, when he appeared on my radio show . . . we didn't meet that day, if you remember, the interview was online. So when he said he'd stayed there I wasn't surprised at first, but then he added that it was three weeks ago. I knew straight away, and I'd probably have said nothing, but Pilar chipped in that the place only reopened ten days ago after its refurbishment. That's when he caved in and said that you were "seeing each other", his words again.'

'What did you say to that?'

'Nothing. Pilar was in full flow by then. She said, "Does that mean that you are sleeping with Nacho's mother?" And he said "Well . . . yes." And still I said nothing, because I was processing it and it wasn't quite so funny any longer. I didn't say anything, but if I had I might have told him that he was a fucking idiot who'd struggle to run a sweet shop far less a country. If a single rival journalist, or any twat with a keyboard and a YouTube station, found out about that connection and saw my byline on a front-page *Saltire* story, they'd have a field day. Okay, you both thought you were giving me a career push, but that could have ended it, and made each of you a laughing stock.'

'Oh my God, Nacho,' Mia exclaimed. 'I never thought.'

'You never thought,' he repeated. 'No, you bloody didn't. Okay, Mum,' he said quietly. 'I'm not blaming you. You thought you were helping me, and I love you for it. But Richard should have known better, he really should.'

'So should I. What happens now?' she asked.

'It's happened already. I called June, the boss, straight away and told her about the spot we were in. We were in luck. The exclusive

Richard gave me, about the Swedish Prime Minister re-scheduling and joining in the ferry link ceremony, it will be second lead in tomorrow's paper, but it hadn't gone to print or online when we spoke, so she's taken my byline off and no damage done. I can still cover the ceremony tomorrow, again without a byline, but we've not to come back on the first crossing. We'll have an extra night; maybe in Copenhagen . . . Pilar wants to do the Hans Christian Andersen experience . . . and fly home probably the day after tomorrow.'

'Tell her not to expect too much,' his mother warned. 'Apparently Hans Christian was a miserable tight-fisted sod who never owned a house in his life. Cameron and I went to Copenhagen once. We did a harbour cruise. Our guide was a world-class cynic, who told us the real Andersen story, and quite a few others, including one about Thundershield, Denmark's great naval hero. The legend was that if the country was ever threatened, he'd rise from his tomb and see off the invaders. Unfortunately, our guide said, he slept through World War Two.' She paused. 'The Tivoli Gardens are okay though,' she continued, 'even though it's really a posh name for a bloody big funfair. Where are you now?' she asked, suddenly.

'Still in the restaurant. Richard beat a hasty retreat though.'

Mia laughed. 'I'll bet he did. I'm surprised he hasn't called me yet. He's probably getting as far away as he can. I hope he didn't stick you with the bill.'

'No, he gave our server his credit card before he left. He didn't even finish his plank steak,' he chuckled. 'So, where does this put you and he now?'

'Relationship-wise?'

'Yes.'

'Probably nowhere. Your father told me something today that had me thinking of chucking him anyway.'

'Do you mean the idea of making me deputy political editor, because Richard's ex hates him? June told me about it when we spoke: then she explained that with you and him together it couldn't happen. But don't bin the guy for my sake, Mum. I told her that I don't want to do politics long-term, I want to do crime. Good luck with the First Minister if you want him. Beneath the veneer he seems like a decent man.'

Mia surprised him by winking. 'I'm not sure I do, want him, that is,' she said. 'I'm breaking in a new accommodation manager: way too young but very tasty. I might take him for a test drive.'

'Mum!'

She laughed. 'Yes, sorry, not appropriate. Actually, I'm joking; I think he might be gay.' She peered at her screen. 'Oh,' she exclaimed. 'I have an incoming call from Guess Who. I think I'd better take it and thanks for tipping me off. Enjoy Copenhagen.'

Twenty-One

Dolça Nuñez Otero was not a newcomer to the executive chairman's office. She had been summoned there once before and entrusted by Sir Robert Skinner with a special investigation. Her success in that project had secured her future with InterMedia and had led to her being given a role that stretched right across the group, even to Italy, in whose language she was as fluent as she was in her own and in English.

Nevertheless, she felt the same trepidation as she stepped into the room, calmed instantly, as it had been before, by the warmth in Skinner's blue eyes as he rose to greet her. 'Chairman,' she said, as she stepped towards him and took the chair that he had pulled out ready for her arrival.

'Hi, Dolça.' They shook hands; an automatic greeting between men in Spain but offered less frequently to women. 'I'm glad you could make it. I'm surprised you're still here though. Don't you have a life outside work?'

She looked him in the eye and smiled. 'They say that cops and lawyers all work to the same principle,' she said. 'Never ask a question if you don't know the answer already.'

'And journalists,' he suggested, 'if they're good enough. As you are, which is why you're here as one of our top investigative reporters. Yes,' he continued, 'I know you have a life outside of the office. I've read your CV, what's on the page and what's between the lines as well. You're a pragmatist. You do what is necessary to get on in life. That's fine with me as long as it never compromises the business, and I believe you're smart enough to ensure that never happens.'

Inwardly Dolça felt a tremor. She had financed most of her university education and her post-grad year by working as a call girl, at the higher end of the profession. *Surely he can't know that?* she thought then looked at him and realised that somehow he did, and that he had just drawn an invisible line in the sand.

'I am,' she replied. 'I've never done anything that compromised anyone,' she added, '. . . apart from one or two who deserved it. Is that what you wanted to discuss?' she continued, briskly.

'No,' Skinner replied. 'We haven't discussed anything yet, Dolça. I asked you to come up because I have an assignment for you. Some might argue that it's personal, because I doubt that there'll be a news story in it, but my view is that in the way that it touches me, it involves the company, so I need to get to the bottom of it.'

She nodded. 'If I can. What is it?'

'Remember that investigation you handled last year? Into a blackmail problem affecting a business part-owned by a woman named Inge Hoverstad? The mother of my son Ignacio's partner.'

'Yes, of course. It was a scam, organised by one of her clients. Is she in trouble again?'

'Not as far as I know,' he said. 'This time I want you to take a look at her husband. His name is Raul Sanchez, and he's an investment banker . . . at least that's what he told me. I took everything about him at face value, but I've had information about him that makes me want to look a bit deeper.'

'Okay. Do you want me to include his wife in the investigation?'

'Don't go looking for her, but if you turn up anything that you don't like, and she's involved, or had any knowledge of it, then yes, look at her background too.'

'And the daughter?'

Skinner winced. 'That would be taking a step too far. Pilar's a nice kid. She and Nacho met at university and they've been together ever since. Christ, she lives under my roof . . . or one of them,' he added.

'What about your son?' she asked, quietly.

'Fuck's sake, Dolça!' he exclaimed. 'He only came into my life as a teenager, but I think I know all of his secrets. Obviously he knows Sanchez, but . . . Look, the odds are that the guy simply dropped my name in a meeting, without asking me first, in the hope that it might help his pitch. The odds are that he's legit. If he is I'll kick his arse gently and that'll be an end of it. If it stretches further than that and Nacho is involved in any way, well, I'll kick it a bloody sight harder.'

She nodded. 'Do have a starting point, sir? Obviously this is sparked by information that's been given to you. Can I go to your source?'

'Yes, you're free to do that. Have you met the *GironaDia* financial team leader, Sonya Arizamendi?'

'No, but I've heard of her. They say she's a very formidable person.'

'She is, and she's also very well informed. You should begin by talking to her, and take it from there in the way you think best. Discreetly, though.' He frowned. 'Sorry, Dolça. I didn't need to tell you that.'

'There's no harm in spelling it out, sir. Okay, I will speak to Señora Arizamendi, but isn't she based in Madrid?'

Skinner shrugged. 'Yes, and you should go there rather than do it on a video call. As I said,' he continued, 'I don't expect to find any more here than indiscretion at worst, but if there's more than that . . . keep it tight and don't worry about expenses, they'll be covered.'

'Thanks, sir, I appreciate that. I will keep you informed on a daily basis.'

'Do that. Anything else? Any other questions?'

'Only one,' Dolça said. 'If I need to, will it be okay to use Jordi Poch?'

He grinned. 'You mean your hacker boyfriend? The one who tried to check up on me last year? After which I had a hell of a job stopping the British security service from putting a red flag on him? That Jordi Poch?'

She smiled, and nodded.

He grinned back at her. 'If you need him, yes, but only on the basis that he does nothing illegal, or stupid.'

Twenty-Two

'Why are some hotel beds so big?' Pilar asked. 'We only need a little space.'

'Very little at the moment,' her partner replied, flicking a few strands of hair from her left eye, 'although I do have one or two thoughts about the matter. You could have two fat people . . .'

'Or one very fat person,' she countered.

'Or lots of people. Orgies and things.'

'Have you ever been in one of those?'

Ignacio smiled. 'I'm afraid not. I've led a very sheltered life. You know well enough, I was brought up alone by my mother. She kept very much to herself . . . understandable, given her illicit business activities, to which I contributed eventually with my skills as a chemist . . . so I had very few opportunities to meet girls. It was the same when I came to Scotland, where Dad was almost as protective as Mum had been . . . until I went to university and discovered a whole new world.' He tapped her on the forehead. 'But then I met you and no longer wanted to explore it.' He drew her even closer. 'How about you?' he asked, raising a provocative eyebrow. 'You've never told me about your past life.'

'That's because I never had one, not in the way I think you mean. Oh sure, I had a couple of boyfriends, but it never went any further than feeling and fumbling. One guy I went out with in my last school

97

year, his nickname was *Burro.* I never found out why, although he did offer to show me. I was a good girl, really, but when I left for university my mother took no chances. She gave me a supply of contraceptive pills but told me to be sensible. I was. They were all still in the packet until I met you, but I've never missed one since.'

'In which case,' he murmured.

'Yes indeed, *Caballo.*' She rolled over, straddling him.

'*Destiny is calling me!*' His ringtone broke into the moment.

'Oh, will you change that fucking thing!' she exploded, laughing.

Ignacio reached out. 'I have to take it,' he said, sadly. 'Might be the boss.' One glance at the screen showed him that it was not. He clicked Accept, and mumbled, 'Yes?'

'Nacho,' the First Minister exclaimed. 'It's Richard. Where are you just now?' he asked, before answering his own question. 'Still in the hotel?'

He checked the time on screen, as his partner slipped out of bed, heading for the bathroom: it showed eight twenty-nine. 'Yes,' he confirmed. 'I have nothing to do before your inauguration ceremony.'

'You're still covering it? Your mother thought you might have been pulled off the assignment.'

'My byline has,' Ignacio told him, 'but I'm here so I will be at the event.'

'I need to see you before that. That big headline I promised you; I've just come from a breakfast meeting with Mrs Mattson, the Swedish Prime Minister. It went well, in that I got the response I was hoping for, and that means I can tell you what it's about. Can you be downstairs in ten minutes?'

'Not a chance. Pilar's in the shower; can you make it twenty?'

'Yes. I can do that. I'll see you in the foyer. By the way,' he added, 'I spoke to Mia. I think we're all right.'

I'm not so sure about that, Ignacio thought, as he joined his girlfriend.

He stepped out of the hotel lift at eight fifty-one, still feeling slightly damp beneath his shirt, Pilar having stopped off at the breakfast floor. Richard Ralston was seated at a small table near the revolving entrance door. He was not alone; Joanie Cooper, his chief spin doctor, stood behind him. 'Take a seat, Nacho, take a seat,' he exclaimed indicating the chair opposite his.

'So, Richard,' the young journalist began as he settled in, facing the First Minister across the round table. The man was excited he realised; his eyes were gleaming and he seemed to reek of achievement. 'What do you have for the *Saltire*?'

'A bloody good story,' Ralston replied. 'Front page material.'

Nacho was hungry, plus, anticipated coitus had been interrupted, but the man was doing his best to please, if not him then his mother. And so he reacted with a smile rather than the scowl that was in his heart.

'Sounds exciting,' he said as he took his phone from his pocket, switched on voice record and placed it on the table. 'Tell me about it.'

'Can't wait. It's a really big deal and the ink's barely dry.'

As am I, Ignacio thought, as he forced excitement into his expression. 'On what?' he murmured.

'Well,' Ralston began, 'it's like this. You may not know this, but the city in which we are sitting has twinning links in place with cities in seven different countries. Scotland isn't one of them, but that is going to be remedied. My people on Glasgow City Council, which we control, have worked up a proposal to twin with Malmo. It's been agreed by both sides, and this morning it was endorsed by Pernil Mattson, Sweden's Prime Minister, herself.'

Ignacio felt an instant sense of deflation; almost shrugged, 'So what?' but restrained himself. 'That's good to hear, Richard,' he said, 'but I can tell you now that my editor will need to be persuaded to put it on page one, far less lead with it.'

Cooper intervened. 'But that's not the whole story. Go on, First Minister.'

Ralston nodded. 'I will, yes,' he continued. 'I know that such arrangements are ten a penny and largely symbolic, but as Joanie says, there's more. To mark the link, Glasgow will build a replica of the Turning Torso. It'll stand on the banks of the River Clyde, on a prime site that's been identified and will be cleared for the purpose. It won't just be a scaled-down copy of the original, it will be identical, and full size. It will have the same plans as the original, the same design and engineering team, and even the same constructor if possible, although that would have to go to tender.'

Ignacio frowned as he considered the details of what he had been told, then nodded. 'I see,' he murmured. 'How would you fund this?' he asked. 'It would be costly, very expensive. The Torso's a complex construction.'

'It will be costly, no question,' the First Minister agreed. 'But we can fund it. The only difference between the Torso here and the Glasgow building will be that while Malmo is predominately residential, ours will be offices. We . . . that is the Scottish Government and the city, have a private investment group lined up to build it, then lease it to the occupant for a hundred years.'

'Who would that occupant be?' he asked. 'A century, Richard? That's a long-term commitment, risky surely?'

'Not at all,' Ralston insisted. 'The occupant will be Glasgow City Council itself. Nacho, do you know the City Chambers? Have you ever been there?'

'No,' he admitted.

'Okay, then I'll explain. The building is Victorian, nineteenth century. It's a magnificent edifice, opulent even, dating back to the time when Glasgow called itself, with justification, the second city of the empire, but it's no longer fit for purpose. The City Council will move its staff to the new building, keeping only the council chamber for its formal meetings, which are public. The rest of it will be devoted to the arts, in ways yet to be determined.'

'Good news, yes, Mr Watson?' Joanie Cooper exclaimed.

'With that twist, yes,' he agreed. 'I'll write it up before the inauguration ceremony and file it. My editor will take it from there. You'll need to discuss positioning with her from now on.'

'Positioning and the byline. You'll agree that it needs one, a story of this importance.'

'Again,' Ignacio said, 'that will be Mrs Crampsey's decision. She might attribute it to our local government editor. Or she might take the view that it's such an overt piece of politicking that she gives it to Sue Bland.'

'God forbid, Nacho!' Ralston gasped. 'She would slaughter it. You've got to stop that.'

He laughed. 'I'm a junior reporter, First Minister; although I've been given this gig I'm still a trainee. But this is all such a great big game that she might give the byline to the sports editor!'

Twenty-Three

Despite her successful project for Señor Skinner, Dolça Nuñez Otero was still unsure of her status within the InterMedia organisation. Yes, she had been given a title, Group Special Investigator, and a position that gave her visibility across its wide range of outlets, available to all of its editors when they felt the need of a focus greater than their own hard-working journalists could offer, but most of her work still sprang from *GironaDia*, the publication that most people outside the organisation regarded as its core.

She knew her own worth, but she felt that she had to demonstrate it to others, and to prove herself every day, to the readership, to her colleagues and most of all, to the big guys on the top floor, Skinner and Sureda. After the initial thrill of her appointment, she had come to realise that in the serious and ever-expanding world of investigative journalism, a club of which any wannabe with a mobile phone and an Instagram account could claim to be a member, status could not be conferred, it had to be earned. And there were those within the Girona headquarters building who remained unconvinced.

Dolça feared, almost assumed, that Sonya Arizamendi would be among their number as she keyed in her email address and sent off her email. She chose to use Castilian Spanish, rather than the Catalan she had learned since joining the company. In days gone that had been the official language of *GironaDia* but under the ownership of the Aislado family its influence had spread beyond the boundaries of the autonomous region, to the extent that two separate and yet identical editions of the newspaper appeared every day. 'Catalan may die one day as a language,' Xavi Aislado had told a Parliamentary audience in Madrid, at the height of the unrest following the region's unilateral declaration of independence from Spain, 'but as long as I am here it will always be on life support.'

Good morning, Sra Arizamendi, Dolça's message to the Financial Editor began, *I have been given an assignment by the top floor, and it has been suggested that I should begin by speaking to you. I would rather do this face to face, if you can spare me some time. At the moment I am in Girona but with the Ave, I can be in Madrid this afternoon. Okay?* She had signed it, *Dolça Nuñez Otero, GSI.* She preferred the abbreviation believing that her full job title was clumsy, ill-suited for the age of the acronym.

She closed her laptop, picked up her personal phone and checked her WhatsApp messages. The first was from her mother, Gabi, asking, testily, when she was planning to come home to Cordoba. 'The hotel is so much work, now that your father is no longer with us, but you are so busy these days. It would help me a little if you could come back, even if it's only occasionally. And Pancho misses you too.'

Dolça did not miss Pancho at all. He was a dog, a mangy mutt that subsisted on scraps from customers' plates, his value measured in rats caught. She did miss her father, however. He was no longer with them because he had moved to Sevilla with one of the hotel employees one month after Dolça had graduated from university. Fredo Nuñez had married into the Otero family only to find that actually he was wed to its business, and in a form of servitude that had him working in an ancient, overheated, unventilated kitchen for more hours than would have been legal if he had been an ordinary employee, although effectively he was. Juan Otero, Gabi's father, had died when their daughter Dolça was fifteen, but that had not eased Fredo's burden; far from it, as the old man had been a form of demilitarised zone between him and his wife and mother-in-law. Fredo had spent a further seven years sweating over his coal-fired range, before making use of his secret weapon, an invest-ment bond that had been an off-the-books legacy from his father-in-law, and cashing it in to open a tapas bar in Sevilla with the forty-year-old Angela, a Welsh ex-pat who had been making the hotel beds for eight years and sharing hers with him for five.

Their tapas bar was called 'Graham Parker's' for a reason so obscure that as Angela put it, 'only an utter geek would ever work it out.' It had taken Jordi Poch less than three minutes. Dolça's second WhatsApp was from him, replying to a voicemail message she had left on his phone the evening before. 'I'm in France,' it read. 'Where do you want me?'

She smiled as she typed in her response. It was laborious, as her fingers were too thick for comfort on the small keyboard. 'France is fine for today. Tomorrow, I'm not so sure. Let you know. You may need your scuba gear.💕' She and Jordi had an unconventional rela-tionship, but it was founded on pure trust. When she had been paying her way through college with her evening activities, he had been aware from the start. While he did not approve, he had insisted on vetting her customers before she ever met up with them, and there had been several occasions when dates had been can-celled as a result of one of his 'deep dives' into the clients' affairs.

She was in the act of sending the message when P!nk inter-rupted. 'Fuckin' Perfect' was the ringtone on her business phone, chosen because it was guaranteed to snap her to attention, wher-ever she was and whatever she was doing. She picked it up and looked at the screen. Its message was '*Sin identificador llamada*' but she took it anyway. 'Nuñez.'

'Dolça,' a female voice replied. 'Sonya Arizamendi. I have your email. It's fairly guarded, but your name got my attention. What's the situation and why is Hector Sureda turning loose his attack dog?'

'Is that what they call me?' she asked, but with no hostility. Her colleague's tone had been friendly enough.

'So I hear, from people in other publications, not ours.'

'Could be worse,' she conceded. 'Sureda's bitch wouldn't be very nice, though, if that's what they really say.'

'No, it's not,' Arizamendi assured her. 'You have respect.'

'Good to know, but it's not Hector Sureda who's given me this task.'

'No? Then who?' She paused. 'Ah,' she murmured. 'The Highlander, is it? Sir Robert?'

'Got it in two,' Dolça confirmed. 'That's his nickname?'

'It is, but only behind his back. They say he's very tough, that he can't be killed, hence the name. Did he give you this job personally? Not through Sureda?'

'I think, no I know, it came from Sureda originally, but Skinner briefed me himself, just like he did with the Lieda business last year. He's not that tough, incidentally.'

'No? I hear stories.'

'They're probably true, but all they mean is don't cross him.'

'I'll remember that,' Arizamendi said. 'Your investigation,' she continued, 'I think I can guess what it's about. Of course I'll talk to you . . . but you don't need to come to Madrid. Today I'm in Barcelona, for one of those junket lunches where top business people give each other awards that their staff have won for them. Can you meet me at midday? At the Palau de la Musica?'

'Sure, I can make that. I'll see you there.'

Twenty-Four

'Is it a very big story?' Pilar asked.

Ignacio held up a hand. 'Minute, please,' he murmured, his eyes focused on his laptop and he keyed in the last paragraph of his copy. He went back to the beginning, read it through for accuracy and errors, until finally he nodded and sent it on its way to the *Saltire* news desk. That done he looked up. 'Ralston thinks it is,' he replied. 'I'm pretty sure it'll make waves in Glasgow, but the rest of Scotland? I'm not so sure. Yes, June will put it on the front page. Where? Second lead at best, I'd say.'

'It sounds big to me,' she said. 'Another of those Torsos, in the heart of Glasgow. But won't it need planning permission?'

He nodded as he closed his laptop and pulled his breakfast tray across the table. 'Yes, it will, but from Glasgow City Council, which the nationalists control. The numbers are tight, but most likely it'll go through. But if there's opposition, he can always call it in for Holyrood to decide. He controls that too, so ultimately Ralston's the planning authority himself.'

'If you were a Glasgow voter, would you want it? I could imagine some people hating it. I've only been there a few times, but there are so many iconic buildings there.'

'Sure, the university on the hill, the art gallery and the City Chambers that Richard's project is going to replace. But there are some modern icons too; the Hydro, the Transport Museum, even the BBC building and the thing they call the Squinty Bridge. Plus it has three football grounds that hold more than fifty thousand people each.'

'What about the height?' Pilar argued. 'The Malmo Torso is a hundred and ninety metres.'

'The Science Centre Tower is a hundred and thirty,' Ignacio countered. 'If they build them fairly close together, height won't be an issue either. It'll be controversial, sure, but I actually like the idea and I reckon lots of younger people will too . . . not that it'll matter. Richard wants it, so Richard will get it.'

'What else does he want?' she asked.

He laughed. 'Apart from my mum, you mean?'

'Nah, he already has her. What does he want to be?'

'I think he wants to be a big man in Brussels. That's what his ex-wife, Sue Bland, believes and I think she's probably right.'

'Doesn't he want to be the first President of Scotland?'

'If he does, he might find it tough getting there. Dad might run against him.'

Pilar's eyes widened. 'Seriously?'

'Probably not, but he and I discussed independence one time, and I remember him saying that government is the business of politicians, while a head of state needs integrity at a level they can never hope to attain because of the very nature of their job.'

'Wow. El Presidente Bob!'

He grinned, and shook his head. 'Never happen.'

Somehow, during their discussion Ignacio had cleared his plate. He picked up his phone to glance at the time. 'Nine twenty-eight, two hours to the inauguration. Now we're not going back on the ferry, you don't have to come. If you want to you can, but there could be a problem if you want to stay with me. I suspect that the Prime Minister being there will mean a higher level of security. So far, nobody's looked at my press accreditation, but I'm sure they will today and since you don't have any . . .'

'Worry not, my love,' she assured him. 'There are quite a few shops in the centre below us that I still have to explore, so I will be very happy to stay here while you watch them cut the ribbon, or whatever it is they're planning to do.'

Twenty-Five

'Are you ready for your big day?' Mia McCullough asked. She smiled at her tablet screen, as Ralston drew himself up to his full height and squared his shoulders.

'Yes, and ready to do our country proud,' he replied. 'I'm sure you were going to call to wish me luck,' he added, 'but I thought I'd beat you to it.'

'And now you'll never know whether I would have or not,' she pointed out. 'But I would,' she lied.

'That's good to know. We are all right, Mia, yes? You and me.'

'Yes, we're fine. When you're home in a couple of days I'll show you just how fine. I like the jacket, by the way: very Scottish. Are you wearing a kilt as well? Can't see that far down.'

He shook his head. 'No, that would have been too much. I'm wearing trews.'

'Jesus,' she laughed, 'that's worse. If you wear a Glengarry as well you'll look like a fucking soldier.'

'It's for the Swedes really. I want to emphasise the Scottishness of the event. This really is a big deal; Pernil being there sends out all sorts of messages. She was very helpful when we met over break-fast. She let me run with a story that I gave to Nacho an hour ago; a bonus on top of the ferry launch . . . and it'll be a *Saltire* exclusive.'

Stop trying to impress me, for fuck's sake, she thought. Mia was still unsure about the future of her relationship with the First Minister. She liked the man, but that was it. He was kind and the sex was not quite as dull as she had described it to Skinner. The fact that his marriage was over, bar the paperwork, meant that she had no moral concerns, and Lowell Payne's discreet warning would help them maintain their privacy. But long term? That was a different matter.

'Okay,' she continued, 'you're in your regalia. What's Ms Sweden going to wear? Will she and the Trade Minister turn up in spangly seventies catsuits?'

'I hope not. That would hog all the headlines.' He paused. 'Love, I'm not alone here,' he told her. 'There's someone with me you might like to meet.' He turned away from the camera and made a beckoning gesture. 'Jens, come over here and say hello to my lady.'

Ralston stepped back from his phone, revealing his garish tartan trousers and allowing a second man to come into shot. 'You've heard of him, I know,' he said, 'now meet Jens Pilling, the CEO of RocLine, which is going to be linking Sweden and Scotland in a few hours' time.'

Indeed she had heard of him, but not through Ralston. Her late husband Cameron's extensive investment portfolio had included a sizeable minority holding in the shipping company of which RocLine was a subsidiary. He had sold it, at a pleasing profit, a few months before his sudden death, having observed to Mia that Pilling's involvement had kept the business strong in a market that was under pressure.

'Good morning, Mrs McCullough,' he greeted her. 'How is Dundee?' he asked. 'I hear that it's undergone quite a transformation in the last couple of decades.' Pilling was short and stocky, with a heavy beard, black but grey-flecked. His eyes seemed to drill into her.

'It has,' she agreed, 'but I don't live there. I never did. I own its radio station, that's all . . . but maybe not for much longer,' she added. 'My son seems to have lost interest in it, and mine is waning. If I had the right offer I might sell.'

'There would be interest surely.'

'There has been, but not from a bidder I would trust to run it the way I have. It's a local radio station, still holding its head up because of its local content, and I'd want to ensure that continued if I sold.'

Pilling frowned. 'Mmm,' he murmured. 'We're always open to diversification. Maybe I should take a look.'

'How much do you know about radio, Mr Pilling?'

'Nothing,' he admitted.

'Then thanks but don't bother. You stick to shipping and I'll carry on being Mia Sparkles for a while longer.' She read his frown. 'My presenter name,' she explained, as her attention turned back to Ralston. 'Okay, my dear, on you go and make your piece of history . . . and straighten up that tie!'

For all Richard's charisma and sophistication, she recognised that there was still something gauche about him, and it made him attractive in a little boy way. He didn't make her insides tremble as Bob Skinner still could, if she thought about him that way, but she liked him; sometimes that was enough. Perhaps she would keep him for a few miles more.

Twenty-Six

'I can understand why the people of Barcelona are flaky about the impact of tourism,' Sonya Arizamendi remarked, as Dolça Nuñez placed a tray on their table in the courtyard of the Palau de Musica. 'This place is not one of the top attractions,' she continued, 'but the last time I tried to visit the Sagrada Familia, I was frightened, literally, by the number of people crammed into that space. I'm a *Madrileña*, I live in the capital city, which is beautiful, and with more cultural assets than here. I tell people that if they can do only one thing in Madrid, go to the Reina Sofia Gallery and stand for an hour in front of Picasso's *Guernica*, admiring its passion, its truth and its sheer genius. If they can do two, go to the Prado. If they have time for three, do the Santiago Bernabeu stadium tour. We have all of that, and more,' she declared, 'but we experience nothing like the hysteria that you find here.'

'I can say the same about Cordoba and Sevilla,' Dolça agreed. 'Barcelona is a freak show.'

Arizamendi sipped her coffee, then picked up the sugar capsules from the saucer and slipped them into her pocket. She was about to do the same with the biscuit, but relented, unwrapped it and ate it. 'Are you single, Dolça?'

'At the moment, yes,' Nuñez replied. 'Why?'

'Do you have a tin in your kitchen that is full of little cylinders of sugar?'

'Absolutely.'

'Do you ever put sugar in your coffee?'

'No.'

'Me neither. But one day,' she declared, 'I will bake a cake. Now,' she continued, 'what does The Highlander want to know?'

'It relates to a man named Raul Sanchez.'

'Ah!' Arizamendi exclaimed, 'I wondered if it might be him. That was the name I passed on to Sureda, when he visited the *GironaDia* office in Madrid last week. Now that I think about it, I'm not surprised that you've been unleashed.'

'What is the background?' Nuñez asked.

'Skiing, believe it or not. There is a big project being proposed for the Sierra Blanca in Andalusia . . .'

'But there are lots of ski runs there already, surely.'

'Yes, there are, and that is the problem for the developer. The existing operators are dead against it, as you can imagine, but the new group has an option on a stretch of virgin mountainside that's even higher than the slopes that are operating at the moment. They want to put in not a ski-lift but a funicular railway line leading up to the runs and to a new hotel complex. It will be an all-year-round resort, in use even outside the ski season and by people who wouldn't dream of using a ski-lift to access it. Eventually, they say, they're going to build a theme park, some sort of fucking Disneyland in the sky.'

'Why haven't I heard of this before?'

'If you lived in Granada you would have,' Arizamendi said. 'It's big news there with the mountains being so close. For now it's slightly smaller news in Madrid, as the ministers for sport and the environment are taking a look at it. There are hearings before a committee at the moment and that's where Sanchez comes in. My interest,' she explained, 'is in the money. Where is that coming from? Who is actually behind the project? I have been working on that for weeks but I'm no closer than I was at the beginning. The proposer is a company registered in Spain, but that is owned by another company, registered in Switzerland. I can't get near finding out who owns that.' She paused, returning to her coffee, spooning some of the chocolate powder from the top. 'To see if I could get a clue,' she continued, licking her lips, 'I went along to a hearing last week before the Parliament's environmental group. The chief witness, if you want to call him that, was Raul Sanchez, on behalf of clients, he said. The chair asked if he would name them, but he said "Not at this stage." He pitched the project as hard as he could, to a very cynical audience, I have to say. He was asked several times who else was involved in the project, but named nobody, just said that his principals were people of substance. When he was asked to list supporters outside the promoting company, he was vague about that too. That was when the chair said she'd heard enough and was minded to close the hearing. And that was when he said that he was confident that a major Spanish institution would be on his side. He said that he had a close relationship with the Presidente of InterMedia and said that he was confident of the group's editorial backing, at the very least.'

Nuñez leaned forward, sharp-eyed. 'Did he name Sir Robert?'

'Not at first. But when the chair asked him, "Do you mean Señor Aislado?" he shook his head and said, "Not him; I refer to his successor Señor Skinner. I have his ear and I believe he will support the project."'

'How did the chair react to that?'

'She said that if he does, Sanchez could bring him along to a future hearing to argue for it. Then she closed the meeting.'

'Did you speak to him afterwards? To Sanchez?'

'I tried to. I called out to him from the public benches . . . there is no press area in that room . . . said who I was and asked if we could have a word outside. I don't know whether I was a trigger, but he was out of there in seconds. I, on the other hand, was stuck in the crowd. It's a controversial issue, so there were a few protesters in the room. By the time I got outside, Sanchez was disappearing into the distance.'

'Did you go after him?' she asked.

Arizamendi frowned, with a small shake of her head. 'Fuck no, Dolça. It wasn't a big story for me, not in the great scheme of life. My job is international and there are far more significant things happening abroad than here. Because the chairman had been mentioned I made a mental note to let head office know, but next day Hector Sureda turned up out of the blue, on a tour of inspection or whatever it was. I told him, and that was duty done. Until you called.'

'Have you tried to contact Sanchez since then?' Nuñez asked.

Arizamendi shook her head. 'No, I haven't. The Sierra Blanca project will be decided by the Andalusian Parliament in Sevilla, so it's not an active story in my orbit. And even if it was it wouldn't be at the top of my to-do list, not with everyone in the business community chasing the side effects of having a nut job heading up the world's biggest economy.'

'I need to find out as much about Sanchez as I can, Sonya. Can you give me any ideas on how to go about it? I've looked at the socials already, and at LinkedIn. There are hundreds of Raul Sanchezes, but I can't match any to him. I've tried to find him through his wife's profile . . . her name is Inge Hoverstad . . . and through their daughter, Pilar. They gave me nothing, but a link back to Ignacio Watson Skinner, the chairman's son, Pilar's partner. That's how he has the chairman's . . . The Highlander's ear.'

'This sounds like a man who doesn't want people to know too

much about him,' Arizamendi observed. 'There are occasions when that can be legitimate, but in my experience, there are many more occasions when it is not. What have you been told about him?'

'Sir Robert understands that he's an investment banker. That's what Sanchez has told him.'

'Then . . . forgive me, Dolça, why doesn't he simply ask him to elaborate on that?'

Nuñez smiled. 'Because he used to be a cop. A cop who is now starting to think like a journalist . . . a very dangerous combination.'

'Indeed. Right, I would suggest that you look for your man in one of two places, The Banco de Espana itself, which regulates everything, and the Spanish Banking and Finance Institute, to which a serious person in the financial industry would belong. You should find him in either or both. If you don't, I suggest that you go back to the top floor and ask for permission to be unconventional yourself.'

'Thank you,' she said, 'but I believe I have that already.'

Twenty-Seven

'Can you take me to the new passenger ferry terminal please? Is it far from here? I have to be there in forty-five minutes, latest.'

Having been there for only a couple of days, making his way by bus or on foot, other than on the trip to and from the airport, it dawned very suddenly on Ignacio Watson Skinner that, for a journalist, he was remarkably uninformed about the layout of the city of Malmo. That truth was confirmed by the expression on the face of his taxi driver.

'You will not realise this,' she said with a grin, 'but you have just handed me a blank cheque. Yes, I can get you there in forty-five minutes, and you would only catch on very near the end, but the truth is a young guy like you could get there on foot in fifteen, twenty, tops. Go past the train station and you're almost there. In fact you don't need to go past it. From there the new shuttle bus will take you straight to the quayside. Go on,' she told him. 'Do that. It wouldn't be fair of me to take your money.'

He shook his head. 'No, I got in your cab so it's only fair that I stay. In fact, you can take me for a thirty-minute tour of the city, as long as you don't get tied up in any traffic jams.'

'We don't really have those,' she replied. 'Okay, the scenic route it is. We'll let you see the castle, the people's park, what passes for our beach, although it's pretty crappy, and we can finish at the Torso, although you can see that from pretty much everywhere.'

'You can skip it,' Ignacio said, as she moved smoothly away from the kerb. 'I've seen that close up, from the inside even. I was there yesterday with our First Minister and your Trade Minister.'

'Your First Minister?' the driver repeated. 'If you don't mind me saying, you don't sound Scottish.'

'I am, though. One hundred per cent and proud of it. But I was brought up in Spain, whence the accent. Listen, I'm a journalist. I'm here to cover the inauguration ceremony for my newspaper, the *Saltire*. Can I ask you something as a Swedish person?'

'Sure, go ahead.'

'What do you think of this new link between Scotland and Sweden? What do Swedes in general think of it?'

He saw her frown in the rearview mirror. 'Good question,' she conceded. 'This Swede will think it's great if it improves her business, if it brings her more customers. I'm assuming there's been some sort of market assessment done, and that the effect will be positive overall. But,' she paused for a second or two, 'it's a car ferry, so I'm not expecting too much. Swedes in general? Well, they split into two camps; those who like Pernil Mattson, our Prime Minister, and those who don't. She's a very divisive lady and very ambitious too. A lot of us think that if Pernil's for it, there must be something in it for her, and the only thing that can be is that she believes it will give her more leverage in Europe, where her real ambitions lie. She says she wants to put Sweden up there on a par with France and Germany. Fine, but her enemies see that as meaning she wants to dine at the same table as their leaders. I don't study these things but I heard a radio discussion last week in the cab where a Scottish woman said that your fellow just wants to be in the same fucking room . . . pardon my English . . . and that he sees Sweden, and Denmark, as a pathway there.'

Ignacio whistled softly. 'Can you remember her name?' he asked. 'The Scottish woman?'

'Not all of it,' the driver replied. 'But I'm pretty sure her first name was Susan.'

'Bland?' he suggested.

'That's it! No friend of your guy, that was for certain . . . unless "divisive opportunist" is a compliment in English, which I don't think it is.'

'No. Sue Bland hasn't paid Richard Ralston a compliment in the last twenty-something years,' he murmured, smiling. 'Are there any other issues that I should be aware of?'

'There's the choice of operator, that's one. RocLine. It's Norwegian. That hasn't gone down well with those who give a damn. There are a couple of Swedish operators who might have been interested, but Jens Pilling was given the franchise, after the Scots put him forward.'

'He paid for some of the new terminal in Edinburgh,' Ignacio volunteered.

'I didn't know that . . . probably because Pernil decided not to tell us.' She looked in the mirror again. 'Is that enough for you? Can we get on with the tour now?'

'Sure,' he agreed. 'Show me Malmo.'

Twenty-seven minutes later, the cab pulled up at a crossing point within the port area. The driver pointed left. 'I could take you all the way down,' she said, 'but you have time, and Pernil seems to have fixed the weather, like everything else, so you should walk to get a feel for the place.'

He looked out of the window as he pressed his credit card to her reader. 'Jesus,' he murmured, 'the Torso really is that close.' The great twisting skyscraper towered over them; it could have been no more than a quarter of a mile away.

'Yes. Walk down that roadway. The terminal is at the end.'

'Will do. What's your name, by the way?'

She tapped her permit, which was displayed to passengers. 'It's on there. Frida.' She handed him a business card. 'In case you ever come back to Malmo.'

Ignacio thanked her and set off down a long straight avenue, with blue water on one side, and on his left a cobbled road, beyond which, to his surprise, he saw blocks of housing, six storeys of red brick, some with steel-faced floors above. His research had told him that most of the housing was for rental under the ownership of an autonomous authority. As he walked on, he wondered what the waterside property waiting list was and how high a rent they would command.

He had not gone far before he was passed by the first of the shuttle buses of which Frida had spoken. It appeared to be full. Another followed soon after, and then a third. Joanie Cooper had told him that the first crossing, on which he and Pilar had been meant to sail, before being made to walk the metaphorical plank by his mother's indiscretion, was fully booked. Paying customers, he wondered, or had the operator packed the ship with complimentaries?

The road took a slight bend, and opened out to reveal the ferry terminal. The vessel was moored there, and the passengers from the third shuttle bus were making their way up the ramp. Three platforms had been set upon the dockside. He saw Lena Rapace standing on the one on the right with the Mayor of Malmo beside her, and up to twenty others. On the stance to the left, he saw his friend Aggie, standing out from another dozen reporters and cameramen. The third platform was empty, but its purpose was clear. It had no seats, only a microphone on a stand and a black column topped by a slanted Perspex screen; autocue, Ignacio realised. It faced the other two, and the backdrop it offered to the cameras was that of the ferry, in front of which another group of spectators looked on.

Realising that his approach might have been too casual, he picked up his pace as he headed for the media plinth. Trying not to look flustered, he bounced up three steps, where he was met by Joanie Cooper, and a solemn man in grey trousers and a blue blazer with yellow piping around the lapels. He was holding a sheaf of papers, one of which he handed to the newcomer. 'The Prime Minister will be speaking in Swedish,' he explained, feeling clearly that introductions were unnecessary. 'This is a translation to English.' He smiled weakly. 'Maybe it should be Scottish,' he said. Behind him Joanie Cooper rolled her eyes as she handed over another text, Ralston's. 'He won't stick to it,' she warned. 'He never does. He's a nightmare that way.'

Ignacio leaned towards her. 'In that case I'll suggest to my mother that she has a stand-up comedy night in the hotel. I'm sure he'll go down well.'

'Come on,' she whispered. 'That would be an even bigger nightmare. Got to say though,' she added, 'he's been much less so since he started seeing your mum. Be nice when I don't have to worry about keeping them out of the press . . . says she to a journalist.'

Nacho grinned, amiably. 'Just as well we're on the same side.' He moved into the centre of the group, where Aggie had been keeping a space for him. He noticed that their minders from the previous day had given up any pretence of being press officers and were standing opposite, close to the Trade Minister, who was in turn seated next to Peter Dunbar and a bearded man that he recognised from photographs as Jens Pilling. Their position was not the only sign of added security. On his walk to the site, he had seen a police sniper on the roof of the nearest block of flats. Looking around he could see three other armed officers. How many more, he wondered, were hidden from sight?

'You counting too?' Aggie asked him quietly.

Ignacio nodded. 'All Prime Ministers have that sort of cover, don't they?' he whispered.

'I don't know. Maybe. But our Pernil, she isn't your average Scandi-pol.'

As she spoke, heads turned on the platform opposite. The press group followed suit as a long black Mercedes limousine cruised into view and stopped beside the third platform. Their view was mostly blocked, but they saw the head and shoulders of a man, wearing sunglasses and with an earpiece, as he jumped from the front passenger seat and opened the rear door for Mattson and Ralston. They climbed the three steps to their stage, turning to face the audience as their car pulled away.

The Swedish Prime Minister smiled as she moved to the microphone. 'God morgon, alla,' she began, 'mina landsmän och våra gäster. Good morning, everyone, my countrymen and our guests.' She turned towards Ralston. 'And good morning to you, First Minister, the father of this new link between our two great nations.'

That's an addition, Ignacio thought, as he checked the translated text that he had been given. Nations, indeed. Richard will fucking love Scotland being called a nation, as much as Westminster will hate it.

She turned her eyes forward, focusing on the autocue screen. 'Skottland,' she continued, 'har alltid varit stolt . . .'

Reviewing the moment later, Ignacio was unsure whether he was first alerted by the sudden unexpected movement or by the gunshots, as one of Lena Rapace's black-suited minders stepped towards the politicians, arm outstretched, pistol in hand, firing as he went. The onlookers screamed, in no discernible language; terror has its own unique sound and its own instinctive reaction. Everyone, even the stoic Aggie seemed to be diving for cover, everyone but him. He was transfixed, consumed by what was happening, understanding, as he came to realise later, that what was happening was history and that to be its witness was a perverse privilege from which you did not turn away. And then many more firearms crackled; the would-be assassin first seemed to be frozen in midstride as bullets from all angles tore into him, then thrown to the side, as his head seemed to explode in a splash of red.

As Ignacio looked towards the platform he saw that Mattson was down. She was on her right side, writhing, twisting and screaming; her white jacket was blood-stained. Next to her, Ralston was fallen also, face down; then with what looked like a huge effort he pulled himself up, not far, but far enough to stare across at the press platform, and to make eye contact with Ignacio, open-mouthed and, the young man thought, pleading, 'Come to me, come to me.' Then he fell forwards again, and his body seemed to spasm.

Some police officers had reached the platform already; others were on their way. Their priority was evident as they surrounded Pernil Mattson, protecting and comforting her. The stricken Scot was ignored.

Personal risk did not occur to Ignacio as he set out to follow them. He was much closer to the ministers' platform than to the VIP stand; it took him only a few seconds to cover the ground and throw himself upwards, on to the stage, a fragment of common sense making him keep both hands in the air hoping that all of the trigger-happy cops would realise that he was unarmed. All but one did: he was in mid-air when he felt a hot flash of pain tear through his right buttock. Then he landed, covering most of Ralston with his body, yelling 'Family! Family!' while tensing himself against another shot, until a voice above him said, 'Okay, it's good, but I think you're too late.' He looked up, to see the man; it was Mattson's protection officer, who had opened the car door for his charges, who had become victims. He had a pistol clasped in both hands. A cuff of his shirt protruded from the sleeve of his jacket, and it was stained with blood. 'Do what you can,' he murmured. 'I've got you. The minister said in the car that his girlfriend's son was here today. I'll bring one of the medics across as soon as I can. For you too; you've been shot, although it looks like only a flesh wound.'

Ignacio nodded, then leveraged himself on to his elbows, looking down at Ralston. He felt strangely detached, and numb, literally. A *sign of shock?* he wondered, but he felt grateful for it, for calm was what he needed to be in the moment. The First Minister's eyes were still open; they signalled astonishment rather than fear. There was blood in his mouth; every breath seemed to be a great gasp.

'Nacho?' The sound was a gurgle more than anything else.

'Yes, it's me, Richard. Easy now, the paramedics will be here any minute.'

But too late, he thought as the dying man gave the faintest of nods, and squeezed his arm, hard, as if he knew it was his last connection with life.

Ralston coughed, sending blood spraying over his comforter's face. 'Tell mother I . . .' he gurgled, as he drew a last drowning breath. 'Blav'n,' he whispered. And then he died.

Something flooded through Ignacio in the same moment. It could have been grief, it could have been the onset of terror as he contemplated his own recklessness, it could even have been the guilt of relief that he was still alive.

Still propped up on his elbows, he looked to his right, towards Pernil Mattson, who was no longer moving. A medical team had arrived in seconds, from an on-site ambulance, and were working on her, fitting an oxygen mask, which he took as a sign that she was still alive. Unexpectedly she turned her head to the right and looked at him. Her gaze was a question. He guessed that his answer was in his eyes, for tears came to hers.

Through the shock, and the stress and the distress, Ignacio's own pain began to make itself felt. He experimented by clenching his buttock and realised very quickly that it was a bad idea. He would have liked to call for aid, but Mattson was still the medics' top priority. *Keep it at bay!* he told himself. *Work. Fuck! Yes! Work!*

Twenty-Eight

Newspaper editors rarely took calls from individual staff members. Lines of communication between reporters and department heads were clearly established. Video calls were received less frequently.

When June Crampsey's computer told her that she had an incoming video call she frowned. She might have rejected it had it been from anyone other than Ignacio Watson; instead she clicked Accept . . . and then recoiled at the image filling her screen. The young reporter was covered in blood. 'Boss,' he said, 'record this, and get it on air if you can.'

Crampsey gasped, hit the record button instantly, then called Dave Armstrong, the *Saltire* online manager. 'Dave, I'm copying you into a WhatsApp live video. Do what you have to.' Instructions in place, she went back to Ignacio. 'Whatever this looks like,' he told her, 'wait for thirty seconds, and consider it a broadcast.'

While she counted off the seconds, she could see her reporter compose himself. 'This makes me think of Tiananmen Square,' she told him, 'a terrible event but also a landmark piece of journalism. Seize the moment, son.'

He nodded, drew a breath and began. 'This is Ignacio Watson,' he began, 'reporting live from Malmo, Sweden, where what appears to have been an attempt to assassinate Pernil Mattson, the Swedish Prime Minister, has also claimed the life of Richard Ralston, the First Minister of Scotland. Ms Mattson, whom I can see, appears to be alive and is receiving medical help as I speak, but there is no doubt that Mr Ralston is dead. He passed away in my arms, less than two minutes ago. I am still beside him; the blood you can see on me is his. The two ministers were here to inaugurate a new ferry link between Malmo and Edinburgh, Mr Ralston's brainchild. Ms Mattson had just begun to speak when the assassin struck. He appears to have been a security officer attached to Sweden's Trade Minister, Ms Lena Rapace. I saw him leave her and move towards the stage, firing a pistol as he went. He managed to get off several shots before he himself was brought down by police marksmen. As I speak Ms Mattson is being taken away on a stretcher towards a waiting ambulance.' Ignacio switched cameras on his phone, displaying the scene for a few seconds as the Prime Minister was evacuated. The edge of a pool of Ralston's blood was in shot, but he made no mention of it, before bringing himself back into shot. 'Reporting on a dark day for Scotland,' he said, 'Ignacio Watson, the *Saltire*.' He paused for a few seconds. 'And tell Mum and Dad, I'm good. Was that okay, boss?' he asked.

Dave Armstrong's voice cut into the call. 'That was better than okay, son,' he said, his voice trembling. 'It went out live on the *Saltire* platform, and it'll be carried, with subtitles where necessary, on all the group outlets. Also, unless I'm told to the contrary, I'll be making the footage available to the BBC, STV, Sky News and every other broadcaster who asks for it. You could get a fucking Pulitzer for this, mate.'

'What's a fucking Pulitzer?' Ignacio asked.

'So young, so brave, so innocent,' Crampsey sighed. 'Deal with all of that, Dave,' she instructed. 'Nacho,' she continued, 'I'm almost afraid to ask this, but is Pilar there?'

'No, she is not, thank the Lord. She went shopping instead. Boss, can I sign off? I think I need to phone my parents before the medics come for me. I didn't want to mention it on air but I've been slightly shot myself.'

Twenty-Nine

'You are all right?' Mia asked her son. She tried to keep her voice steady, but she was close to being overwhelmed by the news that he had just given her.

He had made a voice call. He had reviewed his own recording and, although he knew that eventually she would see the TV footage, Ignacio wanted to protect her for as long as possible from the sight of him bathed in her lover's blood. He had told her only the basic fact that Ralston had been killed, making no mention of his own actions or of his injury. 'I'm good,' he lied. 'I was close to the shooting, but I'm fine. More to the point, are you?'

'I don't know,' she answered, her voice quavering, her vision blurred with tears; in the midst of the drama it came to her that she had not cried, not once, in over twenty years, since the birth of her son, not when Cameron had died, not even at his funeral. 'Right at this moment, I do not know. We were close, Richard and me, but I wasn't deeply in love or anything like that. You could say he was on probation, but I doubt that I was ever going to marry him. He did make those sort of noises, and I expected him to ask me again once he'd cast his wife off into her nunnery, but I'd have said no. At least I think I would have,' she added. 'Are you sure you're okay?' she asked again.

'Sure, sure, sure.' As he spoke a scream-worthy pain shot through

128

his leg. His gurney had hit a crack on the pavement as he was wheeled towards an ambulance by two paramedics. He clenched his teeth as hard as he could.

'What about Pilar?' Mia asked.

'I'll call her, after I've called Dad. She might know already, but be unable to contact me. I left my personal phone in the hotel and she doesn't have the number for this one. Neither does Dad, although he'd be able to get it out of June Crampsey in two seconds. I'll phone him as soon as we're done.'

'Go on then, do it. He needs to hear it from you first.'

'I will . . . but one last thing. Just before he died . . . I had reached him by then . . . Richard spoke to me. He said, "Tell your mum," and then he said one word that I could hardly make out. It sounded like "Blav'n", whatever the fuck that means.'

'It means nothing to me,' she said. 'Is it even a word?'

'To be honest I have no idea; he was drowning in his own blood by then . . . sorry, Mum,' he moaned, 'I shouldn't have told you that . . . but my best guess is probably "I love her". That would make most sense.'

'It would, because he did. And tomorrow, maybe I'll love him too, once my head's together.'

Thirty

'Nacho, what the fuck?' Bob Skinner exclaimed. 'I've just had your big sister on the phone, positively hysterical about some footage she's seen, and Hector Sureda's been in here telling me I have to look at it too.'

'Have you done that yet?'

'No. I was just about to when you called.'

'Then do it, Dad, and call me back. It would be a lot easier for me than to have to go through it again by telling you myself.'

Skinner's phone went silent, but just as he reached for his computer mouse, another call came in. 'Xavi,' caller ID revealed. He sent a 'Call you back,' response, then cancelled and clicked on the link that Sureda had sent. His eyes widened as his son's report played out on the computer screen. As it ended, he realised that his heart was racing. He reached for his coffee mug, but thought better of that. Instead, he replayed the video, trying to remain dispassionate and analytical, as if it was just another crime scene among hundreds that he had visited. He froze Ignacio's wide-angle shot, trying to take in as much detail as he could: the pale profile of Pernil Mattson, as much as he could see of it beneath her oxygen mask, suggested that she had been sedated and that her condition was under control; to the right of the frame, he saw a figure in a dark suit, on his back. When he zoomed in he realised that part of the man's head was

130

missing. 'The gunman,' he murmured. 'Fucking suicide mission. Probably a crazy, but the Swedes will determine that.' The blood on the edge of the frame; it made him shiver. Whose was it?

He picked up his phone and called Nacho, on video. He was answered in seconds, but only on audio. 'Switch your camera on, son,' he pleaded. 'I need to see you.'

In an instant, his screen was filled by a shaky image of Ignacio, lying prone on a trolley, his head on a pillow. His face was still caked with blood, although it had dried, but he seemed calm. 'Where . . .?' Skinner began.

'In an ambulance, on my way to hospital,' he murmured. His eyes were dreamy and his voice was slow. 'They've given me a shot of something nice.'

'You're lying on your side,' his father observed.

'That's because I've been shot, Dad. Just a little bit,' he giggled as if he was drunk. 'Not by the guy in the suit, he was finished by that time. I did something reckless; I tried to get to Richard when he was down. Everyone else was running away at the time, so the cop on the roof thought I was another hitman. Matti, the Prime Minister's protection guy, told me. He protected me too; he stood over me in case the guy took another shot. I had my hands open when I ran so that everyone could see I wasn't armed, but . . . the cop got it wrong. Just as well he failed his practical, eh?' To Skinner's astonishment, his son laughed. 'I'll have an extra crease in my arse for the rest of my days but the paramedic who came to me said it looks as if it's only a flesh wound.'

'Thank God for that,' Skinner said. 'It won't save the guy who did it, though, when I get to him. If he stays on his force, and that'll be a big if when I've had my say, he will never handle another firearm, never.'

'Calm down, Dad,' Ignacio drawled. 'The guy was doing his job . . .'

'Not very well; Mattson and Ralston must have been hit by then.'

'Yes, they were, but, look, he made a call. You'd have done the same thing.'

'I'd like to think I wouldn't. But if I had . . .' he gave a deep sigh, 'I wouldn't have missed, so I suppose, yes, let's be thankful that he wasn't up to it.'

'That's better. Keep cool, Dad, okay?'

'I'll try,' Skinner murmured. 'Now, what haven't I seen on TV? What didn't you record?'

'I got to Richard,' Ignacio replied, quietly, 'but he was unsaveable. It's his blood you see on me. It was . . .' His smile was gone, his eyes darkened.

'Yes, okay: don't say any more, son. Don't relive it, not right now; you will, later on, for ever like as not. I do, son; I relive far too many things. I want you to know I'm proud of you. You ran towards the danger, not away from it. Have you called your mother?'

'Yes, but audio only and I didn't tell her I'd been . . .'

He nodded. 'Understandable. Leave that to me. Listen, I'll be there as soon as I can.'

'Dad! You don't need to.'

'Are you fucking serious? Of course I do. No arguments. Stay quiet, let them treat your wound, and concentrate on recovery.'

'Yes, but first, Pilar,' Ignacio said. 'I need to call her now.'

'Yes, do that. I'm sorry, I hadn't thought of her being there. See you soonest.'

Skinner ended the call. He swung his chair around and stared out of the window. 'Stupid boy,' he murmured, but with relief on his face. 'It would be a lot easier if I'd bred caution into my sons.'

He raised his phone once more and called his oldest daughter. She was calmer than she had been before, but still far from 'Ice Cold Alex' as one of her acquitted clients had labelled her in a comment after his trial. He did his best to assure her that her half-brother was safe, and indeed, something of an instant media celebrity, but something in his tone told her that he was holding back. 'Pops,' she said, 'I know you better than anyone else on the planet. Tell me all of it.'

'Okay, he was nicked in the gunfire. Only a flesh wound they say.'

'How?' she demanded. 'What was it there? The fucking OK Corral?'

'When Ralston went down he ran to him,' her father told her. 'He went into the line of fire.'

'Why the hell would he do that? Wait till I see him! The bollocking of a lifetime is coming his way! But why, why?'

'Because Richard Ralston and his mother were in a relationship.'

She fell silent. He waited. 'They what?' she yelled. 'That fucking woman! She's like a red stripe running through our lives.'

'Baby, baby, baby! In no universe was this Mia's fault. In this one she's a victim too. Cut her some slack, please.'

'That'll be the day. Shagging the First Minister fits right into her behaviour profile, but only because . . .' She stopped in mid-sentence.

'Only because what?' he asked quietly.

'Only because you aren't available! She still has her eyes on you, Pops. She always has, since she resurfaced, even when she was married to her notorious husband. The only people in our circle who don't realise that are you, Sarah and maybe Nacho . . . although I'm not so sure about Sarah.'

'Alex,' he sighed. 'You're talking nonsense, lass. I know how much you love your brothers and sisters, all of them. You're not thinking straight right now. Tomorrow things will look different.'

'Pops, I tell you . . .'

'No, enough. I have to go now. Someone else I need to speak to.'

He sat for a few minutes, thinking, until finally he returned

Xavi Aislado's call. 'Sorry,' he said, as his friend answered. 'I was catching up with my son, and trying to calm my daughter down.'

'How is he?' Xavi asked.

'In an ambulance, on his way to hospital. He was shot too. He says it's superficial, but I won't be happy until I've seen for myself. I'm about to book the next flight to Sweden.'

'No, you're not. The Cessna is fuelled up and on the runway at Girona, with a flight plan filed. Pick up some clothes and get there.'

'Xavi,' he protested, 'this is private business, not company.'

'The hell it is,' Aislado exclaimed. 'Ignacio is a *Saltire* reporter, plus he's a fucking hero. Get your ass to the airport, and on to that plane. But don't take off without me. I'm coming too.'

'Xavi, you don't need to do any of that.'

'Ah, but I do. For two very good reasons. One, you are my best friend, and two, although you would always deny it, you need support too.'

Thirty-One

'My diagnosis was confirmed this morning,' Chief Constable Neil McIlhenney told his deputy and best friend. 'They call it postural orthostatic tachycardia syndrome.'

'What?' Mario McGuire exclaimed.

'POTS for short. It's very common in people with long covid, but now they're saying I might not have that. Whatever, it's a bastard, but, and here's the good news, it's a treatable bastard. They're not sure how long it'll take, but they say I'll be back.'

'That's good to hear, but you're best off where you are for now, buddy. All these command courses that you and I have done over the years, all the role-playing and exercises, I don't recall a single one that was built around the assassination of a First Minister.'

'No, me neither,' McIlhenney agreed. 'But this one's on foreign soil, so that'll ease the burden.'

'You might think so, but never has as much shit been shat by as many people as is happening this morning. And when those doing the most shitting are those at the top of the ladder, that's very awkward for those low down, gravity being what it is. I've had the Lord Advocate and the Justice Minister on to me within the last half hour, both saying the same thing, giving me the same order.'

'Eh? They can't give you orders, Mario. You're the acting chief constable . . .' He paused in mid-sentence as a distant voice interrupted. 'Be a darling, Lou,' McGuire heard him call out, 'and tell him to fuck off. Okay, well tell him I'm stuck on the toilet, anything you like, but get rid of the sod. Thanks, you're a darling.' He sighed. 'That's the Justice Minister on to me now. He didn't even like Ralston, the whole country knows that. Probably positioning himself already for a run at his job.'

'For sure. Have you seen the bulletin, Neil? Young Ignacio's report from Malmo, with him covered in blood yet holding himself together?'

'Yes,' McIlhenney told him. 'Massive. How must the big man feel?'

'Jeez, that's a good question. He's a father first and foremost, but anyone that put one of his boys in danger, God help them. I wish he was here. What do you think he would tell me if he was?'

'He'd tell you the obvious. We, Scotland, need to be involved in the investigation, if only as observers. He'd tell you to contact the Swedes and ask if you can attach officers as observers and to assist as necessary. You know all this already, mate. But just one thing; the Home Secretary has to do it. Whatever Ralston might have pretended, foreign affairs aren't delegated to Holyrood. But that shouldn't be a problem, as we both knew her when she was First Minister herself and married to Big Bob. I still have her personal number from back then. Do you?'

'If I had it, I still will,' McGuire said, 'although I'm not sure. I never delete the numbers of the living. If I don't, I'll come back to you. Assuming it's agreed, who should I send?'

'That's fucking obvious too, isn't it?'

'Yeah, I suppose it is. Christ, what would I do without you, man?'

'Everything you're going to do. I'm just your comfort blanket, that's all.'

'You always were, chum. Christ, wouldn't it be good to be the Glimmer Twins again, two mid-ranking CID guys out on the batter without a care in the world.'

McIlhenney laughed. 'We still are, and don't you forget it. But there is one other thing that maybe you haven't processed yet. Given the current mania for public enquiries into everything, the Scottish Government is bound to set one up into Ralston's death. With an eye on that, we need a Scottish pathologist . . . and I don't need to tell you who that should be.'

Thirty-Two

'How did you find out I was here?' Nacho asked. He was lying on a bed, in a cubicle in the emergency department of Skane University Hospital. He was still on his side, dressed in a hospital gown, but he had been sedated and the pain had abated.

'My mother called me,' Pilar explained.

'Inge? How did she know?'

'From your father,' she said. 'When he learned that you were wounded, and that probably I did not know, he thought it best that I hear it from her, so he contacted her. She got to me just in time. I was having a coffee in the Triangeln shopping centre when she reached me. One minute later, the programme on the TV was interrupted and there you were, with blood all over your face, on the screen. I couldn't hear you very well with all the background noise, but there was a caption, subtitles . . . it said in Swedish: *Mattson skott*. I didn't need a translation because all around me the people were shocked. Some were crying, others were screaming. I think I might have been doing both. Then your boss called me and your mother. June told me where they were taking you, so I went up to the hotel, washed off my smudged eyeliner and came straight here. At the hotel they were terrific. When I told reception what had happened, they were so good. The manager got in his car and drove me straight here. There were police outside but he talked

138

to them, explained who I was, and I was brought here. I was terrified, baby, all the way, until I walked in here and saw you alive. With the blood all over you and everything on TV, I didn't know what to expect, but I was fearing . . . even though I'd seen you speaking on television . . . I just didn't know. There's lots I still don't know for sure. Richard, is he really dead? My mum said he is. Is it true?'

'Yes. That is for sure. When I did that report his body was beside me.'

'The blood on your face? Was it yours?'

'No, his. He had no chance.'

'And the Prime Minister? What about her?'

'She's in surgery now; everyone's working on her they told me. Once they're finished with her, they'll take me into theatre. But I don't know how she is. She was conscious back there, but she was badly wounded, that was clear.'

'She's touch and go,' a voice said. Pilar looked over her shoulder and saw a short, middle-aged woman standing just inside the cubicle's curtain. 'That's what they're saying, but their faces tell me she'll make it.'

'Aggie,' Ignacio murmured. 'You're okay? And the rest?' He looked back at Pilar. 'This is my friend,' he explained. 'She's a journo too.'

'The rest are okay,' Aggie replied. 'We all did the sensible thing,' she explained to Pilar. 'We hauled ass out of there. None of us will ever be war correspondents, I'm afraid. This one, he did the opposite. We got out of the line of fire, like normal people do. When I looked back your crazy boyfriend, he had done the opposite, and was covering the poor damn Scottish guy. Why, for fuck's sake?' she asked him. 'You're a fucking hero but I'm angry with you.' Then she grinned. 'Mostly because you scooped us all. You wait; right now, Mattson's still the story, but if she recovers . . . and we pray that she does . . . tomorrow it'll be you. Already, most of the people in the press room want to talk to you, to get your story, but they're all restricted.'

'Then how did you get here?' Pilar asked.

'Because I'm better at my job than they are,' Aggie replied, cheerfully, then looked back at Ignacio. 'How are you feeling, kid?'

'Stoned,' he murmured, with a faint smile. 'I don't know what they shot into me but it's fucking good. Everything's fuzzy, everything that happened. Apart from Richard dying, it's all just a blur. I was going to watch my report again on my phone, but they wouldn't let me.'

'That's good,' the veteran observed. 'Trust me, you don't want to watch it, not yet, maybe never. Not that you'll have the choice.' She shook her head. 'Natural born hero. I dunno.'

'The shooter?' Ignacio asked. 'What about him? Was he the only one?'

'They're saying nothing yet. The security service is in control of the situation, and they're as tight with information as a fish's ring, which by definition has to be watertight.' She drew a breath, then continued. 'But they don't control the Trade Minister. Lena Rapace has my number; she uses it to leak information whenever she thinks it will do her some good, or an enemy some harm. She serves in Mattson's coalition government but they belong to different parties so she feels a little exposed by the fact that it was one of her minders who shot her boss . . . and potential future rival down the line. That's why she called me a little while ago. The shooter's name was Rogne Andersen, with an "e". He was a former member of the Swedish military SOG, that's Special Operations. He'd only been with the protection group for a couple of months.'

'Who attached him?' Ignacio asked. 'Where did she find him?'

'Lena had no hand in his appointment. Like all these guys, he was placed there by the security service.'

'Which is now running the investigation,' he said.

'Exactly,' she agreed. 'It's now investigating itself.'

'Are you going to run the story?' he asked.

She shook her head. 'I can't. I've got to live here. At best, my career would be compromised if I upset the security guys. At worst, it would be over. But,' she continued, 'you can.'

'Me? How would I get away with it?'

'Son,' the journalist laughed, 'you can do anything you fucking like. You're the hero of the hour, and even better, you're not Swedish.'

He peered at her, a little woozily. 'Can you find out where my phone is, and nick it back? I don't know how long I'll be out of it after they operate on my arse.'

'Ignacio!' Pilar cut in. 'Don't even think about it!'

'It's okay,' Aggie said, reassuring her. 'I'm not going to do that. The story will keep for a day or two. Lena's not going to tell anyone else and neither will the security service investigators. Get your ass fixed first. That is where you were shot?' she asked. 'Really?'

'Yes,' he said, wincing at the memory and as the sedative's effect began to taper off. 'Maybe you could find out the name of the cop who did it, so I can thank him for not being a better shot.'

'Shot in the ass? By a cop? Can I use that?'

'Be my guest,' Ignacio acknowledged. 'I owe you one. But not before Mattson's out of danger, and then don't quote me. Make it "Sources close to the investigation", that's all. I'll use the same line when I run your story.'

'You guys,' Pilar moaned, frowning deeply. 'Poor Richard is dead; we saw him this morning at the hotel and now he's dead. The Prime Minister is in surgery in this hospital, with people trying to keep her alive. You, Nacho, with an untreated bullet wound. And yet here you are, talking about stories as if it was just another day.'

'It's part of the job, young lady,' Aggie said, serious all of a sudden. 'It's a safety valve; it keeps the nightmares at bay. If we didn't have it, we'd all be drunks or suicides. As more than a few of us are or become.'

'Cops are the same, love,' her partner added. 'Just ask my dad.'

Thirty-Three

'Mario, this is a surprise,' the Home Secretary exclaimed. Watching her on TV it had occurred to McGuire that her Scottish accent had been eroded just a little by her years in Westminster, but one on one, on his phone, Aileen de Marco sounded unchanged from her days as Scottish First Minister and, briefly, Bob Skinner's wife. 'I was expecting a call from somebody in Edinburgh, but from a politician or a civil servant, not from a police officer.'

'I think they're all in shock,' he said. 'Nobody else knows what to do, so I'm doing it.'

'Not Neil McIlhenney?'

'The chief constable's on the sick,' he explained. 'I'm standing in for him. His timing's always been impeccable.'

'So it appears,' she concurred. 'It's unimaginable, what's happened.'

'Funnily enough,' Mario McGuire observed, 'Neil and I were just saying much the same thing, but we weren't speaking figuratively. Nobody's trained for this.'

'In future I will see that they are. How can I help?' de Marco asked.

'I need the Scottish police service to have a presence in Sweden,' he replied, 'access to the investigation they're bound to have set up by now. I can make contact directly with my opposite number in

Stockholm, or in Malmo, but they'll be treating this as a Swedish national emergency. I'm not saying they won't take Ralston's death seriously, I'm sure they will, but their focus will be on who tried to kill their Prime Minister and why. It might take a request at Government level to get us a seat at the table and Scotland is rudderless at the moment. And not only because they've all got their heads up their arses, Aileen. Ralston was the head of a minority administration; he doesn't have an automatic successor.'

'If he had, he or she wouldn't have access to Sweden either,' she pointed out. 'Mario, I'm actually ahead of you in this. Ten minutes ago I had a conversation with Kasper Lundberg, my opposite number in Stockholm, and made that request . . . on Scotland's behalf, not mine,' she added, quickly. 'He accepted it without hesitation. Since then I've asked my Permanent Secretary to contact his opposite number in the Scottish civil service. Word would have filtered through to you eventually, but I can tell you now that the Mattson shooting investigation is being run by the Swedish Security Service. Technically that's a wing of the National Police Service, like your equivalent, but it's bigger, with more autonomy, led by a director general rather than by a senior police officer reporting up the line. Lundberg said that he'd be happy to have two Scottish observers on-site; they'll be observers but he'll make sure the Swedes share with them. The only proviso is that the lead officer must be of assistant chief constable rank, minimum.'

'Shit!' McGuire muttered. 'I can't go, so that means Lowell Payne, and I'd rather not send him.'

'Isn't he . . .?' she murmured.

'Yes. He's your ex-husband's brother-in-law, from his first marriage,' he confirmed. 'I know this is a tenuous link to Lowell, but . . .' He hesitated for a moment. 'Aileen, there was another victim in the shooting, although it hasn't been revealed yet, not least because the Swedes are a bit embarrassed about it. I assume you've seen the live TV report from the scene, yes?'

'Yes,' she confirmed. 'Yes, I have. The BBC news channel is running it.'

'Right, it doesn't reveal this but the young reporter who broke the story, and whose footage is going global, he was also wounded in the attack, although he was mistakenly shot by a cop, not by the gunman. He works for the *Saltire*, which is part of the InterMedia group, now chaired by said ex-husband. He gave his name as he signed off the broadcast. Did you happen to catch it?'

'Yes,' de Marco said. 'He's got a Spanish forename: Ignacio Watson wasn't it?'

'Yeah, but, his full name is Ignacio Watson Skinner.'

She fell silent, for at least five seconds. 'Are you saying he's Bob's son?' she asked, once she had absorbed the news. 'The one that he only found out about when the boy was eighteen, after he and I had split?'

'The same.'

'Jesus Christ and General Jackson!' the Home Secretary moaned. 'The main job of the people you send will be keeping Bob's hands off the investigation! He's bound to go there.'

'I expect he's on the way,' McGuire agreed. 'That's why I've got to be careful who I choose. Whoever it is needs to be able to manage him.'

'That's a small field you're talking about. You and Neil maybe but not many others. How about Sammy Pye?' she suggested. 'I remember how highly Bob rated him. Has he reached chief officer rank yet?'

'Sammy's dead, I'm afraid, Aileen. MND.'

'Oh dear,' she sighed. 'I didn't know that.'

McGuire shrugged. 'No reason why you should have. The fact is, I have the ideal man for the job. Even with the Swedes' requirement I can still make it work, I think . . . that's if my powers as acting chief allow it.'

'Let's hope they do. By the way, I asked Lundberg about repatriation of the body.'

'I was getting there,' he said. 'I expect the Swedes will want to do the autopsy, but everyone here is clear that we want a Scottish pathologist to be involved.'

'So do I and Lundberg guessed as much. He volunteered it and I said you would nominate. I'm guessing . . .'

He smiled. 'Either her or the Glasgow guy,' he chuckled.

On the line, he heard her quick intake of breath. 'Look, Mario,' the Home Secretary said, 'I know I'm not in your ministerial chain, but I'd be grateful if you could keep me in touch, quietly, with what's going on, for partly personal reasons. I've met Pernil Mattson and I like her; I'm praying that she makes it. I'll contact her privately once her medical status allows, but for now, I'd like to be in the loop, informally.'

'Sure,' he promised. 'What about Downing Street?' he asked. 'Prime Minister, First Minister: both of them are heads of government. Should I report to Brady's office as well?'

'I don't think so.' He thought he heard a chuckle, or maybe not. 'No, I'll handle that.'

'Fair enough, if you say so. All that stuff's way above my pay grade anyway . . . and I'm happy about it.' He grinned, as if they were in the same room. 'How are the corridors of power anyway, Aileen? I've read all the speculation about your future, given Brady's age, about you having one foot in the door, and yet . . . it seems like only yesterday that you were part of our lives here . . . socially as well as politically.'

'Maybe yesterday to you,' she said, 'but it seems like a long time ago to me. But I confess that part of me does miss those days. We had some good nights, you and Paula, Neil and Louise, Bob and me. You're all fine, you four, yes? I know he is, in his new jet-setting life.'

'Beyond fine, I'd say,' he replied. 'Paula's sensational at being a mum. Neil's older two are both at uni now, and their wee fella's growing apace. Bob? You have to think of his new job as a new suit. When he put it on it was maybe a wee bit big for him, but he's grown into it and now it's straining at the seams. But,' he sighed, 'personal matters aside, I wish you were still here politically, Aileen. Richard Ralston was the last vestige of class and ability in the Scottish Government, in my very private opinion. I've had two of those on the phone this morning; numpties, both of them.'

'I agree with all of that, but I am still there, Mario,' she pointed out. 'Westminster hasn't devolved everything. I had to fly the Scottish nest,' she confessed. 'You know that. My life wasn't my own any more, and after what happened with Bob . . . more my fault than his,' she laughed, 'but don't ever tell him I said that . . . and then with Joey Morrocco, I was a bit, let's just say I was emotionally unstable. I had one small fling that Bob was able to cover up for me, but it was a clear sign that I had to go south if I wanted to have any political career.'

'How are you now?'

'Fully focused, you might say. I've been on the tabloid front pages once, but never again, so my private life is spotless. Actually, it's non-existent.'

'And your public life?'

'What do you think? One of the things I liked most about you, Mario, was your complete lack of ambition. I'm the opposite, and that will never change.'

Thirty-Four

Most visitors to Madrid feel embraced by the *Plaza Mayor*, the great public square that is the heart of the Spanish capital. As she sat in one of its cafés, Dolça Nuñez did not; instead she felt frustrated, as if the city and its institutions were thumbing their aristocratic noses at her, a provincial hack.

She had spent the day following up on Sonya Arizamendi's suggestions. She had visited the public records section of the Banco de Espana in the morning, where she had run an exhaustive search of the institutions and individuals covered by its regulatory functions, looking for the footprints of Raul Sanchez. As she expected she had found several people of that name, but none with Jimenez as a *segundo apellido*. Frustrated, she had moved on to the Spanish Banking and Finance Institute, only to have the same frustrating experience.

And then to round it all off, the chairman had gone AWOL on her. She had tried to call him with an update, using the private mobile number he had given her, but had come up with an 'Unobtainable' response. After some thought she had tried the Girona office landline number, only to be told by his secretary that Sir Robert was currently on private business and could be contacted only in emergency circumstances. 'Is this an emerg . . .?' She had hung up before the assistant could complete the question.

Al diablo, she thought. Discretion is one thing, and she trusted Jordi Poch in that respect, but she worried that his name might be on a monitoring list somewhere after his unfortunate attempt to hack into the chairman's, The Highlander's . . . she grinned faintly at the nickname . . . back story. Before she took the action she was contemplating, she wanted to *cubrirse su culo* and, she added to herself, her own arse as well.

Her brow was knitted, but she felt more positive as she signalled to a waiter for another beer, then took her iPad and its folding keyboard from her backpack.

Thirty-Five

One of the great problems of a Scottish national police service, Mario McGuire believed, was the choice of location of the chief constable's office. Put it in the capital, Edinburgh, and it would be too near to the politicians. Site it in Glasgow and it could be seen as too distant from them. Site it in Central Scotland where Mc-Ilhenney and his predecessor, Maggie Rose, had chosen to be and it could be seen as deliberately inaccessible to the middle management and lower orders.

Since stepping into the shoes of his stricken colleague, McGuire had chosen a fourth option, basing himself at the Crime Campus at Gartcosh. It was built on the site of a Victorian steel mill that had survived for a hundred and twenty years until it vanished with the de-industrialisation of Scotland in the Thatcher era. The Campus was cleverly located, close to the M73 motorway, offering swift access to either of the two major cities and to the trunk road network to the north.

The acting chief liked this; it suited his preference for leading from the front, for going to his people rather than summoning them to his presence. Therefore Detective Superintendent Harold 'Sauce' Haddock, leader of Scotland's Serious Crimes team, was unsurprised when McGuire walked into his office unannounced. In truth he had been expecting him, ever since the news broke of

150

the assassination of the First Minister. Wherever it had happened no way would Mario McGuire sit on his hands and let matters evolve. And then, there was the personal element.

'Boss,' he said, rising from his desk. He welcomed the interruption. He had been checking over an update on an armed robbery in Aberdeen, but he had been preoccupied. 'Quite a day, eh?'

'Too effing right,' McGuire agreed. 'And that's why I'm here. We need shoes on the ground in Malmo tomorrow, and I'd like your feet to be in them. As you'd expect, the Swedes' investigation is being run by its Security Service, but their boss is happy for us to be alongside it, two officers allowed.' He paused, smiling. 'Actually I don't know whether he's happy or not, but he's been told from on high. Your brief is to observe; no more than that, but that's all it'll take, Sauce, observation, for it's pretty obvious that Ralston was collateral damage, poor bastard, in the attempt to kill the Swedish PM. Nevertheless we need to be there, and they accept that. My take is that they're embarrassed by what's happened and they want to be seen to be sharing.'

'Too right,' Haddock agreed. 'One of their security guys opening fire on the Prime Minister?' he exclaimed. 'Last time that happened was forty years ago, in India. Having watched Nacho's video report several times, it seems to have been a shambles.'

'You've picked up on the reporter's connection?'

'Of course,' he said. 'I know the boy. We're related by marriage, remember?'

The acting chief gasped. 'Jesus, of course, your Cheeky being his mother's . . . Christ, Sauce, I'd forgotten that with everything that's going on.'

'No wonder. So, even in the state he was in, I'd have recognised Nacho without the caption. I called his editor when I saw it. She told me that he'd been shot himself. How is he?'

'He'll be okay, I'm told. Does Cheeky know about it?'

'I told her as soon as I knew. Actually I went home to tell her; given that she's pregnant, I didn't want . . .'

'No.' McGuire frowned. 'Given that's the case, Sauce, can she spare you for a couple of days?'

'Of course she can,' he said. 'She'll be happy to if I can report back to her on her stepbrother.'

'Good. There's an early flight to Copenhagen tomorrow from Glasgow. It's the best way to get there.' He paused. 'But there's one pre-condition. Probably for their own PR reasons the Swedes want the lead observer to be an ACC.'

Sauce shrugged. 'Okay, so you want me to be number two. I'm not precious.'

The acting chief shook his head. 'I know, but you don't need to be, because you're being given a temporary promotion, here and now. Neil's aware and so are HR. Your warrant card's being prepared now at Gartcosh and will be couriered to your house this evening. Congratulations, acting Assistant Chief Constable Haddock.'

'Jesus, that's a surprise,' he laughed. 'For how long?' he asked. 'Until I get off the return flight, I assume.'

'I haven't thought that far ahead, Sauce. While you've got it, wear it well, that's all I can say.'

'I'll do my best, boss. Thanks. Who's coming with me?'

'That's up to you. Choose someone who'll be up to it. Don't make too big a hole in the command structure, but otherwise, you have a free hand.'

Haddock nodded. 'One thing,' he asked. 'What about the elephant in the room?'

'Ignacio's dad? He's on his way there; he may even be there by now. You might need to stop him trampling Swedes underfoot!'

Thirty-Six

'I'd like to see you and my daughter's partner in this aircraft at the same time,' Bob Skinner remarked, watching his companion making his way uncomfortably toward the exit. The clearance on the Cessna was such that he had to bend slightly and Xavi Aislado was five inches taller than him. 'You're both the same height, and Dominic's chunkier than you.'

'If it ever happens,' Aislado retorted, 'we'll have to take the Gulfstream.'

'Bollocks, isn't it?' Skinner said as the two reached the foot of the aircraft steps and stood on the Malmo Airport runway. 'Two over-privileged middle-aged guys coming off a private flight moaning about the cabin height.'

'I'm just glad to get off,' his friend admitted. 'I hate flying, Bob. Always have done, always will do. That's why I spent the whole flight listening to Silvia Perez Cruz on my earbuds.'

Skinner shook his head, with an ironic smile on his face. 'And yet you own an international media group that owns two jets.'

'No, I don't,' Aislado countered, 'at least I won't once you've signed some legal papers. I'm transferring my interest in the Inter-Media group to a trust. It'll be held for the benefit of Paloma until she turns thirty, at which point it'll be wound up and she'll inherit directly. I want you and Hector to be the trustees, with you as the

153

senior. You'll run the group between you for as long as it exists, although I'll expect you to involve Paloma always: I know you're mentoring her already.' He sighed. 'It's time, Bob. I need to move on after Sheila, throw away the blinkers and do something positive with my life. I need to be an actor rather than just a member of the audience. Green energy is what I choose. It excites me just as much as journalism did when I was young.'

His friend stared at him. 'This is a bit of a bombshell, mate.'

'I know, and I apologise for springing it on you, but it wasn't something that was up for discussion. It's the right thing to do, Bob. You guys are doing a much better job than I ever did. You've grown the business in ways that I never imagined, or Joe did when he took over an ailing Franco-leaning regional newspaper and made it respectable again. You're up for it, yes?'

'Yes,' Skinner said, 'I am, but who governs Hector and me? What if we make a wrong call? Do something that's against Paloma's interests?'

'Not going to happen, but if it did there will be safeguarding provisions in the trust.' Aislado looked around. 'Now, here we are in fucking Sweden. What happens next?'

'We're being picked up.'

'Who's picking us up?'

Skinner frowned as he peered through his sunglasses, then pointed in the direction of a small, straw-haired woman who stood beside a big SUV around a hundred metres away. 'I think she is,' he replied as their co-pilot came to them with the cases he had retrieved from the belly of the Cessna, then started towards her.

'Gentlemen,' she said as they approached.

Skinner smiled at her. 'Agnetha?'

'Yes, sir,' she replied. 'Agnetha Bure.'

He turned to Aislado. 'Ms Bure is one of a ten-person team of correspondents that InterMedia maintains in Sweden,' he explained.

'She's our chief news reporter. As you know, we don't have a printed outlet here, but there is an InterMedia Sweden app and a YouTube channel. I'd have told you all this on the plane if you hadn't been plugged into Silvia Perez. When June Crampsey told me she was giving Ignacio the Ralston ferry assignment, I was worried that he might not be ready for it, being so lacking in experience, so I asked Agnetha . . .'

'Aggie,' she corrected him.

'Aggie . . . to get herself accredited just to keep an eye on him. Without him ever knowing, of course. Have you told him yet?' he asked her.

She shook her head. 'No.'

'But you have seen him, yes? Since he was shot?' he asked, his demeanour changing in an instant.

'Of course,' she replied. 'I came here straight from the hospital. He was waiting for surgery, sedated but just about awake. He is okay, sir; that I promise you. They were prepping a theatre for him when I left to come here. It was a crazy thing he did, sir, running towards Mr Ralston when he went down, and I didn't realise it, not until I turned and saw that he wasn't with the rest of us. I'm sorry.'

Skinner shook his head. 'There's no blame coming to you for doing what he shouldn't have done, but he did have a reason. Did you know that he had a personal connection with Richard Ralston? Through his mother.'

Aggie frowned. 'Not at the time. I only found out from his girl-friend that they had dinner with him the night before. She told me at the hospital when we went for coffee, while a nurse was checking his wound. But she didn't tell me very much, and Ignacio hasn't said either.'

'Listen, I didn't know myself until a day or so ago . . . not that I should have,' he added. 'How's Pilar taking it?' he asked.

'She's good too. She's had a hell of a fright, seeing him all bloody on TV as she did, but being at the hospital, that's helped her keep control of herself. Will there be anyone to stay with her? I could if you want.'

'We're both here for her,' Xavi said.

She looked up at the huge man, assessing him for the first time, puzzled by his peculiar accent, similar to the chairman's but with a different tone. He smiled back, nodding towards his companion. 'And I'm here for him too. I'm his assistant, you might say.'

'Don't let him kid you,' Skinner told her. 'He's the boss, the ultimate boss. This is Señor Aislado. That aircraft we just got off, it's his.'

Xavi smiled again. 'But Bob here, he heads the company that makes the money that fills the tanks and flies the thing, so really, he is the man. I'm a piece of its history already.'

'But getting ready to write some more. Come on, Aggie, take us to the hospital. I need to see him for myself.'

Thirty-Seven

What had become in theory a nine-to-five job for DS John Stirling was turning out to be anything but. He and his partner were down to one vehicle: three days before he had said goodbye to his beloved Lotus Elan SE, which had moved beyond economic repair . . . it also held bad memories of his close call, but John was not about to admit that to anyone . . . but its successor, a red Jaguar Mark Two purchased from a retired professor who dealt in classic cars, was still awaiting a replacement part. Until it arrived, whatever hours Maya worked, he worked also.

At that moment, ten minutes before six, she was on her way back to the office from a raid on a house in Blantyre that was believed to be used by a grooming gang. Five suspects were on their way to detention cells. He had read some of the statements filed by the officers who had interviewed the young victims, and hoped that their abusers were on their way to the first of many sleep-deprived nights. He saw himself as very much a New Age policeman, but there were times when he felt a little old school.

He was contemplating flashing cell lights and hourly welfare checks when his mobile buzzed on his desk and the screen lit up. 'Caller ID withheld,' probably indicated a colleague . . . or possibly a heat-pump sales person . . . either way not good news at that time of the evening but he answered.

'DS Stirling?' a strong and slightly familiar male voice asked.

'This is John,' he confirmed, unable to hide a note of caution.

'Sauce Haddock here.'

'Evening, boss,' he replied. 'I'm sorry, everybody's still out on the Blantyre grooming raid.'

'I know,' Haddock said. 'Lottie's briefed me. Apparently one of the accused had a go at DI Singh with a carving knife. Tarvil broke his arm, which is a bit of a bastard given the extra work it'll entail, with everyone there probably having to be interviewed by the PIRC. But,' he continued, 'it won't be my immediate problem, or yours, I hope. Is your passport up to date, John?'

Stirling was so surprised by his boss's question that he managed simultaneously to frown, smile and gasp silently, before replying. 'It's two years old, sir.'

'Good. Are you up with the news from Sweden?'

'What news?'

'Eh? Have you been in another coma?'

'Sir, I wish I had been,' he exclaimed as his frustration overwhelmed him. 'I've been chained to this fucking desk all day, on my own while everyone else has been away on the Blantyre job, so I've been in an information vacuum. Sir,' he added.

'You know, John,' Haddock replied, 'in a way that's almost comforting, the fact that in this era of instant knowledge, the biggest Scottish news story of this century can break and seven hours later there's a single individual who hasn't heard about it. This is it: our First Minister, Richard Ralston, was shot and killed this morning, at the inauguration of the new ferry link between Malmo and Scotland, by a gunman who tried to assassinate the Prime Minister of Sweden.'

'Fuck's teeth!' Stirling whispered.

'Don't you have alerts on your phone?'

'Disabled, boss.'

'Maybe reflect upon that. Anyway,' Haddock continued, 'as you can imagine, the Swedes had an investigation in place within an hour. The hitman died at the scene. They know who he was but the why of it, they're stuck on that. The bosses, our bosses, in Scotland and in London, need us to be present there, to observe and assist the Swedish Security Service as necessary. The acting chief wants me to be one of them and he's given me *carte blanche* to choose the other. That's why I asked about your passport. I want you with me. Is your personal diary clear? Can you do that?'

The DS's eyes were wide; he was more awake than he had been all day, perhaps even since he returned to work. 'I'd love to, sir. Haud me back, in fact. But have you forgotten? I'm on desk duties only. What about HR?'

He heard a snort in his ear. 'Bugger HR. John. *Carte blanche* isn't a fucking ice-cream flavour. It means I have a free hand and I intend to use it. As part of this thing, for diplomatic reasons, I guess, I've been temporarily bumped up to command rank, ACC. If anybody in a fucking suit tries to tell me that you can't come with me on an investigation of national importance, they're going to find out exactly what clout that carries.'

Thirty-Eight

The SUV was approaching the hospital when an alert on Skinner's mobile told him that he had an incoming email. He had brought his British mobile for the trip, leaving his business and personal Spanish phones behind. Hector Sureda and his secretary could reach him anywhere, he reasoned, plus his UK directory held all the numbers that he was likely to need in Sweden, and his email inboxes were on all three devices.

Discreetly he checked the sender. He was in the back, because only the front passenger seat gave Xavi Aislado the headroom that he needed. *Should have told Aggie to hire a minibus,* he had grumbled privately as they had fitted awkwardly into the vehicle at the airport. The incoming message was from Dolça Nuñez. Chiding himself inwardly for not giving her his travel mobile number he opened it, just as Aggie pulled into the hospital car park. 'Got to look at this,' he murmured apologetically.

The email was in English. *Sir,* it read. *I am in Madrid, where I have been trying to place Raul Sanchez among the banking community. I have been unable to do this because apparently he does not exist. He is not known to the Bank of Spain or to the Spanish Banking and Finance Institute. If he was a legitimate investment banker, he would be.*

Of course he could be simply a very wealthy man investing his private funds and choosing to call himself that as a shorthand way of describing what he does. However that does not seem likely. I think he may be something else. As I think you were aware when you gave me this task, last week Raul Sanchez appeared before a Parliamentary hearing, promoting a controversial new ski and leisure resort in the mountains of Andalucia, an investment of more than a hundred million euro. Its backer is a Spanish-registered company that is owned by a Swiss company, making its ultimate owners virtually undetectable. They could be anyone and their funds could come from anywhere. They could even come from Señor Sanchez himself, but only you, having met the man, can judge how likely that is.

Tomorrow I propose to go to Sevilla, the seat of the autonomous government of Andalusia, to see what is known there, on the record and otherwise, depending on how cooperative the local officials are. While I am doing that I intend to have Jordi do what he does best, to uncover as much as he can about the people who are actually behind the proposal and if possible about the source of their funds. I am not asking for your permission to do this. I am a journalist in pursuit of a story and my methods are my own. Should Jordi or I be compromised I will take all responsibility for my action and will distance myself from the company's editorial direction and from you.

I do not need a reply to this email unless it is to forbid me from going any further. Should you do that I will resign and carry on anyway. I am from Andalusia myself and I do not like the way this smells. I intend to delete this email and I suggest that you do the same.

Dolça

'Fuck me! A loose cannon or what.'

Skinner thought that he had been whispering, but with the SUV's engine silent his voice had carried to the front.

'Who?' Xavi asked him.

Staring at the screen, he paused. He looked at his friend, the man who more than any other had created the business that he felt proud to lead. 'An investigation that I asked one of our staff to handle for me. She's a star, but I can't put InterMedia at risk, or her and her boyfriend for that matter.' He handed the phone across.

Frowning, Aislado read the message. Watching him as he did, Skinner saw him frown, then raise his eyebrows, then frown again and then finally smile. 'Who is the guy? Sanchez.'

Skinner nodded in the direction of the hospital building. 'You'll meet his daughter in there. Pilar. She's Ignacio's partner, fiancée.'

'Mmm. Yes,' Xavi said. 'She is a loose cannon, our Dolça. And so am I, Bob. So are all our best people. And fuck it, so are you. You always were, as the scary detective sergeant I first met, all the way to being chief constable. That's why I brought you in and why I put you in the chair. The best businesses are built by loose cannons, Bob; they're built on risks, and by people who know what they're doing as they take them.'

He looked back at the screen, made a few movements, pressed the delete sign and handed the phone back to Skinner. 'Let her run. Watch her back and, when you need to, support her all the way. But I don't need to tell you. You've been doing that all your life. Come on, let's go and see your boy.'

They left the car park and moved towards the hospital. As they reached the entrance, they saw a group of journalists and TV cameras gathered round a man in blue scrubs who appeared to be reading a prepared statement. They paused as Aggie slipped across to join them, taking a recording device from her pocket.

'What do you think?' Xavi murmured.

'My guess,' Skinner replied, 'the Prime Minister's out of surgery and, because the guy looks pleased with himself, he's the surgeon and she's going to make it. All of which,' he continued, 'InterMedia needs to report, so let Aggie get on with her job and you and me go and find my son.'

He had done some research on the flight and knew that Skåne University Hospital was the third largest in Sweden, a centre of excellence. That gave him comfort, as did their surroundings as they moved inside; the place was modern, clean, and everyone seemed to be moving with purpose. He looked around, spotted an information booth and stepped towards it. Arriving, he showed his passport as personal identification, then explained to the attendant why he was there. Without delay, as if she had been briefed to expect him, although he could not imagine how she had, she gave him precise instructions on how to find the trauma unit.

When they reached it, they needed no further guidance. Opposite the nurses' station, where two practitioners were having a seemingly earnest discussion, there was a waiting room. Its door was open and Pilar was inside. When she saw Skinner, the young woman gasped, then leapt from her seat, rushed to him and wrapped her arms around him.

'Dad,' she cried into his chest, 'Nacho said you shouldn't come.'

'Since when did that ever work?' he asked, embracing her. 'Where are we at?'

'They've only just taken him to theatre,' she said, as she released him and led the two men into the waiting room. 'He's had to wait for hours. The first drugs they gave him had almost worn off, but they said he couldn't have more, because of the anaesthetic. I was angry; I told the doctor "give me a needle and thread and I'll stitch him up myself," but they said it was more complex than that because the bullet had gone through muscle and chipped a bone. The young doctor said he was sorry, but the Prime Minister's injuries were very serious, very complex and everyone was focused on saving her life. He said that if it had been the other way round, that if Nacho had her wounds and she had his, they'd have treated him first.'

She looked up, as if seeing Aislado for the first time. 'I'm Xavi,' he said. 'I'm here for all of you. Bob, I need to book us a hotel. Which one are you in, Pilar?'

'Scandic Triangeln,' she replied.

'I'll try and get us in there too.'

'Your accent,' she asked. 'Where is it from?'

'Half of it's from posh Edinburgh, the other half from Girona. I'm a mix, a half-breed. My daughter's worse. She's three-quarters Scottish. But in her heart,' he added, 'she's pure Catalan.'

'And I am fifty-five per cent Castellano.'

'The other half?

'Not far from here. Mum's half Norwegian.'

'She'll be big on winter sports, then?'

Pilar smiled as she nodded. 'Very. Skiing and ski-jumping too.'

'Where does she ski?' Skinner asked, casually.

'Most often in France. Sometimes in the Sierra Blanca but she says that's not good enough. The jumping she can only do in Norway when she visits our family there.' She grinned again. 'My dad says he'll have to fix it, but he's a dreamer.'

'Is Raul a sportsman?'

'God no. He has flat feet. He's a master of the TV remote but that's it.'

The men's laughter was interrupted by a tap on the open door. They turned to see a woman as she entered the room; she was Chinese, and her scrubs, blue like those of the man they had seen outside, seemed to have come straight from the operating room, as there was a smear of blood on the right sleeve. 'Excuse me, gentlemen,' she said; there was a trace of US American in her accent. 'I am Doctor Fagen. Is one of you the father of my patient, Ignacio?'

'Yeah, me,' Skinner responded, 'and this is his partner, Pilar Sanchez.'

'Then I am pleased to tell you that the surgery is complete, and that Ignacio is repaired and will make a full recovery. The tear was a substantial wound, but there was nothing complex, no organs involved. He has internal stitches, which obviously will dissolve, and external ones that will be taken out in a week or so.'

'You're keeping him in here for a week?' he asked.

She shook her head, then removed her surgical cap, as if she had forgotten she was still wearing it. 'As an inpatient, no, there's probably no need for him to stay that long. As his surgeon I'd like to be satisfied that he's one hundred per cent, that's all. I had to remove a bone chip . . . a small one . . . that the bullet took off the outside of the ball of his femur, but not from the socket itself. I don't believe it will impair his movement now or in the long term, but I would like to keep him here for a few days, just to check that out, and also to let the affected muscle begin to heal. After that I was going to say he'll be free to leave but I expect that the people who'll be investigating what's happened will want to talk to him.'

'Why?' Pilar demanded. 'He didn't see anything that will help them.'

Skinner laid a hand on her shoulder. 'They will though, love,' he said. 'They'll want to talk to everyone who was there, to build a complete model of what happened.'

'Why?' she repeated. 'They know who did it and he's dead.'

'Yes, but they'll want to know why he did it, they'll want to know if anyone else was involved and they'll want to know if it could have been prevented . . . if they can find a scapegoat to carry the can, in other words. There's politics involved and politicians always have to blame someone else. There's a double dose of them in this case, with the Scottish First Minister in a cooling drawer . . . somewhere in this hospital, I'd hazard a guess,' he added, glancing at Doctor Fagen, who nodded. 'How is the Prime Minister?' he asked her.

'Alive,' the surgeon replied. 'Just; we lost her on the table a couple of times. She was hit several times, in the shoulder, both legs and in the abdomen; that was the most serious. It was a very close-run thing, as someone said. I can't go into detail, but it'll be life-changing for her.'

'Poor woman,' he winced. 'I'm just here so I don't know, but were there any other casualties brought here?'

'No, there were only the two. Ms Mattson is in ICU now, and your son is in recovery. You can see him now, although you won't get a lot of sense out of him. Come, I'll take you there.'

As they followed her, Aislado nudged Skinner. 'Hey, Bob,' he murmured. 'What you said about politicians always wanting to find someone to blame. Cops do that too, don't they?'

'No,' his friend countered. 'Cops identify the guilty then hand them over to others for justice. Politicians . . . maybe not all, but many that I've met . . . don't give a shit about that. All they want is to deflect scrutiny from themselves.'

The surgical recovery room was full of equipment for high-dependency patients, but the visitors were relieved to see that Ignacio was not attached to any of it. A bag of liquid from a bedside stand fed into a canula on the back of his right hand, but otherwise he was unattached from anything resembling life support.

As they approached his bed, Aislado bumped against a trolley. The patient's eyes had been closed, but they opened slightly at the sound and then wide in surprise. 'Hey,' he whispered.

'How do you feel?' his father asked.

'*Dolor en el culo*,' he murmured, with a very faint smile.

'Pain in the arse? I'll bet you have. You had a trench dug in it so we've been told.'

'Why are you here?' Nacho croaked. 'You didn't need to . . .'

'Of course I did.'

'How long has it been?' he whispered. 'I think I knew but every-thing's confused now.'

Pilar looked at a clock on the wall behind his bed, doing some mental arithmetic. 'Between ten and eleven hours since the . . . thing,' she said, her voice faltering.

'What thing? I'm just . . .' His eyes closed, then reopened slightly, focusing on his father. 'Dad, but . . . why are you here?'

Skinner glanced at Doctor Fagen, with an unspoken question; she read it and nodded. 'Yes, go ahead,' she murmured. 'Severe trauma followed by a general anaesthetic. He's bound to be confused.'

'I'm here because you were shot, Nacho,' he said. 'That's why you've got that pain in the arse. After it happened . . . immediately after it happened, you called me. Xavi and me, we got on the plane and came straight here. You're in the process of coming out of a full anaesthetic and a surgical repair; as you waken fully you'll remember all those things again. Some of them, you'll wish at first that you hadn't but you'll get over that too. I've been there myself, son, a couple of times. Best thing you can do, is relax, don't force yourself to stay awake, and just let everything happen naturally.'

'Mum?' he whispered.

'I've spoken to your mother. She had a fright like we all had but she's calm. I'm going to talk to her again, as soon as you get back to sleep. Before you do, smile as best you can and I'll take a photo, to show her you're fine. Go on, as if she'd just poured you a drink.'

Ignacio's eyes opened a little wider. He smiled faintly but it was enough. His father snapped an image with his phone, inspected it, and nodded.

'That'll do,' Skinner said, then glanced at the young woman by his side. 'Pilar, do you want to have a couple of minutes with Nacho while I make that call?'

She nodded. 'Of course, I'll stay until he goes back to sleep.' As the two men left the room she took a chair from a stack of three, and placed it by the side of the bed.

As soon as they were outside, Skinner sent the image of Ignacio to Mia's WhatsApp, waited for half a minute, and then followed it up with a video call. It seemed to him that the woman who answered was someone he had never seen before. Her hair was tangled, she wore no make-up and she was smoking a long black cigarette.

'When did you take that?' she asked, urgently.

'Less than a minutes ago,' he replied. 'He's out of surgery, everything's stitched up and no major damage done.'

'How is he?'

'Right now, he doesn't know whether it's breakfast time or Easter, or I'd have called you from in there and let you talk to him. The anaesthetic needs to wear off, but they'll probably keep him sedated for a while. He's just out of the OR; probably they'll move him to high dependency for the night. Before I leave here I'll arrange for a private room for him, for as long as he's here. Mia, I'm only just grasping myself what happened, and what he did.' To his astonishment, Skinner felt himself choking up. 'He saw Ralston go down and he ran to him, not away. Tomorrow I'm looking for the cop who shot him.'

'He sounded okay when I spoke to him earlier. But in that photo . . .'

'He'll be back to something like normal by tomorrow, although he'll be on heavy-duty painkillers, I guess. I'll visit him again, and then find out what's happening about an investigation into the shooting. There is one other thing,' he added. 'I had a message from Sarah, during the flight. Richard's post mortem: it'll happen in Malmo, but . . . she's been asked to do it. She arrives tomorrow morning.'

'Should I come too?'

'I can't stop you, but I repeat, Ignacio is going to be all right. As soon as he's cleared to leave here we'll have him flown back to Edinburgh. How about you take him to your place to complete his recovery?'

She nodded, stubbing out her cigarette and pulling back her shoulders as if she was making a conscious effort to pull herself together. 'I'd like to do that. And maybe you could bring him up, then stay for a day or so. It might be good for him finally to see his parents together.'

Skinner frowned, remembering his daughter's heated words and how he had dismissed them. *When was she ever wrong?* he wondered. 'We only ever were together for one night, Mia,' he reminded her. 'If I did that I'm not sure what we'd be pretending to be, but I do know that our son wouldn't be impressed, not for a minute. He's a grown man, in his own relationship. And as for what his stepmother would say if I asked her for the okay . . . well, I'm not going to go there. Look, Mia, I know that Cameron's death was a big blow to you, and I can understand that you're shocked by what's happened to Ralston, before you had a chance to decide whether there was anything serious between you. You help Nacho heal, that's your job; it's possible he might do the same for you. But don't reach out to me; you're over twenty years too late for that. If that ship was ever afloat, it hit the rocks when you decided that Ignacio, my son, would grow up as a stranger to me. Even in your most duplicitous moments, do you think I'll ever forgive you for that?'

Thirty-Nine

Although her first loyalty was to her hometown, Cordoba, Dolça Nuñez loved Sevilla, all the more so since her father and Angela had moved there. As she woke, she felt its life and its warmth wash over her. She had caught the AVE from Madrid the evening before, and had spent the night in a hotel called *Las Casas de los Mercaderes*, ticking off an item on her bucket list and enjoying a good night's sleep at one and the same time. She had first seen the place in her teens, and had fallen in love with its name and its look. Initially she had not realised that it was an hotel: when she did she had made herself a promise that one day, when she could afford it, she would spend at least one night there. That time had come. Her father and stepmother lived in an apartment above the bar, but it was small and she would have been uncomfortable turning up out of the blue, so, with a smile made even wider by the fact that it was on expenses, she booked a room, a junior suite, the only one available.

Graham Parker's opened at eight; it was on one of the busier streets in the heart of the old city, not far from *Las Casas*. It called itself a tapas bar, because that was what the tourists wanted, but also it had an all-day menu. Where else would she go for breakfast?

She saw her father before he saw her, talking to clients at the

170

pavement tables. Most were casually dressed, but one or two were more formally attired; she guessed they were on the way to work; bankers, professional people, or possibly Andalusian civil servants, whose office was located in an historic building, the *Hospital de las Cinco Llagas*: 'Hospital of the Five Wounds'.

There were two tables left; her father still had his back to her as she took one, dumping the backpack that she preferred to a cabin suitcase on a spare seat. The sound alerted him, he turned, and his usual welcoming smile went up by several levels. 'My darling,' Fredo boomed as he made his way to her.

Dolça stood and hugged him. 'Papa,' she murmured. 'You look so happy, and so busy. Is it always like this?'

'This is a normal day,' he assured her in his Andalusian-accented Spanish. 'It'll get a little quieter soon, then build up again.'

'Does it ever get too much for you?' she asked.

'No, because I'm in charge, because it's mine. Today, I could have more tables out than I have. In the summer, in the crazy season, I can fill all the space I'm allowed. How long you are here?' he asked as she sat.

She shrugged. 'I'm not sure, maybe only today. I got in fairly late last night. I'm on a story for the group, about a thing in the Sierra Blanca. I'm going to the Five Wounds to see what I can find out there.'

'Where did you stay?' he asked, looking a little disappointed.

'Hotel. The Merchant's. I'm on business,' she added, in explanation.

He whistled. 'Very posh. You didn't have breakfast, did you?'

She grinned. 'Hell no!'

'That's good. I'll go fix you up, and tell Angela you're here too. Meanwhile,' he paused, indicating a table on the other side of the space. 'See that guy over there, in the grey suit? His name is David; he works in the government and eats here most days. You say Sierra

Blanca. If you mean the sporting side, that's what he does. I'll talk to him. If your question is something he knows about, maybe he can save you a trip to that maze and you can spend some more time with your old man.'

He left her, circled round the tables, and spoke quietly to his client. The man glanced across at Dolça and nodded. As Fredo left, he folded his newspaper, picked up his coffee and came across to join her.

'Good morning,' David said as he sat in the one unoccupied seat. To her he was middle-aged, pushing forty, and something about him suggested authority. 'Dolça, is it? Your dad said you're a journalist?' His accent was from further north, Madrid probably.

She nodded. 'Yes, I work for the InterMedia group. Have you heard of us?'

'Of course. Who hasn't?' he replied, holding up his newspaper. 'I'm reading one of your titles, in fact.'

'Very good,' she said. 'I don't work for any specific newspaper or news site. My title is Group Special Investigator; that means I go anywhere and do anything that the big bosses tell me. I'm based in Girona, but, as you can see from my dad, I'm Andalusian.'

'And the story you're on now, it relates to Tromso SA?'

She frowned. 'What's that?'

'It's the name of the company that wants to build the new super ski resort on some very precious mountain land,' he told her. 'Its owners are lobbying hard for permission to build it but there's opposition, as you'd expect. Let's face it, there's always opposition these days to anything new; it's like a reflex, and now with social media, it spreads like fire through pine straw in a forest.' David paused. 'I said, its owners, but part of the problem is that we . . . the administration . . . don't really know who these owners are, and because of that we don't know how financially sound the project is. It's an all-year-round resort they're proposing; looked spectacular in an AI visualisation that they showed us last week. But it looked almost too spectacular. The last thing we want is for it to be three-quarters built and then for them to run out of cash, leaving a derelict lump of concrete on top of one of the highest peaks in Spain.'

'Who owns the mountainside?'

'An old noblewoman; one of those types with about fifteen fore-names. It's been in her family for centuries.'

'Does she have a financial interest in the project?'

'No, none at all. She gave the permission on the promise of joy tomorrow . . . which she's unlikely to see, being eighty-nine years old.'

'Can't the developer show proof of funds?'

'They have. Tromso SA is a front. Its ultimate owner is a Swiss company whose bankers have certified to the Andalusian Parliament that it can fund the entire project.'

'So?'

'We still don't know who they are.'

'Does the name Raul Sanchez mean anything to you?' Dolça asked.

'Yes, it does. He's the guy who's fronting the show. He suggests that it's all him, but when he's asked a few key questions he clams up. The Swiss company . . . I'm sorry, I forget its name . . . protects its ownership from scrutiny. Sanchez claims it's him but still hides behind that protection. That's enough for caution on our side, but there's more. We have access to Sanchez's tax returns for the last few years. He's a Spanish citizen, Spanish resident; he describes himself as a financial consultant, a dealmaker, but the income he's declared doesn't suggest that he's anything like he's presenting himself.' David paused. 'And yet,' he continued, 'a significant proportion of our Parliament seems to be prepared to take him on trust. I believe that it might have passed by now but for one thing. We have a general election next year. If members do commit to the project and it goes belly up, with the clean-up costs that would involve . . . well, Dolça, that would be a lot of egg on a lot of faces, and would end a lot of political careers. Is that enough for you?' he asked.

'It is and thank you,' she said, sincerely. 'That's really helpful. I was thinking of going to the mountains,' she added.

He nodded agreement. 'You should. I believe there is actually some preparatory work under way and that the existing operators don't like it. Yes, you go there . . . but now,' he added, taking a pair of ankle clips from his pocket. 'I must go myself. I have just enough time to cycle the rest of the way to the Five Wounds.' He looked up as Dolça's father arrived with a tray, laden with fruit, olives, Iberian ham, other cut meats, a large wedge of tortilla and coffee. 'Can I have my bill, please?' he asked.

'Not today, my friend,' Fredo Nuñez replied as he set his daughter's breakfast before her. 'Not today.'

As David left, walking towards a Brompton bicycle that was chained to a lamppost, he sat in the vacated seat. 'And now, my child,' he said, beaming, 'tell me about your exciting new life in the frozen north.'

'What about your customers?' she asked him.

'Not a problem,' he assured her. 'The waiter can manage,' he glanced at his watch, 'and another starts in two minutes. The business is doing well, love. Angela and I are more management than we are hands-on. She supervises the kitchen; nothing leaves it without her approval. I look after the tables, but I'm more of a head waiter and sommelier than anything else. It's only in the early morning that I like to be seen out front, for the regulars like our friend David. If they leave happy, they spread the word. It's the most effective marketing tool that I have.' He wrinkled his nose. 'Social media is a closed book to me, and Angela, she hasn't got beyond page three or four. Maybe we should hire someone to do that stuff for us, but I'd need to be convinced that the cost was worth it.'

She was silent for a few seconds as she finished the tortilla. 'I can help you with that, Papa,' she said.

'I'm sure you know that stuff better than us, love, but you have your own important work.'

'I wasn't talking about me. I know someone who could run your socials, no problem. Jordi is a wizard; he's a pro.'

'Ah, a boyfriend?'

'He is when he's in town.'

'And when he isn't?'

She smiled. 'That's another matter. I need to talk to him about something else. When I do, I'll tell him about your problem.'

'Will he do it? Will he have the time? And what will he cost?'

'Yes, yes, and for my Papa, nothing. Okay?'

'Sure, love. That would be great.'

'Good,' she said. 'He'll contact you, as soon as he can. I'll call him as soon as I'm full up,' she looked at the tray, which was half depleted but still held enough to feed another hungry customer, 'which will be soon.'

'How long can you stay?' he asked.

Dolça winked. 'You sound like my mother.'

'God forbid!'

She laughed. 'Papa, after speaking to David, I think I need to go to Granada, and probably up into the mountains. But when I can, I'll come for a week, I promise . . . and maybe even bring Jordi. Of course,' she added, 'you and Angela could always come to visit me in Girona.' She reached out and tapped his signet ring, which bore the crest of FC Barcelona. 'Then you could go and see your beloved football team.'

'Ah,' he moaned. 'I shouldn't; I am a curse. Every time I watch them here, against Sevilla or Real Betis, they lose. You done?' he asked, looking at the tray.

She nodded. 'I wish I wasn't.'

'Then I'll finish it.'

As he headed for the kitchen with the leftovers, she dug out her phone from her backpack, and called Jordi Poch using WhatsApp video. 'Are you still in France?' she asked as he picked up. As was his habit, his camera was switched off.

'Yes,' he replied. 'I can see that you're not in your office, so where are you?' She switched on her phone's cameras, giving him a street view. 'Those trees I can see, are they orange trees?'

'Yes, but they'll have been harvested a couple of months ago.'

'Sevilla then. Are you at your dad's place?'

'An inspired guess,' Dolça chuckled. 'He'll call you soon. You're going to help him with the social media for his bar. You'll be paid in food.'

'Does he deliver?'

'No. You have to collect,' she replied, switching cameras once more. 'But first InterMedia has a money-paying job for you, one that's approved at the top, the only proviso being that you don't cross any red lines . . . or don't get caught doing it,' she added. 'I need you to do a deep dive into a man named Raul Sanchez, his professional and social history, and his involvement with a company called Tromso SA. Then . . . and this is where it may be more complex . . . I want you to open the door of a Swiss firewall and find out everything about the company that owns it, that means who its principal is and where its money originates . . . that's if there is any and the whole thing isn't just a big con.'

'Okay,' Jordi said. 'While I do that what will you be up to?'

'I will be in the Sierra Blanca, seeing if anyone is left on the ski slopes at this time of year. Good luck and keep in touch.'

Forty

'This is quite a structure,' ACC (acting) Sauce Haddock observed to DS John Stirling as their car crossed the border from Denmark into Sweden. They had been anticipating a train journey to Malmo, but to their surprise they had been greeted at the arrivals gate in Copenhagen Airport by a driver, a courteous gesture from the Swedish Security Service, of which they had been advised in a text to Haddock as they disembarked from their flight.

'Sure is,' Stirling agreed. 'Scotland doesn't have a dual carriage-way road from its capital city to the English border, while the Swedes and the Danes have this.'

'As I remember, that's a point Ralston was careful to make when he negotiated the ferry link.'

'What did you think of him, boss?' the DS asked.

'I'm not a separatist,' the ACC replied, 'but I've got to admit that I saw what he was trying to do, look to Scandinavia rather than down south; independence by another route, as the BBC's Scottish Political Editor said in his TV obituary. What'll happen now he's gone, I wonder?'

'Only God knows,' Stirling suggested, 'and He's probably not sure either. Let's just get Ralston back home, so everyone can move on, that's the view in the papers I've read. That's really why we're here, boss, isn't it? We've got no real locus in the Swedish investigation; their PM was the target. Our First Minister was collateral damage; end of story, literally for him, unfortunately. We're here to observe the autopsy, give any input we can . . . which will be fuck all in practice . . . then get the body back to Scotland. Yes?'

Haddock frowned. 'Yes, that's all very true. It's probably why the Swedes were so kind as to send this nice car for us, to emphasise our guest status, and keep us sweet at the same time. Except . . . collateral damage or not, he was still killed on their ground, in an operation for which they provided security. That being so, we do have an interest in knowing what went wrong.'

'I wonder why they insisted on an ACC coming over,' Stirling pondered.

'Guess? They wanted a person from head office rather than a someone who's involved in active investigations. Call me cynical, but I'll bet I'm right. If so, tough shit; they've got both, backed up by our brightest young DS into the bargain. And something else they haven't realised. There's another shooting victim, but I doubt that they realise who he is, or who that's unleashed.'

'You mean Sir Robert?'

'I do, and speaking of whom . . .'

Haddock took out his phone, checked the signal, selected a number and called. 'Gaffer,' he said as it was answered.

'Sauce,' Skinner answered. 'I was wondering when I'd hear from you.'

'You knew I was coming?'

'Of course. Mario called me last night. Who've you got with you? Who's your bagman?'

'John Stirling, DS Stirling.'

'Lazarus? Good call. I'll look forward to seeing him again. Congratulations on the promotion, by the way. Mario told me about that too.'

'Temporary, Gaffer,' Haddock cautioned. 'It's for this trip only.'

'It's for as long as the Police Authority says,' Skinner countered. 'Mario had to get their approval, but in these circumstances it'll be open-ended. There's an ACC vacancy right now, with Stallings going early, and there are no obvious candidates at chief superintendent rank so . . .'

'Nah, it won't be me; I don't have the experience.'

'Well, if it is,' Skinner said cheerfully, 'you heard it here first. It isn't all about experience, Sauce. I used to have a hand in these appointments, so I know. Now,' he continued briskly, 'when are we meeting the Swedes?'

'Gaffer,' Haddock murmured, 'there can't be a "we", you know that. This is an investigation of a massive failure in Swedish security, so . . .'

'You can say that again, Sauce!' he exploded. 'It was such a failure that one of their guys almost killed my son. His head's on a figurative fucking pike for a start! Or at least his career is.'

'Which is why you can't be there,' the ACC told him, patiently. 'You must know that.'

'That's what the book would say, the one that you and Mario play by; mine sees it differently. Okay,' he sighed. 'I won't make life difficult for you, but remember, when you meet the Swedes, these aren't cops you're dealing with, they're security people. They have a different mindset and they play by a different set of rules; that is if they have any rules at all.'

'I'll bear that in mind,' Haddock promised. 'The programme is that we check into our hotel then meet the investigating team this afternoon. By then I expect they'll have interviewed most of the witnesses.'

'There's one they haven't seen yet and that's Ignacio. I would know, because the hospital's briefed to let me know when they try.'

'Maybe they won't.'

'Come on,' Skinner said. 'They're bound to, unless they're completely disregarding Ralston's death, which is hardly likely.'

'I suppose,' Haddock conceded. 'How is Nacho, by the way?'

'He's okay. I'm at the hospital now. I was with him when you called, but I've stepped outside. He's had an uncomfortable night. It may have been just a flesh wound, but it was a big one and in an uncomfortable place. He's on pain control, but they're weaning him off the sedation, so he's not as good as he appeared yesterday. I think reality's dawning on him as well. He was in a bit of a dream state yesterday. This morning he understands that a man died in his arms.'

'And his mother? Have you been in touch? How's she?'

'Under control, I think. She and Ralston weren't together long, and it might only have been a fling, probably was, but with Nacho too . . . she's had a double whammy big time, poor lass. She might need looking after too.'

'Cheeky's going to see her today,' Haddock told him. 'She can still fit behind a steering wheel,' he added. 'She's taking Samantha, of course. Mia's her step-granny after all. The wee one'll be a distraction if nothing else. What about the girlfriend?' he continued.

'Pilar's good,' he said. 'Getting over the fright she had. Xavi said he'll look after her today.'

'Xavi?' the ACC exclaimed. 'Xavi Aislado?'

'Yeah, he insisted on coming . . . in case things went badly with Nacho, I think, although he didn't say so. Now,' he continued. 'I have to go. You know Sarah's doing the post mortem?'

'Yes, the DCC told me.'

'You mean Mario,' Skinner laughed. 'It's first-name terms among the command ranks, Sauce. She's flying in as well, but coming from Spain she's had to fly to Copenhagen. I'm going across the bridge to meet her.'

'That'll be the bridge that we've just left, courtesy of the

Swedish Security Service,' Haddock said. 'Cops must rate higher than pathologists.'

'That will not be forgotten,' Skinner growled. 'Cheers.'

'How was he?' Stirling asked as the call ended.

The ACC smiled. '"Volatile" just about covers it. Anything could happen.'

Forty-One

Xavi Aislado was smiling as he stepped back into the hotel. He felt refreshed by his morning walk around the streets of Malmo, by the crispness of the morning air, and by the sheer buzz of people. It was only recently that he had begun to venture out of his estate. It was a long time since he had been in a city of any size, with the exception of a visit to London for Paloma's graduation, and even then he had flown in and out of Biggin Hill on the same day on the company aircraft. It had taken a couple of years of gentle pressure from Bob Skinner, and to a lesser extent Hector Sureda, but finally he had been persuaded that the premature end of Sheila's life should not shorten or constrain his own.

He checked the time as he looked around the lobby, concerned that he was late for his prearranged meeting with Pilar, only to see that he was five minutes early. Finding a coffee machine for customer use, he made himself a cappuccino, sat on what would have been a high stool for the average person but was at an ideal height for him, and waited for her arrival.

Fifteen minutes later, Pilar had not appeared. Making allowances for the terrors of the previous day, he made himself another coffee, latte for a change, and resumed his perch, glancing through a tourist magazine that had been lying in the reception area.

Ten minutes later, he was still alone. Reluctantly, he called the number that she had given him the evening before, but there was no reply. He was frowning a little as he took the open-walled lift up to the ninth floor but from the beginnings of concern rather than irritation. Xavi could not remember being irritated by anyone in well over thirty years, not since his brief football career, when as an eighteen-year-old rookie goalkeeper . . . 'Big Iceberg' to the Heart of Midlothian fans . . . he had broken the jaw of a thug of a veteran centre-forward named Mulligan.

Reaching her room, he rapped on the door. 'Pilar,' he called out. 'It's Xavi. Have you forgotten we were meeting at eleven?' He waited for it to open, but it did not, nor was there any sound of activity behind it. His concern went up a notch. He had taken a shine to the girl, not only as his friend's prospective daughter-in-law, but because of the name she shared with one of his idols, Pilar Rosa, from the early days of InterMedia, his first mentor, the woman who had taught him most of what he knew about being a journalist.

He knocked on the door again more forcefully. 'Pilar, are you there?'

He stood there for another minute before taking the lift back to the lobby, where he went straight to the reception desk. 'Do you have any way of checking a room?' he asked the staff member on duty. 'I had arranged to meet Miss Sanchez from Nine One One, here, half an hour ago. She hasn't come down, but she doesn't appear to be in her room either. I'm concerned about her, enough to want someone with a pass key to open her door.'

The young man shook his head. 'No need, Señor Aislado,' he said.

'You recognise me?'

'I saw you when you checked in, sir, you and Sir Robert. Neither of you are easily forgotten. I know who Miss Sanchez is, and in fact she was here. She came down around ten minutes before eleven, smiled at me then took a seat at one of the tables in the window. She hadn't been there for more than a minute, when two men came in from the street and approached her.'

Xavi frowned. 'Two men?' he repeated. 'Can you describe them?'

The receptionist shrugged. 'Unexceptional, is all I can say. In their thirties, casual clothing but still well-dressed, if you understand me, well-groomed. If I had to guess, I would say that they could have been cops.'

'Whatever they were,' he snapped, 'what happened?'

'They spoke to her. They were too far away for me to be sure, but I think one of them might have called her "Señora" when he began, because she looked in surprise. They exchanged a few words, and then she got up and left with them.'

'When she went,' he asked, 'did she seem reluctant?'

'No, absolutely not, she went quite willingly; of that I am sure. Why, sir? Is there a problem?'

'Jesus, I hope not. Could you see where they went, after they left?'

'From this position we can only see to the left side of the square outside. I don't recall seeing them go in that direction.'

Xavi blew out a deep breath. He took out his phone, found Skinner's UK number and called it, only for it to show 'Unobtainable' almost instantly. 'Damn it,' he murmured, but he knew that Skinner had gone to collect his wife from Copenhagen Airport, the type of building where signals can be unreliable. He turned back to the receptionist, who remained unflustered. 'When Ms Sanchez checked in, was she asked for a phone number, as we were, or did you simply take her partner's?'

'Let me check,' he said. He left his post through an opening in the panel behind him.

As he waited, Xavi considered possibilities. Nacho could have taken an unexpected turn for the worse, and she could have been called to the hospital. The investigation into the shootings of

Mattson and Ralston could have summoned her for interview as a witness . . . doubtful because she had not seen the attack. She and Ignacio had dined with the First Minister the evening before his death, but that was too tenuous to be likely.

'I have it here, sir.'

He turned to find the receptionist . . . or duty manager, as his lapel badge declared . . . brandishing a registration form. He took it, punched the displayed number into his phone, and waited. A ring tone sounded, four times, until the call was rejected. He tried again, but was cut off almost immediately.

Okay, he decided. *We have a problem.*

'Do you have CCTV in the hotel?' he asked.

The duty manager nodded. 'On the ground floor and in the corridors.'

'What about outside?'

'Yes, we have a camera covering the immediate external area.'

'Does it record?'

'Yes. We erase after two weeks.'

'I need to see it, now,' he said.

The young man's confidence was shaken, for the first time. 'Señor Aislado, I don't know. Normally we would only give the police access to recordings.'

From his great height, Xavi frowned down at him. 'This isn't fucking normal . . .' he peered at the lapel badge, 'Gabriel, is it? You're going to let me see the footage now, and then we'll think about the police.'

Xavi Aislado had one icon in his life; his grandmother, Paloma Puig i Garcia, who had brought him up, and made him what he had become. Nobody had ever said 'No' to Grandma Paloma; nor, he realised in those moments, had anyone ever said 'No' to him.

Gabriel did not become the first. Instead he opened a concealed gateway in the reception counter and beckoned him to follow.

The office behind the public area was mostly open plan, but the monitoring screens had a room of their own, with a large multi-screen display, surveyed by a middle-aged woman. She wore a lapel badge also; her name was Anna Schmit, and she was Head of Security. She and the duty manager spoke in Swedish, but it was clear that she was reluctant to break protocol. However, it was evident also that he outranked her. Finally, with a grunted 'Okay', she reached for a mouse and isolated the front exterior camera. She looked up at Aislado. 'When?' she grunted.

'Ten forty-five on.'

She scrolled back the footage to the specified time, then let it play. The camera was located above the revolving doorway; its display was wide angle. After a minute or so, a silver car came into shot from the left and halted, directly in front of the exit, on a spot reserved for taxis. The two men who emerged from the front seats matched Gabriel's description, well-dressed, well-groomed. *Maybe too well-groomed for cops*, Aislado thought.

'Let me see them, please; best shot,' he requested.

She froze the screen as they stepped towards the entrance. Both were unsmiling. They had an air, he reckoned, of two men on serious business. 'Okay,' he murmured.

Four minutes later they reappeared in shot, with Pilar following. One man moved round to the driver's seat, on the offside; the second opened the rear passenger door. He held it for Pilar, allowing her to slide into the back seat. She entered, then . . . for a second he seemed to close the door, but suddenly, without warning, he ducked his head and followed her, slamming it shut behind him. An instant later the car took off, so quickly that an approaching driver was forced to brake sharply. As it moved out of sight, there was a glimpse of Pilar's face, mouth open as if in protest, eyes wide as if in fear.

'My God!' Gabriel gasped. 'What was that?'

'An abduction,' Xavi said quietly. 'Anna, can you scroll back and freeze on the registration plate, please.'

She did as he asked; as the image froze, he took out his phone and snapped a picture of the plate.

'What do we do?' the duty manager asked. His earlier composure had shattered.

'You don't, I do.' Already Aislado was in his directory retrieving the number that Agnetha Bure had given him before their pick-up. 'No questions,' he said as she picked up. 'Nacho's partner has just been snatched from her hotel, the Scandic Triangeln, by two men in a silver Volvo saloon. I'm going to send you an image of the plate. You have all the police contacts here, I guess, so you'll get to the right person faster than me. Don't ask me why, I haven't a clue, just get things moving and call me back. We need to track that car soon as possible. I'll wait here, at the hotel, for the police.'

He ended the call without allowing Aggie to say a word, then drew a deep breath, realising, perversely, that regardless of the circumstances, he had not felt so alive in years.

Forty-Two

As she emerged from the International Arrivals doorway in Copenhagen Airport, Sarah Grace Skinner looked a little uncertain as she surveyed the throng of waiting greeters. Most of them were holding up signs, but not one bore her name, as far as she could see. She made her way past the crowd, wheeling her case awkwardly, with the straps of her cabin bag around the twin pillars of its handle, and her medical bag in her left hand.

'Let me take that,' her husband said, stepping out of nowhere and grasping the suitcase handle.

'Where were you?' she exclaimed.

'I had you under surveillance,' he replied. 'And you didn't spot me. I used to be pretty good at that: seems that I haven't lost my touch.'

She squeezed his arm. 'You and your bloody boys' games.'

He grinned. 'No, the truth is I was outside, making a phone call. This building's a bit of a signal-free zone.'

She looked around. 'So this is Denmark. How do we get to Sweden? Rail? That's what the investigation coordinator told me.'

'Indeed?' Bob remarked. 'Then cops do outrank pathologists, it seems. They sent a car for Sauce and Stirling. There's no danger of us taking the train, love. The locals told me it's unreliable, and you have to be at the hospital on time, so I hired a car through the hotel . . . and a driver,' he added. 'He picked me up from the hospital and he'll take us back there, after a stop-over at the hotel so you can drop off your luggage.'

'And freshen up,' she interjected. 'I took off from Barcelona not long after sun-up, and I had a rush to catch the connecting flight. To use my favourite Scots word, I must be mingin'.'

He leaned closer to her and sniffed. 'Can't argue with that,' he said cheerfully.

'Bastard.' She dug him in the ribs. 'But first things first. How's Nacho?' she asked, suddenly serious.

'Not as great as he was last night; post-op pain's kicking in.'

'And how are you?'

'Not as good as I was last night. His surgeon told me something this morning that I wish she hadn't. He was shot by a police sniper on the roof of a multi-storey block. Given the angle of the wound and the point of impact, if the building had been one storey higher the bullet would have gone through his spine, likely outcome paralysis.'

'Or worse; add on a stoma bag and possibly a bladder reconstruction. The surgeon didn't tell him that, did she?'

'God no, and she won't.'

'She better not, or she'll have me to answer to.'

As she spoke they arrived at their taxi, an immaculate Mercedes saloon. The driver greeted them; he loaded Sarah's luggage into the boot, and would have taken her medical bag, if she had allowed it. They were pulling away from the taxi rank when she spoke again. 'How is everything now? I gather from the media that the Swedish PM came through surgery, but she's still critical.'

'She'll make it, Nacho's surgeon said,' Bob replied. 'She might have one of those bags, though. And one kidney less.'

'What about the shooter? He was killed, I read.'

'Yes. Ignacio said he was already down when he ran towards Ralston. I was wondering, will they ask you to do that autopsy too?'

'They'll be wasting their time if they do. I don't mind being a witness at a Fatal Accident Inquiry in Scotland, which I believe legally there will have to be, but I'm not letting myself be tied into a Swedish process that could be endless.'

'Understood,' her husband said.

As the taxi left the airport and joined the highway, she linked her arm through his. 'What about the ferry?' she asked. 'I mean the thing happened as they were doing the opening ceremony. It was ready to sail, with all the passengers on board. Surely it didn't?'

He shook his head. 'No. No way could they have done that. They took the passengers off and put them up in hotels all over Malmo. There was talk of flying everybody home, but Pilling, the owner of the line, said that it would have to sail sooner or later anyway, and unless someone could show him legal grounds for a further delay, it would sail tomorrow or the day after. Shit, who's that?' he murmured as a buzz on his phone warned him of an incoming message. He took his mobile from his inside breast pocket and opened it. As he read the contents, Sarah saw an expression of pure amazement appear on his face.

'Fuuuuck,' he drawled in a whisper. 'What the hell next? It's a text from Xavi. He says that Pilar appears to have been kidnapped from the hotel.'

'Eh?' Sarah exclaimed. 'Who would want to do that? And why?'

'I have no idea,' he replied. 'But I'm going to find out and this time nobody better try to stop me!'

Forty-Three

'I was expecting something bigger,' John Stirling remarked, as the car pulled up outside an unexceptional building in the heart of Malmo. 'I did a bit of online searching,' he explained. 'I found the Police Authority building. It's on the edge of the city, in a more open area, and it's a big bugger, the size of our Crime Campus at home, maybe even bigger.'

'We're not dealing with the police,' his boss reminded him. 'State Security are running the investigation. It's not unnatural if they have their own space.'

'If we were in Edinburgh . . .' the DS began, as their driver stepped out.

'We might be running the investigation in theory, but in practice we'd be calling in our own security service, MI5, especially if one of our guys had gone rogue, and playing by its book. My guess is that's why the Swedes insisted on an ACC presence; sensitivity.'

'You mean they think you're less likely to go blabbing their secrets in the pub than I would be if I was here on my own?'

Haddock grinned. 'Pretty much, yes.'

'Gentlemen,' their driver said. 'Follow me, please.' He had not spoken throughout the journey, after introducing himself and showing them credentials identifying him as Matti Lower. Stirling was sure that his silence was his way of demonstrating that he was not a tour guide.

As he led them into the building, the officer seated behind a desk in the lobby emphasised his status by standing and saluting.

'Where are we going?' Haddock asked him as he led them to an elevator.

Lower made a gesture with his thumb. 'Up,' he replied.

They rode the lift to the third floor. They stepped out and were led along a corridor to a door with a keypad. Their escort punched in six figures, very quickly, his hand hiding the sequence, then stood aside.

Stirling's eyebrows rose as they stepped into a space that was less than half the size of the Glasgow squad room in which he worked. He had expected a buzzing hive of activity but all he saw was a young woman seated before a keyboard, a second desk and alongside it, beside a window, a table with four chairs.

'This is it,' Lower said. 'This is the inquiry headquarters. I'm sorry for my boorish behaviour on the way across, but I didn't want to get into discussing details until we got here and you could see for yourself.'

'Where is everybody?' Haddock asked.

'We are everybody,' the Swede admitted, as the three men sat at the table. 'I am the deputy head of the Security Service and Helen is one of our IT specialists.' He nodded, acknowledging the Scots' surprise. 'I know, you were expecting a room full of screens and people. We have that, but it's in Stockholm. We can do everything we need to do there, so it made no sense to move a contingent down here. This isn't a conventional homicide where the cops would turn up with a mobile headquarters. Our first duty here is to protect our Prime Minister against any second attempt on her life, and we're doing that at the hospital . . . not that there will be one,' he added.

'I get that,' the ACC conceded. 'So why are we here and not in Stockholm?'

'Because we don't want you in Stockholm, Mr Haddock. That's the truth of it.'

'Call me Sauce, please. Everyone in Scotland does.'

'Very well, Sauce, and I am Matti. Look, your interest is here,' he explained. 'Your First Minister's body is here, alongside his assassin, Rogne Andersen. He'll be autopsied this afternoon, and then your pathologist will do the same with Mr Ralston. Once she's submitted her report, you can take him home for whatever process you have to do there. I'm sure that Mr Pilling, the head of RocLine, will take the casket back on the Edinburgh ferry, when it sails, so that you can arrange a dockside ceremony, if you wish. Or you fly him home and do something appropriate at the airport. A better question,' Lower continued, 'would have been, why am I still here? This is why. Ms Lena Rapace, the Trade Minister, has taken over as acting Prime Minister in Ms Mattson's absence. She was her deputy, so you can understand that Lena is personally embarrassed that one of her bodyguards did this. She has ordered me to stay here, as the "face" of the investigation if you like, something that is unique for a member of the State Security Service. I suppose I am also the conduit between us and the Scottish and UK interests . . . and as such, how can I help you, Sauce? What do you need?'

'You're giving me what I need, Matti; frankness. That said, Mr Ralston wasn't the only Scottish victim yesterday. There was another, a young journalist, who was wounded. Right now he's in hospital; we'll want to see him.'

'No problem,' Lower responded, 'but it won't be today. Obviously I need to talk to him also, but the only way to him is through his surgeon, a very formidable-sounding lady called Doctor Fagen. I spoke to her before I left to collect you, but she said "Not today". I can wait, but I'd like to see him for personal reasons. I don't need to tell you this but I will. I was there, Sauce, in the middle of the shooting.'

Stirling frowned and intervened. 'Sorry, sir, but why? Is VIP protection part of State Security?'

'Yes, by one of our divisions; the assassin Rogne Andersen, we recruited him. That's why our focus is in Stockholm, because that's where the disaster originated. But, that's not why I'm . . .' Lower hesitated, then looked at Haddock. 'Off the record?'

The ACC nodded. 'Okay. I'll stop you if I feel compromised, yes?'

'Agreed. I was in Malmo yesterday because we had picked up a whisper, a very faint whisper, of a threat against Lena. That's why she had protection for the Ralston visit, two protection people posing as press officers.' He winced. 'One of them turned out to be the fucking threat himself, but he had passed all kinds of vetting so . . . Anyway,' he continued, 'for that reason I decided, that is my director did, that I should go to Malmo the day before, as a precaution. So, I was there. Moving on . . . When the First Minister's visit was arranged it was through Jens Pilling, the ferry owner. He's an important man, in Sweden and Norway; without him, it probably wouldn't have happened. Lena was there because of him, not because of Mr Ralston. Things only changed when your First Minister pulled a rabbit out of his hat, a proposed twin link between Malmo and Glasgow with a symbolic element.'

'The Turning Torso?' Haddock asked. Lower nodded. 'Yes, we were briefed about that before we left, via Mr Dunbar, the First Minister's adviser.'

'Good, so you'll understand how that changed the dynamic and made it suddenly an event that merited the Prime Minister's attendance. That was arranged very quickly, so quickly that her security detail . . . she was in Brussels at the time under EU protection . . . didn't have time to get there. With me being on the scene already, I was asked if I could cover . . . I'm firearms trained, and I had my service weapon with me . . . so I did. I was in the car with Pernil and Mr Ralston, I opened the door to let them out, and I was close when Lena's bodyguard went rogue. I reacted, and so did several others. He went down quickly . . . although not quickly enough, sadly . . . but in the middle of it all I was aware of the young man running towards the stage. The sniper on the roof assumed he was a second assassin, fired and hit him, but I was close enough to see that he was unarmed. I stood over him, guarding him as best I could, until it all calmed down. That's what happened.'

Haddock looked at him. 'Yes,' he murmured. 'Thanks, Matti. I have a personal interest in that too. It's one of the reasons I'm here, with my new temporary rank. I know the boy, Ignacio Watson; but I know his father even better.'

'Why is that?'

'Because he used to be my boss: Sir Robert Skinner. My ex-chief constable; my mentor if you like.'

Lower stared at him. 'Skinner?'

'You've heard of him?'

'Who in our world hasn't? He's a fucking legend. A few years ago I did a security course in a place in England. He was a speaker there; very impressive and very formidable. Very connected too, I heard afterwards. Something he has probably taken into his new role in life . . . yes, I know about that too. That young reporter is his son?'

'He is. That being so, Bob's here, in Malmo. Obviously Ignacio's his first priority, but now he's in recovery, I'm surprised he hasn't been battering on your door already.'

'Jesus,' the Swede murmured. 'That would be the last thing I need. If he sees how we are here . . . Are you in touch with him?'

'He's been in touch with me, Matti, asking if I can get him access to the investigation. To be honest, when my acting chief chose me for this job, Skinner management was one of his reasons.

I'll do my best to keep him away from you, but no promises. He already has limited access . . . which I'm sure that nobody's told you about. The Scottish pathologist . . . actually she's American but let's not split hairs . . . she's his wife.'

Lower's eyes widened as he absorbed the news. 'She's the young reporter's mother?' he exclaimed.

'No. Bob's marital history is as complicated as the rest of him. Ignacio's from an earlier relationship.'

'As a pathologist, how is the lady?'

'Professor Grace is as good as they get,' he promised his colleague. 'That's why she was asked to come. This is our head of government she's opening up, remember.'

He nodded briefly in acknowledgement. 'She's welcome here, don't worry.' He paused. 'Look, Sauce, speaking for Sweden, we are appalled as a nation that such a thing could happen to a guest on our soil, but it has. Even worse that a man who wanted to build bridges between our two nations is an innocent victim of an individual whose motives are not yet clear to us.'

'We understand that. So does Bob Skinner, I'm sure. But it's personal for him, with Ignacio's involvement. I'll do my best to keep him at bay. Can I help you in any other way?'

'Yes,' Lower replied, instantly. 'You mentioned Mr Dunbar, Mr Ralston's adviser. I can't find him, or his media person, Ms Cooper. They were both at the ceremony, but when the chaos was over and the scene was contained, they were gone. You said he briefed you. Where was he?'

'Oslo. He was in Oslo, with Jens Pilling, the RocLine owner. Ralston's private office in Edinburgh established his location yesterday. Pilling's plane was on the ground at the city airport and he had a car and a driver at the scene. After the shooting, when he was told by a police officer that Ralston was dead, he took charge. He got Dunbar and Cooper, he took them to the airport and flew all three of them to his home in Oslo. They're cloistered there. Why do you need him?'

'I don't really, it was just a loose end that needed tying off. With his boss out of the picture, he's pretty much a nonperson now.'

'Okay.' Haddock checked the time. 'I think that's us done for now. When's the autopsy?'

'Fifteen hundred hours,' the Swede said. 'At the hospital. They'll do Rogne Andersen first, with Professor Grace as an observer, then she'll take over for Mr Ralston.'

Forty-Four

Dolça Nuñez leaned back in her seat and gazed up at the outline of the Alhambra set against a clear blue sky. She had expected the place to be packed with tourists but there were none. *A pity but a blessing*, she thought.

She had been halfway to Granada by train, thinking of her homeland, and wondering whether, given the roving nature of her job, she could ask Skinner or Sureda if she could base herself in Sevilla, when a call had come in, from someone not on her contact list. She had taken it anyway, discarding her newspaper, and had been surprised.

'Señora,' the caller had begun, 'this is David, from the café. I hope you don't mind me calling you; your father gave me your number.'

'Not at all,' she had replied. *A little old for me*, she had thought, *but not unattractive. And there were a couple of clients who made him look by comparison like his Michelangelo namesake.*

'That's good. I confess that it was exciting for me to meet a member of the press. The life of an Andalusian civil servant is a little like existing in a glass bubble. You, on the other hand, are involved in everything, you see everything and you meet real people.'

'It's not that great. I have just read about a colleague, someone on an InterMedia newspaper, who was covering a story in Sweden and who was shot. Around twenty journalists have been killed in Ukraine. Fate doesn't discriminate, most of them were Russian.'

'Then be careful.' David had sounded anxious. 'We wouldn't want anything to happen to you. Maybe my glass bubble's not so bad. Anyway. Why am I calling? You must be wondering. This is it: after I left you this morning, it occurred to me that there is someone who can tell you more than I about the Tromso business. His name is Juan Calera, and he is a delegate to . . . a member of . . . the Andalusian Parliament, for the area where they want to build the resort. He knows more about it than anyone; he's the guy you should speak to. I've called him and he says he's quite happy to speak to you. You said you were going to the mountains.'

'I'm on my way there right now.'

'That's great because, as it happens, he's in Granada today. Suppose I set up a meeting?'

'Please do. I'll be there in just over an hour.'

Ten minutes later he had called back. '*Paseo de los Tristes*, junction with *Calle Monte de Piedad*, three fifteen – good?'

'Great.'

'Then I'll confirm with Juan . . . and Dolça . . . maybe next time you're in Sevilla we could have breakfast together.'

'Thanks,' she had said, 'and maybe.'

And I'll tell my dad not to spit in your coffee, she had thought with a smile.

The Walk of the Sad, she mused as she looked around the crescent-shaped terrace. *I wonder what made them so miserable. Was it because they'd just come from Pawnbroker Street around the corner?* She chuckled very quietly. *Maybe it's the name that scares visitors away, or maybe it's quiet only because of the time of day, when the pawnbroker is closed.*

Her elaborate train of thought hit the buffers as a shadow fell across her table. 'Miss Nuñez?' She turned and looked up. 'Juan Calera. You may be expecting me?'

Automatically, she stood. 'Of course, welcome, please sit.'

Looking at the Member of Parliament as he lowered himself

carefully into a seat, and laid his walking pole beside it, she wondered how long he had been in office. White hair swept back from a domed forehead; his lined face was tanned and his nose was a great hooked beak. But his blue eyes were bright and sparkling, and suggested a gateway to a store of wisdom.

'Would you like coffee?' she asked. 'Americano? Cortado?'

He smiled as he raised a hand. 'It will happen,' he murmured. He made himself comfortable on the hard stacking chair; no sooner was he settled, than a waiter appeared, unbidden. He placed a glass of beer in front of him, on a coaster and with a second placed on top of the glass. 'Thank you, Jimi,' Calera said then turned towards Dolça. 'You see? It's a ritual. I come here, I sit down and Jimi brings me a beer. I don't need to order. When it is finished he brings me another. When that is finished . . . I think about it. The second coaster? That's to keep the flies off. And now, my dear, what do you want to know about Tromso and its fun palace in the sky?'

'What can you tell me?' she countered, as he took his first drink from the glass. 'When I was given this assignment, my brief was to look at the people behind it, but now I find that I need to know about the whole project. I followed the man and then I found this, the Tromso project.'

'You're talking about Mr Raul Sanchez? My new best friend?'

'Yes, that's the man.'

'Well, he is from Madrid, he supports Rayo Vallecano, his wife's name is something Scandinavian that I can't recall, and he has a daughter named Pilar who is his main topic of conversation. He describes himself as a banker, but that word covers a treasure house of sinners and sins. All that I learned over just one lunch meeting with him in a decent restaurant in the city centre.'

'Saints and sinners. Do you see Tromso as a sin?'

The old Parliamentarian smiled, and took another mouthful. 'Dolça,' he said. 'I have been in public life for a long time, and I'm elected, which makes me quotable. Being quoted can be good at certain times and in certain circumstances . . . for example when one is running for re-election as I may be next year . . . but not always. Good or bad, it's always best to control the narrative. You are a journalist, not very experienced yet from your age and from what I found out about you in preparing to meet you. But by now you must have learned the basics. If I answer your question directly, yes or no, it will become a quote. Let's keep them general, yes?'

She felt herself flush. 'Yes, sorry. Sir, nothing you say will be quoted directly in anything I write, I promise you.'

'Nah, quote me if you like, as long as they're my words, not yours. What is my view of Tromso's proposed new ski resort? I have seen the geologists' reports on the proposed ski runs. I have seen the route of the funicular that would service them, and the resort. I have seen the environmental impact studies. I have seen the detailed plans and AI visualisation of the new hotel and spa. I have no objection to any of it. But,' he added, 'I'm an old man and my attitudes are those I was raised with. I don't stand to attention and grab a banner when some red-faced kid stages a protest strike. However, those who do deserve as much respect as do I.' He paused, as if gathering her full attention. 'Of course there is a third interest group, the existing players in the Sierra Blanca ski and leisure industry . . . I use the word because that's what it is, a full-blown industry; okay, not the equal of the French or Swiss, but on the other hand with the added value of being close to the Mediterranean coast, which is popular even in winter. There are several of those players, not just the operators of the existing ski facilities, but the hotels that support them and live off them in winter. That group is one hundred per cent against . . . but as someone said in English many years ago, "They would be, wouldn't they?"'

Dolça pursed her lips, one of her unconscious gestures. 'How do you see the balance of opinion? How does it stand at the moment?'

'Among the decision-makers?'

'Yes.'

'My assessment, which is probably more than a guess, is that on balance they are in favour of approval. Anticipating your next question, Will it be approved? To be honest I don't know. Tromso's weakness is its opacity, its shyness, the unwillingness of the people hiding behind Raul Sanchez to show themselves and their money.'

'How do you, the Andalusian Parliament, that is, know there are people behind him?' she asked.

'Honestly? We don't,' Calera admitted. 'We're just sure of it. Yes, Sanchez is the only listed director of Tromso, but the money, we are asked to believe, is held in the Swiss company behind it. Sanchez insists that it's him; he says that he's the head of a consortium of investors.'

Dolça frowned. 'I've been looking into that. The Swiss do have a register of shareholders in their companies.'

'Of shareholders owning twenty-five per cent or more,' he corrected her. 'Sanchez can hide, no question. It's weakening him in the eyes of the Parliament, but at the end of the day, an investment of that size in Andalusia is very attractive. Add on to all that his claim to have media backing.' He smiled, into her eyes. 'Would I be wrong in believing that's what triggered your interest in this man and in his project?'

'No,' she admitted. 'You'd be on the mark.'

'He's in with the Aislados? If so, their wealth would pretty much validate the project.'

She shook her head. 'Not necessarily them; the older Aislado has retired, and his daughter has only just finished university. Media backing.' She repeated his words. 'What exactly did he say to the committee?'

'I don't know myself because I wasn't there, but . . .' Calera stopped in mid-sentence. His glass was empty; Jimi stood beside them with a replacement. 'Thank you,' he murmured as his supply was replenished. 'Sorry,' he said as the waiter left, 'I should have asked whether you would like another.'

'Thank you,' she replied, 'but I'm good. You were saying?'

'Yes, I wasn't there but I was told that he said he had a high-level source in the InterMedia group and . . . he didn't say he had its backing, but that's what every member of the committee assumed that he meant. If not the Aislados, Miss Nuñez, then who? Sureda?' Calera mused. 'He's the CEO, isn't he?'

'Yes, but not the boss. That would be the executive chairman, Sir Robert Skinner.'

'Ah!' the old man exclaimed. 'The one you journalists call The Highlander? It's him?'

'Yes, he has a relationship with Sanchez, but it's personal, not on a business basis. My boss has a son, Sanchez has a daughter, and they're together.'

As she spoke, she recalled the name of her young colleague, the *Saltire* reporter who had hero status after broadcasting live from Sweden, after being wounded. Ignacio, Skinner had called him. Ignacio, the *Saltire*, Scotland. No coincidence, surely.

'Are you all right, Dolça?' her companion asked. 'Is something wrong?'

She shook herself, returning to the present. 'No, sorry, a sudden thought of something I'd missed, it's okay. Because of that relationship,' she continued, 'that's how Sanchez knows Sir Robert, that's all. I believe I'm free to tell you that when my boss was told that the company had been mentioned in that context, it was the first he had heard of it.'

'And would I be free,' Calera asked, 'to convey that knowledge to my colleagues on the Tromso committee?'

She gulped. *Judgement call, kid*, she thought. 'Yes,' she told him after a moment, 'I believe you would.'

'Then I will, discreetly, but for background knowledge only, not to be repeated.'

'Will that kill the project, do you think?'

For the first time, the old man frowned, although the skin on his forehead barely wrinkled. He shook his head. 'No, not directly,' he replied. 'Nobody wants to be blamed for that by the others. There's an election next year, and that's a major factor. Unless your boss is so annoyed with Sanchez that he has you or someone else write an article blasting Tromso . . . do you think he might?'

Judgement call Number Two. 'Between the two of us, I don't.'

'If not, they'll take it that InterMedia isn't against it, and that'll be enough to keep it alive. Whether they would give it Parliamentary approval would be another matter. I believe that we will eventually. If my colleagues choose to wait for the endorsement of the electors, I would not be surprised. But if they decide to proceed to vote now, I believe it would come down to only a few votes . . . and one of them would be mine.'

He raised his second glass. 'Is that enough for you to report back?' he asked.

It was Dolça's turn to frown. 'Not yet. It's very helpful, but I should see the location for myself. I think I'll hire a car, drive up into the mountains and speak to some of those hotel operators, to put the finishing touches to my story, if I get to write it, and to breathe some clean Andalusian air while I can.'

'Speak to six different hotel owners and you may have six different stories at the end of the day. Speak to the person who runs the ski facility and you'll have the broadest view on the mountainside. But yes, go there, my dear. It's most beautiful at this time of year.'

Forty-Five

Xavi Aislado was waiting at the first-floor lift of the Scandic Tri-angeln as Skinner stepped out. 'Is Sarah settled in?' he asked.

'She doesn't have time for that. Quick shower, do her hair, and dress professionally, then we're out of here. We have to be at the hospital for three. What's happening here?'

Aislado led him from the elevator towards an alcove over-looking the foyer where three people were seated: Agnetha Bure and two other women. 'Detectives,' he said. 'They turned out pretty quickly when Aggie called them. We haven't got very far, though.'

'Okay,' Skinner murmured as he took a seat. 'Who's in charge?'

The older woman raised herself from her chair, briefly. 'I am. Sergeant Detective Mary Blix, and this is my colleague, Constable Ulla Forsell.'

'Ladies. I assume that Xavi's briefed you on who I am and where I fit in.' They nodded. 'Very good. How far have we got? Is there a possibility that the guys who took Pilar were official? For example, could they have been operatives working on the Security inquiry into yesterday's shooting? I'm aware that the investigation wants to interview my son, when his surgeon gives the okay. Could it be that Pilar's on the witness list too?'

'They're not cops,' Blix declared; she spoke English with an accent that might have been acquired from American television. A Columbo *fan?* Skinner wondered. 'That I can tell you. I can't say for sure that they weren't secret squirrels, for those guys have their own rule book, but I doubt that it includes driving a car with stolen plates.'

'Granted on that one. What are you doing to find it?'

'Everything we can, sir, but with your background, you'll understand how limited we are. We've alerted every patrol vehicle there is, and we have civilians in our monitoring centre looking at street camera footage. We're relying on a little more than luck, but there's no denying we're going to need it.'

He nodded. 'I know. How about the hotel footage? Can you lift images from that to help identify these men?'

'We have a technician trying to do that right now; Ulla and I looked at it as soon as we arrived here, from the outside camera and another in the foyer. I can arrange for you to see it, but I'm sure you'll reach the same conclusion as us. These are not amateurs, I would say. The one who comes in first is wearing sunglasses. He makes a very quick scan of the lobby area, spots the camera, then quite casually removes the shades. At that point his colleague follows him inside, as if it was an okay signal. From then, both men keep their faces pretty much out of shot.'

'Pros,' Skinner agreed, as his professional senses kicked in. 'Does that give you comfort, Sergeant Blix?'

'I don't know, sir. Should it?'

'It did to me, when I was in your job. Pros don't panic. They'll have a plan before, during and after; they'll know what their personal limits are. You, or your negotiators, can deal with that. A couple of guys off the street, just given a job to do? Hell no, they're too unpredictable. One clear and audible warning, then put them down, with whatever level of force the situation justifies.' He looked at the detectives. 'You don't have much experience of this type of incident, do you?'

Each shook her head. 'No, sir,' Ulla Forsell confessed. 'Mostly we investigate robberies, fraud, commercial crimes, things like that.'

'We were the duty officers when the call came in,' Blix admitted. 'But we are trained,' she added.

'I'm sure you are, and I respect that,' Skinner assured them. 'I think what I'm trying to say is don't feel embarrassed by a new situation or too proud to ask for advice.'

'Understood,' the sergeant said. 'Do you have any suggestions?'

'Motive?' he suggested. 'These guys walk in off the street and pick the woman up. It's not a random kidnap, no way. She was targeted, but why? Pilar's tied into the shooting in only one way. She had dinner with Ralston the night before he died. Did he say something to her and Ignacio that someone wants to know? But no, Ralston was random, he wasn't the target, so how does that work? Answer: it doesn't. In that case look somewhere else. Focus on the girl herself . . . she's only a girl to me,' he explained, 'as she was when she and my son met.'

'What's her family situation?' Forsell asked. 'Who are her parents? What do they do?'

'They live in Madrid. Her mother's in public relations, her dad's in commercial finance . . . but he's a bull-shitter,' he added. 'Plus, they're a couple of thousand miles away from Malmo.'

'What if . . .' Blix mused. 'You two gentlemen are important figures, as Xavi explained to us. Could it be that Pilar has been abducted to get to you? Do either of you, or your company, have any enemies?'

The two men frowned at each other. Aislado shook his head.

'He says "no",' Skinner said, 'and he doesn't, personally. Me?

I know where mine are, those that are still around. But the company, InterMedia? Given what we do and where we do it: everywhere, here included.' He glanced at Bure. 'Right, Aggie? We probably have even more enemies than we imagine. If she's been taken by one of them . . . you keep on looking, but if it's so, I'm sure we'll hear soon enough.' He slapped the table. 'And now, I'm out of here. Xavi, if anything shifts, please keep me in touch.'

Forty-Six

'Should we go in?' John Stirling asked Haddock, as they peered through the glass wall of the room in which Ignacio Watson Skinner lay. He was propped up on an array of soft pillows and appeared to be asleep.

The ACC shook his head. 'Not without someone's permission, and I doubt that anyone will be granting it. The lad's a good colour, that's the main thing. Come on, let's find our way to the autopsy viewing gallery. We can't be late for that.'

The route to the mortuary area was circuitous, but with a little guidance from a staff member they found their destination . . . only to discover that they were last to arrive.

'You guys took your time,' Bob Skinner declared, glancing at his watch.

'What the f . . .' Haddock gasped in surprise, staring at Mattie Lower. 'I thought you were . . .'

'Not something I would normally have done,' the Swede conceded, 'but there has been pressure on my political masters. The British Home Secretary.'

'Not pressure,' Skinner protested, with only a hint of a smile. 'Just a request. I won't get in the way, I promise.'

'You are all right with an autopsy, sir?' Lower asked him.

'I've had experience. I've never been at one that I liked, but I'm okay. No,' he corrected himself. 'There was one that I enjoyed; I only went along to make sure the bastard was really dead.'

'Bob!' A female voice with a sharp edge came from the speaker array in the ceiling. 'Stop pissing about! We're ready to go here.'

It was Lower's turn to stare at Haddock.

'His wife,' the ACC explained, quietly.

'Thank God,' he murmured. 'Professor Eriksson, are you ready to proceed?'

'Yes, thank you.' Both pathologists were suited, masked and booted as they looked up from the floor of the autopsy room towards the observation deck. They stood between two examination tables upon each of which a naked male body lay. 'We will begin with the examination of Rogne Andersen,' Eriksson said. 'I will lead, and Professor Grace will observe. When we move on to Richard Ralston, the roles will reverse. By the way, we are not strangers, Sarah and me. We have been bumping into each other at teaching conferences for years. I am deeply jealous of her gig in Barcelona,' he added. His eyes wrinkled above his mask. 'Okay, let's see what we have here. The body of an apparently strong and well-muscled male aged thirty-three, who was brought here having sustained multiple gunshot wounds while in the process, we are told, of inflicting several himself.' He walked around the body for several minutes, examining each of its many wounds, occasionally pushing, with not inconsiderable strength, the subject on to its side to look at others. Sarah followed him, but from a distance, looking on but saying nothing. Finally he stepped away. 'Henrik,' he exclaimed. There was a third person on the floor, a man in green protective clothing, rather than the professors' blue. He stepped forward with a scalpel, made a Y-incision in the subject, and opened him from the chest to the groin.

Haddock was standing close to Lower as the preparation began. He sensed a slight convulsion and found himself wondering how many post mortem examinations the security official had actually seen. *Probably not his everyday line of duty*, he guessed. He leaned close, and whispered, 'Could be worse, Matti. This place is ventilated. On the floor we'd be getting the smell as well.'

Eriksson stepped in once again, ready to begin the detailed dissection. 'I have observed eighteen gunshot entry points from several angles but only six exit wounds. Those include a single, catastrophic head shot, that would have done the job all on its own. The number of wounds tells us that the armed police and security officers around Mr Andersen reacted quickly to his unexpected attack on the Prime Minister and by extension Mr Ralston, who has the misfortune,' he added 'to be joining us here today. The pattern indicates that they also acted instinctively, without proper appraisal of the situation. What I'm saying here is that they panicked, therefore we're lucky there were no civilian fatalities, given the indiscriminate nature of their fire.' He looked up at the observation deck. 'Mr Lower,' he called out. 'I gather you were at the scene. How far away was Mr Andersen from Ms Mattson and Mr Ralston?'

Above him the Swede frowned. 'Ten metres, approximately,' he replied.

'That being the case,' Eriksson continued, 'can we be certain that Ms Mattson was not hit by any of this reckless and almost random gunfire?'

'Fortunately, we can. Six bullets were recovered from the Prime Minister and all of them were matched to Andersen's firearm. There were no exit wounds, so nothing hit her that wasn't recovered.'

'What was the weapon?' Skinner asked, interrupting.

'A Glock 19,' Lower told him.

The Scot whistled. 'Hit by six nine-millimetre bullets, she's a lucky lady to have survived.'

'I saw her before I came here,' the security officer countered. 'Right now, she wouldn't agree with you.'

'No, but she will. How many rounds were left in the Glock magazine?'

'Five.'

'Plus one in the chamber. That leaves three of Andersen's rounds unaccounted for. I'm here looking down at Ralston's body but I don't see that many wounds.' He looked down at the Swedish pathologist. 'Sorry, Prof, I'm holding you back.'

'Not at all. Let me see what I can dig out of Andersen. God knows, the scene was so confused that maybe he shot himself a couple of times in the panic and confusion. That was a joke,' he added, 'but I have actually seen it: a drunken armed robber.' He turned to his assistant. 'Henrik, I have examined the internal organs in situ. Perhaps you would now remove and weigh them, while Professor Grace and I consider what we have seen so far.'

Above them, the four observers gathered together. 'Mr Lower,' Skinner began. 'You were there, I believe. Is there any chance that one of these random bullets hit my son, and that it wasn't the cop on the roof?'

'No, none at all. By the time Ignacio reached that part of the scene, half of Andersen's brain was being splattered over our Trade Minister. Your boy was definitely shot by the sniper.' He looked at Haddock. 'Is there anything you'd like to ask?'

'Plenty.' He glanced to his right. 'How about you, John?'

'Like to say, sir,' the DS declared, 'rather than ask, if I may.'

Lower shrugged. 'Go ahead.'

'Okay.' He drew a breath, and began. 'So far, sir,' he said, 'we've had vague information about the guy who's currently being emptied out down there. He was an ex-special forces recruit to the protection unit, we've been told in the report you sent us before we got here, and there was a suggestion that he might have been suffering from PTSD. Having just been assessed for that myself, and knowing how it works, that sounds to be more of a guess than anything else . . . or a cover-up. The fact is special forces guys are assessed for PTSD potential before they're accepted. If your man Andersen emerged from SF service with stress disorder, he was a member of a very small group. It would probably have been noticed on assignments or training. If it was, that would have led to him being stood down from duty and would for sure have been marked up when he applied to join your protection team. So . . .'

Haddock started, as if to intervene, but Skinner put a hand on his sleeve. 'Let it play, Sauce,' he whispered.

Lower was smiling but his eyes were icy. 'Are you saying I lied to you, Detective Sergeant?' he murmured.

Stirling shook his head, emphatically. 'No, sir, I am not. I have no doubts that you told us what you were told yourself. All I'm doing is pointing at a flaw in its logic, that's all.'

'You're saying my boss has been bullshitting us both?'

'Too bloody right, sir,' he snapped. 'That's exactly what I'm saying. If I'm out of order, my ACC's going to have my nuts, but I'm over the edge now.'

The other man laughed. 'You're safe,' he sighed, 'and I apologise, to both, to all of you, because I didn't believe it either when I wrote it. In Sweden security operates at more than one level, as I'm sure it does in your country.' He glanced down. 'Let's get this over, then I'll go further.'

Below them Henrik had finished his meticulous but gruesome work, and the two pathologists were studying the organs that he had removed. They worked for over ten minutes murmuring occasionally to each other, before Eriksson looked up to the observers. 'As far as we can see,' he declared, 'of the eighteen entry wounds I mentioned earlier, two of these shots hit the lungs, one nicked the right side of the heart, but faintly, scarring but not penetrating the wall. It is I imagine lodged somewhere inside the torso, for there were no exit wounds in that area, and a fourth is lodged in the liver. We have those four, and the one head shot. We have the six exit wounds, including the head shot. I've always been shit at arithmetic, but on that basis I would expect to recover another eight rounds from the body, none of which would have stopped him in his tracks on its own.' He glanced at Sarah and then up once more, towards the observers but with his eyes on Lower. 'I've believed for most of the time I've being doing this job that the routine issuing of firearms to police patrol officers, supposedly for the public protection, all too often has the opposite result. This afternoon we are only considering the shots that hit Andersen, and their effect. Can you tell me, Mr Lower, how many shots were fired in total by police officers during the neutralisation of this gentleman as a threat?'

'No, Professor,' the Swede admitted. 'I can't.'

'Will you or someone else be determining what that number was?'

'I won't; maybe they will be in Stockholm.'

'Then you had better make sure they do, because in my official report I will be asking the question. God, Matti, it's a miracle that we don't have a queue of dead spectators outside waiting their turn. Okay, that's my spleen vented, now we'll go and look at Andersen's. The cops missed that too.' He turned towards the table, but paused. 'If the Scottish witnesses would like to take a break,' he said, 'we'll let you know when we're done with Rogne here and ready to start on your Mr Ralston.'

Forty-Seven

'You know what?' Dolça told the ski-lift manager, whose laminated badge identified him as Guido, as the late-season customers made their way through the shed, strapping themselves into the gondolas in which they would be lifted to the top of the slope. 'I have never imagined,' she said, 'taking pleasure from strapping planks to my feet and sliding down a mountain, but I have to admit that the surroundings are pretty spectacular.'

'Truth?' the man replied quietly. 'Me neither, but you're right, up to a point. It's a beautiful place to spend the winter.'

'What's the point?'

'This is a nice day. We're over three thousand metres high here; when it isn't . . . it really isn't. If the conditions are too bad the call will be made to close the slopes, or possibly just open the nursery, the beginners' area, but it can be a minute-by-minute decision and staff have to be out here to make it. However the good days outnumber the bad, and the money's decent, better than it is in Switzerland or in France. Plus the hours of daylight are limited and the labour pool is smaller so the staff here can have night jobs.'

'Doing what?'

'Bar work, in a hotel: there are dozens around here. They have their own Facebook group, so when there are job vacancies, the word gets spread around fast. Collectively, together with the ski-lift operators, they're a powerful organisation.'

'How do they feel about the Tromso project?' Dolça asked.

'How would you feel if an anonymous entity turned up out of the blue,' Guido countered, 'with a plan that was pushing the environmental boundaries, and was going to take half your business?'

'As much as that?'

He nodded. 'It's that big. The industry here is just the right size. It operates at full capacity as it is. If you double that capacity, in theory that's good. In practice, it's very dangerous because the transport infrastructure can't be doubled. It's fixed as it is and the journey itself takes longer and is more complicated than it is to the ski resorts in France, Switzerland and the north of Italy. It's not like Field of fucking Dreams, lady. You can build it, but they won't come.'

'In that case,' she conceded, 'I wouldn't like it.'

'No. But it's not without hope. It's still got to be approved by the Parliament in Sevilla. There are endless committees but they still can't make their mind up. Have you heard anything different?'

'No, I haven't. My source says that the shape of the politics . . . the timing of the next Sevilla election and the current state of the parties makes it possible that they'll just keep talking for a year, and take no decision.' She looked up at him. 'Do your bosses know where the money's coming from?'

'Not that I hear, and I'm not at the bottom of the food chain around here. There are rumours, of course. I believe there's a man from Madrid who's the public face of the Tromso organisation. True?' he asked.

'Yes.'

'Here,' Guido made an all-encircling gesture, 'they think he's a front for Russian money, being shovelled in through Africa. That's the best guess they can come up with.'

Dolça frowned. 'But it is only a guess?'

'So far. But if it is so, and their front man from Madrid . . . What's his name?'

'Sanchez.'

'If Sanchez can't deliver soon: he might find there's pressure on him of a kind that he really does not want.'

Forty-Eight

'My God, Bob,' Raul Sanchez moaned. 'What am I going to tell Inge? What am I going to tell her mother?'

'Tell her that the Swedish police have good people working on this, in spite of everything else that's gone on here in the last twenty-four hours. Tell her I'm here too, I have access and I'm on top of it. Plus Xavi Aislado is here, so the situation has the full weight of InterMedia bearing down on it.'

'But why, Bob? Why? Who would take our baby? She's an ordinary girl, we're an ordinary family.'

'Neither why nor who are obvious at the moment, mate,' Skinner said. 'I wish I could offer you more comfort. As soon as I can, I will.'

'Should we come to Sweden?'

'No!' he exclaimed. 'Trust me to handle this for you.'

'Okay,' Sanchez sighed. 'I can't vouch for Inge, but I'll do what you say. This must be just as bad for you, with your son being shot, and now his partner missing.'

'Nacho's going to be okay, and so is Pilar. You're right, she's a member of my family too, and I trust the police to find her. The men who took her left a trail. We have them on camera when they conned her into going with them. These people always think they're a step ahead of the game, but mostly they're a few behind. I'll call you as soon as I have news, Raul. Meantime, hang in there.'

He ended the call and turned to Haddock and Stirling. 'Sorry, that had to be done. Hold on again, please: one more call that I should have made earlier.' He selected Aislado from his contact list. 'Xavi,' he said, as they were connected. 'Can you get on to Blix? Something I should have asked earlier. I know the guys were care- ful to locate the camera then avoid it, but: does her department have access to facial recognition software, and if so did the first one into the foyer show enough for them to do anything with it?'

'I will do,' his friend replied. 'How are things where you are?'

'Bloody. Sarah's still waiting in the wings.' He glanced at a wall clock. 'Shouldn't be much longer now. It's probably time we went back in there.'

'Straightforward, though?'

'With Andersen, not exactly. The guy's like a colander. As for Ralston, I can tell you now he's going to be much more question- able. There's something not right about him.'

'Who's going to ask the questions?' Xavi asked.

'That's why Sarah's there. I'm already working on the answers.'

'How can you be doing that?'

'Because I've seen the footage on my son's phone. He's a natural reporter. He wasn't just running towards the action. He was filming it as well.'

Forty-Nine

'I know,' Sergeant Detective Mary Blix said, pre-emptively, as her contact in the monitoring centre picked up her call. 'I've given you an impossible task: find a silver Volvo in a Swedish city, and now I'm hassling you about it. I'm sorry, but this is a potentially serious situation.'

She paused. She gasped. She smiled. '*Strandgatan?*' she said. '*Ja? Ahh. Ja. Okej.*' She ended the call and turned to Constable Forsell. 'We have something,' she said, then returned to her phone and keyed another number.

'Mr Aislado,' she exclaimed. 'I have something for you. They found it, the monitoring people; they found the silver Volvo on their recording, and they were able to follow it. It headed west, through Gamlastaden and then on towards the Limhamn area, near the Oresund. It was last seen going on to a roadway called Strandgatan, very close to the sea, where the city coverage runs out.'

'Well done them,' Xavi said, 'but that sounds like a trail that's gone cold. Since then, couldn't they have swapped the number plates back to the originals? Also if they were heading towards the Oresund as you say, surely they could be in Denmark by now?'

'Yes, they could,' Blix admitted, 'but . . . I don't think so. If I was heading for the bridge from where they started, I'd have gone to Hyllie, and joined it there. It's possible, I'll grant you, but if you were leaving Sweden, Strandgatan isn't a route you'd take.'

'Unless you knew where the cameras ran out?' he suggested.

'Possibly, but if they were planning to cross the bridge what would be the point in being evasive, when you'd be seen at the toll payment points?'

'Changing the plates?' he suggested.

'The toll-booth cameras would show the passengers, including the girl. But if we get to a point where we have to look at every silver Volvo that crossed today from Sweden we will.'

'What if they swapped cars at Strandgatan?'

'Then we'll find the original and get DNA from it. Mr Aislado,' Blix said, 'I'll be blunt. If they're going to kill the girl, they'll do it in Sweden. They may have done it already. I hope not, but for now all we can do is our best. And I can see another reason for taking that route: that close to the sea, there are caravan parks, and camping sites, lots of them. Towing caravans, static vans and lodges; they're all very busy in high summer, but we're weeks away from that. If you want to keep someone hidden: that would be a good place to do it.'

'That sounds logical,' Xavi conceded. 'A possibility. What are you going to do?'

'Obviously,' the detective replied, 'when Ulla and I were called to the Scandic, and learned what had happened, I reported straight back to my boss. She told me to do what we've done, take statements from the hotel staff, then report back. I have no experience of this situation and neither has she, so I am fairly sure she'll have been talking to her bosses, to cover her ample backside. I'm about to report back, as she ordered, and I'll recommend that on the basis of what we know, we have officers knock on every door in all the Strandgatan area, also go to the camping parks, check on the parked and static caravans and open all of them if we have to. After yesterday, sir, the reputation of the Malmo police is in the shitter already. We can't have them pull the chain on us!'

Fifty

Haddock led the trio back on to the observation deck to join their Swedish colleague. They had been expecting to find Professor Eriksson coming to the end of the Andersen post mortem, but they had been over-optimistic. The little pathologist was still hard at work, and the subject was still wide open on the table. Behind her mask, Sarah seemed impassive but Skinner could tell that her patience was wearing thin. As he checked the time, he could understand why. Four hours had been allocated for both autopsies but the intricacies of retrieval from the gunman meant that three of them had elapsed already, and he knew very well that his wife could not, would not, be rushed in her work.

Unexpectedly, an incoming call to Lower's phone brought matters to a head. It lasted for over two minutes, for most of which the Swede listened, only speaking as it ended. 'Okay, I'll be downstairs: five minutes? Yes.'

'I am sorry, gentlemen,' he told the three Scots. 'The examination of Mr Ralston must be postponed until tomorrow. Sir Robert, will that inconvenience Professor Grace?'

'Not if it means that she'll have enough time to do a proper job. She has nothing booked for tomorrow, and we have another crisis to manage, on which your police colleagues are working already.'

'Should I be interested?'

'I would say so,' Haddock replied, 'but you seem to be in a rush.'

'I am. If I may explain briefly, my colleagues in Stockholm have been turning Rogne Andersen's life inside out. They have discovered that he has been meeting in secret with a group that he seems to have met during his military service, an extremist Islamic outfit with the inevitable grudge against the west. We've tracked them down to an apartment block in Rosenberg . . . a part of the city where Andersen would have stood out. In twenty minutes it will be raided by a group from the very special forces unit in which he once served . . . and I need to be there. I am sorry about this but I must leave.'

'Don't be,' the ACC assured him. 'We have an interest in your operation, remember, lying on a table down there.'

'Thank you. Please explain to Professor Grace, and give her my apologies.'

'Keep your head down,' Skinner called after him as he headed for the door. 'They won't be taking any prisoners,' he added quietly.

'No?' Stirling asked.

'Groups like those, they don't usually give you a choice.'

'What's going on up there?' Professor Eriksson's tinny voice asked from the intercom. 'Where has Lower gone?'

Haddock switched on the microphone and explained.

'Tough on him,' the pathologist grumbled. 'I am not stopping. Sarah, do you want to step out now? We're not going to find anything new here. Yes, the double orchidectomy was a surprise, since it didn't show on his medical records, but there's no potential left for any more bombshells.'

'That's all right, Jo,' she said. 'I'll see it out. Bob, guys,' she called out, 'we'll be another twenty minutes. There's nothing more to be witnessed here. I'll see you outside when we're all done.'

'What's a double orchidectomy?' Haddock asked, as they returned to the anteroom.

'Unfortunate,' Skinner murmured in reply. 'Sauce,' he continued, 'it seems to me your time here's been wasted so far.'

'I know,' the ACC agreed. 'I've been thinking about that, about how to put it to better use. And that, I reckon, means actually starting a formal investigation into Ralston's death. At the very least there's going to be a Fatal Accident Inquiry in Scotland, possibly something bigger with judicial powers given who the fatality was. The autopsy is part of that, but we should probably begin interviewing witnesses as soon as we can. Matti Lower will give us access to his list, at least I hope he will, then there's Ignacio, obviously.' He glanced at Skinner. 'When the hospital says we can,' he added. 'For the sake of thoroughness we should also talk to Ralston's staff. They were his adviser, Peter Dunbar, and his press officer, Ms Joan Cooper. Last heard of they were hunkered down in Oslo with Jens Pilling, the ferry owner.'

'Do we have to do all that, boss?' Stirling asked. 'Ralston seems to have been an innocent victim of an assassination attempt. Like a by-stander caught in a gunfight.'

'You still need to talk to them,' Skinner intervened. 'An inquiry won't simply be the formal means of recording what happened. It'll be interested in apportioning blame. Yes, we know about Andersen, but once the scene went active, could anything have been done that wasn't, that might have prevented Ralston's death? Lower and his mates in Stockholm will be asking that same question, but their interest will be different and their hands might be tied in a way yours aren't. If they do take prisoners, i.e. living witnesses, from this raid of theirs, I'll take that as a good sign. If they don't, I'll be suspicious.'

Haddock frowned. 'What do you mean, Gaffer?'

'I mean dead men tell no tales, Sauce. There was one person on the scene who is just another individual to you, but a hell of a lot more to them. Ms Rapace, the Trade Minister, is now the acting

Prime Minister as a result of Mattson's incapacity, having been her deputy. She's actually benefitted from it, personally. And . . .' he looked from one officer to the other, 'the guy with the Glock, Rogne Andersen, was one of her security guards. If I was the head of the Swedish Security Service and running this investigation, I wouldn't just be looking into his background, I'd be looking into hers, for any evidence of a previous link between them and for any sign of her involvement in his appointment to her team. That's what I'd be doing. Will they? Or will that obvious line of enquiry be left alone?'

'Will it?'

Skinner laughed. 'Sauce, my friend, I'm a born conspiracy theorist and so are you. Every possibility remains open until it's discounted. None should be disregarded. But this is someone else's politics; in this case they're overlapping with ours. I'd be amazed if that potential line of investigation is raised in the Swedish Parliament or media or anywhere else. Or I would have been, were it not for two facts. I'm at the head of an international media organisation with outlets in Sweden, and, my son is lying in this very building having been shot in the incident. Whatever stone the Swedish investigators might prefer not to turn over, that's too damn bad, for I have people who are going to make damn sure that it's looked under.'

'So we should too?' the ACC asked.

'Yes, you should. That's if it's still relevant to your inquiry tomorrow. If it isn't, you won't have a locus.'

'What do you mean "if"?'

'I mean Sarah hasn't done Ralston's autopsy yet.'

His phone interrupted their discussion. He frowned at the screen. 'Xavi,' he murmured. He took the call and listened, frowning all the time. 'Positive,' he said. 'I'd go with Blix's theory. I hope they have enough officers to sweep those sites properly. Thanks,

I might even go out there and join in later on. Anything on facial recognition? Ah, too soon I suppose?'

Haddock frowned at him as he finished. 'Pilar?' he murmured.

'Mmm?'

'Could they have killed her, Gaffer?'

'I hope I'm right,' he replied, 'but no, I don't see it. I can't think of a single motive, and there's this too. Snatching her from a public place in broad daylight, that was risky. Would they have done that if they were going to do away with her? Nah, I don't see it. A hit would have been one man in a biker helmet, walking into the lobby, two in the forehead then out of there and off on a bike. I'm fairly confident about that, but I'm nowhere close to working out why anyone should take the girl.' He blew out a large breath. 'I'm going to have to come up with some ideas very soon, though, lads. As soon as Sarah's ready, we're going to see Ignacio. I'll have to tell him what's happened. He'll be wondering where she is already, because she isn't with him. There's a TV in his room: if he sees anything on it about a missing girl and a big police operation on the outskirts of the city . . . he has a journalist's mind, it won't take him long to make a connection.'

Fifty-One

'It would be too high for me,' Jordi Poch said. 'I'm a boy from Vigo, remember. I grew up at sea level, to the sound of the Atlantic breakers. Any greater altitude than Madrid, I get dizzy.'

'You'll manage,' Dolça assured him. 'I'll bring you here one day, I promise. Maybe we'll go to the Tromso hotel if it ever gets built.'

'If,' he repeated. 'A big one from what I can see.'

'Oh?' she murmured. 'You have doubts?'

'I still haven't found the money. It isn't sitting in a vault with its key in Raul Sanchez's pocket, that's for sure. I've run complete background checks on him, and his family. He's fifty-five, born and raised in Santander, where his father was a doctor. He has two siblings; both of them followed Papa into medicine, but Raul went into banking instead. He joined the Caja Casolana straight from university, and did very well there. So well that by the time he turned thirty-two he was its chief executive. A proper high-flyer, and on the shortlist for a couple of equivalent roles with bigger commercial banks.'

'Do I sense an "unfortunately" coming?' she asked.

'You do indeed,' Jordi confirmed. 'You and me, Dolç, we're too young to really have been aware of the international banking collapse of the late noughties, but . . .'

'I remember my mother moaning when the tourists stopped coming and the hotel takings fell away.'

'Yeah, well . . . at the heart of the crisis was very risky mortgage lending, of which the Spanish Caja sector, and executives like Sanchez, were particularly guilty. All over the country . . . and not only in Spain . . . those mutually owned savings banks were on the point of collapse, effectively bankrupt. The only solution was for them to be swallowed up by the mainstream commercial sector; they vanished while banks like BBVA, Santander and Sabadell came out of the crisis healthier than before. Relief for their depositors, but not for people like Sanchez. Their recklessness in lending to anyone, regardless of wealth, saw them go from hero to villain overnight . . . in Raul Sanchez's case, from being a highly paid executive, with performance bonuses running into the millions, to being a pariah as far as the restructured industry was concerned. Think of him as the banking equivalent of my local football team, Deportivo la Coruna, champion class for a while, now struggling to stay in the second tier. He lay quiet for a while, then reinvented himself. Today he calls himself a banker, but in effect he's a deal-maker, finding cash for people with new business ventures, but without the resources to get themselves off the ground.'

'Whose cash?'

'Mainstream banks, mostly, as far as I can see. Looking at him from outside, I'd describe Sanchez as a financial agent. He assesses a project's business potential, finds a commercial lender, takes a commission from the source and moves on. Sometimes he might take a small equity stake in the business as well, but safely, in the form of share options. He's good at what he does but he's a low-risk operator. Tromso is a step back into the Premier League for him. In practice Sanchez's wife earns more than he does. Her PR business, the one that you and I helped out last year, does very well.'

'Where has he found the money for the Tromso project?' Dolça asked. 'Is it in the Swiss company?'

'That's the thing,' Jordi said. 'Tromso's a shell, but so is the Swiss company.'

'You got in?'

'Babes,' he sighed. 'You ask me that? Of course I did . . . and I found nothing. Sanchez set up the Swiss company himself. I can only guess he did it to create the illusion of a powerful corporate backer. The source of the funds is still a mystery.'

'Not as far as the Sierra Blanca operators are concerned. They're convinced . . . or they're assuming . . . that it's Russian mafia cash. And there is money, for there's some preparatory work going on already.'

'They may well be correct. If they are, good luck. Much as I love you, Dolç . . .'

'Yeah, don't go there,' she agreed. 'But how am I going to tell my boss that his son's girlfriend's dad may have ties to the dark side?'

'Do you need to, at this stage?' he asked. 'You're an investigative reporter on the trail of a story. Doesn't that give you all the justification you need to approach Sanchez directly, and ask him who the Tromso project's backer is, without giving up your boss's name?'

She pondered the alternative. 'I suppose it does,' she conceded. 'Yes, I will. The only downside is that I need to look him in the eye when I do it and that means leaving this beautiful place and going to Madrid.'

'If I met you there tomorrow, would that help?'

'You know, my boy, it might just.'

Fifty-Two

'So this is one of the tourist highlights?' John Stirling murmured. 'This is what I lived to see?'

'That's what the guidebook says,' Haddock confirmed. 'Lilla Torg; here we are completely surrounded by restaurants, Moose-head Bars, gastropubs, fuck knows all what, and yet . . .'

'Me neither, boss, I don't fancy any of them either.' The DS frowned. 'What was the name of that place Ignacio told us about, where he and Pilar had dinner with Ralston?'

The ACC grinned. 'Where he dropped his accidental big reveal about himself and Nacho's mother? It's called the Gustav Adolf; we walked past it ten minutes ago. He said it was pretty good. I don't really fancy eating moose, so let's go there.'

The detectives turned and began to retrace their steps. 'What did you think of the boy?' Stirling asked.

'All things considered,' his boss replied, 'he was better than I expected. Still way too woozy for a formal interview though. We'll need to wait for Doctor Fagen's clearance before we can do that. And for one other okay too,' he added. 'I've never seen the Gaffer as stressed out. With his boy in hospital, and Pilar's kidnapping on top of that, he's almost hot to the touch.'

'Was he serious about the InterMedia papers questioning the investigation into the shooting?'

'Oh yes; be sure of it. He's right too.'

'Could the abduction be linked to the shooting incident?' Stirling looked cynical as he put the question. 'Is that possible?'

'How can it be ruled out? Nacho's reports made him internationally famous. Of course Pilar's kidnapping will be linked to him when it becomes known . . . and it has to leak by tomorrow at the latest, because of the search if nothing else. Yes, I can get my head round the terrorist group being behind it.'

'If that's so, and the Swedes are targeting those same people, could they be putting her life at risk?'

Haddock winced, shrugging his shoulders in a gesture of helplessness. And as he did so, his colleague tugged at his sleeve.

'Look,' Stirling said. He was nodding towards an Italian restaurant, with pavement tables. They were all fully occupied and their customers' attention, almost without exception, had been captured by a television screen. It was showing a news report; footage of black-clad people closing in rapidly on a white five-storey apartment block. The commentary was strained and in Swedish, but the action spoke for itself. The unit disappeared into the building. After a few seconds the image faded, and was replaced by another scene; ambulances, four gurneys, each laden and covered with a white sheet, and a man in an armoured vest, speaking to camera: Matti Lower. He looked sombre, frowning as he spoke.

'What does "*Inga överlevande*" mean?' Haddock asked, reading an on-screen caption.

The DS took out his phone, opened Google translate and keyed in the letters. 'No survivors,' he read.

Haddock snorted. 'Now there is a surprise! What did Big Bob say?'

'He said that if the special forces team took no prisoners, he'd be suspicious.'

'Just as I am, given the sensitivities involved. I don't go so far as to suspect that the acting Swedish Prime Minister could be involved in the shooting of her own predecessor. I can't bring myself to believe that. Assuming she wasn't, what's the first thing she's going to ask when she's briefed about the people who were behind it. "How the hell did our security and counter-terrorism apparatus fail to pick this threat up and prevent it?" Well, Lower's people have made bloody sure there's nobody left to answer that question. But there's still another one for Ms Rapace, one that the InterMedia titles and probably everyone else in Sweden will be asking tomorrow. Did she approve the operation in advance to save national embarrassment?'

Fifty-Three

'How are you this morning?' Bob Skinner asked his son. 'Did you get much sleep, being strung up in that arrangement?'

Ignacio looked up at him; his right leg was suspended in a harness to keep its weight from his healing wound. 'What do you think? It's even difficult to piss in a bottle.'

'Don't say too much about that or they might catheterise you; that's something you want to avoid if you can. How do you feel otherwise? You weren't very connected last night, with the painkillers and everything.'

'I'm better this morning,' he replied. 'I had a fucking awful dream through the night, until I woke up and realised it was actually a memory. That's helped me focus.'

'That's good, because your boss is going to be calling you on WhatsApp. The reality of Ralston's death is beginning to sink in in Scotland. Every news outlet is doing follow-ups, with the *Saltire* leading the pack, as always. June's doing our piece herself, and she wants you involved if you're up to it. Doctor Fagen's given her approval, subject to another examination this morning.' He paused. 'Sauce Haddock and another police officer will need to speak to you as well, later on today. They're here as observers of the Swedish investigation, but also to report back to the Crown Office in Edinburgh. You're a witness, son, as well as a journo . . . and as well as a victim.'

233

'My statement's on record already, in a big way,' Ignacio said. 'It was pretty awful, Dad. Doc Fagen told me that her nurses actually removed fragments of Richard's lung tissue from my face when they were cleaning me up pre-surgery.'

Skinner's eyebrows rose. 'They did? That begs a couple of questions. I hope the autopsy'll answer them, when Sarah's finally able to do it. Meantime,' he continued, 'there's something else we've got to talk about.'

'Yes, there is,' Nacho declared, 'like when are they going to give me back the TV remote?'

'After we've had this chat. In the time you and Pilar spent in this city before the circus arrived, did anything out of the ordinary happen?'

'Apart from the First Minister telling me he was bedding my mother?' he murmured.

'Before that, before he got here. While it was just the two of you, did you see anything, meet anyone, or ever feel like you might have been watched?'

He frowned. 'No, not really. We didn't really do a hell of a lot. Went for an advance look at the Torso, visited the Disgusting Food Museum . . . but not for long, Pilar threw up. Did we meet anyone? We spoke to a guy in a bar called the Dirty Taco, but as you do in a bar, no more.'

'Can you describe him?'

'He was white, medium height: longish dark hair. He was a cop, but very plain clothes from the way he was dressed.'

'A cop? How did you know that?'

'Because he told us. I told him why I was here and he said, "Maybe see you around." I asked why and he said something about event security.'

'Okay, think about this. When you went into the bar, was he there already or did he follow you in?'

'Come on, Dad,' he exclaimed. 'What's this about?'

'It's Pilar, son,' he admitted. 'Two men took her from the hotel foyer yesterday; from what the security video shows, they persuaded her to go with them. From what you're telling me, I think that guy was one of them, because she went with them willingly.'

Ignacio heaved himself upright, fighting against the pull of the harness. 'Then get me out of here,' he shouted. 'I can't lie here while she's in danger.'

Skinner stepped to the bedside and pushed him back down, on to the pillows. 'What are you going to do?' he asked, gently. 'There's a whole fucking police force out there looking for her and pursuing a pretty good theory about where she might be. Xavi got there soon afterwards. He raised the alarm, and he's been monitoring the situation ever since. I'm going straight from here to the police station that's running the search, and I'm going to lean on them as hard as I can . . . which will be very hard indeed. If I have to, I'll join the search team myself. Pilar will be all right, Nacho, I promise you. Since my early days on CID, son, I've had a feel for situations that could go bad. Trust me, this isn't one of them. You stay here, think positive, wait for June Crampsey's call and do what she asks, and then prepare yourself for a formal interview by ACC Haddock. I have a feeling he'll have plenty he needs to ask you, once Sarah's completed her work on Richard Ralston.'

Fifty-Four

'I'm really here as a courtesy,' Matti Lower said as he joined the Scottish police officers on the mortuary observation deck. 'With the elimination of the radical cell last night, we're satisfied that we've taken care of every element of the plot against our Prime Minister's life. I've been recalled to Stockholm as soon as your pathologist has completed her examination of Mr Ralston. Once that's done his remains will be handed over to your custody, for return to Scotland.'

'Noted,' Haddock acknowledged. 'Tell me, Matti, those four people you killed last night; what was their nationality?'

'They were of Iraqi origin.'

'That's not what I asked you.'

Lower gave him a half-smile. 'They were Swedish citizens.'

'What's the Middle Eastern population of Malmo? I'm told the area you raided is known as "Baghdad". Is that right?'

'So I believe, although I'm not from here myself. I believe also that the city's Arab population is around fifty-five thousand ... although it's probably more, as not every Muslim joins a community, those being what they count to produce a total.'

'Had any of your targets, your terrorists, been to Iraq lately, or even at all?'

'I don't know,' he admitted. 'But still, we are satisfied that the plot against Mattson originated in Sweden and has been terminated here. We're still looking at motive. But what's your interest, ACC Haddock?'

'That's pretty obvious, isn't it? Whatever the origins of the attack or its motives, our First Minister is dead as a result. It's a terrible analogy, but Scotland has a dog in the race and I'm here to represent my country.'

'Fair enough, but that's how it is. That's the Swedish position. Now,' he looked down into the examination room, where Sarah Grace stood beside the body of Richard Ralston, 'can we begin or are we waiting for Sir Robert?'

'His interest is elsewhere this morning,' Haddock said. 'Where's Professor Eriksson?'

'We don't need him. This is a purely Scottish matter now. So let's get on with it.' He touched the intercom button. 'Professor Grace, if you will.'

'About time,' she replied. 'I bill by the day. It might be a purely Scottish matter, but I'm here at the request of the Swedish government,' she reminded him. She turned to her assistant. 'Henrik, can you please turn the subject over on to his front.' She stood aside while he performed the task. 'Gentlemen,' she said, when it was done, 'how many wounds can you see?'

Lower stood aside, leaving Haddock to respond. 'One, Professor.'

'Precisely. And it's an entry wound.' She took a long thin probe, inserted it into the bullet hole, withdrew it and measured the depth of penetration. 'Henrik, turn him back, please.' She stood back once more. 'Now,' she continued. 'How many?'

'One, I believe,' Stirling replied. 'But it's much bigger.'

'Yes, Detective Sergeant. That's because it's an exit wound. What does that tell us? Volumes, boys, volumes. For openers, that hole was not ripped out of Mr Ralston by any nine-millimetre pistol cartridge, which means . . .?' She looked upwards questioning.

'He wasn't shot by Rogne Andersen,' Haddock sighed. 'Christ, Sarah, I knew you were going to say that. I just hoped you wouldn't. It's going to get worse, isn't it?'

A pattern of wrinkles around her eyes showed that she was smiling behind her surgical mask. 'Every which way, Sauce,' she replied. 'In the last couple of days, I've only seen one other wound like this. It was a photo taken by my step-son Ignacio's surgeon before she operated to repair the damage done by a high-velocity round fired by a police marksman . . . who is, I believe, after an intervention by my husband, currently packing his bags for a traffic management course.'

'Are you saying that our sniper shot Mr Ralston?' Lower called out.

'In one way, I wish I was, for it would be a hell of a lot easier solution. However, after having a sight of the deceased yesterday, I spent some time last night reviewing the footage from Ignacio's phone. It shows the whole incident very clearly, right up to and beyond the moment when Mr Ralston literally coughed his lungs up and all over the lad. When I saw the body, my immediate assumption was that the deceased had turned his back on the attacker. But he didn't; the video shows that when he was hit, while Andersen was still firing, he was facing the incident. You can see the impact of his wound. You can see the moment when the bullet exits, bursting his chest open, causing the damage you're looking at now. Richard Ralston was shot in the back, gentlemen, not by Rogne Andersen, but by someone else.' She paused, for five seconds and more before continuing. 'Guys, to quote the great Robert Wyatt . . . google if you don't know who he is . . . "Ruth is stranger than Richard". For sixty years, conspiracy theorists have been fantasising about a second gunman in Deeley Plaza, Dallas,

Texas. Undoubtedly that is what you have here in Krankajen, Malmo, Sweden.' She smiled behind her mask, looking up at the silent three. 'While you boys wrangle over jurisdiction, I will now proceed with my detailed examination, but I can tell you right now, that's what my report is going to say.'

Fifty-Five

'I guess this is how the other one per cent live,' Jordi Poch remarked as he looked upwards, admiring the dominating facade of the white, seven-storey apartment block where Raul Sanchez had agreed to meet Dolça Nuñez. 'Top floor duplex in the heart of the city, overlooking the Prado National Gallery. Not bad. Are you sure you don't want me to come up with you?' he asked. 'It's a long way down if he decides to chuck you off that balcony, when he finds out why you're really there.'

'I'll be okay.' She had introduced herself to Sanchez as an Inter-Media reporter who had been assigned to write a positive piece on the Sierra Blanca ski project. Expecting an enthusiastic welcome she had been surprised by his diffidence.

'It's not a good time. I have things going on in my life right now.'

'Oh, come on,' she had cajoled him. 'It's an opportunity. I'll be gentle with you, I promise.'

'Still . . .'

'Please?'

'Oh, okay, if you insist. Twelve thirty tomorrow . . . but be brief. Come to my home; I work from there mostly.'

Jordi frowned. 'You sure?' he asked her.

She patted his chest. 'Of course I am, my sweet boy. Don't tell me you haven't looked into Mr Sanchez so thoroughly that you know him better than he knows himself. If you really thought it was risky you'd be blocking the doorway.'

'True,' he conceded. 'So you want me to wait outside?'

'No, you don't need to. Go to the Prado and study Hieronymus Bosch. *The Garden of Earthly Delights*. Take half an hour to look at a real half-a-millennium-old Dutch painting rather than at a computer screen that was made last year in China. I'll text you when I'm done, and join you there.'

She gave him a half-hearted push, watched him as he walked down the gentle slope, then turned towards the elegant building. A white-haired concierge gazed at her as she stepped into the lobby. She had seen worldly men like him before, mostly when visiting clients in her hidden past, but she had been dressed differently then and so he looked at her in a different way. 'Sanchez,' she said without waiting to be asked. 'He's expecting me.'

'Level six, madam,' he said. 'The elevator is broken, I'm afraid.'

She frowned at him. 'You are joking, aren't you?'

His eyes twinkled. 'Yes, madam, I'm joking. You look very serious; I thought you'd appreciate a laugh.'

Thanks for that, she thought, consciously altering her expression. *Serious is not the way to begin this meeting.*

She rode the lift six storeys up. The concierge must have alerted Sanchez, for he was waiting for her in his open doorway as she stepped into the lobby.

'Miss Nuñez.' His greeting was on the curt side of polite. She replied with a killer smile, that softened it in no way at all. 'I thought it was you,' he said. 'I was looking out for you from the terrace. Who was the guy? A photographer you're going to ask me later if you can bring up? If so, the answer's no.'

His hostility puzzled Dolça. Ostensibly she was there to make his day, to build his pet project up to the skies, and yet his attitude yelled, 'Get this over with and get out!'

241

She followed him into an entrance hall, with twin pillars that had to be authentic marble, through a living room, and on to the terrace of which he had spoken. At its centre there was a small table, with two wicker chairs but only one glass. She was unsure whether he would offer her a seat, and so she took one anyway, leaving him no choice but to follow suit.

'What would you like me to say? That the Tromso project is the best thing that's happened to Andalusia in years, maybe ever? Okay, you have it. It's going to take an industry with potential and turn it into a recognised European leader, placing Spain above France, above Switzerland, above Italy. Okay, you have it.'

Dolça dropped the killer smile. 'Actually, Mr Sanchez,' she said dryly, 'I want to ask you about the money? I want to ask you why Tromso and the Swiss shell it hides behind is maybe the least transparent company I have ever seen? As far as its potential competitors are concerned, it's in the wrong sector. They say it should be listed as laundry, not leisure.'

He stared at her. 'Are you serious?' he gasped. 'This is a fully funded project that is going to do all the things for Andalusia that I have just described and yet it's being treated with suspicion and outright hostility by those self-seeking politicians in Sevilla. And why?' he exclaimed, his eyes widening, 'Because nobody's prepared to grease their fucking palms, that's why! The principal of the project is not that sort of man! Look, Miss Nunez, I don't have much of a professional reputation left but I've put it on the line for this. Every stop I have, I've pulled out. How have I been greeted? With cynicism and bad faith, and now you turning up here prepared to treat me like a gangster. I have a friend in your company, a friend right at the top. He's going to hear about this, young lady, I promise you.'

She let her eyes drill into him for a few seconds. 'What makes you think he hasn't already?' she asked.

Raul Sanchez slumped back in his chair and buried his face in his hands. 'Nobody,' he moaned softly. 'Nobody. I can rely on nobody. Fuck it. And it isn't even my company,' he protested, his voice strengthening once again. 'It's my wife's! The queen of Madrid PR! And what has her involvement been? Nothing, because in this one she wants to operate in darkness. And now, now, what has it brought us? My daughter has been kidnapped, that's what!' And with that desperate wail, he burst into tears.

Fifty-Six

'What do we have, Sauce?' Mario McGuire asked, gazing at his computer screen in the Scottish Crime Campus office he had commandeered for his stint as acting chief constable.

'Possibly a diplomatic crisis,' ACC Haddock told him. 'If you were to tell me that Pontius Pilate had been canonised and was patron saint of Sweden, I'd have no trouble believing you. That's how fast Matti Lower washed his hands of any notion that Rogne Andersen had an accomplice, a second shooter. He's adamant that he and his Islamic friends have all been identified. "A tightly wrapped group," he called them, with no links to anyone else. The Swedish Security investigation is closed and he and his boss in Stockholm aren't about to re-open it.'

'Do you want me to get our Justice Minister involved?'

'From what I've heard or read about her, that would have little or no effect. Plus she's got no locus; her powers don't cross borders. If we want intervention it would have to be the Home Secretary, Ms de Marco. She got the Gaffer a seat at the table because of Ignacio. But, sir . . .'

'I told you, it's Mario.'

'Very good, but Mario, I'm not sure that her intervention would give us anything we don't have already. I haven't seen the intelligence behind Lower's conclusion, but I've got no reason to

244

doubt its existence or to question his judgement. Which brings us to the likelihood, backed by Sarah's autopsy report, that our First Minister was the specific target of the shooter who killed him and that we've got a completely separate murder investigation on our hands.'

'On foreign soil.'

'Exactly, on foreign soil.'

'Which means that it's one for the Swedish police,' McGuire suggested.

'So you would assume,' Haddock agreed, 'but that's a conversation I've had with Lower already. He's taking the view that there are still politics involved, given the new victim's status as a head of government. That should mean it's still State Security business, however, he accepts they're our politics, not Sweden's. *Ergo*, he says . . . and that's a direct quote, he speaks fucking Latin . . . it's appropriate that we conduct the investigation, that's John and me, with the full assistance and cooperation of his people.'

'D'you need help from here? I'll fly officers over if you do: on a private plane if necessary, like footballers. Or like Bob Skinner,' he added.

'I'll shout if I think I do,' the ACC promised, 'but we're already networked into the local force in a strange way through another incident . . . although technically this one has nothing to do with us, since the victim isn't a British citizen.'

'Victim?'

'Pilar Sanchez Hoverstad,' he said. 'The partner of Ignacio Watson Skinner. She's been snatched from her hotel. That's the main reason, I suspect, why the Gaffer isn't breathing down our necks. He's taken up with that.'

With Stirling by his side in the mortuary office they had commandeered, he gazed at his laptop, as their chief took in the information. McGuire's thick, dark eyebrows were locked together in a frown, and his massive shoulders were hunched as he leaned forward on his desk.

'Why,' he began, finally, 'would anybody take the girl?'

'We'll get to that in a minute,' Haddock said, 'but we do believe from something Nacho told us that she was lined up for it a day or so in advance of the Ralston shooting.'

'Where does that take you?'

'I'll bring John in here. He pieced it together.' He glanced to his right. 'Go on, tell him.'

Stirling leaned into shot. 'Just a wild theory, sir, but: Pilar Sanchez is the partner of Ignacio Watson, Ignacio Watson is the son of Mia McCullough, Mia McCullough was sleeping with Richard Ralston. Now he's dead, Ignacio's been shot, ostensibly by accident but he has been nonetheless, and Pilar's missing, abducted in broad daylight from their hotel.'

'Mia was shagging the First Minister?' the acting chief gasped. 'Nobody told me that. Did Bob know?'

'You'll need to ask him that,' Haddock replied. 'The Gaffer still moves in mysterious ways,' he chuckled, ironically. 'I do believe Ralston's close circle must have been aware of a relationship, but Nacho didn't know until Ralston spilled it by accident the night before he was killed.'

McGuire whistled, leaning back, filling his high-backed chair. 'Your wild theory, DS Stirling. How wild do you think it is?'

'No idea, sir. But it's a lineal connection of actual events, the only one we have.'

The chief nodded. 'You know, son,' he murmured. 'I'm really glad those kitchen scissors only hit your gall bladder. Sauce, you know what we have to do, yes?'

'It's done,' Haddock said. 'Half an hour ago. It's one of my temporary responsibilities so I flexed my new rank and ordered protection officers to cover Mia McCullough's home and to shadow her wherever she goes, in case she's the next target on somebody's list.'

'I knew that was a good move,' McGuire declared, 'even if it was dictated by circumstances. There was always a fair chance you'd have been keeping that new warrant card, but catch us the First Minister's killer and it'll be a certainty.' He hesitated, but only for a second. 'Have you told the lady that she's under our umbrella?'

Sauce smiled. 'I plan to ask someone else to break that news,' he replied. 'Somebody who knows her better than either of us do.'

'Mmm. Good thinking, ACC Haddock.'

Fifty-Seven

'Yes, it's true, Dolça,' Skinner admitted. 'It's happened where I am just now, although the police have a news blackout on it, one that InterMedia is respecting. They believe it may be linked to what I'll only call a recent event.'

'Where are you, sir?' she asked. 'Are you going to tell me that?'

'I'm in Malmo, Sweden.'

'Where their Prime Minister was shot? And your First Minister was killed? The place where the *Saltire* reporter with the Spanish surname made himself a hero by reporting live after he'd been shot?'

'That's the place,' he confirmed. 'Now the only thing you don't know is his second surname. Don't share this, even with your boyfriend . . . although the sod would find out anyway if he'd a mind to . . . but that is Skinner. He works under his mother's name for a reason that should be obvious.'

'I had guessed as much,' she admitted. 'From what you told me before. How is he, your Ignacio?'

'He's tough. He has to be, poor guy. He's also angry, and frustrated. He wants to be out there looking for her, but he's literally tied to his hospital bed and will be for another day or so. Maybe longer if they don't find Pilar, but that'd be my choice. How did you leave it with Raul when he told you about her?'

'I gave him my sympathy, ended the interview and got my ass out of there. I felt sorry for him, and that doesn't happen too often.'

'Did you believe him? About the project?'

'About it being his wife's? And him having been thrown under the bus so to speak? I had no reason not to. He'd lost it by then; he seemed completely spontaneous.'

'What do you think he meant about it being her project?' Skinner asked.

'About it being her project? My assumption is that Tromso is her client, but it's controversial so she doesn't want her business . . . her very successful business, sir . . . to be associated with it. Instead she's shoved Raul out front to argue the case in Andalusia, in Sevilla, before the Parliament, even though he doesn't seem to have a financial interest, not that we've been able to uncover. The irony is that he seems to be doing a good job. My contact, who's so old and wise that people call him Gandalf, he thinks there's an even chance of approval this year. That's if I read him right, for his could be the casting vote. What do you want me to do?' she asked, abruptly. 'You told me to look into Sanchez. I've done that. He's a poor sap, but he hasn't betrayed you in any serious way. Is that it? Job done?'

'Is there a story in it,' he countered, 'leaving my connection out of it?'

'There could be.'

'Then as a journalist, you should follow it.'

'It'll mean looking into his wife,' Dolça warned. 'There'll still be a family connection for you.'

'Until Pilar turns up dead,' he muttered. 'Shit, I shouldn't have said that.'

'Why not?' she said. 'I was thinking it. Is there a real chance that she will?'

'In a situation like this there's always that chance. With Pilar, there's been no contact from the kidnappers, so the motive's unknown. But . . .' He paused. 'You know, thinking about it, I went through a police career reacting to dreadful events, after the fact. I saw their victims but I also saw their survivors; of them what I remember most is their disbelief. D'you understand me, Dolça?'

'Yes, I think so.'

'Well,' he continued, 'it's only as I've got older I've come to real-ise that most humans have a switch that prevents us from actually believing that the worst is going to happen, until it does. That's what I was seeing in those folk, so I think what I'm telling you is that as someone with a personal interest in the outcome, I'm the wrong man to ask.'

'Understood. In that case my prayers are with you all. Yes, I do pray,' she added. 'My dad brought me up well. When I was growing up in Cordoba, he took me to the cathedral in the Mesquita every week. I'll carry on with the story, sir. If I find anything you should know, I'll tell you.'

'Do that, Dolça, thanks. I'll . . .'

He was interrupted by an incoming call. He frowned as he saw its originator. 'Sorry, I have to take this.' He switched from one to the other. 'Mia,' he exclaimed, irritably. 'What's up? Nacho's fine. I promised I'd call you if he had a set-back.'

'I know that,' she snapped. 'It's got nothing to do with him. Bob, you know most things, so tell me, why the hell are there armed police in the woods near my house? Loukas Adelfos was stopped by one on his way here. I had to vouch for him. Poor lad got a hell of a fright.'

'Nobody's told me about it,' Skinner said, 'but I can think of a couple of reasons. I'll make a call and get back to you.'

'Do that, please. Nacho really is okay, yes? I tried to call him but his phone's off . . . or he's not picking up, the sod!'

'He's okay, I promise. I won't down-play what happened to him, Mia. Someone says "flesh wound" and we think "superficial" but this was a through and through shot. He will recover, fully, but it'll be more than a day or two.'

'How's Pilar taking it? I tried to call her too.'

He was silent for only a second, but it was enough.

'What?' Mia snapped. 'Is she okay?'

'She's incommunicado,' he replied, thinking fast. 'Given what's happened, the security people are twitchy.'

'Skinner, I know you. You'll say I can't, that we weren't together long enough, so how can I, but I do. And I know that you're lying to me!'

'I'm not!' he protested.

'Fuck off! We both know you are. Now, how is Pilar? What's the matter?'

He sighed, and told her about the abduction. 'The only people who know about it other than the police are Xavi Aislado, me and Ignacio . . . well, her parents do now as well. There's a big search operation going on right now, but given everything that's happened, no public statement's been made. The Swedes' initial assumption, and Sauce Haddock's, is that it's linked to the assassination in some way. People are reacting on that basis, and I'm pretty sure that's why you've got the watchers in the woods.'

'Am I at risk?' For the first time he heard a note of concern in her voice.

'I can't see that, but better safe than sorry, and so on. They won't be there long, I'm sure.'

'I hope not, now that they've got the guy that killed Richard.' She paused. 'Is the autopsy done?'

'Yes, it's over.' He was careful to keep his tone free of any inflection.

'Will they bring him back now?'

'I imagine so.'

'What happens in Scotland?' she asked.

'Legally that's up to the Crown Office. A sudden death of a Scottish citizen in a foreign nation, he determines cause, like a coroner would in England.'

'I meant politically.'

'Parliament will choose a replacement. That's not your world any longer, if it ever really was. How are you feeling anyway, Mia? Just as I can't fool you, I didn't buy it when you suggested that Ralston was just a casual shag.'

'You're not the only one,' she chuckled. 'I had a call last night, quite late on, from the *Saltire* political editor, Sue bloody Bland no less.'

'You had what?!' Skinner barked.

'You heard me. She called the hotel switchboard and they put her through to the house. She wanted my reaction to Richard's death, since we were in a relationship.'

'What did you say?' he barked.

'I had a lot of hot blood running at the time, but I think I yelled, "I bet you're fucking pleased about it!" then slammed the phone down. How did she know, Bob? I know you found out through your family contact in the police, but they're supposed to be hush-hush, aren't they?'

'Yes, they bloody are. It would not have been Lowell Payne's division, be sure of that. I had to tell June Crampsey, for editorial reasons, given her plan for Nacho's career, but no way was it her . . . at least I hope not or she's out of a job. Leave that with me. It'll have to be tomorrow, but I promise I will find out how Bland found out and I will shut her down!'

'You won't be hard on her, will you?' Mia asked.

'I can't promise you that,' he replied.

'Oh, please do, my dear: I don't want you to be hard on the creature, I want you to be fucking brutal. She hated Richard when he was alive, and she's carrying on her vendetta even though he's dead!'

Fifty-Eight

'First of all,' Sauce Haddock began, looking from his table towards the screen through which Mario McGuire, in the Crime Campus, DCI Lottie Mann, in Glasgow, DI Tarvil Singh, in Edinburgh, alongside two observers from the office of the Lord Advocate, were joining the meeting, 'I'd like to thank Mr Lower and his colleagues in Swedish Security for the use of this facility in their Malmo office, and for letting me take the lead in an investigation on their soil.' He nodded towards Lower who waved an acknowledgement. *He practically begged me to take the lead*, the ACC thought.

'Here's where our inquiry stands at the moment. The autopsy that's been carried out on the late First Minister has changed the way we were looking on his death. We are now certain that he was shot by someone other than the rogue protection officer Rogne Andersen. Swedish security has assured us that he and all the other people behind the attack on their PM have been eliminated, and that they had nobody else active at the scene. However, Professor Grace's examination has proved that there was, in her words, a second gunman.' He paused to drink from a water glass.

'I find myself looking at it in a different way,' he continued. 'We have a single crime scene, but two crimes. Each one was planned, each one took advantage of the same unique circumstance, the Malmo–Edinburgh ferry inauguration, but with two separate targets. There's one other distinction between them. Where Mr Ralston's assassination must have been planned some time in advance, the attack on Ms Mattson was more opportunistic. We're told by our colleagues that Andersen and his group had intended to kill her at a state event in Stockholm, on a later date. However when she decided, less than twenty-four hours in advance of the ferry ceremony, to do the inauguration herself, they brought their attack forward, reasoning, wrongly as it turned out, that her protection cover would be much less. A reasonable assumption,' Haddock added, with emphasis, 'as that assassin was part of it himself! In the event he failed, inasmuch as he failed to kill his target. The other plot was successful, sadly, and it's our task to catch the culprit. In setting out on the investigation we're going to make one basic assumption; the target was Scottish, therefore the likelihood is that the motive is also. Mr Ralston was a charismatic figure in Scottish politics, but he was also controversial. His plan to achieve independence by an alternative route to a second referendum, that was no secret. He never declared it publicly, he simply floated it as an idea and invited discussion. However, this afternoon I was sent by Peter Dunbar, Mr Ralston's chief of staff, a copy of the speech that he would have made at the ferry ceremony . . . I'm trying not to call it a launch, folks . . . and it was right there at its climax, set out as his policy and that of his administration. I'm told also by Mr Dunbar that he'd advised Ms Mattson of his intention, and she'd been all for it. In fact, that's why she decided to come to Malmo herself, to endorse it.' Beside Haddock, Lower nodded in confirmation.

'As I said,' the ACC continued, 'Mr Ralston never did acknowledge his strategy publicly, but there was an assumption in Scotland that he would, and that it was only a matter of time. Could that have been a motive? Well, we all know . . . that is, all of us Scots know . . . how high feelings ran during the referendum campaign.

The fact is that the heat's never gone out of the issue. It's a question we'll be asking, but discreetly, through ACC Payne's counter terrorism team. Indeed, I reckon that most of the questions asked in this investigation will be in Scotland, but there are some facts we have to establish here first,' he looked at the screen, 'the mechanics of the crime, for a start.'

'Can I ask you about that, sir?' DCI Mann intervened. 'The guy Andersen, he was out in plain sight, but what about the other shooter? Do you have any idea where he was positioned?'

'Short answer, Lottie, no. As I've said, there was a decent audience for the thing. The public were on the ground between the two ministers on their speaking platform and the ferry. On the other side, there were two more raised daises. One was for VIPs, civic dignitaries including Nicolai Lundqvist, the Mayor of Malmo, Jens Pilling, the Norwegian owner of the ferry line, his guests and also the Trade Minister and now acting PM, Ms Rapace. She was in the front row and Andersen was standing in front of her. The other dais was for the media, and was occupied by a couple of TV crews and some reporters . . . including Ignacio Watson.'

'How about his father?' Di Singh interrupted.

'He wasn't there, Tarvil,' Haddock replied.

'No, sir. But where is he now?'

The ACC frowned. 'Not far away. But on other business. I'll go into that later, but not right now. Going back to the crowds, to the witness pool if I can call it that: apart from those on the ground, the terminal jetty and the ceremony site are overlooked by residential blocks. We know from social media and other sources that some householders were watching the event. The Malmo police are hard pressed just now, on that other matter, but they're going to help us when they can by doing a door-to-door of those homes, to see if anyone can tell us anything useful.'

Mann raised a hand. 'What about the rest of the spectators?

The non-VIPs, the folk on the ground. Can you identify and interview them? Could the perpetrator have been among them?'

'Taking one question at a time. At this moment many of them are at sea. The game plan was that Mr Ralston would do the deed, make his announcement, then he, Mr Pilling, Ms Rapace and others would have boarded the vessel and sailed for Edinburgh. That was delayed, but it's ready to go tomorrow, albeit without Ms Rapace, who obviously finds herself with new responsibilities. As for the perpetrator, yes, they could have been among the folk on the ground, and now they could be anywhere.'

'Can I go back to motive, sir?' Singh asked, and then did. 'You talked about Scottish politics, and the possibility of Ralston's backdoor independence plan provoking a No-voter to take him out. Isn't that theory applicable beyond Scotland? I don't boast about it but I did politics for my OU degree. Historically, Westminster's the headquarters of Unionism; it's called the United Kingdom for a reason. Isn't it possible . . .?'

'You never cease to surprise me, Tarvil.' Mario McGuire's chuckle boomed out from the speaker. 'Yes, it is possible that Mr Ralston was killed by someone from beyond the precincts of the Holyrood Parliament. All I will say about that is that the Home Secretary's aware, and that the branches of the security service that report to her are active alongside ACC Haddock's investigation. Any internet chat, whatever its origin, will be picked up. And that doesn't leave these two rooms,' he added, heavily, 'or someone's head's on the block. Sorry, Sauce, carry on.'

'Thanks,' Haddock acknowledged. 'I've described the scene and the way the witnesses are dispersed. Now our first priority is to pinpoint the shooter's position if we can. It was suggested early on that the police rooftop sniper who, God help him, shot Bob Skinner's son by mistake, might have hit Mr Ralston in another miscalculation. That's been ruled out by the fact that the First Minister was shot in the back. The bullet that hit Nacho was dug out of the paving stones nearby. Swedish forensic teams are re-surveying the area looking for the one that went through the First Minister. Okay, needle in a haystack, but we can make the stack a lot smaller if we can give them an idea of its trajectory. With that in mind, all of the existing video footage that we can find has been sent to Acting Chief Constable McGuire in Scotland. He's going to instruct our technical resources to create a three-dimensional model of the scene, based on a freeze-frame of the instant the bullet emerged from Mr Ralston's chest. That will give us at worst, just by eliminating the impossible, a range of possible trajectories, giving the CSIs a clearer idea of where to look. If we're lucky it will tell us exactly where the killer was when the shot was fired. If we're even luckier,' he continued, 'combined with the video, it'll show us who he is.' He smiled. 'But let's not bank on that. It would take Euromillion odds. That's it, ladies and gentlemen. I'm closing this briefing.' He folded his tablet's cover. 'Now, DS Stirling and I are going to knock some doors in those residential blocks, hoping that the occupants speak English. Before we do that, DCI Mann, DI Singh, if you stay online, I'd like a further word.'

As McGuire and the other observers disappeared from the scene, Haddock left the room with Lower, bound for a Costa machine that he had seen on the ground floor. When he returned, with two cappuccinos, he saw that his Scottish colleagues had been on a similar mission.

'Okay,' Haddock said, as he resumed his place and appeared on the Zoom screen, 'now we're all refuelled, let's crack on. Any thoughts, you two?'

Mann nodded. 'A few, sir,' she began.

'Hey, come on,' he laughed. 'Cut the "sir", ffs. I may be carrying this temporary title, but when we first worked together you outranked me, Lottie, and as for you, Tarvil, you taught me a few things that have served me very well, not least because they're not in any training manual. So, Sauce it will remain, okay, to DI and above. Now, Lottie, you were about to say?'

'I was about to ask, Sauce. This separate investigation into Ralston's shooting, is it public knowledge in Sweden?'

'As of this moment, no it isn't, it isn't anywhere, outside our circle.'

'What if the Swedes leak it?' she asked. 'Do you think they might? If only to get them off the hook for Ralston's death.'

'They don't feel on the hook, not yet, so they don't have a need to. Everyone's buying that the actors against Mattson have all been eliminated, and that's all the Swedish press are interested in. But, there's another question, one that I've already discussed with the acting chief. We didn't want to raise it with the Crown Office people listening in, as they're already in full panic mode, but it's this. Should we pre-empt any leakage by going public ourselves?'

'Did you make a decision?'

'Yes, we did. We're agreed that, without a compelling reason to keep the separate Ralston inquiry confidential, it's our duty to go public on it. We're holding back for now to give the technicians at Gartcosh time to construct the model of the shooting, in case we do get very lucky and find ourselves with a prime suspect. Once that's done, DCC McGuire's ready to make the announcement, probably tomorrow noon.'

'That'll fuck up the football coverage for sure,' Tarvil Singh rumbled.

'There's only one thing that might delay it,' Haddock continued. 'The other matter I mentioned earlier. Pilar Sanchez, Ignacio's girlfriend, she's been snatched. There's a school of thought saying this could be connected to the killing of Ralston.'

'Do you believe that, Sauce?' the DI asked.

'Doesn't matter,' he replied. 'It can't be discounted. If the situation isn't resolved, it could be a factor in the timing of any announcement; we might not want the conspirators, if there is more than one, to know we're on to them. That would be a compelling reason.'

'I can just about see that,' Mann agreed. 'But isn't there a big complication in all this? Don't the press know about it already?' she asked. 'By that I mean Bob Skinner? He's there, he's got a personal interest, and remember he is the press, as the boss of InterMedia.'

Haddock nodded. 'Spot on. And he knows already there was a second shooter. Not just because his wife did the PM, but because he was there, officially as a representative of the Home Office, and saw with the rest of us that Andersen couldn't have shot Ralston. I suspect the only reason he hasn't told his people at the *Saltire*, and in Sweden, to run the story is because Pilar is at risk.'

'How long will that hold?' Singh asked.

'Until she's found, alive and well or otherwise. Meantime, there are other people who need to know the truth. They've been overlooked so far but they have rights. They may have been estranged, but Ralston does leave a widow, Mrs Amy Ralston. Also, he has a son from his first marriage, Daniel, and I believe also a stepson via Amy, named Calvin Knox.'

'Seriously?' the DI grunted. 'Calvin Knox? Sounds like a presbyterian think tank.'

'Yes, no kidding; and to pile on the irony his mother's an Anglican. Immediately after the shooting the DCC assigned family liaison officers to support Mrs Ralston, but they were told she was in retreat in a convent somewhere near Perth. Daniel was offered support too, but declined. As for Calvin, Ralston's man Dunbar says that he believes he's been in a monastery for years. We can disregard him, I think, but the others, the wife and son, need to be interviewed about recent conversations with Ralston. He may have told them something that's relevant; okay, probably not, but the box still needs ticked. And one other person,' he added, 'but I'll do that when I'm back in Scotland.'

Mann peered through the camera, curiously. 'Who's that?'

'Mia McCullough.' He saw her eyes widen, her jaw drop. 'Yes, Lottie, my stepmother-in-law. Unknown to any of us in the family, but spotted by ACC Payne's watchers, she and Ralston were . . .'

'Having it away?' the DCI exclaimed. 'Jesus, the tabloids will eat that.'

'The tabloids are not going to find out. It's not general knowledge. Mia's under police guard at the moment, because of the Pilar situation. Everyone connected's being watched.'

'How long do you expect to be in Sweden, Sauce?' Singh asked.

'That might depend on the Gartcosh reconstruction, but my plan is to fly back tomorrow and leave John here to liaise with the Swedish officers investigating the Pilar abduction.'

'And to keep an eye on Big Bob?'

'I wouldn't put it quite as bluntly. "To liaise with interested parties", might be a better remit.'

'Lucky lad. Listen, John,' the big Sikh called out, 'we've all worked for the big man in the past. You could learn just by watching him cross the street, so see it as a blessing, not a curse.'

'That's true,' Haddock admitted. 'I wish I'd thought of saying that, Tarvil. Okay.' Rounding up, he went on, 'While we're knocking on those doors here, I have a priority task for you two. I need you to contact RocLine, the ferry operator that's running the new link, and get from them the passenger and crew lists for the inaugural crossing when it sails. When it docks in Edinburgh, as it will the next day, everyone on board will need to be interviewed as a witness, before they set foot on shore. They'll include Ralston's man Peter Dunbar, and one Jens Pilling. He owns RocLine and half of Norway besides, from what they tell me.'

'Do we treat him with kid gloves?' Mann asked.

'You treat him as a witness, that's all. I'm sure he'll be helpful, but brass knuckles if he's not. I don't care how important he is.'

Fifty-Nine

June Crampsey was used to the quiet laid-back version of Bob Skinner, the boss who never stood on her editorial toes. A few seconds after taking the call she realised that was not who was phoning. 'Sue Bland.' That was all he needed to say, his tone did the rest.

'What about her?' the *Saltire* editor asked, cautiously.

'How did she react to Ralston's death?'

'Quietly,' Crampsey replied. 'The editorial floor went very still when the first news of the shooting came in. In that minute or so we didn't know how serious it was. Then Ignacio's call came through and at once we were on top of it, breaking the news that the First Minister had been killed. It was pandemonium; people were going crazy, calling anyone and everyone for a reaction to the death. Not Sue, though; she just sat there, calmly.' She paused. 'How's Ignacio doing, by the way?'

'Not great,' Skinner said, 'but I'm keeping an eye on him. Back to Bland, did she say anything at all, once his death was known?'

'Not a cheep. She went to the ladies, in fact. And she switched her phone off: I know that because Daniel called her.'

'Who's Daniel?'

'Her son, hers and Ralston's. When he couldn't get through to his mum he called me to see how she was, but mostly, I think, to find out if there was anything we knew that Ignacio hadn't reported.

He was devastated, the guy. I told him everything we did know, then I had someone dig Sue out of the bog to take his call. I had a good look at her then. I can think of only two reasons for her to have been in there, to cry or to laugh, and I didn't see a sign of a tear.'

'I saw your byline on the obituary. Did Bland contribute?'

'I didn't need her to; she'd have been a lousy witness. I spoke to Daniel instead for personal background. He was very helpful, he clearly loved his dad. Know what he said? That Richard was far too nice a guy for his mother, but too worldly for his second wife. You know, Bob, we hired Sue because she has one of the best CVs in the business, but if that's what her son thinks about her, I'm wondering about her as a representative of the paper.'

'You and me both, and not for that reason alone. Did you speak to Ralston's wife, scratch that, widow, when you were prepping the obit?'

'I tried, but I couldn't reach her. She was sequestered.'

'How about Nacho's mum?'

'Yes,' Crampsey admitted. 'Later on I called Mia, but only to commiserate with her about his injury and to say what a fantastic job he did under unimaginable pressure. I did not,' she emphasised firmly, 'ask her about her relationship with Ralston.'

'Did you tell Sue Bland about it?'

'Fuck no!'

'Well, someone did,' Skinner growled. 'She called Mia last night, asking her to comment on their relationship, as if for a story. Not asking for confirmation,' he added, 'but for comment. She presented it as a fact.'

'She did that without bringing it to me?' Crampsey gasped. 'A compromising story on a dead man who's currently being seen as a lost hero? She used this newspaper as a vehicle for her personal vendetta? She's sacked, Bob!' she snapped. 'I'm not asking for your approval, Chairman. She's fucking sacked!'

'That was my instant reaction too, June, but let's be careful with it,' Skinner cautioned. 'My priority is to find out who Bland's source was. Ralston and Mia hadn't been together long, and I know that she was still cautious about it. His marriage was over, most people were aware of that, and he probably did see their thing as long term, but Mia wasn't there yet. Their relationship wasn't a state secret, but the circle of knowledge wasn't large. If someone within it has spoken to Bland, I want to know who it was, for Mia's sake, but so will the police.'

The editor's news antennae twitched. 'What's the police interest?' she shot back. 'The Swedish investigation's all wrapped up, isn't it?' She heard a breath being drawn. 'Bob?'

'There are things happening,' he said. 'I can't tell you about them, not yet, but the police . . . ours, that is . . . haven't closed their investigation. If someone's been leaking information, they'll want to know why. Let me guess, you're going to tell me that a journalist will go to prison before betraying a source. When you speak to Bland, you can tell her that might well happen. Lean on her, June: I want to know who tipped her off about Mia. I'm sure that the threat of sacking her won't be enough. From what I've heard of the woman she's got the stuff of martyrs in her bones, so you're going to need a carrot as well as a bludgeon. Tell her I know that her source can only be one of three or four people, so it can't be protected for long. Then give her a choice, backed by me. Either she keeps her mouth shut, winds up before a judge, spends next week in Saughton and for as long after that as that judge cares to keep her there, or she gives up her informant and we transfer her to Washington as the *Saltire* US editor.'

Crampsey smiled at his proposition. 'You are a clever old sod, aren't you, Bob? That's an area I've been wanting to strengthen for a while. We're a national newspaper, so we should staff and act like one. The fact is, I've been waiting for the right moment to ask you for an increase in the editorial budget to cover just such an appointment, although I never thought of Bland for the job. To use it as an inducement to spill her source? I think that would work. I know Sue well enough to believe her principles do have a price.'

'Go for it then,' Skinner said.

'I will. She's left for the day, but I'll call her into the office tomorrow morning. Just one thing though, Bob, before I do. Why? Why has this happened? Ralston's dead. What's the point of this leak? What's its purpose?'

'There's only one reason that I can see. It isn't aimed at Mia McCullough. She doesn't matter. It's targeting Ralston himself. For Bland's source, the First Minister being dead isn't enough. They want to destroy his memory as well, to trash his reputation completely. Who would want to do that?' he asked, rhetorically. 'First and foremost, you have to look at his political opponents; those in Holyrood, and maybe further south.'

'Hold on,' Crampsey exclaimed. 'You said that him being dead isn't enough. Are you saying that whoever's leaking the story about him and Mia could be behind his killing as well?'

'Not necessarily, but June, ask yourself this: the Mia story seems to have been given to Bland alone, otherwise it would be all over the red-tops by now. Why? My guess is it's because she was perceived as the person who would do maximum damage with it, given her famous antipathy towards Ralston. If it was leaked generally, the source couldn't be sure how it would be handled . . . if at all; the BBC would have ignored it, probably STV as well. With some newspapers it could have had the opposite effect than Sue had intended. You want an example, take the *Courier*, in Dundee. One, it's a family newspaper, doesn't do sleaze, and also, Mia's one of its significant advertisers with her radio station and Black Shield Lodge, the country house hotel and spa. They'd be more than likely to portray her as a second victim, a tragic heroine, Ralston's way out of a marriage that had failed through no fault of his . . . or words to that effect.'

'Yes,' she agreed. 'I can see that. But, now that Bland's let them down, won't they take the story somewhere else?'

'Possibly, but Mia's prepared now. She has her own PR people; the next call she has will be referred to them. If you ask me, Bland's contact is smart enough to have worked all that out. Sort her out, June. Let me know how it goes.'

Ending the call, Skinner stepped back into his son's hospital room. 'Your boss is asking after you,' he said.

'What did you tell her?' Ignacio asked. He had been freed from his harness but was still on pain medication.

'I told her you were doing fine,' he lied.

'Fine, apart from my girlfriend being missing. Dad, it will be okay, won't it?'

'Yes, it will. I'm sure of it. It's tough, I know, but we just have to sit it out.'

'I want to kill the fuckers, Dad. You know that, don't you?'

'Of course you do,' he said. 'Nacho, we don't talk about it, but Alex was once snatched. She'd got in tow with a guy who wasn't what she thought at all. How do you think I felt at the time?'

'I can imagine. How did it end? I mean I know you got her back, obviously, but how did it end?'

Skinner laughed. 'How do you think? I killed the fucker. The police think they're looking in the right area,' he continued quickly lest his son might think he was serious. 'They recovered the stolen car close to it.'

'They should get DNA.'

'Sure, so if its real owner was involved they'll catch him in no time. Don't expect too much from that. These guys will have worn gloves, and they'll probably ditch the clothes they wore. Facial recognition's the best hope, if one of the guys let the camera see enough.'

As he spoke, his phone signalled an incoming text. He checked it, frowning. 'It's from Sauce Haddock,' he said. 'He's asking if you're up to being interviewed, formally, for the investigation. Are you?'

'Please,' Ignacio replied. 'I have to be doing something, anything. Tell him to come as soon as he likes. It's all back in place now, everything that happened. I don't know if it'll help, but I can tell him.'

'Good.' Skinner keyed in a reply, sent it, then headed for the door once more. 'Another call I have to make,' he murmured, then realised suddenly how tired he was. 'But it can wait until morning.'

Sixty

'Do you know the last time I had a weekend off?' the Home Secretary mumbled sleepily as she took the call. 'I'm doing Kuenssberg tomorrow, and I really was hoping for a lie-in today.'

'You've never had a weekend off,' Skinner retorted. 'You've always been too scared that if you did you'd miss an opportunity.'

'My God,' Aileen de Marco sighed. 'How I don't miss being married to you.'

'I don't blame you. I've never been very good at marriage, until now.'

'That's because you saw it as a constraint, the same as you saw your job. Now you're in one that you really enjoy, you're liberated in every respect. You're a classic Scot,' she said, 'always looking to expand your boundaries, never quite content with your precious homeland.'

'You too, as your political career proves. I knew that back then; being First Minister was never going to be enough for you. Being Home Secretary isn't either. When do you make the big jump into the flat above the office?'

'You're a journalist, Sir Robert. I can't tell you that.'

'You don't need to. You'll want at least a couple of years in office before you go to the country, but you'll want to do that a year before you have to. That means that the next King's Speech, in the autumn, that'll be yours. September; that's when.'

267

'I couldn't possibly comment,' she murmured. 'What else have you been hearing?' she asked.

'Nothing,' Skinner insisted, 'and I didn't hear that. Entirely my own conclusion.'

'You hadn't been speaking to Ralston before he died? You or one of your *Saltire* people?'

'I only ever met Ralston once, at a Holyrood social thing when you and I were married. He was an opposition spokesman then. My *Saltire* person,' he stressed the singular, 'she wouldn't be a very good source, given that her relationship with him was like yours and mine but with major mutual acrimony.'

'You haven't spoken to anyone else?'

'Fuck's sake, Aileen, no,' he insisted. 'Why should you think I have?'

'Off the record?'

'Aileen, love, everything between us is off the record. So, why?'

'Because what you just said is correct, and Ralston knew it. Once his Swedish project was launched, he was planning to dissolve Holyrood and call an early election. I had a go-between who fed him information.'

'If that had happened, he'd have won an overall majority.'

'For sure.'

'Which means that you were shafting your own party in Scotland,' he declared.

'For the greater good. Bob,' Aileen said, 'you're a better politician than I am, so you'll know this already. Brexit's a disaster. In an ideal world, as Prime Minister I would make rejoining the EU a General Election issue, and get the authority that way, but I can't because of those Reform fuckers. They'd eat what's left of the Tory vote or, worse, ally with them. We would probably lose. The alternative? A surrogate. A strongly pro-European Scottish parliament with a majority government doing its own unofficial trade deals with EU member nations and expanding its presence there, from which England and Wales would benefit. In ten years, with Reform undoubtedly having disappeared back up the arses from which it emerged, and Scotland acting and behaving like an independent nation within Europe, we do go to the country with the Big Issue and we win. Get it?'

'Yes,' Skinner said, 'I get it. I get more than that,' he added. 'I get that you're telling me that your dark side had nothing to do with Richard Ralston's murder since he was effectively an agent of the UK government.'

'Of course we didn't,' she protested. 'Why would you even think that?'

'Seriously? You got me into the Swedish investigation so that I could watch your back, we both know that. That investigation's now established that Ralston was killed by someone other than the radicalised security guy. There's a new murder hunt under way. It's not public knowledge yet but it will be, within twenty-four hours.'

'And it takes you to tell me this?' Aileen exclaimed. 'Not the Scottish police?'

He laughed. 'Think of me as part of the Scottish investigation and be happy that you've just been exonerated. Enjoy your week-end off.'

'Fat chance,' she grumbled. 'I'm wide awake now.'

Sixty-One

'Inge Hoverstad,' Jordi began. 'She has no second surname because she's a Norwegian national. She learned Spanish at school in Trondheim, followed it up at university in Oslo as part of a degree in communications, then did a postgraduate in business studies at a college in Madrid. She married Raul Sanchez twenty-four years ago, when he was CEO of Casolana Savings Bank. By that time she had founded a PR firm, Hoverstad Diaz. Ostensibly it's a partnership with a woman named Penelope Diaz, but in fact there's a company behind it and Hoverstad owns it one hundred per cent. Caja Casolana was one of its first big clients. I'd assumed that's when she and Raul met, until I discovered they were actually living together when Hoverstad Diaz was given the contract.'

Dolça smiled over her coffee cup. 'Naughty.'

'Maybe so,' he conceded, 'but you give me work, don't you?'

'Yes, but I'm not planning to marry you. And sleeping at my place when you're in Girona doesn't count as living together, not in my world.'

'It's not a given that Raul was planning to marry her either,' he said. 'She was three months pregnant when they got hitched.'

'But he did. That said, having met the man, I would need persuading that she gave him a choice. Do they have any other children?'

'No, Pilar was a one-off. Pampered kid,' Jordi continued, 'private education, sent to university in Edinburgh to study chemistry.'

'Why Edinburgh?' Dolça asked. 'It's a jump from Madrid.'

'I wondered that too, so I looked deeper. Inge's father is an engineer. When he studied sixty years ago, Norway's technological university was short of places, and didn't have a great international reputation; as a result, the country had a link with Heriot-Watt College, now University, in Edinburgh, and that's where much of its talent graduated. Things are different now. You'd expect that with Norway being oil-rich.'

'No doubt,' she said, impatiently. 'What about her business?'

'Very successful,' Jordi said. 'It reports high six-figure profits every year and has done for the last ten years and more. It has more than twenty active blue-chip clients, and twice that number of lesser firms, in the financial, transportation, manufacturing and leisure sectors. These include banks, insurers, food producers, a couple of big IT names, and a big shipping and trucking company. It has a payroll of eighteen account handlers, plus support staff. Inge runs the Madrid office, and Penelope Diaz is in charge of Barcelona. The staff are all full-time, with one addition; Raul Sanchez. He's named in the accounts as a consultant, advising some of the financial clients.'

'And Tromso, apparently. How is that described on the client list?'

'It isn't,' he replied. 'I can't find any reference to it anywhere. It's not named in the audited accounts, in any of the company's files, correspondence, emails, anywhere. And I have looked everywhere, trust me. If you want to find out how it fits, you'll need to ask Inge.'

'I can try,' Dolça said. 'But I'm not sure she'll take my call. Raul will have told her about me for sure. If she wanted me to know about Tromso, she'd have reached out to me by now. And . . .' she added, 'her daughter is missing.'

'That's true, is it? Are you sure it wasn't just something wild he threw at you, just to get you out of there? After you told me in the Prado, I looked for any media reports about a kidnapping. I couldn't find anything. No internet chatter, nothing.'

'It's true. Steer clear of it. I've been told to, so should you.'

Sixty-Two

Ignacio Watson Skinner had a dark three-day stubble, heavy for such a young man. Looking at him as he and Stirling entered the room, Sauce Haddock ran a hand over his own chin, relieved to confirm that it was smooth and that his electric shaver had been worth the money.

'How are you, mate?' he asked. The two had met before, at family events when Ignacio's stepfather, Haddock's father-in-law, had been alive.

'How do you think, Sauce?' the younger man retorted. 'Angry, frustrated, vengeful, take your pick. And you can add on scared. Dad says Pilar will be okay, but you and I both know he's just saying that. He can't know for sure, nobody can.'

'Not for certain, I admit. But in all his police career, and in mine, neither of us have ever worked on an abduction where the victim hasn't been recovered alive.'

'So where's the ransom demand? There hasn't been one, has there? Is that something that's been kept from me?'

'No, it isn't. I promise.'

'Okay,' Ignacio conceded. 'But these cases you and Dad worked on, were the victims, the female ones, recovered . . . intact, if you know what I mean?'

'Truth?' Haddock replied. 'All but one, but the guy who took her was a psycho. He's still in Carstairs, the state psychiatric hospital, and may well die there. From everything I've been told about the men who took Pilar, they're professionals.'

'Does that make a difference?'

'Sure. It means they've been paid to do it. We're considering the possibility that it could be linked to Ralston's murder. Because of that your mother's being given police protection, given her . . . closeness to him. But that is only one theory. There could be other explanations: ransom could still be one of them. That hasn't been ruled out. Trust me, Nacho. She'll be all right.'

'I'll do my best, Sauce,' he said. 'But it's fucking difficult.' He drew himself up, sitting higher against his pillows. 'Now, you guys aren't here because of Pilar, I realise that, so what do you want?'

'We need to interview you as part of a new investigation,' the DS replied. 'I'm John Stirling, by the way.'

Ignacio's eyebrows rose. 'Wow. You're the guy who was . . .'

The DS nodded, smiling. 'I was, and I'm coming to accept that's how I'm going to be known for a while, just as you're going to be identified as the journalist who broadcast live to the world with half his arse shot off.'

'I know that already,' he chuckled, sombrely. 'My dad gave me my phone back. I haven't posted anything yet, just DM-ed a few genuine friends, but my socials are going crazy. So, what did you mean by "new"?'

'The Swedes have closed theirs,' Stirling began, 'but . . .'

'Andersen didn't shoot the First Minister, Nacho,' Haddock said, intervening. 'Another gunman did. We know now that he was someone else's target. Suppose that Rogne Andersen had been everything he was supposed to be, a specialist police officer there to protect the Swedish Trade Minister, and he had kept his gun in his holster, Ralston would have been shot anyway.'

Ignacio surprised him by smiling. 'Why doesn't that surprise me?' he mused. 'I didn't sleep too well last night, because I was back at the scene, replaying everything in my head like I was sleeping and it was a nightmare. I remember seeing Richard standing there, staring at the guy with the gun, and I remember thinking what a crazy brave fucker he was, not screaming and hitting the floor like everyone else. Then he did, and I remember starting to run towards him, yelling at him to stay down, but then I was hit myself.' He stopped suddenly.

'Take your time,' the ACC murmured. 'Whenever you can.'

Nacho shook his head. 'I'm okay,' he insisted. 'It's a pretty scary movie I'm replaying, that's all. When Richard was hit, it was as if he'd been punched in the back. But at the same time his chest seemed to explode, and he went down, forward, face down. That was when I dived towards him, and when I was shot, but even then I was thinking *"How the hell did that happen?"* because Andersen was being shot to bits by then. Now, when you tell me there was another gunman, I say what I've been saying to myself, "There was someone else. There had to be. There was no other way."' He looked at the two officers. 'Guys, I'm sorry. I should have told you that before. I think Dad might have wondered too, but he didn't say as much. Sometimes though, his silence says a lot.'

'Don't be sorry, man,' Haddock told him. 'You're humbling us. And maybe Bob did work it out . . . I know that he had when the autopsy was done . . . but his only thoughts were for you. Nacho, what we need from you is to formalise that and sign it, for the paper file that we'll have to prepare. The Murder Book, if you want to call it that. You can dictate it, we'll have it transcribed and you can put your name to it.'

'Can my boss run it in the *Saltire*?'

'Not until after the trial. It'll be *sub judice* until then.'

'Do you have a suspect? This is the victim asking,' he added, 'not the reporter.'

'Not a clue,' the ACC admitted. He grinned. 'You going to give us that too?'

'No, but Richard did say something, just as he died, when he coughed blood all over me. That came back to me last night too. It was just a mumble, but he was looking at me when he said it and his eyes were wide, as if it meant something.'

'What was it?'

'It wasn't clear, for his mouth was full of blood at the time, but it sounded like "Blav'n".'

'Blav'n?' Haddock repeated.

'Yes, that's as close as I can get. It means nothing to me, though. It didn't relate to anything he said when Pilar and I met him the night before when he let slip about him and my mother. I wonder now if it might have been a message for her, but I can't think what it could have been.'

'Blav'n,' Haddock said again. 'Might it have been Belhaven?' he asked.

Ignacio frowned. 'Belhaven? Yes . . . yes, that fits. The name's familiar but I can't place it.'

'I can,' the ACC murmured. 'It's a brewery. Given that Ralston was literally fading out of existence, not just consciousness but life itself, with whatever that brings, confusion, desperation, everything else, could it have been the only word that came to him to convey what he wanted?'

Nacho closed his eyes, and thought. 'Yes,' he said, as he re-opened them. 'That could have been. But why a brewery?'

Haddock shook his head. 'He wasn't telling you what it is but where it is: that's my belief. But he was trying to say more than that.'

'Well? Where?'

'Dunbar.'

Sixty-Three

Strictly speaking, Mary Blix knew that Xavi Aislado should have been kept in reception, but the middle-aged giant had a calming presence that she found comforting in a situation that was more serious and stressful than any she had experienced before in her police career.

'We've had no result yet, obviously,' she said, 'but I still believe that the theory we are pursuing is the best hope we have of finding Ms Sanchez. Our problem is that we can't flood the area with cops, simply because we don't have them.'

'Do your best, Sergeant,' he told her, 'that's all we can ask. But if that's the case, are you sure that maintaining a news blackout is still appropriate? Wouldn't it be better to make the public aware and ask everyone to check their property?'

'That's what I said to my boss, but her boss said if we did that, the kidnappers might panic and kill the woman.'

'Does your boss's boss have any expertise as a hostage negotiator?' Xavi asked.

'My boss's boss was promoted from a department that dealt with trans-Scandinavian car theft, a job that, let's say, never got him cold in the winter or sunburned in the summer. There is a view that as a criminal investigator he would need a map, a compass and possibly a mirror to locate his backside. But he's still my boss's boss, so neither of us can overrule him.'

'When I was young I was a professional footballer,' he began.

'What position?' Blix asked, interrupting.

He smiled. 'Goalkeeper. Do I look like Leo Messi? Anyway, I had a manager who fitted that description. He didn't last long in the job, but he did enough damage before he left to see us relegated. That taught me a life lesson, Sergeant. Idiocy's incurable, but it can be costly, so don't suffer it. Sir Robert shares that belief. I'm speaking for him here, but I think I can. You should ask your boss to tell her boss that the executive chair of InterMedia, the international news group, has a personal interest in this situation and that if Pilar is not recovered by tomorrow morning, then its Swedish titles will run the story. And that the coverage won't reflect well on him. Will you do that for us?'

'That would be my pleasure, Mr Aislado. My boss's pleasure too, I think.'

As she spoke, the tablet on her desk sounded an alert. She picked it up and opened an incoming secure message. As she read it her eyes widened. 'Progress,' she exclaimed. 'There was enough data on the hotel CCTV for our technical people to find a match. Here.' She handed him the device.

He took it and looked at the face displayed. A man, probably in his twenties although possibly a few years older, unsmiling, unattractive, with dull eyes, and without a single memorable feature. Beneath the image there was a name, and a note. 'Giovanni Inverno,' he read aloud, but the note was in Swedish. He handed the tablet back to Blix. 'Can you translate?' he asked.

She nodded. 'Of course. It says he's age thirty-one,' she read. 'An Italian citizen, birthplace Turin, but now resident in Hamburg, Germany. He graduated, aged twenty-two, in business administration from the University of Verona. From there he joined the Italian state police as a constable, and served for five years before joining a German company, *Wachtersicherheit*, as a security executive, where he's worked for the last five years. He has no criminal convictions . . . but soon he will,' she added, with a grim smile.

'A clean record,' Aislado murmured. 'In that case why would he be on file?'

'I don't know, but given that his record is up to date, I would guess that Germany requires everyone employed in the security industry to be on file, for vetting by potential clients.'

'That would make sense,' he agreed, 'but if you wanted to stage a kidnapping, you'd hardly take the job to a legitimate security consultancy, would you?'

The sergeant shrugged. 'No, so he must be freelancing. If he goes back to work . . .'

'When he does.'

She and Aislado both turned at the sound of Skinner's voice, to see him framed in the doorway.

'Ah, good,' Blix said, 'they sent you up like I asked. What did you hear?'

'All of it,' he replied. 'It's not *if* he goes back to work, it's when. Why would he not if he has a clean record? The question will be when to lift him. The German police will have an interest. They'll want to know whether this is entirely private enterprise on the guy's part or whether his employer has a dark side to its business. From what I know of the regulated security industry, the latter of those is highly unlikely. But that's their business, yours is to locate the man Inverno.'

'How?' the Swede asked. 'That might not be so easy.'

'It should be very easy. You know who he is. That means you know where he lives, you have his mobile number, the licence plate of his car, the works. But he doesn't know that. Let's say he's been smart enough not to use his mobile on this operation so he can't be located through its signal . . . these days every bugger knows not to do that . . . but you should try anyway. At the same time have the Germans stake out his home address. He and his accomplice may still be holding Pilar somewhere, or they may have left her to be found, or . . . okay we won't consider the other thing . . . but sooner or later he will go home.'

'True,' Xavi agreed. 'Bob,' he asked, 'how does this tie in with DS Stirling's notion? That the kidnap could be linked to the killing of Ralston.'

'It doesn't,' Skinner declared. 'And that makes it even more of a mystery. Also, Sergeant,' he added, 'it piles even more pressure on your force to find the solution. So, let us get out of your way.'

'Thank you,' she said, with a wicked grin. 'My boss's boss will be so glad to hear this.' She winked at Aislado. 'And that's before we tell him about your deadline.'

Sixty-Four

'First and foremost,' Tarvil Singh began, 'my condolences for your bereavement.'

'Thank you, Inspector,' Daniel Ralston replied, leaning back in his chair, gazing at the big detective across a polished rosewood desk. 'That's much appreciated.' He smiled, faintly. 'It's a portentous word don't you think, bereavement. It's part of our Scottish psyche, the need to find a weighty way to express something as basic as loss. But when you think about that one, it's absolutely appropriate. Because I am bereft; my dad's been removed from my life and it's left a great big hole. It's more than just a loss; that can be the simple consequence of a hole in your trouser pocket, a pound coin disappearing down a drain. This is so much more, so sudden, so unexpected.' He shook himself. 'I'm sorry,' he said. 'I sound as if I'm trying out my eulogy on you.'

'Not at all,' Singh told him. 'It sounds right. I'd use that if I were you. Have you done anything about funeral arrangements yet?'

'It's much too early for that. The body's still in police custody, although Scottish now rather than Swedish, ACC Haddock told me. But it's not just that; it'll be more than just a family affair. I mean, he was a public figure, wasn't he? The Parliament will want to be involved, and the party will too. I'll need to talk to Peter Dunbar about that, that's if he can still speak once he gets off that boat. Peter's a notoriously bad sailor. I went with him and Dad to a conference on Arran a couple of years ago. It wasn't all that choppy but he barfed most of the way there. And yet . . .' he shook his head, 'the idea that they should do the inauguration thing in Malmo, then get on the boat and sail away, that was his. He suggested it, and Dad and Jens went for it straight away. That's the sort of guy he is. Peter puts Dad and the party above everything.'

'Were he and your father close personally as well as politically?'

'Joined at the hip,' Ralston replied. 'Dad did some family law tutoring at Glasgow University about fifteen years ago. Peter was one of his students, they were similar types, both committed independence chasers, so Peter became his shadow and has been ever since. God knows what he's feeling, having seen it happen.' He paused and sighed, heavily. 'That said, we all did. I saw that first broadcast on the *Saltire* video feed. Dad had told me to look out for it; he said they had a young reporter there, "of whom more later", he said. I never did get to know what he meant. Do you have any idea?'

'Maybe,' Singh said. 'Did your father share things about his personal life with you?'

'I think Dad shared everything with me. Are you going to ask me about his new girlfriend?'

'He told you that?'

'About Mia, yes. I think he was smitten. I've never met her though. She's a hotelier, isn't she? A widow?'

'Yes. The young reporter, he's her son.'

'My God,' Ralston exclaimed. 'And he was shot too. I should reach out to her. She must be . . .'

'Black Shield Lodge,' Singh volunteered. 'That's the name of her hotel. It's between Perth and Dundee.'

'Thanks. I think I knew the location from something Dad said, but not the name.'

'Were you surprised about him having a new relationship? Given that he was still married?'

'You getting moralistic on me, DI Singh?'

'Hell no, sir. It's something I have to ask, that's all.'

'Sure, understood. How much do you know about the state of my dad's second marriage?'

'Personally nothing. I've had information through the inquiry.'

'Amy's a lovely woman, I like her, I respect her and I wish her every happiness. When she and Dad got together, I believe it was good for both of them. They'd each come out of traumatic marriages and needed healing. Cal and I were only kids at the time, but I think each of us understood that.'

'Cal? Who's Cal?' the DI asked.

'He's my stepbrother; his name's Calvin Knox. We're the same age, give or take a few months.'

'Were you brought up together?'

'No,' Ralston said. 'Cal's father was given custody when they were divorced following his petition. Amy had a breakdown, and the court took the view that she wasn't able to raise him. Bloody nonsense; her lawyer did a lousy job. If Dad or I had been acting for her there would have been a different outcome, I can tell you. Amy was institutionalised because of her first husband's physical and emotional abuse, for God's sake, but as can happen in these cases there were no witnesses, apart from Cal. Her medical records might have told a story, but they weren't presented to the court.'

'Did your father and Cal's ever meet?'

'They met every time Knox came to pick the lad up after a visit. Dad wouldn't allow Amy to be alone with him. Things were stiffly correct between them; even as a kid I remember that, but never . . .' He paused. 'Looking back, Brian Knox's resentment was obvious, but, well, he wouldn't have pushed his luck with Dad. This was never mentioned in his election material, but he was a karate black belt.'

'What does Knox do?'

'He was a farmer.'

'Was?'

'Yes, he's dead. He fell off a mountain in France, on a fiftieth birthday holiday. Dad told me that was the only time he'd ever seen Amy take a drink. Veuve Clicquot, he said; her request. She won't be doing that now that she's a widow herself. She'll be broken-hearted, I imagine. She loved Dad very much. I never heard her say it, but I could tell by the way she looked at him.'

Singh was surprised. 'You haven't spoken to her since your father died?'

'I did try,' he insisted. 'I called the convent the morning after, but they said she was in seclusion.'

'How about Cal? Have you spoken to him?'

Ralston shook his head. 'I haven't spoken to Cal in years. We weren't raised together so we were never close, he and I. He and his mother have taken the same journey in life. Cal's a monk. He lives in a monastery in England, and has done for six years or so, since just before his father fell off his mountain. Dad took Amy to visit him there not long after he moved in. She declared herself happy with it, he said. At that point in her life, she was going to her convent, but only on retreats, for a couple of weeks at a time. Dad believed that seeing Cal, sorry, Brother Something, I've for-gotten his monastic name,' he confessed, 'settled in his place was what made her consider taking orders herself. You know, Mr Singh, Knox must have been a real monster to affect them both in that way.'

'Seems like it. I might run a check on him, just for fun, to see if he was known to us. Mr Ralston,' the DI continued, 'I know that politicians get crap all the time, abuse on social media, offensive letters, angry constituents. Do you know if your father was worried about anything? Had any threats been made against him?'

'None that he didn't laugh off,' the late First Minister's son replied. 'My father was a very popular man, Inspector. Even his political opponents liked him, for all they would rail against him across the chamber in Holyrood. And he liked them back, even the Greens, even though he took the piss out of them incessantly. "Ben and Holly in their Magic Kingdom", he called them once, during a debate . . . you know, after the kids' cartoon series. The place fell apart; even they laughed.'

'I remember seeing that on BBC Reporting Scotland,' Singh recalled. 'Even its political editor had trouble keeping a straight face. Mind you, the politicians didn't have much choice but to laugh. They'd have seemed like po-faced twats if they hadn't. So,' he continued, 'no active threats?'

For the first time, Daniel Ralston seemed to falter. 'No,' he murmured, 'and yet. You know, Inspector,' he said, 'I was stunned when first I heard of my father's death. But I am even more stunned now. When ACC Haddock called me and told me what the autopsy had determined, I was completely blind-sided. An accidental victim of an attack on someone else, as his death was seen initially, I was coming to terms with that and ready to deal with it on the same emotional level as you'd handle road fatality or a plane crash. The fact that someone, or a group of people, set out to murder him? That's something else. It's stirred up feelings inside me that I never thought I could have. Goes beyond anger? You know what I'm saying?'

'You're saying something I've heard many times before,' the DI replied, 'if less eloquently. Don't be ashamed of feeling that way. I know I would. These days, at the conclusion of a trial, after conviction, there are things called Victim Impact Statements. Not everybody likes them, some think they don't belong in what should be a dispassionate system, but I do. I see them as part of the healing process for folk in your situation, as a safety valve of sorts. I promise you this: Sauce Haddock, Lottie Mann, that's my DCI, me, and everybody else on the team, we're all working towards you having your day in court.'

Sixty-Five

'What happens next?' June Crampsey asked.

'In what respect?' Sue Bland countered.

'Ralston's replacement.'

The political editor shrugged. 'There's a procedure to elect a new First Minister. It'll be followed. Most of it will happen behind closed doors. First of all, there'll be haggling among the nationalists over who'd be the best choice. Once that's done, there'll be more haggling, with potential coalition partners. The way the numbers are at the moment, that's likely to be the Greens.'

Crampsey grinned. 'Ben and Holly?'

Bland seemed unamused. 'If you want to call them that, yes,' she replied, curtly. 'The other possibility is a deal with the Lib Dems. That was impossible with Richard in place, given his history with them, but my sources tell me they'd be open to an arrangement with his successor, whoever that might be.'

'Who's your tip?'

'I wouldn't bet on any horse yet. I'll wait until the field assembles.'

'Need there be a coalition? Ralston led a minority government.'

'He did,' Bland retorted, 'but only because half of his policy platform was lifted from the Labour manifesto at the last election.'

'Oh, come on, Sue,' her editor protested. 'You're blinded by your own prejudice. He was an inspirational leader. Even the bloody *Daily Record* said that in its obituary.'

'You sound like my son, in those vox pops he did for BBC and STV. Look, June, did you really need to call me in for this?'

'Have you spoken to Daniel since his father died?' she asked, ignoring Bland's question.

'We'd only argue. What would be the point?'

'You're his mother?' Crampsey suggested, with a touch of irony.

'I don't think you're in a position to chide me about mother-hood, June, do you?'

'Oh, I don't know, Sue,' she countered. 'Some situations are best observed dispassionately. With all your experience, I thought you'd understand that. Evidently not.'

'What the hell do you mean?' Bland demanded.

'You can't speak to your son because he won't tolerate your antipathy towards his father. Your hatred for Richard compromised your ability to do the job we hired you for. That's why I had to send a junior reporter to cover an event that should have been yours. It didn't die with him, it seems. Now it's compromising the reputation of this newspaper.'

'In what way?'

'Why did you call Mia McCullough?'

For an instant Bland's sallow face paled. 'What?' she said.

'You heard,' Crampsey said, quietly. 'You called Mia McCullough, your colleague's mother, and asked her to comment on her relationship with the newly deceased First Minister. Why?'

'Because it was a fucking news story! That's why!'

'For the fucking *Daily Star*, possibly, but not for the *Saltire* without my approval, something I would not have given. Even the dead are entitled to privacy. Ralston's second marriage was effectively over; that was public knowledge. The fact that he was seeing some-one else, very discreetly, was not, but tell me how exposing it would be in the public interest in any sense of the words. Look, Sue, you've compromised the paper, you've compromised your position, and you can't stay in it.'

'What!' she screamed. 'You can't do that. I'll go to the union.'

'Don't make me laugh.'

'I'll go to the chairman!'

'Trust me, you don't want to do that. He's the only hope you have. Sue, we need your source. We need to know who put you up to making that call to Mrs McCullough. Whoever it was is conducting a vendetta against Ralston, and it's still going on. They're trying to destroy his reputation even after his death. The father of your son. What would that do to Daniel? The source, Sue. Who is it?'

'No chance!' she snorted.

'Look, it's not just me who'll be asking this. The police will want to know.'

'Why should they?'

'Because there's a murder investigation under way. A new one, based on new evidence. They will want that name, Sue. I don't need to spell out the consequences if you refuse them. Our judges don't piss about.'

Bland shifted in her seat, frowning, looking past her editor towards the city, at the familiar shape of Edinburgh Castle; from her expression, it could have been glowering back at her.

'What's in it for me?' she asked eventually.

'I fucking knew it,' Crampsey murmured. 'Principles have value. What's in it for you, Sue,' she replied, 'is the biggest get-out-of-jail card . . . literally . . . that I have ever seen, and it comes from the chairman himself.' She set out Skinner's proposal, without saying that it was really an ultimatum.

'Washington?' Bland murmured.

'Washington.'

'Contract?'

'Of course. That's in our interest as well as yours. You don't imagine we could ever trust you after this. New life, new status, away from all your old prejudices.'

'Who would succeed me here? The Hero of Malmo?' she asked, her tone heavy with irony.

'I don't know yet. That's none of your business really. But Ignacio's shown himself to be a better, and braver, reporter than you'll ever be, so he's in with a shout, yes.'

'Joanie Cooper.'

Crampsey's eyes widened. 'The Scottish Government communications director? She's your source?'

'Yes, she's been feeding me information for a while.'

'Why?'

'I have no idea, but she had a down on him. That's quite certain.'

'In that case she's done a bloody good job of covering her tracks. She bad-mouthed you something awful to Ignacio in Malmo. She was so vitriolic he felt that he had to report it back to me. Okay,' she said. 'Washington it will be. I'll show you a contract in a couple of days. Clear your desk here, go home and wait for a call from ACC Haddock, or whoever he sends to interview you. Meanwhile we'll sort out your US accreditation. I'm sure you'll find the White House press corps a lot more exciting than Holyrood's.'

Sixty-Six

Lottie Mann had no clear idea in her mind of what a convent should look like but she had not expected it to be a grand castellated building with a tennis court and a putting green, perched on a hilltop from which it surveyed the city of Perth below. 'I guess being a bride of Christ doesn't mean you can't play tennis,' she murmured to DC Maya Smith as she drove through the gate, past a sign that read 'Anglican Sisterhood of Kindness. Visits by appointment only.'

The car park was on the far side of the building. All but two spaces, marked 'Visitors', were occupied. 'So nuns have cars,' the DC observed as she exited the passenger seat.

'What did you expect them to have? Donkeys?' Mann shot back, checking the time. Ten past midday; they were five minutes early.

They walked round to the entrance, past two women on the putting green. Each wore slacks and trainers rather than gowns. Neither reacted to the police officers' curious appraisals. The main door was half-glazed, with both a button and a keypad: the DCI pushed the former but before it could sound, a figure appeared in the hallway, slim, bespectacled, middle-aged. She was hooded but otherwise clad as casually as the golfers.

'DCI Mann,' she began as she opened the door. It seemed that it was not a question. 'I'm Sister Jane. I saw you as you drove up the hill. You're the only appointment we have today, so I guessed it was you.'

'Me and Detective Constable Smith,' Mann added.

'Ah,' Sister Jane said. 'We weren't expecting two of you. Not,' she added, 'that it makes any difference. We can set an extra place in the refectory for lunch.'

'That's very kind of you, sister,' the DCI exclaimed, 'but we need to see Mrs Ralston in private. This is a formal interview as part of a criminal investigation. That's why DC Smith's here; Scottish law still requires corroboration.'

'Of course,' the nun conceded. 'I should have thought of that. I was a solicitor in my former life. I still am, I suppose. I look after the Sisterhood's legal affairs, such as they are.' She smiled at Smith's raised eyebrows. 'We don't all abandon our secular lives when we begin a spiritual one. For example, Sister Briony was a surveyor. She's responsible for the fabric of the building.'

'How about Mrs Ralston?' Mann asked. 'Mind you, I don't know what she did before she was . . . First Lady, if you like.'

Sister Jane smiled again. 'I've never thought of her with that title, but it suits her; she's exactly that. Sister Trudi was a vet,' she said. 'She qualified before her first marriage, in fact I believe . . .' She paused. 'No, I should let her tell you that. On her previous visits,' she continued, 'she helped look after our farm: now she's here permanently she's going to manage it, to the venerable Sister Alice's relief. It's a smallholding really, on land way behind the house. We grow strawberries, raspberries, leeks, onions, and we have livestock. Hens, a few sheep, and goats. Sister Trudi looks after those and she'll organise the growing of the crops. We have a farmer neighbour; he lends us fit young men to help with the planting, but we do everything else ourselves.'

'What do you do with the sheep and the goats?' Smith asked.

Sister Jane shrugged. 'We sell the lambs and the kids to a

butcher in Perth,' she replied. 'We're not vegetarians, Detective Constable,' she murmured, seeing her reaction. 'There's no evidence that Christ was either.'

Lottie Mann was about to observe that everything about Christ was anecdotal, but she was saved as the nun continued. 'Come now,' she said, 'let me take you to meet Sister Trudi. Midday prayers are over so she'll be waiting for you in her room . . . we don't call them cells,' she explained, 'not in this order.'

There was a staircase behind her, but she led the detectives past it, to a small elevator with a grille rather than a door. It was barely large enough for three, but it took them slowly up two floors, opening on to a wide corridor, where Sister Jane knocked gently on a varnished door. A card reading 'Sister Trudi' was displayed in a brass holder.

The woman who opened the door was as tall as Mann, but much slimmer. The officers knew that she was fifty-three years old, but her face was that of someone ten years younger, with barely a wrinkle. Her dress was similar to the women on the putting green, slacks and a blouse, but she was barefoot. 'Welcome,' she said quietly, 'please come in.'

They followed her into a room that was anything but monastic. It was a bright airy space with a bay window and large enough for an armchair and a small settee, with a table between, on which were a water jug and two glasses. The bed was a single. Above the headboard, a crucifix on the wall was the only Christian symbol on display, other than a framed photograph of a young man in a monk's habit that stood on a bedside table. Looking around, Maya Smith was reminded of a junior suite that she and John Stirling had occupied on a weekend break in Northumberland. The settee was a tight fit for her and Mann but neither felt crushed. Amy Ralston waited as they settled into it, then sat, facing them.

'Ladies, officers,' she began. 'What do I call you?'

'I'm Detective Chief Inspector Mann,' the senior of the two

began, 'and my colleague is Detective Constable Smith, but if you prefer you can call us Lottie and Maya. This is a formal interview, but it doesn't need to feel that way. More to the point, how should we address you, Sister Trudi . . . by the way, and I have to ask just to get it out of my head, isn't that an unusual name for a nun?'

'It is,' she accepted. 'When I joined the order as a novice they suggested I should be Sister Gertrude, but I revolted against that and became Sister Trudi as a compromise.'

'Aren't nuns named after saints?' Smith asked.

'Maybe Trudi will be, one day. But why don't you just call me Amy? She's who you're here to interview after all.'

'Fair enough,' Mann said. 'Do you mind if we record this, Amy?'

'God's our witness, so why should I mind?'

'Thanks.' The DCI placed a recording device on the table and switched it on. 'For the record,' she began, 'I am DCI Charlotte Mann, with DC Maya Smith, interviewing Mrs Amy Ralston as part of an investigation following the death of her husband, Mr Richard Ralston. That's the formality done,' she said. 'We're both sorry for your loss, Amy. Can you tell us, when did you and Mr Ralston meet?'

'Do you know, I'm not sure exactly,' she said. 'I'm a little vague about that. My memories of the time after Brian Knox are like a drifting mist. Richard and I were both what he would have described as post-marital refugees . . . it might be fair to say we counselled each other. After a while it turned into marriage. We loved each other very much. He cared for me in every sense, even when the time came for me to withdraw into this place. Do you want total frankness?' she asked.

'Be as frank as you wish,' Mann invited her. 'It might be relevant, it might not.'

'Very well. We were happy together, always, but with one big difference between us. Richard was a carnal person, I am not. That was beaten out of me by my first husband, Brian Knox. He was a beast of a man, a thug, a monster. Charming to those he wanted or needed to charm, but in his own household a tyrant. That I discovered the hard way, but initially he charmed me. Brian and I met professionally, when I visited his farm one winter, a week before Christmas, as a young vet with a partner in the practice where I started after graduation. It began with flowers, then champagne . . . Veuve Clicquot, always Veuve Clicquot . . . then dinner dates, then dinner, several times, at a flat he owned in Glasgow. On one of those evenings he invited me on a trip to Cheltenham, the National Hunt festival. It was there that I met the other Brian, when he raped me.'

Both police officers started in surprise. 'What did you say?' Mann asked.

'I said that he violated me, Lottie. In our hotel I assumed we'd have separate rooms, but no, we didn't. I realise now that I should have left, but he was still charming, and somehow he persuaded me that it would be all right, as there were twin beds. On the first night it was; we undressed separately in the bathroom. But on the second day he lost a lot of money on a bet, on a horse that fell and had to be put down, poor thing. That evening Brian got drunk. I thought he would sleep it off . . . until I was wakened by a hand over my mouth, and . . .' She stopped, to drink from the carafe.

'Did you . . .' Smith began.

'Did I go to the police? How could I? I was a single woman, with a single man, in a double room, on our second night there. And also I'd been too frightened to resist. There would have been no evidence of forcible penetration. I felt a fool, as if I'd asked for it. While he was still asleep, I packed my bag and left. Two weeks later,' she continued, 'he came to see me, in full charm mode, with a case of Veuve Clicquot and more roses than I had room for. He begged forgiveness, swore that he had never done anything like that before and asked for another chance . . . which I gave him, mostly because by that time I was ten days or so overdue with my period. When I was sure I was pregnant, I told him. Literally he went down on one knee. We were married very quickly, my son Calvin was born six months later and that's when I met Mr Hyde, properly, that's when all the physical and mental violence began, years of it, until I had a complete emotional collapse and was sectioned. It was all a secret, though, even later when I was under medication. Out of fear, shame, I don't know, but I told nobody about it, not even my doctors however subtly they pressed me.'

'You were that afraid?' Smith asked.

'Not only that.' The woman smiled at her but with a look in her eye that chilled the young DC. 'My dear,' she sighed, 'there are some things a person simply doesn't want to remember. If you'd had a hot iron held against your arm for leaving a crease in an evening dress shirt, you'd understand that. Whatever,' she continued, as calmly as before, 'I'd been an in-patient for a year when Brian sued for divorce and was given custody of Calvin. You know, he stole my son's name too. I'd planned to call him Philip, after my father, but Brian went off and registered him as Calvin. It was his idea of a joke: Calvin Knox, a Presbyterian parody. That's when I began to pray; after he did that I prayed every night. No, ladies, not for his redemption: at first I prayed for my son and myself, but soon I prayed that he would die. But not of . . .' She saw Mann reach for the recording device as if to switch it off. 'No, Lottie,' she exclaimed, 'leave it on. Not of something instant, I was going to say, but something that would make him die in pain and fear. Those prayers were answered when the Devil reached out and took him. I believe that when he fell, the Swiss police had some questions about his ropes. If I had been accused,' she said, 'I'd have pleaded guilty and called Satan as a co-defendant. There,' she sighed, 'I've been wanting to get that off my chest for years, to someone other than my confessor.'

Finally Mann did switch off the device. 'Good for you, Amy,' she said. 'Good for you. If that had been me, I wouldn't have had your forbearance. I'd have put a knife in his neck one time he came for me and taken my chances with a self-defence plea. Your way was better: Satan saved us all the cost of a trial.' She turned the recorder on again. 'Can we go back to Richard now?' she asked.

'Of course. Where was I? I said that Richard was carnal, didn't I?' She frowned and for a few moments seemed to retreat into her thoughts. 'There came a time when that side of our life was almost non-existent; and I knew that he was finding satisfaction elsewhere. He was always discreet, but after our separation became formal he did tell me about someone in the office. She was open to a relation-ship, he said, but he thought it would have been inappropriate. Yes, the last time he visited me here, he told me that he was on his way to visit a lady who lives not far from this place, a widow, around our age, with one son like each of us. I asked him if he'd packed his toothbrush. He went red; that's his usual tell. He didn't give me her name, but maybe Daniel will know. He's a lovely man, my stepson, with all of his father's virtues and none of his mother's vices, a mirror image of my Cal, who has what I like to think of as my good nature, but none of his father in him.'

'I've been told your son's a monk. Is that so?' Mann asked.

'Yes, it is, down south. Brother Luke makes pottery in a monas-tery in the Midlands. I have a piece that he sent me. I believe that we led each other, he and I, towards a spiritual life.'

'Do you hear from him?'

'Of course.' She smiled. 'We are allowed to use WhatsApp here. We speak to each other once a week, Brother Luke in his cell and Sister Trudi in her sanctuary. It's celestial.'

Sixty-Seven

'Which country are you in, Sauce?' Lottie Mann asked. 'The background noise sounds . . . I don't know, different.'

'I'm in Scotland,' the ACC replied. 'I flew back to Glasgow this morning, early doors. I had a car bring me straight to the Crime Campus: the DCC's here too. The technicos have finished the model of the Ralston shooting and want us to see it. Tony Davidson . . .'

'Who's he?'

'He's the Chief Scientific Officer, or is it Chief Digital Officer these days? Either way he's part of the management team. He reckons it's urgent that we do look at it, but he hasn't said why.'

'I recognise that name now, from the website. I looked at it last night,' she explained, 'to see if you've been added. You have: "Temporary Assistant Chief Constable Harold Haddock," but no photo yet.'

'Probably,' he suggested, 'because they don't want the public to notice when I get bumped back down in a couple of days. Incidentally, Neil McIlhenney has his eyes on that website. Mario says he's been spending time during his absence redrafting it, cutting out the bullshit.'

'Good for him,' Mann said. 'I look at it as a serving officer and I wonder what the hell Transformation is, and yet it's in an ACC's job title, and it has a civilian director. There'll be punters out there thinking it's something to do with gender identity.'

'Whatever it is, it must be fucking expensive,' a voice in the background commented.

'That's him indoors,' she explained, 'across the breakfast table.'

'He's not wrong,' Haddock replied. 'Say hello to him for me, and sorry as well for interrupting your Sunday. I need a catch-up, that's all.'

'Sure, we understand. To be honest, there's not a lot to report. Tarvil met with Daniel Ralston yesterday, and I went to the convent to see Amy, the widow, Sister Trudi as she is now. Daniel couldn't help much. He's shocked and angry as you'd expect, but he couldn't think of a single person who might have had a lethal grudge against his father. Likewise, Amy. She's a kind of saintly woman. If you ask me she should have gone into her convent years ago. I don't doubt she loved Ralston . . . that's the thing, Sauce, that's what I'm hearing: everybody loved the man. He didn't have any political or personal enemies. Anyway, Amy; her first marriage, the way she described it: I've had a bad experience myself, as you know, but the way she talks about hers, it was awful. It began with a rape and ended with her as a psychiatric in-patient. That husband's dead too, and she confessed happily to having killed him.'

'What the . . .' Haddock exclaimed.

'No, Sauce, she didn't,' the DCI added, quickly, 'unless you believe in the physical power of prayer. Brian Knox died in a climbing accident in Switzerland, something to do with a worn rope. I've got Jackie Wright checking it out, for the record. A death like that overseas would likely be reported to the fiscal. But Knox is long gone. Amy does have another family member though, a son, Cal. His father drove him into a monastery. He's a monk in England. Saintly family all round, even Daniel Ralston, from what Tarvil said.'

'That's good,' he said, 'but you're wrong about one thing.

Ralston did have an enemy; Sue Bland, his first wife. This I got from the Gaffer yesterday; Bland called Mia McCullough the night before last, asking for a comment about her relationship with Ralston. To save her job, and probably her liberty, Bland gave up her source. It was Joan Cooper, Ralston's media woman.'

'Indeed?' Mann exclaimed. 'That squares with something Amy said, that someone in the office had made Ralston an offer he could refuse. We'd better just have a chat with her too. Is she on the ferry with the rest of them, do you know?'

'No, she flew back Friday morning. She should be in her office tomorrow.'

'I could ask Tarvil and Jackie Wright to brace her at home today.'

'That wouldn't advance anything,' the ACC said. 'Draw a breath, all of you. As soon as I'm done here I'm off home to Cheeky and our one and a half kids. Got to go now, the DCC and Davidson will be waiting.'

He ended the call and walked the short distance along the Crime Campus corridor to the acting chief's office. He knocked and entered. McGuire had just arrived; he was dressed for the weekend, in jeans and a Hibernian FC sweatshirt, and was in the act of making coffee. 'Hey, Sauce,' he called out, picking up another Nespresso pod, 'want one?'

'Fuck, yes,' Haddock replied, gratefully. 'Make it a double if you have a mug there. It's quarter to ten and I'm running on empty. I really hate early flights.'

'And I hate getting caught up in motorway roadworks on a bloody Sunday. I'll need to go back the other way, or we might miss the kick-off. My Eamon would give me hell if that happened. But if you want the good news,' he added, 'Neil's been signed off; he's back tomorrow, fired up for his war against management bullshit.'

'Glad to hear it,' the ACC said. 'Even though it'll mean me being bumped back to the ranks.'

'When you're leading the most important criminal investigation this force ever had? Not very likely. He does want to see you though, once his feet are under the desk, maybe Tuesday. How was Sweden when you left?'

'Still anxious, with Pilar Sanchez still being missing. They do have an ID on one of the kidnappers though. All they need to do is find him.'

'And the girl,' McGuire pointed out.

'And the girl, but one will follow the other. Stirling will keep me in touch.'

'And Bob?'

'Still there, pretty much living at the hospital. Sarah's flying home today with Xavi Aislado, the Gaffer's staying with Nacho, just in case there is a connection between the murder and the kidnap.'

'Do you believe there is?'

'No, and neither does John, but it isn't impossible, so Bob's with Nacho and we have security with Mia McCullough.'

'What about Mrs Ralston and the son?'

'She's in secure accommodation as it is, in the convent. The Abbess is briefed to call us if there are any unusual visit requests. Daniel's being kept under discreet observation, without being aware of it.'

'Fine. Let's go see Tony, and we can get on our way home. Grab your mug.'

They left McGuire's office and made their way to another part of the complex, where the scientific departments were located. The Chief Digital Officer was waiting for them, alone in a big open room with several workstations. He was a bright-eyed man in his mid-thirties. 'Nobody's old who does what he does,' the deputy chief had observed to Haddock. 'The science is moving forward every day.'

'Guys,' Tony Davidson exclaimed as they entered. 'You got here, good.'

'We did,' McGuire said, 'but where's the fire?'

'Let me show you,' the scientist replied, turning to a computer screen on which was displayed a very realistic model of a large ferry. 'We've analysed all the data you sent, Sauce, and added in other footage that we've blagged from broadcast sources. We started from this, and worked backwards.' He clicked a keyboard and the image changed, to one of Richard Ralston, in virtually three dimensions, frozen at the instant when the projectile that killed him had emerged from his chest. 'That's the starting point. We might have got no further but for one thing. Yesterday evening the Swedish SOCOs recovered the bullet, lodged in one of the supports of the platform on which the VIP observers were stood. That let us determine its trajectory and gave us this.' He clicked again and the image changed to one that showed the course of the bullet, its fatal passage through the First Minister, its final impact and its point of origin. 'Look at that,' Davidson exclaimed.

'My God,' McGuire murmured. 'The shooter was actually on the ferry!'

'In a cabin,' he confirmed. 'We can't tell you which one, as the vessel was moving slightly with the swell, but after looking at a model we can pin it down to one of half a dozen. But I can't tell you how they got on board.'

'I can,' Haddock said. 'The idea on the day was that Ralston and the Swedish PM would open, inaugurate, bless . . . choose the word you like best . . . the new service, then everybody would get on board and it would sail off into the sun. The passengers had been boarded earlier, although most of them . . . we had thought all of them . . . had come back out to the quayside for a closer view. Clearly someone stayed on board and fired from one of those six cabins, not necessarily their own, but maybe, if the others were locked.'

'Do you see the urgency now?' Davidson asked.

'Too fucking right! Where's the ferry now?'

The Chief Digital Officer held up his phone, displaying an app. 'Myshiptracking says it's just passing North Berwick. It'll dock within the hour.'

'And it's a floating crime scene,' the temporary ACC sighed. 'That means we need the terminal sealed off, immediately, we need all the passengers detained for interview, we need to know their names, we need to know whether anyone who was boarded for the abandoned crossing didn't check in for this one, and . . .'

'And,' Davidson added, 'you need Jenny Bramley and every scene of crime officer she has ready to sweep those cabins. I've arranged that; they're on their way to the site already.'

'Yes,' Haddock agreed, 'but what I was also going to say was that we need every available officer there to begin the passenger interviews. Sorry, Lottie,' he murmured, 'you're going to hate me.'

'So's Paula,' McGuire chuckled. 'With me being an available officer, she's going to have to take Eamon to Easter Road . . . and she hates football!'

Sixty-Eight

'How are things in Scotland, love?' John Stirling asked his partner.

'They've just exploded,' Maya Smith replied. 'One minute before you phoned I had a call from the boss. The Malmo ferry's due to arrive in Edinburgh any minute now, and all the passengers need to be interviewed before they get off the ship. So it's all hands on deck, every available CID officer's been ordered to the scene. The DCI's picking me up in five minutes. I've put you on hands-free while I get dressed; I'm still in my knickers.'

'I wish I was,' he sighed. 'What lit the fuse?'

'They reckon that Ralston was shot by someone on board the ferry. That's all I know for now.'

'How many passengers are we talking about?'

'Potentially hundreds, but the boss thinks that the numbers were restricted with this being the first crossing.'

'I assume they'll have to search the thing too. For the weapon,' he added.

'Full SOCO sweep, the boss said. Love, that's Lottie arriving, I'll need to go.'

'Me too, it seems; I have a call incoming. Good luck, miss you.'

He ended the call and accepted the other, from a Swedish mobile. 'Detective Stirling?' an excited female voice asked.

Instantly, he felt a burst of optimism. 'This is Detective Blix. We found her! We found Pilar. She was in a recreation park, on the edge of the search area, locked in a hut next to a static caravan. She's alive, thank God. She was very dazed and dehydrated, but otherwise she's unharmed. Paramedics are with her now and they're planning to take her to the hospital, the same one her boyfriend is in. I'm going to the scene. Do you want to come with me or would you prefer to go to Pilar?'

'I'll go with you,' he said. 'I want to see where they left her.'

'I thought you'd say that. Are you in your hotel?'

'Yes.'

'Good. I have a patrol car nearby. By the time you get to the door it'll be there.'

Blix was as good as her word. The uniforms in the car offered no small talk; instead they switched on lights and sirens and cut their way through the Sunday traffic reaching their destination in under fifteen minutes, just before Blix herself, who arrived as he was stepping out of the vehicle. Pilar's place of captivity was obvious: the door was open and crime scene officers were already at work.

'She was lucky,' the Swedish sergeant said as she reached him. 'The owner of the caravan, his name is Johanssen, lives in a little place called Vollsjö. He told the first responders that he doesn't visit too often, but this weekend his wife wanted some sea air. He said that he might not have opened the hut, if he hadn't noticed something peculiar. The lock, the padlock, it was new. There's nothing valuable in there so he had left it secured with a chain and a very small lock. When he tried to open the new one with his screwdriver he heard a noise from inside. It was indistinct because Pilar was barely conscious, so he called the police.'

'They just dumped her there?'

A uniformed sergeant wearing gloves and overshoes stepped out of the hut. 'Yes,' he said, 'but they left her water, and a couple of chocolate bars. They had drugged her, the paramedics think.'

'They're sure there were no signs of violence?' Stirling asked.

'She'll be examined in hospital, but none were obvious.'

'Was there any indication of why she was taken?'

'Not exactly,' the sergeant replied, 'but they left this.' He handed Stirling a clear plastic envelope. It contained a hand-written note.

The Scot held it up. '*¿Ves lo fácil que fue?*' he read.

'What?' Blix asked, puzzled.

'Spanish,' the DS said. 'I studied it at school. I'm not fluent but I've got a Higher on my leaving certificate. It means "See how easy that was?" or similar.'

'Why would they tell us that?' Blix wondered.

'What makes you think they're talking to you? I was completely wrong. This has got nothing to do with Ralston's assassination.'

'Then what's it about?'

'We'll need to catch the kidnappers to find that out . . . or rather you will, for now that Pilar's safe, I think I'll be off home.'

Sixty-Nine

'Is that us done?' Mario McGuire asked.

'Just about,' a weary Sauce Haddock confirmed. 'One hundred and thirty-seven people on board, one hundred and thirty-five interviewed. Only Mr Dunbar left, and one other.'

'Thank Christ it was invitation only.'

'It was and it wasn't,' Jens Pilling intervened. Surprised, both police officers turned towards him. 'There were a hundred names on the guest list,' he explained. 'Business leaders from both countries, tourist promotion agencies, cultural ambassadors, civic heads, for example the Lord Provost of Edinburgh and the Mayor of Malmo,' he added, 'and the Lady Provost of Glasgow at Richard's specific request. Before he asked for that she wasn't on the list, but he said it was essential that she was added.'

'What about Santa Claus?' McGuire grunted. 'How come he missed out? Sorry, Mr Pilling,' he added, quickly. 'It's been a long day, and my team lost.'

The ferry owner laughed. 'Only because nobody thought of him. I must chide my publicity people for that. It would have been one fewer cabin to fill. That's what we did, you see. Once all the guests had been allocated accommodation, we put the remaining cabins on offer to the general public.'

'Who did the allocating?'

Pilling looked at Haddock. 'Olaf Guerin, my head of publicity, and Ms Cooper from the Scottish Government. They also vetted the public applicants for the excess cabins, twenty-one Swedes, four Danes, three Norwegians and nine Scots.'

The ACC nodded; he was the youngest of the trio by fifteen years. 'Okay,' he said. 'Let's get the last interviews done, knock off for the night and see what the SOCOs have for us tomorrow, if anything. Where's Mr Dunbar?'

'In his suite,' the Norwegian replied. 'Probably as impatient as we are to get off this vessel.'

'He's last for a reason,' McGuire growled. 'The others, that was just processing. He's different. Sauce, do you want me to join with you?'

Haddock shook his head. 'Thanks, Mario, but no. I've asked Tarvil Singh in, since he's been actively involved in the investigation.'

'Fine. By the way, you said there were only two interviews left. Dunbar's one. Who's the other?'

'Someone called Nicholas Ridley. He checked in in Malmo on day one and was allocated a cabin, but we can't find him.'

'Man overboard?'

'Ah,' Pilling moaned. 'That would be all we need. This venture is cursed; I can feel it already. As are most things I touch these days. I like to keep a low business profile, gentlemen; I find that I get more done that way. I'm on this crossing for Richard's sake, that's all. He sold me this project, he persuaded me that we could create a viable link between Scandinavia and Scotland, one that would benefit all four countries involved. He put Scottish Government money into it, he brought in business investment, I did the same in Sweden. Together we raised sufficient funds to underwrite the crossing for up to two years. With him it would have been a success; without him, I just don't know. We were working on another project too, the renewal of the refinery upstream from Edinburgh that's in danger of closure. With him we might have done it. Without him? I am doubtful. Eh,' he sighed. 'Not just in Scotland am I under pressure. I have another project, a big one, that's under threat, and I find I can do nothing about it. As I believe you Scots like to say, fuck that for a game of soldiers. I'm going to fly home.' He patted McGuire on the shoulder, and left the stateroom.

'Well,' the acting chief murmured, as the door closed. 'It seems there are worse things than being a Hibs supporter. I'm off, Sauce. Get Dunbar done and you head home too.'

Haddock nodded, and headed for Peter Dunbar's suite. Tarvil Singh was waiting for him at the door, looking twice as fresh as the ACC felt. 'I said hello,' the DI told him, 'and apologised for the wait. He said "No worries". I think he's been at the mini-bar.'

'Lucky him.' They stepped into the cabin.

Dunbar was standing by the window, gazing across the wide river towards the great iron rail bridge and Fife beyond. He turned to greet them; fresh-faced, clean-shaven, looking younger than his forty-one years. 'Mr Haddock. Mr Singh. Long day, eh?' His voice was slightly slurred, giving credence to the DI's suspicions.

'We can't deny that,' Haddock agreed. 'And again, I'm sorry we've had to ask you to wait, but we have things to discuss.'

'I'm sure you have. I'm still struggling to come to terms with what happened to Richard.' He flashed them a sad smile. 'Do I need an alibi?'

'I doubt that,' the ACC replied, straight-faced, 'since you weren't on board this thing when it happened, because that's where the shot was fired from. Of course, you could have been part of a conspiracy . . . but let's discount that for now.'

Dunbar touched his forehead in acknowledgement. 'Thanks for that. Do you think there was one?' he asked.

'We don't know, but it's clear that Mr Ralston wasn't as loved as everybody thought.'

'Nobody is.'

'I meant by his close associates.'

Dunbar winced. 'Well, I did love him, and I don't mind admitting it.'

'In that case . . . "Pleased" is probably the wrong expression, but you might be gratified to hear that Mr Ralston said one word before he died, and we believe that was "Belhaven". We take it to have been a reference to you. Correct?'

The man's eyes moistened. 'That's what he called me. We were pretty close.'

'Did he discuss everything with you?' Singh asked.

'Pretty much. I wasn't just a bag-carrier. I'm an MSP too; I was his Chef de Cabinet, a fancy title he dreamed up to give me a bit of status in Parliament, and a seat at the Cabinet table without pinning me down to a specific role. As such, we'd brain-storm together. The Glasgow–Malmo twinning link, for example, with a replica of the Turning Torso being built on the Clyde: I won't claim that it was a joint initiative, but I had input.'

'And the ferry crossing?' Haddock wondered.

'No, that was all him.'

'When he said your name, could he have been trying to send a message?'

'What kind of message?'

'Might he have thought you had something to tell us?'

'If he did,' Dunbar confessed, 'I don't know what it was.'

'Have a think about it. Something that happened that might on reflection have constituted a threat. Someone who might have had it in for him.'

'Are you talking about Joanie Cooper?' he asked, quietly.

'Tell us why we should,' the ACC countered.

'She had a bit of a crush on him, and she didn't make it a secret. Look, I assume you know that truth about Richard's marriage.'

'Yes, we do; one of my senior officers has spoken with Mrs Ralston. We know they were separated and we know why. We also know about his relationship with Mia McCullough. Was anyone else aware, that you know of?'

'Joanie was, for a start,' Dunbar replied. 'Look, this is the way it was: she came on to Richard one night in the office when they were working late. This would have been a few months ago. She kissed him and . . . "offered him further favours", that being a quote from him. He was taken aback and he was embarrassed but, he assured me, he behaved properly. He told her that much as he liked her, he couldn't reciprocate because it wouldn't be appropriate. It wasn't mentioned again and the three of us carried on as if nothing had happened, until . . . Richard met Mia and they connected. Very soon we found out about it. There were messages, phone calls, etc., and that's when things got very icy with Joanie. There was an atmosphere, no question. I spoke to her, reminded her that everything she learned in the office was privileged information, and asked her to behave professionally. I hoped that would have been enough. Are you suggesting that it wasn't?'

'Yup,' Haddock confirmed. 'There was a press leak, after the First Minister's death. It's been traced back to her.'

'Provably so?'

'Yes.'

'Then it will be grounds for dismissal, and I'll have to act . . . or someone will. We're all in limbo until the new FM's elected by the party.'

'Couldn't he have fired her before?' Singh asked.

'It would have been difficult, as she's a civil servant. He and I did discuss it briefly but we agreed that it wouldn't be worth the risk of political embarrassment.'

'I can see that,' the ACC agreed.

'Yes. What we were actually going to do was promote her, take her out of the press office and put her into a senior role in the mainstream civil service, in the Culture and Sport department. If she'd only kept her mouth shut that might still have happened.'

'Too bad for Joanie. Apart from her, could there have been anything else he wanted to warn us about?'

'Nothing comes to mind. There were certainly no specific threats against him. If there had been you'd have known about them at the time. Protocol is, anything like that is reported to your Special Department. Okay, there are odd things we get in the mail that aren't very nice, mostly things you can imagine, occasionally something stranger. Richard never saw any of them. They were reported to me but never made it to his office. We had a foetus once from an anti-abortion group: it turned out to be a dog's.' Dunbar frowned. 'Then there was the rope, I suppose. Yes, that was strange.'

'What rope?' Haddock exclaimed.

'An A4 envelope was delivered one day, Royal Mail first class, posted in Glasgow. The only thing in it was a length of rope, frayed in the middle.'

Seventy

'First of all, señora,' Dolça Nuñez began, 'I'm happy to learn that your daughter has been found and is safe. I wouldn't have asked to see you otherwise.'

'Thank you,' Inge Hoverstad replied, 'but how do you know that? The kidnapping was never publicly acknowledged.'

She smiled. 'I'm a journalist.'

Hoverstad pursed her lips. 'Even so. There was a news blackout in Sweden, and we've had no other calls.'

Dolça conceded. 'My boss told me.'

'But how did he know?' She paused, frowned, gasped. 'Ah! Your boss is Ignacio's father.'

'Yes,' she confessed.

'He asked you to investigate my husband? Why the hell would he do that?'

'Because of something your husband said to the committee in the Parliament in Sevilla. He suggested, not in so many words, but that's how it was taken, that InterMedia supported the Sierra Blanca ski project, which he was proposing. My method was to gather information first, which I did by talking to people in Sevilla, Granada and also in the Sierra Blanca itself. Only then did I approach your husband. Only then was I told by him that actually it's your project. I have my teeth in this subject now, as a journalist, as was

313

always the case. My boss is standing back from it; I have free rein now, in accordance with professional practice, something I'm sure you will understand as a PR person.'

'I see,' Hoverstad murmured. 'Things may not be the same between Sir Robert and us in the future.'

'Maybe your husband should have been more open with him,' Dolça suggested. 'You must know he's not a man to be taken lightly.'

'Mmm, maybe he should,' she admitted. 'Okay, what do you want to ask me?'

'Why have you been so shy, in this case? You're one of the top spin doctors in the country, so why haven't you been spinning here?'

'Because I'm Norwegian. My client, the backer of the project, is also Norwegian. He's a major business figure, but he is very discreet. If I had put my head above the parapet, been visible in this thing, his identity would be blown.'

'Why would that be a bad thing?'

'It would bring nationalism into play. If you've done your research, you'll know that there is already a Spanish ski facility in the Sierra Blanca, one that makes money, although not as much as it might. There are ski facilities in Norway also, but not nearly as successful as those in the southern European nations. Basically what my client wants to do is establish a Norwegian ski industry in Spain, where it will be one of the highest and best equipped in Europe. And one of the most accessible: my client also owns an airline and will introduce new services to Malaga and possibly to Jaen. I am not authorised to reveal his name, but one minute in a decent search engine and you will know who he is. He's a good guy, and he has a record of success. The Tromso project has huge potential. It will create thousands of jobs, permanent jobs, with its year-round potential. No sensible government would turn it down,' she declared, 'but this is Spain,' she added. 'We have very little history of sensible governments.' Inge Hoverstad put her hands on her desk, palms down. 'There,' she said, 'you have it. Now, you have a lot of power in your hands, Señora Nuñez. What are you going to do?'

'If the InterMedia group did support the project,' Dolça asked, 'would it help?'

'Undoubtedly.'

'Then I will talk to my boss,' she said. 'And if he gives the okay, I will write a piece that says so. And then,' she added, 'I will go for a beer with Gandalf.'

Seventy-One

DS Jackie Wright crossed her fingers as she dialled the number on her desk phone. Without a specific name, she had been forced to work from a list, one that had surprised her by its depth. She had assumed that in the twenty-first century monasteries would be few and far between, but her search for 'religious communities' had produced at least a dozen hits.

Having edited out convents, Moreton Abbey in Gloucestershire was the fourth on her list. The first three had received her calls with curiosity, bewilderment, and in the third case a flat refusal to cooperate. She waited as the dial tone sounded, three, four, five, six times, until it was replaced by the start of a voicemail greeting. 'This is More-'. It stopped, to be replaced by a voice that sounded more than a little out of breath. 'Moreton Abbey,' it gasped. 'I'm sorry, we were all in the garden. This is Brother Denzil speaking. How can we help you?'

'Take your time,' the detective replied, as a sudden vision of Friar Tuck in the film *Prince of Thieves* appeared in her mind's eye. 'Get your breath back. I'm Detective Sergeant Jackie Wright from the police in Edinburgh. I'm trying to contact a member of your order. He's known to me as Calvin Knox.'

She waited for a few seconds; eventually Brother Denzil was able to respond normally. 'I'm afraid that name means nothing to me,' he said, 'but it wouldn't necessarily. In this monastery we leave our former names at the door. For example, I'm Denzil here, but in the secular world I was Douglas.'

'I see,' Wright sighed, as a cloak of pessimism settled on her shoulders.

'But,' the monk continued, 'that said, I do know some of the brothers' given names. Calvin, though? Not that one; can't think who he might be.'

'He's Scottish if that helps.'

'Not really; we have a few of those. Brother Matthew, for example. He says he's here by mistake. He insists that he mixed us up with Buckfast Abbey.'

'Is there anyone you could ask?'

'The Abbot would know, I suppose. But he had a heavy session on the mead last night, so I won't be approaching him in a hurry. Instead,' he continued, with a chuckle in his voice, 'I'll just go to his office and look through the files. We really are an anachronism, Sergeant. Nothing here is digital; everything's on paper. It's a bloody wonder it isn't papyrus. Listen,' he continued as she grinned, 'I would ask you to hold on, but I have no idea how long I'll be, so give me a number I can call you back on.'

'Of course,' she said. 'Thank you, Brother.' She recited her mobile number. 'That'll be much quicker than coming through the switchboard.'

'We don't even have one of those. I'll be as fast as I can.' She hung up, thinking how out-dated that description sounded. As she leaned back in her chair, she realised that Sauce Haddock had just come into the open-plan office. Heading for his own room, he paused at her desk. 'Hey, Jackie,' he greeted her. 'What are you up to?'

'Tarvil's got me looking for a monk in a haystack. Richard Ralston's stepson.'

'Good, we need to speak to all the family members.'

'Yes, Tarvil's at a care home in Dunbar this morning. Ralston's mother lives there. Daniel, the son's gone with him. I don't envy them; she's pushing ninety and she has dementia.' She paused. 'By the way, congratulations, sir.'

Haddock grinned. 'Temporary, Jackie, temporary.'

She looked up at him with a raised eyebrow. 'Aye, sure.'

He wrinkled his nose. 'Not bothered either way,' he assured her. 'I'm happy here with you lot. It gets me out plenty too; once you're done with Calvin Knox, there's a job for the two of us that needs doing. We need to bring in Joanie Cooper: for formal questioning, not a job that can be done on a video call.'

The DS stared at him, surprise evident. 'As a suspect?'

'Person of interest at the moment. We'll see how it develops.'

'Very good, boss.' 'Sauce' no longer seemed appropriate, she thought. 'I'll get through this as fast as I can.'

Haddock had just reached his glass-walled room when her mobile rang.

'Denzil here,' the monk said, as she answered. 'I've found your man,' he announced. 'As I thought, his details were on file. The Abbot and his predecessor had the sense to file alphabetically. It didn't take me long at all.'

'Thanks, that's great. Can I have a word with him? Is he available?'

'Well, no. I'm afraid you can't. Mr Knox, as I must call him now, not Brother Luke, left here five years ago. His vocation didn't last long, only eighteen months. There's a note on his file that says he went to attend to some family business and never returned. We never heard from him again.'

'That's weird,' Wright exclaimed. 'His mother told my DCI that they communicate often, by video call. Maybe he's gone to another order,' she suggested.

'If he had we'd know. This life isn't like moving from one car showroom to another, as I used to do, back in what it's now fashion-able to call "the day".'

'But his mother told DCI Mann that he makes pottery in the Midlands. He even sent her a piece.'

'Not here he doesn't,' Brother Denzil assured her. 'We grow soft fruits in polytunnels, and that's the extent of our commercial activity. He probably bought it at Prinknash Abbey. They do that kind of touristy stuff,' he said, with a sniff in his tone. 'I'm really sorry, Sergeant, but your search seems to be at a dead end. It's been good to talk to you, though. If you ever need advice on a used Honda, or a Toyota, I'm your man.'

Seventy-Two

'How are you feeling?' DS John Stirling asked.

'One hundred per cent better than I did yesterday,' Pilar admitted, 'when the man who owns the hut found me. Rehydration and a night's sleep. They are miracle cures.'

'And a change of clothing,' Ignacio added from his bedside chair, grinning.

'Let's not go there,' she told him. 'But he is right,' she added, for the detective's benefit. 'Nacho's Dad brought me these things from the hotel. What I had on when I was taken, that's in the hospital incinerator already.'

'That's good,' Stirling said, 'but how do you feel emotionally? It must have been a scary experience.'

'I don't think I had time to be scared,' she confessed. 'It all happened very fast. They told me they'd been sent to take me to Nacho, and I recognised one of them as someone we'd met in a bar, so I accepted it. I was hardly in the car before the one I knew got in beside me, rather than the front seat. I thought that was odd, then he put a damp cloth over my face and I passed out. Everything afterwards was just a haze.'

'And how are you?' the DS asked her partner.

'More relieved than I've ever felt before. And I feel liberated,' Ignacio replied. 'I was going crazy in that bed.'

'Tell me about it,' Bob Skinner laughed. 'There are patients and there are im-patients. He's one of the latter, no doubt about that. We appreciate your visit, John. You've been a support to all of us and it won't be forgotten . . . by us or by others,' he added. 'Have you been recalled yet?'

'I'd expected to be, now that Pilar's been rescued, but the ACC wants me to stay on for a bit, to be present at the interview with the kidnapper. That's another reason I came actually, to share some good news that I had earlier on from Mary Blix. The man the Swedes identified, Giovanni Inverno, got back home to Hamburg last night, and was lifted straight away by the German Police, under a European arrest warrant. He was taken completely by surprise, apparently. He hadn't a clue that he'd been identified. There are a couple of formalities to be dealt with, but they expect to have him here for interview tomorrow morning.'

Skinner's expression darkened. 'I wish I could be there,' he growled. 'But I did have a conversation with your friend Matti Lower of State Security, asking him to throw the biggest book they can at him. In Edinburgh, I'd have done him and his mate for attempted murder.'

'Did he say anything when he was arrested?' Ignacio asked.

'*Wer zum Teufel bist du,*' Stirling replied. 'That's what Blix told me. It means "Who the hell are you?" apparently.'

Seventy-Three

'That's a bit of a surprise,' Haddock agreed as Jackie Wright finished her account of Brother Denzil's revelation, en route to the home of Joanie Cooper, the Scottish Government's official spokesperson. They were in the back seat of a patrol car, with a uniformed driver, a privilege of rank that the temporary ACC found a little embarrassing but had used to avoid any problems with the capital city's notoriously restrictive anti-car policy. 'Could he just have moved from one monastic house to another? Is that possible?'

'It is, but he didn't. I didn't stop there. I went through the list I had and eliminated all the other possibilities.'

'Are you certain that list was exhaustive?'

'More than,' she replied. 'Quite a few of the places on my list didn't have full-time residents. People went there on retreats; not just Christians either. I came across a couple of places that offered respite . . . their description . . . to Buddhists, Hindus, and even in one case Rastafarians.'

Haddock whistled. 'I'm trying to imagine their Evensong,' he murmured.

'Me too. What do we do about Calvin Knox, boss?'

'I'm asking myself that; probably nothing much. Maybe we go back to Amy Ralston to clarify what she told DCI Mann and DC Smith. It doesn't need to be two officers this time.' He frowned.

322

'We know that Ralston was targeted but we're nowhere near determining a motive. Joanie Cooper's the closest we have to a suspect
and I don't really fancy her. I mean, it's a big leap from being huffed
because Ralston wouldn't shag her to hiring a hitman to take him
out. Depending on what we get from her I might go for a chat with
Mrs Ralston myself, and with Daniel. I need to get a feel for this
investigation, Jackie. Dunbar was adamant that there had been no
political threats. If he's right, it was either a fanatic . . . and nobody's
claimed it as they would have almost certainly . . . or, the motive
must be domestic. That means we need to focus on family members and friends, associates. Calvin Knox qualifies as one of those,
but after what you've found out about him, it seems that he's been
doing his best to hide from his family. Given his up-bringing, who
can blame him? We'll look for him,' he said, 'but he's for later.
Cooper's our immediate priority, and,' he looked out of the window,
and upward, 'we appear to have arrived.'

A Holyrood HR official had provided Cooper's address, a first-
floor apartment in a twentieth-century brewery conversion in
Calton Road, barely a quarter of a mile from the Scottish Parliament. She had confirmed that the spin doctor had been expected
in the office that morning, but had not arrived. Nor had she been
contactable by phone.

'Ms Cooper was very close to the First Minister,' the executive
had told Haddock. 'We imagine that she's in great distress, as we all
are, so nobody's surprised by her absence. Not that it would be an
issue anyway,' she had added. 'She's a department head, and reports
to Mr Dunbar.'

Who had heard nothing from her, the ACC knew, since she had
flown back from Jens Pilling's bolthole in Oslo, a courtesy flight on
the same aircraft that had brought Ralston and his two aides to
Malmo. The only certainty since then was that she had been col-
lected in Edinburgh by a government car and delivered home.

'She has a short commute to Parliament,' Wright observed as they surveyed the building. 'Lucky her.'

'Her luck's run out,' the ACC said. 'When we're done with her she's going to have to face the consequences of tipping off Sue Bland about Mia McCullough. That will be a sacking offence, for sure. Which makes me think,' he murmured. 'I'd like you to take the lead in the interview, Jackie. I have a loose connection with Mia; she's an in-law by marriage of my wife. I'm only here because there's nobody else available, with Tarvil and the rest on catch-up time off after yesterday.'

The DS nodded. 'Will do, boss, but let's find Cooper first.'

The entrance to the building was a green door, with six squares of obscured glass at the top. To the right there was a panel of buttons, listing apartments and their occupants, with a speaker and a camera above.

'2c J Cooper.' She pressed the button for five seconds. A full minute elapsed. She pressed again.

'We need to get in,' Haddock declared.

'Boss, we don't have a warrant,' Wright pointed out. 'And she could be at Tesco, anywhere.'

'We need to get in,' he repeated. 'I feel it, Jackie. Raise one of the neighbours.'

'They'll all be at work. There's nobody on benefits living in this place.'

'This is 2025, post-Covid. There will be at least one home-worker in there, probably more. Do it.'

She pressed the buzzers one by one, from the top down. The first three went unanswered, but '2e A Mathieson' drew a response. 'Yes?' a testy male voice exclaimed.

'It's the police, sir,' Wright replied. 'I'm Detective Sergeant Wright with Det . . . Assistant Chief Constable Haddock. We have a meeting with one of your neighbours but she's not answering. We're concerned. Will you let us in, please?'

'She?' the man repeated. 'Sounds like Joanie. You're on camera; let me see some ID and I'll let you in.'

The DS took out her warrant card and held it close to the lens. A few seconds later there was a click as the door's latch was released.

The detectives stepped inside almost directly on to a narrow flight of stairs, leading to a first-floor landing. They had barely reached it when a middle-aged man appeared in a corridor on their left, barefoot, clad in jeans and a red tee-shirt with 'Canada' emblazoned across the chest. 'Drew Mathieson,' he said. 'Let me show you the way to Joanie's place. This isn't the most conventional building.'

He led them in the direction from which he had emerged, past his own apartment and up two more short stairs, arriving at a dead-end: 'Flat 2c J Cooper'. There was a knocker on the door. Mathieson seized it and rapped twice, hard. 'Joanie,' he called out, 'it's Drew. Can you come to the door, please. There's people here to see you.' He looked over his shoulder, at Haddock. 'I didn't like to say "police",' he whispered. 'You know.'

'Sure,' the ACC said. 'Understood. Can you hear Ms Cooper from your place when she's at home?' he asked.

'Just about; the sound-proofing could be better. She's got wooden floors and if she wears heels . . . not that she does often . . . I can. On Saturday night I heard her. Since then, nothing. We don't live in each other's pockets, you know. We're both single and we both value our privacy.'

He nodded. 'Look, Drew, we need to get in there if she doesn't open the door very soon.'

'Then you're in luck,' Mathieson told him. 'Joanie and I keep each other's keys, in case of emergencies. Since she hasn't answered by now, this could be one of those. I'll go and get it.' He turned and rushed off.

'What do you think?' Wright murmured as he left.

'Nothing good.'

Seconds later Mathieson returned, brandishing a Yale key. He was about to open the door, when Haddock put a hand on his shoulder. 'Let me.'

He slid the key into the lock, turned it . . . and met stiff resistance. He tried once more pressing harder. 'Damn it!' he hissed. 'She's immobilised the lock.'

'I've got chisels,' the neighbour offered.

'This is quicker.' He took four steps backwards, ran at the door and slammed the sole of his right foot against it. The lock shattered and it swung open.

'Jesus!' Mathieson whispered. 'I've never seen that done before.'

'And I've never done it before,' Haddock admitted. 'Not for real, but as a probationer, you're taught. Jackie, stay here with Drew, please.'

He knew what he would find as he stepped into the flat. The only question in his mind was where. The living space was large and open plan with ample light from high windows, but no street view at all. An armchair and a sofa faced a big wall-mounted television. A small dining table with four chairs sat close to the kitchen area which was all white units and appliances with a contrasting black granite work-top, with a black draining block by the twin tubs, a block of Kitchen Devils with one knife missing, a bowl of apples that had lost their shine, and a white envelope. Everything was neat and tidy; no unwashed dishes or crockery, no food waste, the antithesis of his own place in his single days, before Cheeky and Samantha and he-who-was-to-come, whose name would be Robert Cameron Haddock-McCullough, although only his creators knew that.

He realised that he was postponing the moment and so he moved on. A guest bedroom was next; there was a flowery duvet on the double bed but no indication that it had ever been used. Beyond, there was what an estate agent might have described, if inappropriately, as a family bathroom. Both had large skylights. Finally he came to Joanie Cooper's private space, her en-suite bedroom, which did have a window, looking down to a courtyard: undrawn floor-length gold curtains, a king-sized brass bed with a yellow duvet, custom-made fitted oak furniture and a dressing table and stool.

He had expected to find her in bed; instead she was in the en-suite bathroom, in the tub. There was a small table beside it, on which stood an empty bottle of Marques de Caceres 2015 Gran Reserva, of which the last dried traces were in a tall crystal glass beside it. The missing knife from the block on the kitchen work surface lay on the bath mat. Haddock hoped she had bled out quickly.

From the pocket of his jacket he took blue overshoes and gloves, and slipped them on. Returning to the living area, he picked up the envelope from the work surface and slipped it into a plastic enclosure, then made his way to the door.

The protective coverings told Wright all she needed to know. 'Call it in please, Jackie,' Haddock said, quietly, with his back to Mathicson. 'Get the SOCOs here soonest, plus a pathologist and a mortuary wagon. For now, we have to treat it as a crime scene, but I'll be very surprised if it is.' He handed her the envelope in its sterile case. 'This needs to be processed for prints and DNA, but I want to see the contents as soon as it's opened. I'll look like an idiot if it's a shopping list, but again it's long odds against. Would you wait here, please, for everyone to arrive, while I take Drew back to his place and have a chat with him. Also, could you call the Holyrood HR people and get next of kin details.'

'Yes, boss,' she murmured, then turned to the neighbour. He was stunned, grey-faced, beyond comprehension. 'Mr Mathieson, could you go with ACC Haddock, please.'

'Is . . .?' he whispered. She nodded in reply.

The two men left her there and made their way down to Mathieson's home. Unlike the Cooper apartment, it did have a view, across the well-maintained gardens of the white-painted Scottish veterans' residences. 'More conventional than upstairs,' the ACC observed.

'Most of them are,' the owner said. 'The developer went to town on one or two, that's all.' He had recovered some of his composure. 'She really is dead?' he asked.

'Oh yes,' Haddock assured him. 'Obviously you were friends as well as neighbours, trusting each other with your keys. I'm sorry for your loss.'

'Thanks. It'll take a while to sink in, I imagine. What happened? I mean, how did she die?'

'Suicide. Obviously,' he added, 'we'll need to rule out everything else, but that's how it presents.'

'What did she . . .? I mean, how did she die? Overdose? She didn't hang herself, did she? That would be awful. When I was a kid my parents had a neighbour who did that. Apart from being a bloody awful way to go, I always feel sorry for the people who find them. I mean finding somebody like that, the memory, it's never going to leave you, is it?'

The ACC gazed out of the window. 'You're right there,' he said. 'When I was a PC, a rookie, the first body I ever found was a hanging victim. I was in the Meadows with another cop, why I cannot remember, but it was a foggy night, a real pea-souper like we don't seem to get any more, and we almost literally bumped into this bloke, hanging from a tree. I'll never forget that, I promise you. But you can rest easy, Drew, Ms Cooper didn't do that. She did it the

Roman way, got in a warm bath, drank a decent bottle of wine, and opened her wrists. Very efficiently too; the wounds were precise, and in the right place.'

'God,' Mathieson whispered. 'I don't know how to feel. At the moment I'm just . . . just . . . You guys, you must have to do this stuff all the time.'

'Not me, not DS Wright. The uniforms catch most of those calls. What do you do, Drew?' he asked, changing the subject, keen to move on.

'Graphic novels. I write them; my associate's the illustrator.'

'Successful?'

'We do okay but we have to keep up with the times. Just as self-publishing and e-books changed the traditional publishing industry . . . and turned a lot of shite out into the market in the process . . . my fear is that AI's going to fuck us. My pension fund's full though.'

'Did you and Ms Cooper discuss your work?'

'Not much,' he confessed. 'I know what she did, though, and who she worked for. I wonder if that's why she did it. In fact, now I think about it, I imagine it was.'

'What do you mean?' Haddock probed.

'Ralston. The First Minister. Him being dead.' Mathieson frowned. 'She worked directly for him, you see, and not always in the office. With it being so close, they'd go over stuff here in Joanie's place, away from the mob, she said. Not so much lately but there was a period when he was here quite a lot . . .' Mathieson paused, drew a breath and blew it out. 'Ah, what the fuck,' he exclaimed. 'They're both dead so I might as well tell you. They had a thing for a while. They'd work here at night . . . well, maybe they did, maybe they didn't, but there were a couple of mornings I heard the door go early and it wasn't her that was leaving, for I'd hear her moving about afterwards. There was even one morning, about a year ago:

I'd a breakfast meeting with our publisher up in the Balmoral Hotel, so I left early. I bumped into Ralston on the stairs, tie in his pocket and in need of a shave. That might have been the last time I heard him around: certainly it was the last time I ever saw him here. And after that, Joanie, well, she was never quite the same.'

Seventy-Four

'Fuck's sake, John,' Lottie Mann sighed. 'I'm in fucking Morrisons' fucking car park. There really is no such thing as a fucking morning off, is there?'

'I believe there is, ma'am,' Stirling replied. 'But it's so long ago since I had one that I've forgotten.'

'Touchy,' she chuckled.

'You mean "touché"?' he suggested.

'Is that French for "smartarse"?' the DCI retorted. 'No, I did mean "touchy", but I must apologise. You've got every right to be, left out there on your own in Malmo. But I know you're not calling me to bitch about it, so what's up?'

'I'm only calling you because the ACC's unavailable. First call was to him. I spoke to one of the DCs in Edinburgh. Something's up there but he couldn't tell me what.'

'If it's big we'll hear about it soon enough. Come on, I've got freezer stuff here and I don't want it to melt.'

'I suppose. The thing here: the Swedish forensic officers think they've identified the cabin from where Ralston was shot. They found probable gunshot residue, hair samples, and more. Obviously the window, the porthole, had been opened. It's secured and made watertight by two brass screws, and they were able to recover partial prints and DNA from both of them.'

'Whose cabin was it? Do they know?'

'It was given to a man called Nicholas Ridley. He was one of the supplementary guests added to the manifest. We know that he checked in on Day One, because that's when the cabins were allocated.'

'Yes!' Mann hissed. 'Nicholas Ridley. When we interviewed all the passengers in Edinburgh yesterday there was one name on the manifest that we couldn't find: Nicholas Ridley, that was it. The ship's purser told us they were less scrupulous in checking passengers in for the rescheduled crossing. They got everyone out of there as fast as they could after the shooting, so fast that they were allowed to keep their cabin keys. How did they let them know the time of the rescheduled crossing?'

'Text.'

'Boom! That means we have a number for Mr Ridley. Why's that name familiar?' she wondered.

'There was a Tory Cabinet minister of that name in the eighties,' Stirling volunteered. 'Also he was one of the Oxford Martyrs.'

'All of Thatcher's ministers were martyrs in the end, weren't they? Right,' she said, 'I'm off home to dump the frozen greens and Dan's Cornettos, then I'm straight into the office. I need to check how Ridley got on to the passenger list. Also,' she paused, thinking. 'John,' she continued, 'he may still have the weapon, but after what he'd done, surely he had to get rid of it. Yes?'

'Yes,' the DS agreed. 'The Swedish security chief told the ACC and me that they got everyone off the site so fast that their luggage was left on board.'

'And it was all X-rayed when the ferry docked yesterday, so, how did he get rid of it?'

'Either he slipped off the boat carrying it . . . risky, therefore unlikely . . . or he dropped it out of the window.'

'I agree. You're still in Malmo. Ask your contact there . . . what's his name?'

'Matti Lower.'

'Ask him to raise his game and get divers down there, pronto, as he should have done as soon as we knew about the second gunman. Fuck me, if he was one of ours he'd be feeling Mario McGuire's hot breath on his neck even now!'

Seventy-Five

'What's your gut saying, Sauce?' Tarvil Singh asked, leaning again the door of the ACC's office, which he had just closed. 'Could there be a chance of third-party involvement?'

'My gut's saying none at all,' Haddock replied. 'It's straightforward to me. The woman had just committed career suicide by trusting Sue Bland not to give her up, and she knew it. There was a voicemail from Bland on her phone, saying "Sorry but I had no choice". It was timed well before her death. Add the door being locked from the inside and the place being pretty much intruder proof. It's a suicide, mate. When I get to see what's in that envelope it may tell us why she did it, but we probably know most of it already.'

'Any other stuff on her phone?'

'Only work calls, apart from the one to Bland. Key, there is absolutely nothing there that links her to Ralston's death. I must have another conversation with Dunbar, though, because his story's in question. It's possible that on those occasions Drew Mathieson told me about, they really were working late, so late that he kipped in the spare room, but the fact is that Ralston had a place of his own near the Parliament, going back to the days before he was First Minister, a mews house that was more or less next door to Cooper's

334

place. He could have walked home in the time it would take him to get undressed at Joanie's. No, the only thing my gut's telling me is that maybe the late Richard's armour wasn't quite as shiny as everyone thought.'

'Hump her and dump her, like the song title from that shock-rock group a few years ago?'

'Elegantly put, mate,' Haddock said. 'But yes, people might think so. And when she learned about him and Mia, her reaction would be understandable.'

'Yes,' Singh agreed. 'Meanwhile,' he continued, 'I came to tell you that I've had information from the procurator fiscal in Glasgow about Brian Knox's death in Italy, his climbing accident; very interesting information it is too.'

He pointed to a chair. 'Sit down and tell me.'

'Right,' the DI said, seating himself. 'Knox was killed on a mountain called *Polluce*, or Pollux if you want the English version, on the Italian side of its border with Switzerland, at the top of the Aosta Valley. Climbing was the guy's main sport . . . unless you count wife-beating. He was experienced and had a lot of significant routes on his record. He was climbing with two local guides when he fell off. They swore that he was properly roped up and had done nothing wrong; watching him, they said, it was obvious that he was a good climber and not a risk-taker. That's what they told the investigating judge in Italy. Nevertheless, the Italian police did a thorough job, as they do on all mountain accidents. That involves seizing the dead climber's ropes, under the judge's order. When they looked at Knox's, they found that it had broken, snapped. When they looked even closer, they saw that it hadn't frayed on a sharp rock . . . proper climbing ropes don't do that anyway . . . it had been cut, halfway through, not with a knife, but with a saw-like blade, making it hard to detect even by an experienced climber who'd be likely to check his kit before he went out. That put the guides under suspicion for a while, but they swore that they'd never met Knox before they went on the mountain. Still, they tested the rope for DNA, to check theirs weren't on it. When they did, they found Knox's all over it, as you'd expect, and one other. That wasn't found on any database, anywhere, but that doesn't matter, not at all.'

'Why not?' Haddock asked.

'Because it shows a filial link, and Brian Knox only had one son.'

The two detectives looked at each other across the desk. 'Jesus, Tarvil,' the ACC whispered, 'how did the Italians react to that?'

'Their lead investigator, a bloke called Rocco something, I forget his other name, he wanted to extradite Calvin Knox, but the investigating judge said there was no evidence that he'd ever been in Italy, or that the rope had even been cut there, so . . . he passed the buck, sent the papers to the PF in Glasgow and that was that as far as he's concerned.'

'Next question . . .'

'Yes, how does that link to the broken rope that was sent to Ralston in the mail?'

'That too,' Singh said, 'but it's not the one I was going to ask. Everything the PF had from Italy is in the box he sent to me, but it doesn't tell me what his office did about the buck once it had been passed. There should have been a criminal investigation in Scotland. I've looked for it in our system, but there's nothing.'

'No? Call the fiscal back, then.'

'I did,' the DI replied, 'but he said he'd only talk to you, or to the DCC. I think he has strange ideas about his place in the pecking order.'

'Fact is, Tarvil, he's pretty high up; all CID officers are equal in his eyes. If he said that, he's got a reason for it. Leave it with me, and I'll get in touch with him.'

'Okay, Sauce, will do. Do you want me to get back to Dunbar about the rope that came in the mail?'

'No, that'll be for the two of us. We need to know what else he hasn't told us about his late boss.'

Seventy-Six

Malmo Remand Prison was the most discreetly sited that John Stirling had ever seen. It was in the city centre, so close to the police building that he and Matti Lower reached it on foot in under fifteen minutes. From the street there was no clue that it was a place of incarceration. It was only when they turned into an alley and reached a massive gate, with a door cut in its centre, that its nature became evident.

'I know,' the Swede said. 'You're asking yourself how this can be secure, but trust me it is; you can't see it from the outside, that's all. It's short stay, a halfway house. Our suspect will go to court later today. He'll be formally accused, if the prosecution case is complete, in which case he'll be transferred to prison to await trial, either that or he'll be sent back here for a few days until they are ready to go ahead.'

Lower pressed a buzzer beside the entry door, identified himself, stated their purpose, and they were admitted. After passing through airport-style security procedures, they were led into the heart of the centre and up a flight of stairs to a windowless interview room. They had been expected, Stirling realised, because Giovanni Inverno was there before them. He wore the orange jump-suit that seemed to the Scot to have become standard uniform for detainees everywhere and was handcuffed to a heavy table. His eyes looked sleep-deprived, and there was a dark stubble on his chin.

'Good morning,' Lower began. 'We will speak in English, which I'm told you understand, for my colleague's benefit and because mine is better than my German.'

'Where's my lawyer?' Inverno asked.

'Waiting for you at the court,' the Swede replied. 'You'll have plenty of time to talk to him there. He's a public defender, I'm afraid. We advised your employers in Hamburg of your arrest, but they were very quick to wash their hands of you. They deny any knowledge of your operation. I believe them; I have colleagues in Germany who can vouch for them.'

'Fuck them. I'm saying nothing.'

'You don't have to, my friend. All you have to do is listen while we spell out for you where you're at. First, be in no doubt that you are done, as your associate will be when we catch him. You were seen on camera engaging with Miss Sanchez, your victim, in her hotel. You were seen following her into your stolen car and we have already established that you can be linked by fingerprints to the place where she was abandoned. If you were a goose you are cooked, as the English say. My colleague here is Scottish so maybe that should be haggis. Time to start helping yourself, Gianni. Give us your accomplice. Who is he?'

The Italian shook his head, and yawned.

'No sleep for you for a while, I'm afraid,' Stirling told him. 'I've been reading up on Swedish criminal law. For what you've done, the absolute minimum tariff is four years. But the prosecution will add on the fact that it was obviously a conspiracy, because we know that you stalked her, that you approached her and her boyfriend in a bar. Then they'll consider your drugging her; that's a serious physical attack. All that adds to your sentence. From what I'm told we're up to eighteen years already. But then you pumped some more narcotics into her and you dumped her. You abandoned her in a place where she was only found by accident, a place where she might have lain for weeks, a place where she might have died an awful death from dehydration. That takes it all the way up to a life sentence, mate, and all you've got on your side is a public defender. Yes, he might be Clarence Darrow. On the other hand, and maybe more likely, he might be Clarence the cross-eyed fucking lion, but still smart enough to know a loser when he sees one, and simply abandon his client to the court's mercy, of which there will be none. That's your future, pal.'

'Bullshit!' Inverno whispered.

'No,' Stirling said, firmly. 'That's where you are.'

'I'll give you the other guy.'

'Fuck off!' the DS snapped. 'Don't throw us peanuts. The only bargaining power you have lies in the name of the person who paid you to kidnap Pilar Sanchez.'

Inverno shook his head, his eyes glistening. 'I can't,' he whispered.

'For your own sake, you have to. We will work it out, you know. You're an experienced security professional with no criminal record. Organised crime doesn't recruit people like you; wouldn't even try, it'd be too risky. We will find that person, Gianni, and when we do, you really will be done. Stuck in a Swedish prison, maybe even one in the north, where the winters are balls-aching cold. Isn't that right, Matti?'

'Absolutely,' Lower confirmed. 'And I can fix it, that location.'

'Fuck!' Inverno hissed. 'Okay. If I give you a name, you'll go easy on us both?'

'Easier on you,' the Swede conceded. 'I can't guarantee any-thing for the other, not without a name.'

'Okay.' The man's face twisted into an expression that was close to pain. 'It was my brother, my brother Guido.'

'Where will we find him?'

'Where he works. In Spain.'

Lower leaned back sitting straight in his chair. 'Thank you,' he murmured. 'You will not be charged with anything today. You will be taken to court and remanded here for as long as it takes to arrest your brother and bring him to Sweden. When we have him, we will take it from there.'

The two officers stood and left the room. Outside, in the corridor, Lower smiled. 'John,' he said, 'that was excellent. It would have taken me at least a day to get there. Hey,' he chuckled, 'would you like to come and work for my department? I'm sure I could arrange a transfer, even if it was only a secondment at first.'

'No disrespect, Matti,' Stirling replied, 'but you'd need to second my girlfriend too, but she's very much a Weegie girl.'

'Weegie? What is Weegie?'

The DS grinned. 'She's from Glasgow,' he explained, 'and her roots there are deep.'

'Maybe I get a spade . . .' He paused as a tone sounded on his phone. He took it from his pocket and peered a little myopically at the screen. 'More good news for you,' he said as he put it away. 'The divers have found a sniper rifle, disassembled and in its case. It wasn't difficult for they knew exactly where to look. The crime scene analysts are saying that the case was virtually watertight. They have high hopes of recovering prints, that's if there are any, if the shooter didn't wear gloves, and DNA, which almost certainly there will be. A good day, John. Two for the price of one.'

Seventy-Seven

'I don't take kindly to being summoned to a police office, Detective Superintendent,' Lionel Darch drawled. 'If not for the fact that I'm due at the Crown Office this afternoon, you'd have been coming to me.'

'That's ACC Haddock,' Tarvil Singh growled, leaning his bulk towards the procurator fiscal.

Darch frowned at him. 'Acting,' he snapped.

'Shh, gentlemen,' Haddock murmured. The Glasgow procurator fiscal was a grey-haired Crown Office veteran, one of the school, the ACC recognised, that saw the police as their servants rather than their agents, as in law they were. 'He's right, Tarvil,' he said. 'I could be deactivated at any time, just as Mr Darch could be posted to Inverness or Lerwick if the Lord Advocate thought he'd be a better fit there.' He paused to let the implied threat sink in. 'Let's get down to business,' he continued, gazing at the fiscal, 'that being the ongoing investigation into the murder of the First Minister, which I'm conducting, whatever my rank, reporting not to any fiscal but to the Crown Agent and the Lord Advocate.'

'And what progress are you making, may I ask?'

'No. You may not. Instead you can explain something to me, a matter that's probably tangential to the inquiry, but needs clearing up nonetheless. You were asked by DI Singh,' he continued, 'for

342

information about the death of a man named Brian Knox, in a climbing holiday in Italy. You sent him a box of information and exhibits that explained the facts, but left a big unanswered question.'

'Oh yes?' Darch drawled.

'Yes. We've seen it, that evidence. It makes it pretty clear that a crime was committed, a homicide, in fact.'

'Mmm. It was probable, but the issue was where. Knox died in Italy, so logically, it was there, but that's not how my opposite number in Aosta saw it. It involved a rope that had been tampered with, but his view was that there was no evidence of that having been done in Italy, since Knox had brought his gear with him from Glasgow. We haggled for a bit but he, Judge Baldini, had the stronger hand, so I agreed that I'd examine the productions myself, consult the Crown Agent and come to a view.'

'We've seen the productions,' Singh said, 'and it took us little or no time to come to our view . . . that at the very least there were grounds to detain the victim's son, Calvin Knox, for questioning, as he was known to have handled the rope that broke, the rope that had been partially cut through.'

'That's right,' Haddock agreed, 'but there's no record among the material you sent us of any such interview ever taking place. I'll be blunt, Mr Darch, I'm smelling fish here, and not very fresh either. What happened?' he asked, bluntly.

Darch shifted, in his chair, and in his attitude. 'Edinburgh happened,' he replied. 'I discussed the case with the Crown Agent. I was proposing handing the papers to the police, and letting them question Knox junior, and I was expecting his agreement, but he told me to leave it with him. I was only a depute then, standing in for my boss, who was on leave, so I didn't feel able to argue. I did what I was told, and a couple of days later he came back to me. He told me that the Justice Minister had intervened. He had heard of the case because of the Italian involvement, he said, and asked to see the papers. Two days later he told the Crown Agent that it was entirely reasonable that Calvin Knox could have handled his father's ropes, but unreasonable to assume that he had cut them. On his instructions, I marked the case "No Pro", no proceedings. If it had been up to me, I'd still have had Knox interviewed, but I did what I was told. There; that's your question answered.' Darch rose to his feet. 'Do you have any more before I leave?'

'Just the one,' Tarvil Singh said. 'Who was the Justice Minister, in case we need to talk to him?'

'Good luck with that one,' the veteran fiscal snorted. 'Back then he was still on his way up the ladder, and very wary about snakes; fact is, I assumed that was why he did what he did. It was Richard Ralston.'

Seventy-Eight

'I'll give you a file with all the information relating to your treatment,' Doctor Fagen said. 'When you get home you should make arrangements to have the stitches removed, and to have your rehabilitation monitored. You can do that, Ignacio, yes?'

'It's done already,' Skinner told her. 'He'll go to a private clinic in Edinburgh, where he'll be seen by a trauma surgeon. The rehab will be done by a physio in North Berwick, near where he and Pilar live. She's very good, I've used her myself. I want to thank you, Doctor Fagen, for all you've done for him. If any of us can repay you in any way, let me know. You have my number already.'

'It was my duty,' she replied. 'But also my pleasure,' she added. 'Given that your wife is a forensic pathologist I'm not sure what she could do for me, but if I ever need a reference for a job in the UK, I may call you.'

'Or in Spain. Or even the USA. I know people there who know people there.'

She laughed. 'I'm Chinese. I may give the USA a miss for a while. When do you fly?' she asked.

He grinned. 'Whenever I tell the pilot. Our plane should be back at Malmo Airport by now.'

'You'll have the file in fifteen minutes, tops.'

'Thanks, doc,' Ignacio called after her. 'You'll be in my book.'

'You what?' his father exclaimed.

'Kidding, Dad. But I do have an offer from a Swedish TV company that wants to work up a drama series based on the shooting. It came through my work email. They want me to be a script consultant. What do you think?'

'From the little I know of that world, tell them you want executive producer status or they can fuck off. They don't know about the second gunman yet. When they do, their series will get a lot bigger.' He looked at Pilar. 'They don't know about your involvement either. There could be something in it for . . .'

He broke off as his phone sounded. 'Dolça,' he murmured, looking at the screen.

'Sir,' the young reporter said, as he accepted her call. He sensed her excitement at once. 'It's over, the Tromso story. It's done.'

'I'm not surprised,' he replied, 'but tell me how.' As she spoke, he switched his phone to speaker mode, full volume.

'There's been an arrest. A man named Guido Inverno; he's Italian and his company owns three hotels in the Sierra Blanca region. He organised the kidnapping of Pilar Sanchez, by his brother and another man, as a warning to her parents to dump the Tromso project. But tell me, please, why are you not surprised?'

'There was a note left with Pilar when she was dumped by her kidnappers,' Skinner told her. 'It was in Spanish. We're in bloody Sweden, Dolça. Pilar speaks fluent English, so does my son, her partner, and so, I like to think, do I. Therefore that note could only have been directed at one person, her father, the public proponent of the new ski project. I told my Policia Nacional contact that much even before the kidnapper was arrested.'

'I met the man,' she confessed. 'I actually spoke to him at the foot of the ski slope. I thought he was the ski-lift manager. There's a quote from him in the piece I've written and sent to Señor Sureda.'

'Is it published?'

'Not yet. I asked him to hold it until the Sevilla Parliament votes on the project tomorrow. My contact there called me to say that Inverno's arrest makes it virtually certain.'

'In that case, tell Hector from me to run the story now, billed "Exclusive". If we wait, every bugger'll have it. And Dolça,' he added. 'Well done, kid; great job.'

'Thank you, sir,' she said. 'This might be a good time to ask you something. Since I'm an InterMedia group correspondent, with a brief that can take me all over Spain, do I have to live in Girona?'

Skinner laughed. 'As far as the company's concerned, and I speak for everyone involved, you can live wherever you like. But wherever that is, based on current performance, don't expect to be at home too often.'

As he ended the call, he realised that his son was gazing at him, with a smile on his face. 'You know, Dad, you need to be careful. Listening to you there, you're beginning to sound like a proper journalist.'

'Fine,' he said. 'Given the people I'm working with now, I'm going to take that not as a warning, but as a compliment.' He pocketed his phone. 'Okay, you two,' he continued, 'you got all the baggage you brought with you?'

'And more,' Pilar announced. 'I've been shopping, remember?'

'Christ, let's hope the aircraft hold's big enough.'

The door opened behind him as Doctor Fagen returned. 'The file,' she announced, handing Skinner a folder. 'Hard copy rather than a memory stick, in case your Scottish doctor can't open the digitised X-rays. Also,' she continued, 'before you leave, Sir Robert, the Prime Minister has learned that you're here and has asked if you would look in on her.'

'Of course I will,' he promised. 'It's good that she's fit for visitors.'

'She's a remarkably strong woman, physically and mentally. Don't stay too long,' she warned, 'but it did seem important to her that you visit.'

Seventy-Nine

'What do we know about the Knoxes, father and son?' Lottie Mann asked. 'The father, the brute we've been told about, was a farmer, yes?'

'That's right,' Maya Smith confirmed. 'I know quite a lot about him now, little or nothing about the son, but while you've been talking to John in Sweden, I've been speaking to an official in the National Farmers Union. He knew Brian Knox; he described him as plain-spoken and not particularly likeable. He was surprised when I told him he'd been accused of domestic violence, but he did say that he never talked directly about his wife and was "openly disdainful", and that's a quote, of his son. He said the boy was a wimp; "a poof" he even called him at a farmers' dinner when drink had been taken. That and, I quote again, "a fucking mummy's boy". And last but not least, at the last dinner he attended before he died, as "Friar fucking Tuck". However, it didn't stop him leaving everything to Calvin when he fell off the mountain.'

'What happened to the farm?'

'It's operated by a tenant now, a family that NFU Scotland helped place there. It's owned by a limited company; it was even when Knox was alive. Pretty much all of his assets were vested in it. I've pulled his will from the public record in the Sheriff Court.

What he actually left to Calvin was a one hundred per cent shareholding in the company, cash and investments worth close on four million, personal belongings, and a duplex apartment in Broomhill, in the west end of Glasgow. I did a check on the property register; the place is now in Calvin's name, but the council tax is paid by the company.'

'What do Calvin's income tax records say?'

'I'm still waiting for HMRC to tell me that, but I know from the statutory accounts that are filed every year by a small practice in Hyndland that he's been drawing a hundred grand in dividends from the company every year. Before that, when his dad was alive, he was on the company payroll, although according to the accountant I spoke to, a guy who went to school with Brian Knox, he didn't actually do anything other than run errands.'

Mann perched her frame on a corner of the DC's desk. 'So,' she summed up, 'we know that Calvin Knox is independently wealthy, lives in Broomhill and probably never got his hands dirty in his life. We know that he's been letting his mother believe that he still leads a monastic life, but he actually bailed out as soon as he inherited his father's wealth.'

'And we know that he handled the rope that was cut halfway through,' Smith added.

'But we don't know when. You know what I'm seeing, Maya? I'm seeing him fraying the rope and then checking into his monastery to pray,' she smiled grimly, 'that it would wear all the way through. That's as good an alibi as you could ask for. Agreed?'

'One hundred per cent.'

'I wonder what he has this time, for that's not going to be so easy to arrange.' She looked down at Smith. 'John gave me an update on the weapon the divers found. It's hand-made, probably by one of a dozen names on an Interpol list, silenced, and easily assembled. They found prints, but they're not in any database. Neither is the DNA they recovered, but it does match that on the rope. There's no doubt about it. I need to call Sauce to let him know for sure that Calvin Knox killed the First Minister . . . his stepfather.'

Eighty

'Sir Robert,' Pernil Mattson greeted Skinner as he was admitted to her hospital room by the security officers outside. Her voice was hoarse, an after-effect of intubation, he knew. 'Thank you for coming to see me. I know you must be keen to get your son out of here and home. I envy him; they tell me I am looking at another month, at least. Did Doctor Fagen look after your boy?' she asked.

'Yes, she did,' he confirmed as they shook hands.

'Then he's lucky. She's just taken over my case, at my insistence after hearing nothing but negativity from the chief surgeon. He told me that I would have this bag thing for life, which was not what I wanted to hear. She has taken another look and has promised me that there's another procedure possible and that it will make it unnecessary.'

'That's great.' He smiled. 'Will it be possible for you to go back to work?'

The Prime Minister laughed. 'Yes, but I was always going to do that. No way will I let Lena Rapace have a free run. Now,' she continued, 'there's something I want you to do for me. I was told about you by my aides and I've looked you up, on my tablet. You have quite a profile. I sense that people tend to do what you say.'

'Hah,' he snorted. 'I have a couple of wives, one ex, one current,

352

who'd tell you different. In my career, though, I admit that I tend not to give them a choice.'

'Good, because I want you to be my ambassador to Scotland, to the Scottish Parliament. You have heard of Richard Ralston's plan to twin Malmo with Glasgow?'

'Yes, I've been told about it.'

'And about the idea of a replica of the Turning Torso, beside the river?'

'That too.'

'How do you feel about it?'

'I went to school in Glasgow,' Skinner said. 'And to Glasgow University. For a brief period, through circumstances, for I never wanted to be, I was even its chief constable. It's a place that's full of historical evidence of its development, from the old Merchant City, to the crane that's a memorial to the great shipyards, to the new era, with the Hydro Arena and even the thing they call the Squinty Bridge. You can walk through it and see its evolution over a couple of hundred years and more. But now? I sense a danger that its growth might be stagnating. I believe that Glasgow needs the Torso, or something else of that magnitude, as the spur to the next stage. I'm for it, unquestionably.'

'Wonderful. In that case I'm sure that with your personal influence and your media power, you will be able to ensure that it gets built.'

He shrugged. 'No guarantees, but if I can I will.'

'You will, and one more thing. It must be named after Richard Ralston.' Mattson frowned and her eyes showed pain. 'Richard was a great man, you know, a real visionary, streets ahead of any other politician in your country, even your ex-wife.' His reaction made her pause. 'Yes, I really did look you up,' she said. 'I knew Richard for years. Our politics are similar so we would bump into each other at conferences. And yes, I know, he had his weaknesses;

between us I was one of them for a while.' Skinner remained expressionless at her revelation, but with an effort. 'Yet still he was a good man, a great man, a nice man. He'll be replaced, as we all are, but not by an equal, or anything like it, not for a while.' She paused. 'Do they know who shot him?'

Skinner nodded. 'I had a word dropped in my ear half an hour ago. They do; now they have to find him. He's done everything in plain sight so far. Possibly that's where he's hiding too. He's a clever guy, this one.'

'Was it political? Like with the fanatics who tried to kill me?'

'I don't believe so.'

'Then what?'

'I'm not privy to all the evidence,' he admitted, 'but as you said; Richard Ralston had his weakness.'

Eighty-One

'All secure, Lottie,' the leader of the armed unit called out, as he opened the main door of Calvin Knox's apartment in Broomhill. It had been kept under discreet observation for three hours and only when the team were as sure as they could be that it was unoccupied had entry been forced, through the back door.

Detective Constable Maya Smith seemed awed as she gazed at the cream-coloured sandstone frontage of the five-storey Victorian tenement, with its intricate carving, false balconies on the upper floors, and minarets on the roof. 'That's something else,' she whispered.

'That's Glasgow,' Mann said, in a matter-of-fact way. 'It'll have wally closes as well. A grand place to live, but just think of the main-tenance cost over the years. That building'll be listed for sure, Category B minimum. Big sash windows, all original wooden frames, none of your UPVC crap, and all needing painting every few years, with health and safety insisting on scaffolding for pretty much every job above head height. Plus it was built with Victorian plumbing, maybe with gas rather than electricity. All the original features have been ripped out and retro-fitted with varying levels of skill, so you don't quite know what you're getting. Love at first sight, Maya, but move in unprepared and you're liable to find that it's a fucking monster, like Calvin Knox's dad, only impossible to kill.'

In the DCI's childhood, she had visited the neighbourhood often, as her mother's bridesmaid had lived there. She had thought of it as moderately posh and it still remained so, an enclave of the management class rather than professional, although the racial profile had altered over the years. It was on the fringes of Hillhead and Hyndland, but without the air of intellectual superiority to which those areas were accused of aspiring.

She and Smith climbed the twelve steps to the entrance, where Inspector Riley Kyumu waited, armour-clad but with his visor tipped back. His ancestry was Kenyan but his accent was west of Scotland. *He puts vinegar on his chips for sure*, Mann recalled having told herself at their first meeting.

'As we thought,' he said, 'the place is clear, but we'll speak out here, Lottie. He's got Ring cameras on both doors, the upstairs landing and the downstairs hall. They were all active so the bugger knows we're here, or will as soon as he monitors them. We've unplugged them all, but there might still be one we haven't seen, so we're better outside. There's no signs of recent occupancy; the fridge is empty, apart from half a dozen Coronas and a couple of wrinkly limes. Looking at the postmarks on the mail behind the door . . . and there isn't much, hardly any junk . . . he hasn't been here for three weeks.'

'Did you look through the place?'

'We took a quick look for nasties, but we didn't find any. To save you time, he eats and works downstairs. Upstairs he sleeps, watches telly, and plays video games in another room. The place could have four or five bedrooms but it only has the one. The big front room downstairs is his office, and his gym, for there's a treadmill.' Kyumu shook his head. 'The kit in there's ridiculous,' he chuckled. 'There's an Apple Studio desktop, and a twenty-seven-inch monitor. It looks like about six grand's worth. The whole place is a rich self-indulgent single man's paradise, with just one oddity, and it's a big one.

Downstairs too, there's what might have been a utility room, or even a maid's room when the place was built. Now, it looks like a chapel. There's a wee altar, with a gold crucifix and a picture of Jesus above it, a cushioned thing for him to kneel on, and an optional extra on a stand at the side: an Apple iPad. Is he doing God stuff on YouTube, do you think, Lottie? Has he got a direct line?'

'He has,' she replied, 'but it might not be to Heaven. Come on, Maya, let's see what's in there.'

Eighty-Two

'Thanks for meeting us, Mr Dunbar,' Haddock said, as he and Singh faced the politician across the threshold of the late First Minister's Calton Road bolthole. 'It was important that we see you again; some questions are best asked face to face.'

He winced. 'I get it. When I heard about Joanie's suicide, I thought you'd want another chat. This is as discreet a venue as we can find. I've been using it myself since Richard's been in Bute House, the official residence. Come on in.' He held the door wider allowing the detectives to step inside.

The house was small, made even smaller by Singh's bulk, and the furniture mostly flat-pack, but it was comfortable. 'Sit down, guys, please,' Dunbar told them.

Haddock took an armchair but the DI demurred. 'I'm good,' he murmured. 'I'll stand.'

'First and foremost,' the ACC began, 'this is not public knowledge . . . only the pathologists and the two of us know . . . Ms Cooper's death was not a suicide. Post-mortem examination showed a drug called Propofol in her system. It's an anaesthetic, used as a relaxant and in surgery. She was injected in her right upper arm, in a place that she couldn't have reached herself, and there was enough of the stuff in her to have rendered her unconscious or at the least fully compliant.'

358

'My God,' the politician whispered, 'I thought you were certain.'

'I was,' Haddock admitted. 'With the door locked from the inside and the windows pretty much inaccessible, I thought that was a cert. Then two things happened. First, we took Ms Cooper's sister to the scene, at her request. She took one look at it and said, "No! Joanie was born untidy and she'd have died untidy! And she was afraid of knives." She assured us that while her sister had all the gear, she never cooked for herself from scratch. It went back to a teenage accident, one that left a scar to back up the story. When she ate alone at home, it was always ready-meals.'

'That's true,' Dunbar confirmed. 'In the office, if we worked late she'd leave a trail of pizza boxes and Big Mac wrappers.'

'Yeah? Well, her sister insisted that someone else had cleaned the place. She even took a look in the toilet. That was spotless too, also out of character, she said. Anyway, in the light of that, I took another look at the place and I found what I'd missed the first time around. The place has a back door.'

'Where? I've been there a few times with Richard and her and I never knew that.'

'Maybe, but it does. You might take it for a cupboard, with a simple lock, but actually it leads down to the building's garage.'

'And Joanie didn't have a car,' Dunbar added, 'so . . . But if I didn't know about it and you missed it, how would anyone else have known?'

'That's the second thing that happened. The conversion is too old for the plans to be accessible online, but the developer's still in business and they can be viewed, in detail, on his website. Our people established that it had been, from an IP address in Glasgow. The internet's a housebreaker's playground, you know.'

The politician buried his face in his hands. 'Give me a moment to take all this in,' he murmured. 'Richard was murdered. Now you're saying that Joanie was murdered too. By the same person?'

'We believe so.'

'Why?'

'This is where I need to ask you about Mr Ralston's private life. It's been suggested that he and Ms Cooper did have a sexual relationship. Is that true?'

'Yes, they did,' Dunbar admitted, 'for almost a year, until Richard came to understand discretion, and cooled it with the election coming into sight. Mr Haddock, DI Singh, I have to tell you that my friend was the most charismatic man I have ever met, and I loved him deeply. However, and sadly from my viewpoint, he was also the most resolutely heterosexual. That's what went wrong between him and Bland. She was shagging that academic, but she still saw herself as a woman scorned,' Dunbar snorted. 'As for him, put those two qualities I've mentioned together and he could get into the knickers of women wherever he went. And he did. I could name some names, but I won't, not even under oath. He was a real crossbencher in Parliamentary terms, although he did draw the line at trying it on with Aileen de Marco, not because he didn't fancy her, but because even a black belt of his standing wouldn't want to have her then husband on his trail. Richard loved women, simple as that, and when they parted it was usually on good terms. As it was with Joanie, until he took up with Mia McCullough. I believe now that with Richard and Amy's marriage due to be dissolved next year, Joanie had been biding her time. When she found out about him and Mia, she became vindictive, and finally, as I had believed until now, suicidal.' He looked sideways at the ACC, then up at Singh. 'Well?' he asked. 'Do you have a suspect?'

'We're not going to go there,' Haddock told him. 'But we have one more question. A man named Nicholas Ridley was among the people who applied for a cabin on the first ferry crossing, and he was allocated one, after a request by Joanie Cooper. Do you know who asked her to get him on to the list?'

'Yes, I do,' Peter Dunbar replied. 'It was Richard, he did it. Because he was asked to.'

The ACC stared at him for a second. 'In that case . . .' he continued, until the other man raised a hand.

'I want to stop there if you don't mind,' he declared. 'Rather, I want to suspend this discussion, to be resumed tomorrow morning, in Perth, at the convent of the Sisterhood of Kindness. It's time you understood.'

Eighty-Three

'Is our boy home safe?' Mia McCullough asked, as her call was connected.

'Yes, he's back,' Bob Skinner told her. 'Pilar too. They're both fine, and settled back into their apartment. I said they could come into the big house, but they say they're fine where they are. Nacho's recovering well; the trick will be stopping him from overdoing it when I go back to Girona tomorrow.'

'Would you mind if I went down to Gullane for a few days? Loukas can take care of Black Shield Lodge.'

'Aye, sure. Is that your new manager guy? What's his name again? You told me but it's gone.'

'Loukas,' she repeated. 'Loukas Adelfos.' Mia was aware of a gasp, the silence. 'What's up?' she asked.

'Are the cops still looking after you?'

'No, they were withdrawn yesterday.'

'Right,' he said, firmly. 'I want you to lock yourself in the house, and if he shows up, do not let him in. Get it? Don't let him in!'

'Bob!' she exclaimed. 'What is it? You're scaring me.'

'Good, that'll be a first. Just do what I say, and to be on the safe side, get out that highly illegal firearm that Cameron had, the one I never knew about officially. Get it and make sure it's in working order.'

'But Bob, Loukas isn't even here.'

'Maybe not, but he could come back. Do what I say and don't fucking argue!'

He cut the call and dialled Sauce Haddock, only to be told that his number was unobtainable. He called Mario McGuire to be told that his was switched off. He called Lottie Mann, and was connected.

'Sir,' she said. 'What can I do for you?'

'You can get armed cops back out to Mia McCullough's place, soonest, to protect her and to arrest her new accommodation manager if he shows up. His name's Loukas Adelfos, she told me. I did a bit of Greek at high school, Lottie. In English that means "Brother Luke"!'

Eighty-Four

'You just made it,' Alex Skinner said, nodding towards her wall clock. 'In fact, you're lucky I'm still working on my court appearance tomorrow, or I'd have been home by now. What can I do for you, Mr Adelfos?'

Her mystery client smiled back at her. 'The time has come when I require your services, Ms Skinner,' he replied. 'You're about to act for the defence in what's going to be the biggest trial in Scottish legal history. I'd like you to take me to the nearest police office, which I believe is in Torphichen Place, and witness my arrest. But first,' he added, 'I'd better tell you my real name.'

Eighty-Five

'That's a weight off everybody's mind,' Haddock said, at the wheel as he and Tarvil Singh left the Friarton Bridge, turned off the M90 motorway and headed towards the centre of Perth. Until then, since leaving Edinburgh, they had talked of nothing but families, golf and football, having agreed to keep their minds clear and uncluttered before the renewed meeting with Peter Dunbar.

'Yes,' the DI agreed. 'It could have got bloody if it had turned into a manhunt.'

'It could have got bloody difficult too. Who would we have been looking for? Lottie told me last night that when they got into his computer, they found a Wise bank account in the name of Nicholas Ridley, with a virtual card and the same in Revolut for Loukas Adelfos. There's more stuff in there too; a whole string of WhatsApp calls between him and his mum.'

'In whose name?'

'His own. His avatar thing, it's a fucking angel, believe it or not.'

'I'd believe anything about that guy,' Singh declared. 'The balls of him, having Alex Skinner walk him into Torphichen Place to give himself up to cops that didn't even know they were looking for him. I'm told that the PC on the desk thought it was a piss-take, until Alex gave her a hard stare and told her to call your mobile. Why did she do it, d'you think?'

'What?'

'Walk him in there like he asked. Why did she not just call us and have us pick him up at her office?'

'Because her dad told her to,' the ACC replied. 'She made Calvin a coffee, went to the ladies and called the Gaffer from there. He warned her that she was dealing with an unstable personality, and that while he was smiling she should do whatever he asked.'

'What if he'd stopped smiling?' Singh asked.

'She'd have fucking tasered him, I suspect,' Haddock said. 'Alex is a criminal defence advocate. She'll have had some really serious people in her office, so you can bet that her dad will have made sure she can protect herself.'

'Or she could have sent for her boyfriend,' the DI suggested.

'No. Dominic's not what he was.'

'Thank goodness for that. We all know what he was.'

'I didn't mean that. I've been hearing things from people who've seen him recently.' He braked, unexpectedly, then turned the car sharply to the right. 'Sorry,' he said. 'Almost missed our turn-off.'

The road climbed sharply until they reached their destination. 'Just like Lottie said,' the ACC remarked, as they passed the tennis court, where an energetic foursome were at play.

Haddock turned into the car park, to find Peter Dunbar waiting for them. 'Thanks,' he said, as they emerged. 'Do you like the surroundings?'

'Not what we expected,' Singh admitted. 'It reminds me of that big hotel just as you come into Pitlochry. It's about the same size too.'

'And the same vintage. It was built for an importer of tea, tobacco and maize who made his fortune through the port of Leith, but didn't like to live there.'

'He must have had a big family.'

'None. His brother inherited the place when he died. A couple

of generations later one of his descendants established the Anglican convent of the Sisterhood of Kindness. The lady you're about
to meet is the founder's great-granddaughter.'

He led them round to the entrance where, rather than ringing
the bell, he keyed a code into the pad and opened the door.

Haddock looked at him. 'You've been here before?'

'Several times, with Richard. Come on.'

They stepped into a hallway and carried on, to the left and
along a short corridor, at the end of which there was an open door,
framing a woman in a white hood, wearing a tweed skirt and a
Barbour gilet over a green polo-necked jumper.

'Peter,' she exclaimed. 'Blessings upon you, you woeful sinner.
These will be your policemen, I assume.'

'Assistant Chief Constable Haddock and Detective Inspector
Singh.'

She smiled. 'You don't have to tell me which is which.' For a
reason that he had been unable to explain to the ACC or even to
himself, the DI had chosen to wear his turban, something that normally he only did when visiting his traditionalist parents.

'Gentlemen,' Dunbar said, 'may I introduce Mother Teresa, the
Mother Superior, head of the convent.'

'Sometimes known as Rosemary,' she added. 'Come in,' she
said, leading them into a large drawing room with bay windows on
two sides and a view of the tennis court, which was no longer in
use. 'The sweaty sisters have finished, thank goodness,' she said.
'That would have been a distraction.' Catching Singh's expression,
she grinned. 'Did you expect them to be in long dresses? No, the
Anglican faith has accepted that nuns still have legs. Sit down
please, gentlemen. Peter's brought you here for a reason that I will
now explain. This is a convent; it is an establishment where women
live spiritual lives. They come here for periods of healing and res-
toration, some only once, some on multiple occasions. Some, as is

the case with poor Sister Trudi, take holy orders and live out their lives here. "Why here?" you're asking yourselves. "It's nice, but it's not your conventional nunnery." Well, no, it isn't. And yet it is, because we really do devote ourselves to God here, but at the same time . . . Mr Haddock, Mr Singh . . . the Convent of the Sisterhood of Kindness is also a private psychiatric hospital, and I am its consultant psychiatrist. I effected the change from its original purpose when I came here eighteen years ago. Until then I was Doctor Rosemary Moore, working in an NHS hospital in Edinburgh and frustrated by its place in the pecking order, while also chairing the family trust that my great-grandfather set up.'

'A bit like those places you hear about in England?' Singh ventured.

'Wash your mouth out with something caustic,' Mother Teresa said, severely. 'I'll grant you that some of "those places" do offer quality mental health care, but they're seen generally as places where celebrity cokeheads go to dry out. If that perception ever befell this convent . . . not that it could . . . I would close it.'

The DI touched his turban and smiled sheepishly. 'Sorry.'

'Forgiven. Now, let's talk about poor Sister Trudi, the widowed, twice widowed, Amy. I so wish that I had been here when your colleagues interviewed her. She was not herself when they saw her, not the self she has become. Richard's death knocked her off balance for a few days; the good memories faded, with the bad ones coming to the front.'

'I've heard the recording of the interview,' Haddock told her. 'Bad is an understatement.'

'Exactly,' the psychiatrist nun said. 'Happily, she's back in balance. Let me tell you the real story of Amy Ralston. I met her in the early years of my tenure here, when she was introduced to me by one of the few of my former colleagues who knew what I was doing. She had been found in a shopping mall in a highly emotional state, showing classic symptoms of paranoia. She was sectioned under the Mental Health Act, in Glasgow, where my colleague saw her and had her transferred to Sisters of Grace. At first she wouldn't speak, she'd say nothing at all. But gradually she began to see me as a friend and not a collaborator with her brute of a husband, as her paranoia had led her to believe. When she did come to trust me, when I began to recover her and she told me the full horror of the way she'd been treated, I did something mildly unprofessional, although,' she added, 'I could justify it as I was legally her guardian. I found her a solicitor. He was keen to sue for divorce, on the ground of emotional cruelty, but Amy refused. I sided with her because of her mental condition. Then Knox sued for divorce himself. It all went through fairly quickly, but with Amy still an in-patient here, he was granted custody of their son. We didn't like that, the solicitor and I, but there was nothing to be done about it since Amy wouldn't let us lead evidence of abuse.'

Haddock raised a hand, as if he was interrupting a lecturer. 'Who was the solicitor?'

Mother Teresa's eyebrows rose below her hood. 'I wondered how long it would take you to ask that. It was Richard Ralston. Although he was in politics back then he was still in legal practice.'

'I see,' the ACC said. 'The story I heard was that she was one of his constituents when they met.'

'Made up,' Dunbar confirmed.

'She was,' the nun continued, 'but the truth is they first met here. Amy's condition began to improve until finally I judged her fit to return to secular society. She knew nobody on the outside, nobody at all; she'd been her husband's prisoner, literally. When she was found in that shopping centre she had the house keys in her possession. She'd found them, got out, and walked fifteen miles to Newton Mearns.'

'Didn't Knox look for her?' Singh asked.

'Not for over a week. I'm quite sure he was hoping she'd be found dead on the Ayrshire moors. To him that would have been convenient. When finally he did, Amy was with me and I knew enough about him to keep him at bay. Once Richard was brought in he was no longer a concern. I've never met a saint,' she said, 'not a real one, but Richard was close. Yes, he was flawed, but he had such compassion. When Amy was ready to leave here, I told him, and he looked after her. She had a divorce settlement from Knox, which helped Richard find her a place to live, well away from Ayrshire. He even found her a job, with the PDSA. I was a little surprised when he told me they had married . . . I thought it would have been once bitten, twice shy for him,' she explained, 'but he really did love her, as she came to love him.'

'She came back here on occasion, I've been told,' the ACC said.

'Yes, she did, on retreat we called it, to mask reality.'

'Which was?'

'She began to regress. As Richard reached Cabinet rank it took up more and more of his time, and she began to fear that she was losing him. The paranoia began to return. He countered that by bringing her back to me. For a while it worked, her retreats would restore her but, when he became First Minister, well, all I can say is that she faded. They had a physical life, of sorts, but, well, just of sorts. And Richard had other women. He and I did discuss his life, you know. I was his counsellor too. He couldn't help it, gentlemen. That was his psychiatric condition. Yes, I would describe it as such. Now, finally, Amy has been consumed by her own. But she's no longer paranoid. She no longer feels hunted, she feels fulfilled. She has absorbed God into her being. We nuns do that, to an extent, but Sister Trudi doesn't have normal limits. Today she believes that she's in Paradise. She believes that she's an angel.'

The room fell into silence for over a minute, until Haddock broke it. 'And Richard?'

'She believes that she's the guardian of his soul. Since he died, she's been serene, not grief-stricken, because she really does believe he's with her. And as a nun, rather than a clinician, I cannot say that she's wrong.'

'How does she feel about her son?' the ACC asked.

Mother Teresa smiled. 'Brother Luke? They meet. Even angels can use WhatsApp. They speak regularly, online, she in her room, he in his cell in his monastery. He sends her gifts occasionally, things he's made. It's a good relationship.'

'The problem is, Mother,' Haddock said, quietly, 'Brother Luke left his monastery five years ago. His cell is actually a bedroom in a house in Glasgow.'

'What?' she gasped, hands going to her mouth. 'I don't believe it.'

'We can take you there if you like. Is there a chance that his mother might be aware of it?'

'That he's been living a lie? No, absolutely none. She isn't capable of understanding it.'

'Have you ever met Calvin? Brother Luke.'

'No, never. Where is he now, do you know?'

'He's in custody in Edinburgh. Once we've put the last pieces in place in our chain of events, he'll be charged with the murder of Richard Ralston and of a woman, Richard's former colleague and former lady friend. The question we're trying to answer is who manipulated who? We need to see her now, Mother. We need to talk to Sister Trudi. As her consultant, will you allow that?'

'I will, but on two conditions. I have to be there, and you must not tell her that her son's been deceiving her.'

'The second'll be more difficult than the first,' the ACC told her, 'but yes to both. Will you ask her to join us here?'

'No, it must be in her room. She's got to be comfortable in her surroundings. Let's go, but only you and me, Mr Haddock. She mustn't be overwhelmed.'

'Agreed,' he said, 'subject to my own condition. If corroboration is needed of any evidence I might have to give in the future, under oath, you're it. Would that compromise your duty to your patient?'

'Chum, my patient's an angel. How could it?'

Mother Teresa led the way. They bypassed the lift . . . 'The stairs are better for you, and they're faster.' The Mother Superior rapped on Sister Trudi's door, then keyed in the entry code. 'If necessary, although it never is, someone can be confined,' she explained. 'But I don't have people here who're a risk to others. Sister,' she exclaimed as they stepped into the room, 'you have a visitor. This is Mr Haddock, he's a police officer.'

'It seems that I'm popular with the police,' she said. 'Do come in. Can I make you a cup of tea, Mr Haddock? Or coffee?'

'Coffee would be good, thanks, with a drop of milk if you have it.'

'Of course. Mother Teresa?'

'Same here, thank you, sister.'

Haddock watched her as she filled two cups from a Nespresso machine, while frothing milk from a small fridge in an attachment. When they were ready he stepped across and took them from her, handing one to the Mother Superior as they seated themselves.

'How are you, sister?' he began.

'Blessed by the grace of the Lord,' she replied, quietly. 'My Richard is safe in His arms, free of sin, free of this world.'

'When did you see him last?'

'I'm not sure,' she confessed, 'but he phoned me every Friday, without fail. He would tell me about his week, what he had been doing, who he had seen, what he was going to do.'

'Did he tell you about his trip to Sweden?' the ACC asked her.

'Yes, of course. It was a very big thing in his life.'

'But that was where he died.'

'Yes, that was where he became free, Mr Haddock, that was where his troubles came to an end and where his sins were forgiven.'

'What sins, sister?' he asked. 'He was a good man, a great man, they're saying now.'

'Sins of the flesh,' she said quietly. 'The ladies he slept with. They were wicked and they tempted him, Brother Luke says, and he had to be freed from them, and now he has been and is at peace.'

Haddock found that her calmness was having the opposite effect on him. He glanced at the Mother Superior, but she was expressionless. 'Brother Luke is your son, sister,' she said, 'and he's in a monastery. How would he know of his stepfather's sins?'

'My son,' Sister Trudi murmured, 'yes, I suppose he is, but he's transcended that. Now he's my guide and my guardian angel . . . and he's a prophet. He said that the fate of his father, the beast who was my husband, had been placed in the hands of the Devil, and . . . the Devil acted, broke the rope with which he was climbing and took him down to Hell.'

'What did he say about Richard?' the ACC asked.

She looked at him, clear-eyed and with a slight smile. 'Brother Luke said that he was an abuser too, but in a different way. He said that he had betrayed me and that he had abused his position by his acts with those women but that he had done it out of weakness not from evil. He said that his fate and theirs should be placed in the hands of the Lord, as his father had been given to the Devil. And as we see, God has given Richard back to me, when he was moving away.'

Fuck me! Haddock thought. It took an effort not to say it aloud.

'Sister,' he continued, 'before the ferry ceremony, where he died, Richard asked that a man named Nicholas Ridley be given a cabin for the crossing. Do you know why he did that?'

'Yes,' she replied, 'he did it for me, because Brother Luke asked me to. He said he had a friend, the brother of a Brother, who would be in Sweden and wanted to be there. Brother Luke is kind that way, Brother Luke is good.'

Eighty-Six

'And Brother Luke is batshit crazy,' the newly confirmed Assistant Chief Constable Harold Haddock told Mario McGuire and Bob Skinner, in his Edinburgh office. 'Mother Teresa made me promise that I'd get her appointed by the Crown Office to assess his fitness for trial. Can I do that?' he asked the DCC. 'I'm not quite sure.'

'The chief can, now he's back.'

'So can Peter Dunbar,' Skinner added, 'now he's been lined up as the new First Minister . . . and to deliver the Glasgow Torso, or Ralston Tower, as it'll be called.'

'That's good,' Sauce said. 'Mother Teresa reckons she'll have a field day with him. From what was said and from what I told her, she reckons we could be dealing with multiple personalities. He actually had fake documentation, passport and driving licence for Nicholas Ridley and Loukas Adelfos . . . those were Greek . . . and another for Hugh Latimer, another of the Oxford martyrs. On top of that, we're retrieving all his WhatsApp video calls with his mother since she's been in the convent. It's all there, the whole story. We just have to study it. Now he's on remand, he's talking quite freely to Lottie and Tarvil, under caution. He wanted to decline legal representation, but given his mental status the Crown Office wouldn't allow it.'

Skinner smiled, as if relieved. 'But it's not Alex, Mario, not my daughter. She's been recused because she's a potential witness.'

'That's right,' Haddock confirmed. 'One of Cal's revelations is that Mia McCullough survived by the skin of her teeth. He admitted to killing Joanie Cooper, straight away, as soon as it was put to him. He's pleased with himself about that, Lottie says, pleased with how he did it. When she asked him about Mia, he said that he was on his way to kill her when he was stopped by a cop in the woods. He thought about going back for another try, but he decided it would be too risky. He'd never wanted to be caught, you see. Walking into Torphichen Place was always part of Brother Luke's plan. That's why he used the Greek identity when he got the job at Black Shield Lodge.'

'A proper one-off,' Skinner murmured.

'That's what Mother Teresa says too. Her view is that the guy who should really be on trial is Brian Knox, only the bastard's dead. She believes that the abuse that Amy and Calvin were subjected to was unsurvivable, and that it drove them both literally crazy. She told me that when this is all tied up there'll be a book to be written about it, by somebody else though, for she can't.'

'I might know the very person.'

McGuire looked at him over the frame of his reading glasses. 'Ignacio?'

'Hell no, he'll be too busy. June Crampsey's given him a new job, crime correspondent, like he wanted. No, I was thinking of someone else. She's in Spain but I might fill her in on the story so far and send her to cover the court appearance, for there will be one even though Calvin won't be fit to plead.'

'Will you find her a publisher too?'

'Fuck off, Mario. Don't you know that InterMedia does that too?'

'Indeed?' Haddock murmured. 'When I write my memoirs I might come looking. There'll be a story in them that neither of you

know about yet. Gaffer, you should tip off your crime correspondent son about this. When I ordered a full search of the place in
Broomhill the team did just that, a hundred per cent sweep. They
found a trapdoor that led to a lower level where the services are,
and there they found signs of digging. So they dug themselves, and
found two bodies buried, both female. They'd been there so long
that we reckon it must have been Brian that put them there, not
Calvin. That being the case, tomorrow the folk who rent the farm
are going to find cadaver dogs all over the place.'

'Fuck me, Sauce,' Skinner laughed, 'as an ACC you're the gift
that keeps on giving. And stop calling me Gaffer!'

RAISING READERS
Books Build Bright Futures

Dear Reader,

We'd love your attention for one more page to tell you about the crisis in children's reading, and what we can all do.

Studies have shown that reading for fun is the **single biggest predictor of a child's future success** – more than family circumstance, parents' educational background or income. It improves academic results, mental health, wealth, communication skills and ambition.

The number of children reading for fun is in rapid decline. Young people have a lot of competition for their time, and a worryingly high number do not have a single book at home.

Our business works extensively with schools, libraries and literacy charities, but here are some ways we can all raise more readers:

- Reading to children for just 10 minutes a day makes a difference
- Don't give up if your children aren't regular readers – there will be books for them!
- Visit bookshops and libraries to get recommendations
- Encourage them to listen to audiobooks
- Support school libraries
- Give books as gifts

Thank you for reading.
www.JoinRaisingReaders.com